PREDATOR

DOMINION

THE SHADOW DIRECTIVE, BOOK 1

R.D. Brady

Scottish Seoul Publishing, LLC

BOOKS BY R.D. BRADY

Stand Alone Novels:

Hominid

Extinction Threshold

The Vienna Deception

Storm Rage

Operation Kringle

The Shadow Directive Series:

Sanctuary Kingdom

Final Payout

The Belial Series (in order)

The Belial Stone

The Belial Library

The Belial Ring

Recruit: A Belial Series Novella

The Belial Children

The Belial Origins

The Belial Search

The Belial Guard

The Belial Warrior

The Belial Plan

The Belial Witches

The Belial War

The Belial Fall

The Belial Sacrifice

The Belial Rebirth Series

The Belial Rebirth

The Belial Spear

The Belial Restored

The Belial Blood

The Belial Angel

The Belial Templar

The Belial Cipher

The Belial Devastation

The Belial Ghosts

The Belial Covenant

The Belial Heart

The Belial Witnesses

The Belial Trial

The Belial Sons

The Belial Fate

The Belial Alpha

The Belial Omega

The A.L.I.V.E. Series

B.E.G.I.N.

A.L.I.V.E.

D.E.A.D.

R.I.S.E.

S.A.V.E.

The H.A.L.T. Series

Into the Cage

Into the Dark

The Steve Kane Series

Runs Deep

Runs Deeper

The Unwelcome Series

Protect

Seek

Proxy

The Nola James Series

Surrender the Fear

Escape the Fear

Tackle the Fear

Return the Fear

The Gates of Artemis Series

The Key of Apollo

The Curse of Hecate

The Return of the Gods

R.D. BRADY WRITING AS SADIE HOBBES

The Demon Cursed Series

Demon Cursed

Demon Revealed

Demon Heir

Demon War

The Four Kingdoms

Order of the Goddess

Exclusive Content

Exclusive content is available only to members of R.D. Brady's mailing list. Sign up today!

B.E.G.I.N. – prequel novella (A.L.I.V.E. Series)

Belial Sacrifice - alternative ending (The Belial Series)

Dust – full length novel (The Unwelcome Trilogy)

Extinction Threshold - novella

Begin the Fear – prequel novella (Nola James Series)

Vienna Deception – excluded scene

Members who sign up for R.D.'s mailing list are also the first to hear when she has a new release and to preview book covers. Don't miss out!

Welcome to Sanctuary Kingdom!

Here at Sanctuary Kingdom, our mission is to safeguard the future of our planet's most endangered species.

We are dedicated to the protection, conservation, and rehabilitation of wildlife through innovative breeding programs, cutting-edge research, and global collaboration.

Our goal is to create a sanctuary where endangered species can thrive and be nurtured back to health, with the ultimate aim of reintroducing them to their natural habitats.

We strive to educate and inspire our visitors about the importance of biodiversity and the critical need for conservation efforts.

Together, we can restore the balance of our ecosystems and ensure a sustainable future for all living creatures.

Thank you for joining the fight and have a wonderful visit!

CHAPTER 1

Flicking a glance over the group in the conference room at the Amphibian Axis Building on the grounds of Sanctuary Kingdom Park, Darby Ellis noted that there was not a single seat available. In fact, a number of reporters lined the sides of the conference room and a few stood along the back wall.

The packed house was not a surprise. Sanctuary Kingdom now rivaled both Disney and the Universal parks for daily attendance. Anytime Sanctuary Kingdom held a press conference, people clamored for news.

Nerves danced along Darby's skin as she stood to the side of the small stage at the front of the room. It was an effort for her to avoid running a self-conscious hand over her dark hair. She'd hurried here this morning and hadn't had a chance to look in the mirror before she'd had to begin the presentation. As one of the reporters aimed his camera her way, she tried not to grimace. The park uniform of a dark navy blue polo shirt with the Sanctuary Kingdom logo and the boxy navy blue shorts was not exactly her favorite look. The yellow RFID park bracelet was her only jewelry.

Luckily though, she was not the main attraction. No, that was the large twenty-foot screen that allowed all the reporters in attendance a perfect view of the latest addition to the park's entertainment offerings: Axolotls.

Although in reality axolotls were only twelve inches long, this axolotl filled nearly the entire screen. With webbed feet, a dorsal fin, and a tail, the adorable white axolotl with pink feathery gills that sprouted from its head looked as if it was smiling.

The photo was not a manipulation or the cartoon image the park would be using in its marketing and entertainment endeavors. No, this image was just how the axolotls looked: perpetually smiling.

Axolotls were truly adorable-looking creatures. They were unusual in that they were frozen in time in the teenage stage of development, giving them a cuter, sweeter appearance. Or at least that was the case with the ones in captivity. The ones in the wild were brownish-gray. Still cute, but not quite as cute as the white-and-pink version.

Tapping on her microphone, Darby smiled at the image as she spoke. "Not only are we thrilled to announce the opening of the Axolotl exhibit, but I am beyond pleased to announce a new addition to the Sanctuary Kingdom's *Fantastic Friends*: Abby the Axolotl."

The image on the screen shifted to a cartoon version of the Axolotl. Giving everyone a beat to take in the image, Darby continued. "Abby Axolotl will be joining the rest of the *Fantastic Friends* next season before she stars in her own spinoff series."

The image shifted again depicting the well-known image of the *Fantastic Friends*. There were seven of them: Eddie Elephant, Leo Leopard, Teddy Tiger, Jillie Giraffe, Sandra Panda, Pascha Polar Bear, and of course, little Ping Pika. Each of the animals had been carefully hand-drawn with large expressive eyes set in adorably friendly faces.

Fantastic Friends was a runaway hit for the park. It had been created by the park's co-founder, Gabe Sullivan years ago as a book series, which then had been turned into a massively popular cartoon. The series told the tale of a group of young animals who banded together to save the environment. Abby was the latest addition, and she was the beginning of a new series that would focus on water animals.

The whole park was based around the characters. Almost every exhibit depicted at least one of the characters. The merchandising of the series was by far the most lucrative revenue stream within Sanctuary Kingdom, both at the park, online, and in stores.

Another image flashed on the screen behind her. A light chuckle rumbled through the crowd. Darby flicked a glance over her shoulder and couldn't help but smile at the cartoon image of Abby on the screen behind her wearing a Sanctuary Kingdom hat. A carousel of images from the *Fantastic Friends* then flicked across the screen along with a short clip of Abby meeting Ping Pika, one of the most popular Friends.

As the last image slipped from the screen, Darby strode to the lectern in the center of the dais, an image of the *Fantastic Friends* grouped together behind her. "Of course, we're not just adding a new cartoon character."

"Although that will make the park a lot of money," someone called out good-naturedly.

Darby grinned. "True. But as you also know, that is not the primary objective."

There were a few good-natured laughs from the group. She raised her hands. "Or at least not the only objective. Axolotls are the latest addition to the breeding program.

"There are only about a hundred adults still living in the wild. The rest can be found in zoos and private homes around the world. They are critically endangered, and Sanctuary Kingdom is working on breeding them and repopulating their habitat. So far, we've been able to spawn axolotl eggs."

The screen behind her shifted to the real photo of the smiling axolotl as Darby answered more questions about the program.

There were lots of questions.

The press on the new Axolotl exhibit had been hugely successful. The public had embraced the idea.

That was not a surprise. It was almost easy to get support for cute-looking animals. Less cute endangered animals, like the Proboscis monkey with its massive elongated nose or the Madagascan aye-aye with its creepy eyes and claws, were much tougher sells.

A hand raised in the front row. Darby gestured to Chip Holster from the *Tennessee Tribune*. He stood up. "So we've heard that you guys are getting into genetic engineering with that secret research center of yours." Chip wiggled his rather impressive eyebrows.

Darby chuckled. "If you're looking to get a visit out there, Chip, I'm afraid the answer is still no. Many of the animals residing there, as you guys know, aren't used to humans. We need to keep the interactions to a minimum until we can get them acclimated."

"Yeah, yeah," Chip said. "But how do we know you're not re-engineering? Are you trying to turn this place into another Jurassic Park?"

"I assure you, there will be no baby T-Rexes running around," she said, grinning at Chip's word choice. "We are not trying to reanimate any long-gone species. But I am allowed to tell you that we are contemplating genetically engineering some species that have recently gone extinct in an effort to bring them back."

There was a stir among the audience.

Darby continued. "As you all know, the extinction rate is currently one hundred times the natural rate, in large part due to human activities. Sanctuary Kingdom's goal has always been to help the environment. Our scientists are currently examining which species' loss has most negatively affected the environment and are looking into what bringing them back could do."

"But won't they just go extinct again?" a reporter asked from somewhere toward the back. Darby was unable to make out exactly who it was.

"That's why the animals we create are going to be heading to one of our preserves located across the globe. We have seven—wait, sorry, I mean eight. I keep forgetting there's a new one." Focusing on her laptop, she pulled up a slide and sent it to the screen behind her. Glancing over her shoulder, her chest tightened at the name: The Joel Sullivan Animal Preserve.

Joel had died six months ago, the husband of Sanctuary Kingdom's co-founder, Gabe Sullivan. It had been a tough blow to Gabe. He'd gone into seclusion and then busied himself being anywhere but at Sanctuary Kingdom.

Shoving her own grief aside, Darby turned her attention back to the reporters. "The preserves have been established on six continents and will be used to help assimilate and build the numbers of these incredible animals. Technology is partly responsible for the disappearance of these creatures, but now technology can help bring them back."

Scanning the room, she leaned forward over the lectern. "There's a great deal of good that Sanctuary Kingdom has done and will continue to do. We know that animals being removed from the natural life cycle of the planet has had incredibly damaging effects.

"By reintroducing them, we can hopefully ameliorate some of those effects. Just look at what the introduction of wolves in California did to the ecosystem there. That's what we're aiming for—to simply make the world a better place."

The journalists jotted down notes on their computers, their heads bent. As they did, Darby caught sight of a woman standing at the back of the room: Wendy Miller, the assistant to the head of special events. Wendy gave her a nervous smile. Darby's stomach dropped, and it was an effort to keep a groan from slipping past her lips.

Oh no.

CHAPTER 2

THE LARGE, CAVERNOUS, 2,000-SQUARE-FOOT WAREHOUSE WAS QUIET AS Kevin Young slipped into his chair in front of his console. He flicked a glance at the giant hand-painted banner hanging from the rafters: NATURE'S JUSTICE, OUR MISSION. The EcoAct symbol—a globe with a pawprint on it—had been painted in blue and green in the bottom-right corner.

The warehouse was located just a few blocks south of Syracuse University in a commercial area. It had been unused for a few years before EcoAct took it over.

Kevin wasn't sure what it had been used for before. The oil stains on the ground suggested it had been a garage of some sort.

There was a small office in the back that they'd set up as a kitchen. But the main space held only eight six-foot tables, four with computer monitors. The others were used for non-computer work and as places for people to eat.

Normally, the room was full of EcoAct members, but today most were on site down in Tennessee. Kevin was the only one working from the warehouse. As he sat, he glanced uneasily over his shoulder. He hated being in the middle of a large space. It was a stupid setup.

A few other members were still in town and could be called if Kevin needed help. They would arrive in a couple of hours to start breaking down the space. Until then, it was entirely his.

Rolling his shoulders, he contemplated dragging one of the tables closer to the wall but finally decided against it. He'd have to take apart and reassemble his whole setup if he did that.

Besides, quiet is good. I work better in the quiet, he reminded himself. Plus, it was true. He liked to work without distractions.

Joining a group was unusual for him to say the least. He was not someone who sought out company. In fact, for the four years prior to joining EcoAct, he'd spent almost all his time in the basement of his parents' home. His mother had finally said that he needed to get out. She didn't care where he went, as long as he left the house.

Feeling the ticking clock of his parents' growing annoyance with him, he'd started looking for something to join as his resentment simmered. His parents had never recognized the genius that was their son. He was special. He wasn't meant to be like other kids with a nine-to-five job. No, he was meant to live inside machines, to manipulate them, to unlock doors that others wanted to keep closed.

I am the locksmith, he thought as he reached for his energy drink and took a swig.

Only a week after his mother's final ultimatum, complete with an employment application for a local fast food place, a random social media post led him to EcoAct. He'd never really been into animal rights. Honestly, he didn't care about animals at all. But EcoAct was looking to up their game, and that interested Kevin.

Of course, he hadn't jumped at the offer immediately. He'd done his research. The group had been all talk with a few small protests every now and then. They were definitely small ball.

But their leader, Todd Sharp, had been researching how to move to the next level. Kevin had investigated other terrorist groups that sabotaged equipment, contaminated water supplies, destroyed energy utilities, and even deployed biological agents. When Kevin had met Todd, he saw the same need to make something of himself, to be recognized, in Todd's eyes that he saw in his own reflection.

After a few conversations, Kevin saw the potential. From that day on, Todd, Kevin, and a few other higher-ups in EcoAct had worked tirelessly on today's plan.

But I am the reason it is going to work.

Cracking his knuckles, he tucked his head toward his keyboard and ran some quick diagnostics. He'd already run them, but he was filled with nervous energy. He needed to do something. He flicked a glance at the clock. Almost time.

Smirking, he sat back. *Well, Mom, looks like I'm finally doing something.*

CHAPTER 3

As Gabe Sullivan drove along the long road leading to Sanctuary Kingdom, his mind was once again blown by the fact that he and his sister had created all of this. Years ago, they'd had a simple sanctuary. It had belonged to their grandparents. He'd loved visiting and then living there.

Once he was old enough, Gabe had started doing lots of social media about the sanctuary. Slowly, he'd built a following.

And then one of his videos had gone viral, and that was it. A short time later, he'd created the *Fantastic Friends* and the popularity of the sanctuary had skyrocketed.

But his sister Martha, who'd never really cared too much about the sanctuary, had been the one who saw how to take Gabe's modest fame and turn it into an opportunity. She knew that combining education and entertainment was the key to making money.

Now they brought in over thirty billion a year through not just Sanctuary Kingdom but their line of hotels, a water park, and their latest addition, a movie studio. He remembered searching his couch and car for coins when he was in college, needing money to eat, and now Latham Parks grossed nearly twenty million a day.

And all because I wanted to help keep animals safe just like Grandma and Grandpa.

He smiled, wondering what they would think of all this. His grand-mother would no doubt say there was too much fuss, although she'd be beyond proud of them. His grandpa would beam and probably lead the park's daily parade every chance he got.

Although the image left him feeling both nostalgic and amused, the amusement soon faded. They were long gone. And Joel . . .

No, don't think about Joel, he warned himself, turning his attention back to the road as he took a shaky breath.

Easing the car down the tree and flower-lined row, he tried to get back some of the excitement he used to feel. He used to love making this drive. Now, it just left him feeling unsettled.

Passing through the private entrance at the eastern gate of the Sanctuary Kingdom Park, a hollow fluttering erupted in Gabe's stomach. Placing his hand on it as he made his way to the VIP parking lot, he pulled into the spot reserved for him. There was only one spot closer to the walkway that led to the Dominion private entrance, and that spot was taken by his sister's white BMW.

Turning off the engine of the Mini Cooper, Gabe made no move to get out of the car. Instead, he sat with his hands on the steering wheel, staring out over the park.

Beyond a small retaining wall a few feet from the parking lot, the land sloped toward the Euphrates, the man-made river on the southern end of the park. The river teemed with life as electronic sensors and unseen nets kept the populations within it carefully contained.

Beyond that was the Dominion, the crown jewel of this particular property. It housed all the corporate offices, but also the high-end shops, restaurants, and a five-star luxury resort. It was set on an island in the middle of Sanctuary Lake. Somehow it was the perfect blend of wide, vast windows that overlooked the water and parks and yet also generated of feeling of an ancient temple.

Dominion had been his sister's idea. Almost all of this had been his sister's idea. She was the one with the head for business. Gabe was the one with the heart for animals. Together, the two of them had built this incredible destination. People traveled from all over the world to see the animals and enjoy the attractions.

He'd never foreseen any of this. He'd just wanted to help endan-gered animals and continue the legacy of his grandparents. Martha, though, knew that the only way to help was to make sure they had enough money to make a difference.

And now they did.

Gabe knew that they were doing a lot of good, much more than even his grandparents had been able to do with their animal sanctuary. But sometimes it all just felt so wrong, as if they were commercializing rescue efforts.

Letting out a breath, he shoved away the thoughts. No. They were doing good. They gave billions to animal relief efforts across the globe and had eight animal sanctuaries where animals were safe from the encroachments of the modern world. In fact, Gabe had just come back from opening their latest one.

And a large part of him wished he was still there. It had nothing to do with the park. Part of him was just looking for a reason to put the car back into gear and turn around.

As he pulled his hands from the steering wheel, he noted they were shaking. Rolling them into fists, he took a deep breath. This place was so full of memories, and he did not want those particular memories. He flicked a glance to his right. The parking spot for his husband, Joel, had had its placard removed.

No new one stood in that spot. Instead, there was a "No Parking" sign. Gabe stared at it, his heart feeling heavy. *I miss you, Joel.*

The maudlin thoughts started to creep across his mind, but once again, he shoved them away. No. It had been six months. He'd locked himself away from the world for that time, jet-setting from different animal sanctuaries, opening the new one, doing everything to keep from coming back here, to keep from remembering the day-to-day with Joel.

But it was time.

In fact, today was probably the perfect day to return. Darby was here giving a press conference this morning, and then she would be giving a private tour to Mama Sue and Linc. He couldn't think of a better way to face his first day back at the park without Joel.

Mama Sue, Linc, and Darby might not be blood, but they were family. A little bit of family was exactly what he needed.

An image of his sister flashed through his mind. Well, his chosen family at least.

CHAPTER 4

THE LARGE DISPLAY AT THE FRONT OF THE CONFERENCE ROOM SHOWCASED six mottos:

Reviving Nature's Wonders
Conservation in Action
Bringing Back the Wild
Together We Can Save Them
The Future in Our Care

At the bottom was Sanctuary Kingdom's current motto: *Your Visit, Their Survival.*

Stan da Vinci, in his usual bow tie and round glasses, gestured toward the screen. "We explored all possible variations of the motto, but our current one still performs the best. The second most popular was *Reviving Nature's Wonders.*"

Martha Latham studied the mottos as Stan continued to talk, discussing the demographics of the focus group and the need for more diverse groups for future research, but Martha had already tuned him out. She knew that their original motto would be the most successful.

Her eyes focused on the last possibility: *The Future in Our Care*. She could have told them that one wouldn't work. It smacked of guilt and worry about what was to come.

You didn't want people coming to a vacation spot thinking about climate change and deforestation. You wanted them thinking that they were saving the world, not focused on what was wrong with it. It was a very fine line to walk, one that Martha had learned to traverse with expert care.

Sanctuary Kingdom was a vacation destination, but it was one that people could feel good about visiting. A portion of all proceeds from the park went to conservation efforts. In fact, prior to the park's opening, she had worked out a deal with the Tennessee state legislature and the federal government so that all expenditures were considered charitable donations. It made it so that people could literally write off their vacations on their taxes.

That tax benefit had been a huge boon to their ability to compete with the major parks. Now they were on par with Disney and Universal, and Martha intended to surpass them in the not-too-distant future.

Sensing that Stan was winding down, she returned her focus to the conversation as he said, "So we'll keep doing the research, and I do think we can incorporate *Reviving Nature's Wonders* into some of our in-park advertising and evaluate the effect while we explore additional variations on the motto for a larger advertising effort."

With a non-committal grunt, Martha looked over at Shandy Johnson, the director of conservation efforts. Shandy was thirty-nine years old, smart, and perpetually harried. She lived and breathed animal conservation.

"How are the axolotls acclimating?" Martha asked.

"Very well. Hopefully, within another two weeks, we'll be able to get the full number into the exhibit. For right now, though, we have six that are good to go."

Stan hit a button, and a picture of the axolotls appeared on the screen. Even Martha had to admit that the marine animals were cute. They were absolutely begging to be turned into a cartoon. And that was exactly what they had done. "Stan, how's the response to the spinoff of *Fantastic Friends*?"

"Great. Adding a water line has been phenomenal and really opens the door." Stan reached forward and pressed a button on the remote. An image of the *Fantastic Friends* appeared on the screen. With their large expressive eyes and sweet expressions, they were a merchandising gold mine.

Next to it was a group of another six animals, all water-based. The newest group was still in flux: a dolphin, a seahorse, a crab, an eel, an octopus, and an axolotl were depicted. There was also a whale, an octopus with massive cute eyes, and little frogs.

Martha tilted her head, studying it. "Not quite as cute as the original cast members, are they?"

"No, this is still in mockup. Abby Axolotl looks great, though, and Ollie the Octopus as well."

They'd been mixing and matching different animals, trying to find the right combination. Her brother hadn't been around to add his thoughts. This is where he was missed. Creatively, he had no equal.

The image changed, and now it was only Abby Axolotl. Martha grunted her agreement. The axolotls were cute with their perpetual smiles.

"Okay, keep playing around with the other options. Abby's good to go, Ollie's close, though have someone adjust his coloring a little bit. Let's work in an episode where the *Fantastic Friends* interact with the two of them, and then we'll see where we go with the other ones."

Stan made a note on the legal pad next to him. "Sure thing."

There was a younger man in a suit and tie at the end of the conference table who piped up. "Is it really necessary to create a spinoff?"

Everyone in the conference room went silent as they turned their heads to the man and then back to Martha. She focused on him, narrowing her eyes. "Remind me again, who are you?"

"Jeff. Jeff Kling from the marketing department."

Martha's eyebrows rose. "You're from the marketing department and don't understand why expanding *Fantastic Friends* is necessary? People come here because their kids insist that they come here. People come here because *Fantastic Friends* is the most popular cartoon in the world. So yes, expanding *Fantastic Friends* is necessary."

"I get that. But shouldn't we be helping the animals more? I mean, shouldn't we be focusing on the most endangered, like the black rhino?"

Martha drummed her fingers on the tabletop. "And how do you propose we do that? Grab some picket signs and take turns guarding them on the animal preserves? How would you suggest that we save the black rhino?"

"Well, I mean, there has to be a different way that we can—"

Barely pulling back her annoyance, Martha cut him off. "Do you know how much money Latham Parks provides to conservation efforts?"

Looking around the table, Jeff searched for allies. Everyone kept their eyes averted. Finally, he shook his head.

"Two billion dollars every year. That number is always growing. That does not include the required donation for anyone using our name or images of any of our characters through Sanctuary Kingdom. Literally billions of dollars are generated for conservation efforts across the globe. So tell me, do you think we should play around with a winning formula just because you think a rhino should be on a poster?"

Jeff winced. "No."

Martha nodded. "All right, that's it for today. Everyone's got their assignments."

A collective sigh and a few nervous smiles erupted across the table as everyone grabbed their things. As Martha stood, her gaze pierced into the man at the end of the table. "And what was your name again?"

"Jeff?" he asked, nervously halting halfway to standing.

"Well, Jeff, you're fired."

CHAPTER 5

THE JOURNALISTS WERE SET TO GET A TOUR OF THE AXOLOTL DISPLAY IN THE Amphibian Axis Building following the press conference. Darby had planned on leading that tour, but Wendy's appearance meant that was probably unlikely to happen. As the journalists filed out of the conference space, Darby met Wendy at the back of the room.

"Everything okay?" Darby asked.

Wendy gave her a nervous smile. Despite being only forty-four years old, there was something incredibly grandmotherly about Wendy. She had a nervousness about her and a need to ensure that everyone was taken care of. She was a very kind woman, which made the fact that she was the assistant to Claire Askins, the special events coordinator, all the more surprising. Claire could be described with many terms, but "kind" was not one of them.

"Oh, yes, yes, of course, Darby. Well, actually, no, there is a small problem. Claire needs you to give a VIP tour this morning."

This morning was supposed to be a one-off. Technically, she wasn't supposed to be working at all on Mondays. "I'm not working today. I agreed to come in and do the press conference, but that was all I was supposed to be doing today."

"I know, I know. But she's got a very special client and she really needs them to have a great tour. Sian was going to do it, but her daughter went into labor last night, so she's been at the hospital with her since then. Poor thing's been in labor going on twelve hours now."

Wincing, Darby felt a great deal of sympathy for Sian's daughter. She sighed. "Ansell can't do it?"

Wendy gave Darby a look. She chuckled in response. Ansell was one of the other tour guides, but he was, to put it delicately, boring.

"It would be considered overtime, so you'd get time and a half for it," Wendy said hopefully.

It would be nice if that didn't make a difference, but sadly, it did. Money was extremely tight right now, and any extra she could make would definitely be appreciated. She sighed. "Okay, well, after I escort the reporters back to Dominion—"

With a wince, Wendy cut her off. "Actually, I brought Levi out to do that." She looked over her shoulder.

Darby could just make out the tour guide's tall frame in the hallway directing the reporters toward the axolotl exhibit. "So I can give you a lift back to Dominion," Wendy finished.

Trying not to snap at the poor woman, after all she was just the messenger, Darby shook her head. "No, that's okay, I'll walk."

Her eyes full of understanding, Wendy said, "Okay. And I'm sorry, Darby."

"I know. Thanks." Darby gave her a tight smile and turned for the exit, trying to tamp down her annoyance. Claire had been pushing more and more duties onto her. The extra money was good, but it was seriously eating into her time.

Oh shoot. Darby stopped and turned back. "Mama Sue and Linc are coming today. I was going to take them on a private tour."

"I'll make sure that I find someone to take them," Wendy said quickly.

Disappointment crashed through Darby. It was good her foster mom and brother would be able to see the new axolotls, but Darby had really wanted to be the one who took them. Her shoulders drooping, she blew out a breath, "Yeah, thanks."

Reaching the lobby, a few journalists turned her way. She plastered a smile on her face and straightened her shoulders. Passing a few of them with a professional smile, she headed for the exit.

Reaching the vestibule, she stopped to take a deep breath. With each breath she took, her resolve strengthened. *Okay. I'll take these VIPs on the fastest tour they've ever had. Then I'll join Mama Sue and Linc.* She could do these tours in her sleep, she'd done them so often.

So yeah, a quick tour and then she'd be done for the day.

CHAPTER 6

THE RESTRICTED GATE AT THE BACK OF SANCTUARY KINGDOM WAS NOT labeled. To find it, you had to know it was there.

Commander Adrian Felix of the Defense Threat Reduction Force, a special program under the auspices of the Department of Defense, drove along the private driveway with complete confidence, even though this was his first time here.

His second-in-command, Sabrina Gutierrez, shifted uneasily in the passenger seat. Short with coiled muscle and close-cropped dark hair, the two of them looked like siblings and had been on more than a dozen missions together. He knew her well. Uneasy was not a look he saw on her often.

"Something up?" Felix asked.

Sabrina shook her head. "No. I just don't really like animals."

Felix barked out a laugh. "Then you might be a little unhappy on this mission."

"Yeah, well, as long as they stay behind their fences, I won't have any issues."

Felix grinned. "I'm pretty sure that's the entire point of a zoo. They stay in their place, and we stay in ours."

He flashed his badge at the manual security gate. His badge glowed green before the gates opened. As he drove through, his mind focused on the mission ahead. His higher-ups were getting impatient and wanted an update on the program.

Initially, Felix hadn't been supportive of this particular project. He thought the government funds would be better spent on improving training programs to make soldiers more lethal. Specialized units were more effective these days than mass training, so the goal should be to bring everyone up to the special-teams level.

Of course, no one cared what a soldier thought about the battlefield. Decisions were made by armchair administrators who'd never actually stepped foot on a field of war and barely knew their ass from their elbow.

Felix had lost too many people in too many fights to believe the scientists would come up with a magic solution. But he didn't argue when given orders. Following orders was what made him an effective soldier.

And even though he wasn't a big science guy, he had to admit he was intrigued by this new line of research. The goal was to increase aggression in soldiers. That could be a game-changer. Special teams were already hardened and ready for combat, but the grunts? He'd seen more than a few of them turn tail and run at the first sign of trouble.

If they had a way to increase aggression in a fight, they could cut down training time dramatically. Part of the training was just getting them used to the violence they would face so that when confronted with it, they could react effectively.

Smaller, more lethal groups were the wave of the future, and if this research allowed the ability to turn aggression on and off, it would be revolutionary. Felix couldn't help but think of the berserkers from the old Norse tales. The legendary warriors were said to fight in a trance-like fury. The fearsome Vikings were supposed to be a terror to behold. They fought with a wildness and viciousness that was unparalleled.

They were impressive. If these experiments went well, they would have the means to create a berserker for the modern world. The ability would, in essence, turn off their humanity and focus only on the goal. Plus, with the problems soldiers faced when coming home, this showed promise in reducing PTSD and other integration difficulties, because allegedly, memory was affected. The goal was for the soldiers to not remember what they had done.

He'd also read about the long-term hopes for the program. If all went well, they were going to offer the first stages of the program to inmates. They would give them some training, make them part of the program, and then drop them behind enemy lines to see what happened.

Felix smiled. He was all for it. He'd rather not risk the lives of good, patriotic soldiers. But using people who had already harmed the country? Yeah, he had no problem putting them in the crosshairs.

CHAPTER 7

ANNOYANCE ROLLED OVER MARTHA'S SKIN AS SHE STRODE DOWN THE HALL toward her office. Her assistant, Kelly Holmes, hurried along after her. Kelly was a few inches shorter than Martha's five six. With Kelly in flats, Martha's heels only accentuated the difference.

"Make sure everything is in place for the Japanese Prime Minister's tour tomorrow. Double-check that we have the correct golf clubs for the charity tournament this weekend."

Martha hated golf, but she was excellent at it. The golf course was, sadly, where many deals were made, and she always had to put on a good show. This weekend, she would be golfing with senators and other movers and shakers in the business world. She wanted to see if she could get a more beneficial tax structure put in place for the park and lay the groundwork of support for the aquarium.

She'd been pressing the senators for months now and knew they were on the cusp of giving in. Her marketing team, with the exception of the now-unemployed Jeff, had done an excellent job of playing up how well it would spin with the politicians' constituents. She was just going to push that angle a little more to seal the deal this weekend.

"Yes, it's all set. I'll have your new golf clubs waiting for you on site," Kelly said.

Stan called from behind, "Martha, got a minute?"

No, she thought sourly but found herself turning, nevertheless. Her days were jam-packed from sunup to sundown. But she always managed to make time for the people who were actually good at what they did, and Stan was most definitely one of them, the hiring of Jeff not included.

Hustling down the hall toward her, Stan gave Martha a quick smile. "I was wondering if we could get Darby back for this campaign. With Jeff not here and—"

She cut him off. "Darby's where she's needed."

Picturing her brother's little pet, Martha tried to rein in her annoyance. He'd taken the girl under his wing and promoted her way too quickly. It was true she seemed to have a knack for marketing, but the truth was the girl seemed to have a knack for everything. Wherever she was planted, she bloomed.

Stan's face fell. "It would really be helpful."

Martha bit back her own annoyance. She wasn't sure what it was about Darby that rubbed her the wrong way. Maybe it was the fact that Gabe treated her like a little sister much more than he'd ever treated Martha. Or maybe it was the fact that the girl seemed to just land on her feet no matter what happened to her.

"I'll take it under advisement. Anything else?"

"No, no, that's it."

Without another word, Martha turned on her heel and made her way to the elevator. Three floors later, she was striding down the hall to her office. The doors opened as she approached. A small smile slipped across her lips. Everyone in the park wore an RFID bracelet, including the staff. Martha's was encoded so that whenever she approached her office, the doors would unlock and swing open for her. But they would do it only for her.

At the center of the room stood a sleek executive desk, an impressive piece of craftsmanship in polished wood with subtle metal accents. Behind it, a high-back ergonomic chair, upholstered in rich black leather. The desk was impeccably organized, with dual curved monitors and a few essential items neatly arranged.

To the left, a modern conference area had been created, featuring a minimalist table surrounded by sleek pale gray leather chairs, all positioned to take advantage of the sweeping views outside. A large flat-screen TV hung on the adjacent wall, ready for presentations and video conferences, while a smart-home control panel allowed for seamless adjustments to lighting and climate.

The decor was a masterclass in understated elegance. Abstract art pieces adorned the walls, their bold colors and shapes adding a touch of sophistication without overwhelming the space. A few select accent pieces—a sleek sculpture on a side table, a designer vase on a shelf—added personality and charm, or at least that's what Martha had been assured by her ridiculously expensive interior designer.

Striding inside, she hit a button on her desk and the doors swung shut. She let out a breath, annoyance still rolling through her as she pictured that little know-it-all. She was so sick of these environmental types telling her how to manage her park. People had no concept of what it took to run a place like this.

Of all the amusement parks in the world, 20% accounted for 90% of the revenue. Less than 5% of all parks made a billion a year. Essentially, there was Disney, Universal, and then everyone else—at least until Sanctuary Kingdom had come along.

What people also didn't realize was that in order to play in the big leagues, you couldn't just have a park. You needed everything that went along with it. You needed the merchandise, you needed the stores, you needed the entertainment, and you needed the hotels. Most importantly, you needed the kids.

Fantastic Friends had been her brother's brainchild. He'd created it fifteen years ago, and it had taken off like wildfire. Initially, her brother's thought was to take the proceeds and put them back into the small animal sanctuary that their grandparents had created. But Martha had seen the bigger possibilities. She knew that *Fantastic Friends* could be the springboard to making a true impact on the world.

Now they had twelve themed hotels, four dozen restaurants, half a dozen sports centers, a massive new research center, five different amusement parks, animal-themed movies, conservation areas around the world, small kid-themed parks, all with animal exhibits, and shopping areas.

So many shopping areas.

The park was set up so that you couldn't go from one exhibit to the next without seeing something to buy. Anything that they could slap an image of the *Fantastic Friends* on, they did.

And it had paid off.

Journalists had often written about them as if they were an overnight success. Martha scoffed. There was nothing overnight or quick about their success.

Kelly buzzed in from the outer office. "Um, you have a call from Archer Fitzgerald."

Picturing the aide to Senator Freddie Markham, Martha grimaced. The kid was right out of central casting: thick dark brown hair, bright blue eyes, lean, Brooks Brothers suit. She didn't know his background, but she would not be at all surprised if a country club was a large part of it. Grabbing the phone, Martha slapped a smile on her face. "Archer, how are you?"

"Good, Martha, good."

She gritted her teeth. He was maybe twenty-two and always spoke as if he was on the same level as her. "So what can I do for you today?"

"I just wanted to let you know that the team will be arriving a little early. They're ahead of schedule."

Martha stopped flipping through papers. "How early?"

"They've already arrived."

Trying and failing to keep the snark out of her response, Martha gritted her teeth. "Thanks for the heads-up."

"No problem. Talk soon." He disconnected the call.

Hitting the intercom button, Martha said, "Get me Roger. Tell him I'll meet him at the cart."

"Will do."

Standing, her gaze flicked over to a picture of her and her brother on the corner of her desk. The two of them were eight, with their arms wrapped around one another, giant grins on their faces.

He would not approve of the DOD project. But Gabe wasn't in charge of the park. He handled the PR, the entertainment, the lighter side. It was Martha's job to keep the doors open and the engines running.

And that's exactly what she was going to do.

CHAPTER 8

BREATHING DEEPLY, DARBY STEPPED OUT OF THE AMPHIBIAN AXIS Building and made her way toward Dominion. When she'd put some distance between herself and the Axis, she couldn't help but flick a glance back at the new home for the axolotls. The building was designed to look like the entrance to a cave on the side of a lagoon. There were exotic colorful flowers winding around the massive doors.

Cute animals with big eyes peeked out from behind the greenery. The animals were part of a scavenger hunt for kids in the park. If they found all of them, they were given a commemorative cup. And, of course, each one made the park money.

In fact, every piece of the park had an angle to make people spend more money. To complete the scavenger hunt, parents had to stay at the park longer. The longer they stayed, the more they spent.

With a shake of her head at both the brilliance and mercenary nature of the ploy, Darby headed along Tigris Way. Each of the streets inside the sprawling Sanctuary Kingdom was named after a famous river. The rivers, in turn, were named after famous natural preserves. She glanced over at the Caledonia, which ran just behind the amphibious exhibit. She smiled as a trout peeked its head out and then disappeared again under the water.

The sound of the *Fantastic Friends* theme song played over the loud-speaker.

In a forest bright and green,
With a river sparkling, the air is clean.
There's a team of friends who love to play,
But when nature calls, they save the day.

The theme song played every thirty minutes, and although Darby should probably be sick of it by now, she had to admit that it was awfully catchy. She found herself humming along and then even softly singing the words of the chorus as it played.

"Fantastic Friends, Fantastic Friends,
Together we stand, together we care.
Fantastic Friends, Fantastic Friends,
For the Earth, we'll always be there."

She smiled. It still amazed her that all of this had come from Gabe's imagination. He was full of creativity. Although, Martha did deserve the credit for the park.

Darby's thoughts soured when she pictured the co-CEO. She was not as warm and friendly as Gabe. But without Martha, as Gabe always pointed out, none of this would have been possible.

Realistically, Darby knew that was true. But she couldn't make herself like Gabe's sister. Part of the problem was the woman really just didn't seem to like Darby, even though Darby had really tried with her.

Blowing out a breath, she shook her head. *No negative thoughts, focus on the good,* she reminded herself. She'd just started a new mental approach to the day to try and tamp down her increasingly anxious thoughts.

Okay, feel the air, feel the ground under my feet. Breathe in the moment, breathe out the stress.

It was kind of hokey, but it did seem to help. She turned and watched the blue water of the Caledonia River flow by. It ran along the western part of the park. There were four man-made rivers in the park and one man-made lake, Sanctuary Lake.

The landscape was lush and full of flowers, carefully maintained to not look perfectly manicured but natural. The ice cream kiosk was shuttered just up ahead. All the rides were silent as well.

Set in eastern Tennessee, Sanctuary Kingdom had become one of the number one vacation spots for tourists from the United States and beyond. With the parks, the hotels, the water parks, the movie studio, it was quickly rising through the ranks of parks.

But that wasn't what Darby loved about it. She loved the fact that it did good. A portion of every single dollar taken in by the park went to conservation efforts. Solar and green energy were used throughout the park, which meant that it drew very little energy from the grid. Composting and recycling were all part of the park's process.

And honestly, it was just nice to walk around. The park was closed on Mondays until one, so no guests would be coming for hours yet. It allowed the park to do training, gave staff some time off, and allowed for VIP group tours. That particular policy had helped land them on Forbes Top 100 Companies to work for.

It was like a utopian city plunked down in the middle of what could be a dark and difficult world at times. Darby liked to leave her worries at the gate when she stepped in.

Today, though, that was proving a little more difficult. Her duties were becoming more and more demanding.

Prior to Joel's death, she'd worked with Gabe, and honestly, it had barely been work. When they'd met years ago, the two of them had hit it off. The park had not been the same without him.

She felt guilty for begrudging Gabe his mourning time. She checked in with him every week and had spoken with him every other week. He was still grieving Joel, and Darby understood that. Seeing the two of them together was electric, and Joel's loss had left a huge hole in Gabe's life.

But Darby missed her friend. She really hoped he came back soon.

Her phone beeped, and she pulled it out. It was a message from Claire. *Ballroom. Ten minutes.* Shoving her phone back in her pocket, Darby repeated the mantra that she'd started two months ago when the demands on her had increased: *I love my job, I love my job, I love my job.*

Then she blew out a breath, thinking about her bank account and the bills the next couple of months were going to bring, and decided to switch it: *I need my job, I need my job, I need my job.*

CHAPTER 9

KEVIN'S KNEE JIGGLED, MOVING UP AND DOWN QUICKLY AS HIS GAZE constantly strayed to the clock. His smile deepened as he imagined what was to come.

The power right at his fingertips was incredible. He itched to just go and get it all started.

No, no. Patience. You didn't do all this work just to jump the gun. Do this right, and you are set. Your name will be legendary.

He smiled as he sat back, imagining where he'd be this time next year. In school, he'd been a loner and the target of more than a few bullies. They were all stronger, all more popular.

But now, Kevin was the strong one. In the olden days, physical muscle was king, the guy who could swing his sword the fastest or wield a sledgehammer or do something else that involved brawn had been the top dog.

In the modern age, though, it was the computer nerds who were kings. They could get into systems, they could create whole worlds. They could make the powerful bend the knee. Or, in Kevin's case, they could destroy them.

Today was the first step to being that destroyer. If today went well —and he had every expectation it would—EcoAct was going to take their reign of terror on the road. Todd's plan was to close down every zoo in the United States, and then across the world.

But that wasn't Kevin's plan.

No, once he'd shown what he could do, he was going to use Beowulf as his calling card full time. Beowulf, the slayer of monsters, just like Kevin slew the technological beasts arrayed against him.

Already he'd linked the moniker to his previous hacks. After today, that was how he would be known. Kevin Young was his past. Beowulf was his future. Once he pulled this off, people would line up for his services. Money would never be an issue.

Yeah, a year from now he'd be sitting on a beach surrounded by gorgeous women. The kid that everybody made fun of, the kid that nobody wanted to sit next to—he was coming into his own. And he was going to make sure that everybody respected him.

CHAPTER 10

FELIX PULLED TO A STOP IN FRONT OF THE DOOR TO THE FOSSEY CENTER. Stepping out of the truck, he looked around. The research area looked a lot like the bases he'd been on over the years. There was a sameness to every building, all pale concrete with solar paneling along metal roofs. Only the words on the white signs by the front door were different.

He glanced back at the other members of his team, all former military and now on contract with the DOD. They took up the three rows of the Suburban. All were dressed in jeans and dark T-shirts that accentuated their tight muscles.

Noticing Bobby Proctor sitting in the second row with his head back and eyes closed, Felix nudged his chin toward him. "Santos, wake up Bobby."

"I'm awake. Just resting my eyes," Bobby said, cracking one eyelid open with a grin. "Had a late night. Definitely worth it."

"Yeah, I'm sure you and your hand had a great time," Santos said, opening the door.

Instead of taking offense, Bobby grinned as he followed Santos out of the vehicle. "He is my best friend."

Shaking his head at the banter, Felix stepped out and stretched his back. It had been a four-hour drive from DC, and they had only stopped once. His gaze roved over his five-member team. Bobby was a former Ranger. Santos was former recon as was Urich Friedland, the quietest member of the group. At age thirty-three, Urich was tall and looked like a Tarzan actor. He probably wouldn't say more than one or two words the whole day.

Marissa Benson was the smallest member of their team, but she was solid muscle. It wasn't her muscles that had gotten her on the team, though. She was former Army intelligence and an absolute whiz at all things electronic.

Sabrina was his second-in-command and could be relied upon in a pinch. The team had been together for six years now and had been in more than a few dicey situations. He hadn't expected that when he and Sabrina created their private military group. Working for the DOD, he'd expected easier gigs, not harder.

This gig, however, had proven to be a cakewalk. They were little more than errand boys. For right now, that was fine. They needed a little bit of a break from the rough and tumble.

Stretching his heavily tattooed arms above his head, Santos grimaced. "This meeting going to take long?"

"Why, you got somewhere to be?" Felix asked.

Santos grinned in response. "Actually, I was hoping I could go check out the park once we're done. Never had a chance to visit."

Turning his gaze toward the amusement park beyond the research area, Felix raised his eyebrows. "Once we finish up the meeting, I'll get some guest passes. We can spend the day."

Bobby slapped Santos on the back. "Ya hear that? Boss is giving us a vacation."

CHAPTER 11

DOMINION WAS SET ON THE MAN-MADE LAKE ON THE WESTERN EDGE OF Sanctuary Kingdom. Darby had always loved the look of the place. It had a strong Polynesian influence in its design, with dark wood and greenery everywhere, but it was also open with lots of windows letting in tons of Tennessee sunshine.

It featured high-end shopping, an exclusive hotel called the Kingdom, a beach, and an events center with the Emporium Theater. Darby passed the marquee display for Cirque du Soleil, which was currently in residence. A different entertainer was highlighted every three to four months. Entertainers were dying to get in here. There was a ton of good press, and the shows were always sold out.

Then there were the restaurants. There were a few casual kiosks for people who were just wandering through Dominion, unable to afford a room or shop in the stores. But then there were the high-end restaurants with celebrity chefs. Darby knew that part of Martha's plan was to get a Michelin-star restaurant here.

And Darby had no doubt that the co-CEO of Sanctuary Kingdom would accomplish it. If there was one thing she could say about Martha Latham, it was that the woman was driven. If she had a goal, she would find a way to make it happen.

Martha and her brother were polar opposites. Gabe always seemed to bring out the best in people, always *looking* for the best in people.

Martha walked around like a crocodile looking for weaknesses that she could prey upon. Darby had witnessed more than one browbeating that had caused a staff member, male and female alike, to burst into tears.

Thoughts of Gabe caused her heart to squeeze a little bit. After talking nearly daily, these last couple of months had been hard. She knew that Joel's death had completely destroyed him, and she wanted to be there for him. But he wanted to curl up in a dark space and shut out the world. She understood. Losing Joel, it hadn't been easy for anyone who knew him.

She'd been relieved when Gabe had agreed to go as the Latham Park representative for the new animal sanctuary. Him getting out in the world was exactly what he needed. Joel's death was absolutely tragic, a hit-and-run. Joel had been out for a morning jog. The car had come out of nowhere. They never found the driver.

Even more terrifying, Joel hadn't been meant to be running alone. Gabe was supposed to have been with him that morning.

Darby could've lost both of them. Even the idea of it sent a shiver up her spine. But Gabe was okay.

Or at least alive.

When he returned to Sanctuary Kingdom, she'd make sure that his first few days did not have a single hiccup. The other members of the staff, who loved Gabe just as much as she did, would help in that endeavor.

Smiling, she nodded. Yeah, when Gabe finally came back, she'd make sure that there was nothing upsetting that could derail his return.

CHAPTER 12

As the doors to Martha's private elevator opened, they revealed the head of Sanctuary Kingdom's head of security, Roger Collins. A former Washington, D.C. cop, he had a full head of bushy white hair and a similarly bushy mustache. No matter the time of year, he had the same ruddy complexion, which Martha attributed to an unhealthy drinking habit. As it never interfered with his job, though, she never commented on it.

As she stepped into the elevator, he inclined his chin. "Ms. Latham."

"Roger. Are we all set?"

He nodded but didn't say anything more.

The two of them descended to the first floor, and Roger got behind the wheel of Martha's personal cart. It moved a little faster and was a bit more comfortable than the carts available for the rest of the guests at the park. It had cost a pretty penny, but as the CEO, she figured she deserved it.

As soon as they pulled away from the Dominion, she turned to her head of security. "Cameras?"

"They've been shut down at the research center. No one saw the group coming in and no one will see them leave. Plus, the research area is on a skeleton crew. We should be fine."

That was true. A few people might have seen them, but they would be dressed in plainclothes so no one would realize who they were. They'd entered through the north gate, which was highly restricted and required special permission to access. Weeks ago, she'd sent badges over to Archer to allow them entry.

It did not ease her annoyance at the fact that they had arrived early. Due to the classified nature of this endeavor, they needed to ensure that there was no record of their presence and no recordings. Knowing when they were coming, however, would have made that much easier.

As Roger drove, Martha did not pay attention to the landscape rushing past as they made their way down the perfectly designed path. Instead, she reviewed her notes for the legislation she'd be pushing this weekend.

Ten minutes later, as they approached the research center, Martha finally looked up from her phone. They were just passing the game section on the northernmost part of the park. There was a massive arch above the entrance to the area with the words MONKEYING AROUND! emblazoned across it. Some of the larger games had massive stuffed versions of the *Fantastic Friends* arranged along their booths, enticing players young and old to bring them home. Across from the game section was GEORGE'S PLACE, the orangutan house.

Each area had a massive placard announcing it's name. In fact, there were signposts pointing to each section of the park every hundred feet or so. Signage was critical in a park this large, as was branding. If something could have the name Sanctuary Kingdom slapped on it, it did.

But there was no park signage at the entrance to the Latham Park Research Center. Most of the park was designed to attract the eye, to entice people to approach. The exterior of the research center was designed to do the exact opposite. It had been designed so that people barely even realized it was there. Plain white buildings, no adornment, with high, yet uninspiring landscaping in front of the section rendered the area practically invisible.

Employees called the area "Oz" because it was where the magic happened. In the movie, Oz didn't have any magic. No, he had science. *Just like we do*, she thought with satisfaction as the guards opened the gates to allow her entrance.

Driving through, her gaze shifted to the one small sign on the right-hand side of the drive: LATHAM PARK RESEARCH CENTER. The area consisted of twenty buildings: ten labs and ten buildings that were a mix of containment areas, offices, supply sheds, and even a cafeteria with overnight accommodations.

Access to the research area was carefully controlled. The subjects of the experiments were highly sensitive—not just the DOD's but all of them. Animals that had just been brought into the park spent time in the quarantine cells at the research center as they acclimated to the zoo environment.

In fact, the entire research center contained acres and acres of fenced-in land. It was a sprawling area, nearly the same size as the rest of the zoo. Animals new to captivity, once cleared by the scientist, were acclimated here before they were put on display.

Glancing at her watch, Martha debated for a moment and then decided that being the DOD hadn't bothered to tell her they were arriving early, they could wait a little bit. She gestured to the exhibit on the right. "Pull up there."

Roger did, and Martha stepped from the cart. She strode into The Leakey Building. Each of the buildings on the research center campus was named after a famous naturalist or biologist. The Leakey Building was for their high-altitude research. Inside, she stepped through the door, into a small foyer, with offices to the right and labs to the left.

But straight in front of her was a massive viewing window. She stepped to the edge of it and noted the mountainous terrain that had been replicated inside. The air inside had a lower oxygen rate than where Martha was standing, equivalent to the air found at 10,000 feet.

Scanning the scene, she spied the small creature that looked somehow like a hybrid of a bunny and a gerbil moving across one of the ridges with it's almost perfectly round ears.

There were more than 30 different species of Pikas, found from North America to the mountains of China. Climate change was quickly destroying the availability of habitable land for many of them, pushing them closer and closer to extinction.

But for some reason, they were denied categorization as endangered. Gabe made an executive decision to begin a breeding program for them to help shore up their numbers so they didn't have to reach that critical point. He and Joel had been working on creating a habitat for them just before Joel's death. It had been opened just two months ago. This group here were the Ila Pika species, which would be added to the exhibit of Pika already in the park. They'd stay here until they'd acclimated to captivity.

Ping Pika was part of the *Fantastic Friends* exhibit and had been a huge hit. After Ping's introduction, interest in pikas had exploded, and so had the money donated to preserving them. That was good.

On the downside, however, a huge black market had been created for people who wanted pikas for pets. But pikas were not designed to be pets—not just because they were wild animals but because many of the species could not handle lower altitudes. Martha had read more than one horror story of a pika being caught and brought down to lower altitudes, only to die.

There was a full campaign in effect now around the small mammal, reminding people not to collect the pikas, that doing so would only kill them.

But Marthas interest in them wasn't simply altruistic. No, her view was decidedly more mercenary. Pikas had a unique biology. They could dial up or down their biology to adapt to the oxygen levels surrounding them.

As the planet heated up, pikas were moving to higher and higher elevations to compensate. The trade-off was that they were getting less oxygen, and genetic variations had been seen in those higher-level animals to allow it. This discovery stunned the scientific community: genetic changes were believed to take thousands of years. But the pikas indicated that they might take much less time.

Cracking that particular scientific nut would be beyond lucrative. If they could figure out how to speed up genetic changes, the options would be unlimited, and so would the money. Narrowing her eyes as the little pika burrowed into an opening and another one came to join it, she smiled. *You, my little friend, are going to be an absolute cash cow.*

She turned for the lab to get a quick update, and then it would be on to her next cash cow.

CHAPTER 13

THE BALLROOM AT THE DOMINION WAS LOCATED ON THE MAIN FLOOR JUST down from the Emporium Theater. Ten-foot-tall, golden-engraved double doors welcomed guests into the sumptuous space.

The room was vast, with a ceiling that soared forty feet high. Crystal chandeliers hung like majestic crowns, their golden light casting a warm, inviting glow over the entire space, making the intricate gold-leaf designs glimmer.

Rich, dark velvet fabric embroidered with golden threads depicting scenes of wild savannas, dense jungles, and exotic wildlife covered the walls. Lions, peacocks, and tigers seemed to come alive in the detailed tapestries, their eyes catching the light and giving them an almost lifelike presence.

In the center of the room, a grand dance floor stretched out, its surface an exquisite mosaic of golden tiles. The perimeter was lined with luxurious seating areas, each arranged around low tables inlaid with mother-of-pearl and gold. Plush, deep-cushioned sofas and chairs, upholstered in fabrics of rich emerald green and sapphire blue, provided a comfortable yet stylish respite for those taking a break from the festivities.

During events, at one end of the ballroom, a raised platform would hold a magnificent buffet, the tables draped in white linen and accented with gold. Large, ornate ice sculptures of elephants and giraffes would tower over an array of gourmet dishes, each more delectable than the last. The scent of exotic spices and fine cuisine would fill the air, mingling with the subtle, earthy fragrance of fresh flowers.

Currently, the room was being set up for this weekend's wedding. The animal theme was carried through even in the smallest details. Gold-rimmed glasses and plates bore delicate etchings of leopards, elephants, chimpanzees, meerkats, lions and bears. Napkin rings in the shape of coiled serpents held silk napkins embroidered with tiny golden bees. Even the waitstaff wore uniforms that hinted at the theme, with golden buttons and animal-print accents adding a touch of whimsy to their polished attire.

In the corners of the room, life-sized statues of animals in gilded metal stood sentinel, their eyes studded with precious stones that caught the light and added a regal air. A massive gold-framed mirror reflected the entire scene, doubling the grandeur and making the ballroom seem even more expansive.

Although it was early on Monday, the ballroom was abuzz with activity. A stage had been set up in the center of the dance floor, and on it, the *Fantastic Friends* dance troupe were rehearsing their number for the big wedding this weekend. The troupe was really talented, and their costumes were much more streamlined than the bulbous mascots that walked the park taking pictures with people.

On stage, Ping Pika was flung into the air before being caught by Leo Leopard before being tossed and caught again, this time by Pascha Polar Bear. Darby smiled at the athleticism and grace in the movement. All of the dancers were professionally trained, and it showed.

"No, no, no." A blonde woman stormed up to the stage and shook her head. "It's not big enough. She needs to go higher."

Stopping just inside the doors, Darby shook her head, watching Courtney Coughlin, this weekend's bride, standing with her hands on her hips. Long blonde hair, a perfectly made up face, she was stunning and absolutely horrible.

Following behind her was her fiancé, wearing his chinos, no socks, loafers, and a bright pink polo shirt with the collar up. He was looking down at his phone, which tended to be his usual stance.

Lance Seabrook was the heir to Seabrook Inc., the top yacht manufacturer in the world. His bride-to-be was an influencer who had struck gold with a makeup line that she sold through TikTok. Their wedding was scheduled for next weekend, and Courtney and Lance both had given new meaning to the term "bridezilla."

Courtney conferred with the choreographer while the dancers left the stage. Spying her, Leo Leopard headed toward Darby, pulling off his mask to reveal his dark hair and sparkling brown eyes. Juan Rivera grinned at her as he grabbed his water bottle and joined Darby.

"How's it going?" she asked, nodding toward the engaged couple.

Standing beside his betrothed, Lance's head was nodding even as he kept his gaze on his phone, while Courtney's hands were up in the air dramatically as she spoke with the choreographer.

Juan settled in against the wall next to Darby. "Remind me again why I do this?"

"For the applause and the big bucks?"

"No, no, that's not it," he mused.

"For the complete lack of recognition and the poverty wages?" she offered.

Straightening, he snapped his fingers. "That's it!" His grin faded as he looked down at his costume. "I had dreams of being my generation's Elvis."

"Elvis?" she asked.

He shrugged. "My mom loved him. I grew up listening to him and watching his specials over and over again." The grin slipped from his face as his eyes widened. "Uh-oh. Wicked Witch of the West incoming."

Darby flicked a glance over her shoulder. Claire Askins, the head of special events, was striding toward her. Her tightly curled black hair shone, and she wore a bright fuchsia suit tailored perfectly to accentuate her slim figure.

"Run away. Run away," Juan warned before he hustled back toward the stage.

"Maybe you should do the same," she called after him, eyeing Courtney, who still looked annoyed.

He grinned at her over his shoulder. "And miss all the excitement?"

Shaking her head, Darby turned toward Claire and plastered a smile on her face. "Hi, Claire. I hear there's a VIP tour you want me to give."

Claire stopped right in front of Darby and looked her over with a sneer. Darby looked down at her own outfit self-consciously. Nothing was out of place and there were no noticeable smudges or stains.

"Yes, yes. We have some special guests that need to be taken around personally," Claire said in an annoyed tone. Darby tried not to take it personally. Claire seemed perpetually annoyed with the world.

Flicking a glance at Courtney and Lance, who looked very busy with the choreographer, Darby let out a sigh of relief that at least she wouldn't be stuck with them for the day. "Great, so who am I taking?"

Dread pooled in Darby's stomach as Claire indicated the stage. "The couple who will be getting married this week. There's also another high-level guest who will be joining you." Claire gestured toward the man who stepped through the main doorway.

As he strode into the room, he stopped to talk with someone, a smile on his face that didn't quite reach his eyes.

And she would know that face anywhere: movie star Augustus King. She struggled to hold in her groan. *Great.*

CHAPTER 14

ALTHOUGH FELIX WAS BY NO MEANS A SCIENCE GUY, THE LAB AT Sanctuary Kingdom looked seriously state-of-the-art. There was no smell of animals when you stepped inside. Everything was pristine, with dark tiled floors and bright white walls. The rooms they passed had wide observation windows and inside, the rooms were lined with pristine equipment. Nothing was out of place and everyone he saw was focused on their jobs.

Ahead of them, a nervous guy who'd introduced himself as Ned led the way. Ned looked like he'd never done a push-up in his life. In fact, just the appearance of Felix and his crew seemed to make him want to run and hide somewhere in a corner.

It wasn't an unusual response. Each of his people gave off a "don't mess with me" vibe, and Felix himself gave off the biggest one.

Stepping into the lab at the end of the hall, Felix noted that the scientist in charge was standing at a lab table, muttering to himself as he stared at a monitor. He'd never met Dr. John Cadman but had read up on him. The guy looked like the older brother of Ned, and apparently, they had the same workout routine. He was gaunt, on the edge of emaciated.

It wasn't due to a particular lifestyle choice, at least not a conscious one. According to Felix's report, the doctor got so wrapped up in his research that he often forgot to eat; he even had to be rushed to the hospital for fainting twice.

Apparently, not much of a learner, despite all those degrees.

Felix dismissed the doctor immediately and focused on the two other guests. The tall guy with the bushy mustache was the head of security for the park. Despite that title, he was not the power broker in the room. No, that position belonged to the woman standing next to him. No doubt she had been the one who'd had them cool their heels in the lobby for thirty minutes.

Perfectly styled in a dark gray suit with her blonde hair pulled back in a tight bun, she had blue eyes that were a little paler than her brother's, and her features were a little too small for her face. She was a striking woman—not beautiful, but there was something arresting about her.

He walked toward her. "Ms. Latham? I'm Captain Adrian Felix."

"Martha," she said as she extended her hand.

He was surprised at how strong her grip was. He was a big believer that handshakes revealed a lot about a person.

"And this here is Dr. John Cadman and my head of security, Roger Collins." She gestured to the two other men.

Although Felix shook the head of security's hand, he merely nodded at the doctor. He was pretty sure that if he shook his hand, he'd break the bones in it. "All right, Doc. What have you got to tell us?"

With a sigh, the doctor picked up his tablet. Apparently, the man was a little put out at having to provide an update. "So, I'm going to assume no one here understands how aggression affects the brain."

Not waiting for a response, the doctor continued. "The brain chemical serotonin has been implicated in all types of aggression. Adding serotonin to fruit flies has resulted in increased aggression. The fruit flies will enter other flies' territories, either because they don't care or they don't recognize the boundaries."

Bobby perched his hip on one of the lab tables. "Don't really care about fruit flies, Doc."

Cadman glared at him. "You should. Humans or animals—studying these creatures has led us here today."

Taking a breath, the doctor continued. "We know that damage to the prefrontal cortex is associated with aggression, but since we don't want lasting damage, that's our focus. Now we're interested in the hypothalamus. Do you know what that is?" he asked Bobby smugly.

Felix let out his own sigh, mentally counting to ten. Then he stared the scientist down. "Located deep within the brain, the hypothalamus is the control center, keeping the body in homeostasis. It is also believed to serve a regulatory role in aggression."

"Yes, yes, that's right," the doctor stammered, some of his confidence shifting back into insecurity. "So, we have implanted electrodes in specific subjects to stimulate the hypothalamus and see if we can create aggressive episodes."

"How many animals?" Felix asked.

"Over a hundred, spread across species throughout the park."

CHAPTER 15

Augustus King was the star of Sanctuary Kingdom's runaway hit movie series, Guardian of the Wild. He played the swashbuckling animal sanctuary hero, Jax Ridley, always jetting across the globe to save animals in high-end locations.

Visually, the movies were stunning, and they were entertaining. Plus, they'd made a huge amount of money for animal research efforts across the globe.

Standing over six feet tall, he had the muscular build all action stars seemed to have. His looks were a striking combination of Asian and Caucasian features from his mixed-race parentage. Grudgingly, Darby had to admit she liked that he always brought his mom to award ceremonies and movie premieres.

This was not the first time Darby had seen Augustus King. He'd been on the park's property a number of times over the years. She had not had the pleasure of meeting him on any of those visits.

But she had taken a number of celebrities on tours over the years. Each tour left her feeling less excited for the next until she absolutely dreaded taking anyone with any sort of media following. In her experience, the image they showed the public when there were cameras around was very different from the person they were to people they viewed as staff.

Feeling Claire's gaze on her, Darby felt her cheeks flush. She'd been so caught up in staring at Augustus King and thinking of all the horrible interactions she'd had from past celebrity tours that she hadn't heard what Martha had said. "Sorry. What was that?"

"I asked if that's a problem."

The tone of Claire's voice made it clear that it was not supposed to be a problem. Whatever baggage Darby was dealing with, she needed to zip it up and pack it away. "No, not at all. I just need a minute. I was planning on taking my family on a private tour."

Claire's eyes narrowed. "And I assume you got permission for that?"

Once again, it was an effort for Darby to keep her smile in place. "Yes, of course. Gabe signed off on it. I just need to speak with them quickly and let them know about the change in plans."

"Very well. But make it quick. I'm sure they want to get started with the tour soon."

While Claire and Darby had been speaking, Courtney had moved away from the choreographer. Now it was just Lance. Now, with an annoyed look on his face, Lance stepped away from a heated argument with the choreographer, and strode over to his fiancée. Instead of going to her though, he stopped at a tripod and double-checked the phone attached there. He nodded to Courtney.

Immediately a smile burst across her face. "Hi, fans! Today is such an exciting day. We're at Sanctuary Kingdom, doing a last-minute review of the wedding preparations. And it is going to be amazing!"

She reached out her hand. Lance stepped into the shot, wrapping his arm around Courtney's waist, then kissing her cheek before he smiled at the camera.

"We are so excited, right, sweetheart?" she asked, beaming at him.

He smiled down at her and then at the camera. "Absolutely. And we want to give a special shout-out to Sanctuary Kingdom for making all of this possible."

Leaning into him, Courtney's grin grew wider. "Yes, and there's a discount code on my page for all of my followers. And remember, when you spend money here, you're saving animals across the globe!"

The two of them stood frozen for another moment before Courtney stepped away from Lance, flipping her hair over her shoulder. "Okay let's see how that looks. I swear, I feel so gross from all the negativity here."

"Don't worry baby. It's all going to be great," Lance crooned as he headed for the camera.

Trying not to look shocked, Darby turned her attention to a much better view. From one of the other doorways, she saw an older African American woman in a wheelchair being pushed in by a tall teenager in cargo shorts and a navy-blue-and-green-striped T-shirt—Mama Sue and Linc, her brother.

Next to her, Claire was explaining how important this couple's wedding going off without a hitch was. From the corner of Darby's eye, she saw Mama Sue wave. As Claire looked over at the couple, Darby waved back at them and held up one finger.

As Claire prattled on, Darby surreptitiously scanned the room, wondering who she could get to keep them entertained until she was free.

CHAPTER 16

A HUNDRED ANIMALS HAD RECEIVED IMPLANTS? ANGER SIMMERED UNDER Martha's skin. "I never approved that."

Frowning, Cadman stared at her. "You already approved some of them so I just added a few more of the same species. Higher numbers make for better tests. Even a hundred is small, though."

Narrowing her eyes, Martha was tempted to fire him on the spot. But this one wasn't some arrogant PR guy. He was critical on a number of other projects as well. She'd need to ease someone in as she eased him out.

Yes, Cadman's days here were numbered. He'd stepped way over the line.

When the government had first explained its intent behind the project, Martha had been reluctant to get involved. Making money was one thing, but actually endangering animals was something else altogether. She might not love them like her brother did, but she certainly didn't want to actively harm them. Eventually, though, she saw the benefits that the program could offer, particularly the financial ones.

But she had stipulated that she needed to be the point person for every single test subject. Not a single animal was allowed to be implanted without her approval. For the most part, she had no objections, except for one case where Cadman had wanted to try the implant on an older primate, George the orangutan.

Martha had put her foot down. George was not to be touched. While she and her brother had struggled to find their footing as adults, she still loved him. And she knew how much he loved George. George was a no-go zone.

As for the others, she didn't have any problems with them. Each had been taken over to the research center under the guise of being examined for possible enrollment in the breeding program. Electrodes were placed deep in the brain on the hypothalamus. At the push of a button, an electronic signal would be sent, stimulating the area.

But she'd only approved two dozen implants.

Unaware of his impending unemployment, Cadman continued. "All implants were completed as of Sunday night. In the last week, we've conducted the preliminary tests. All the implants are working properly."

Rolling her hands into fists, Martha stared daggers at Cadman. "I wasn't informed of that either."

Cadman shrugged. "It's standard protocol. Besides, it wasn't an official test. I just checked to make sure that they were working, and it was done at night. There was no risk."

"That was not your call to make, Doctor."

Meeting her gaze, he quickly looked away, finally seeming to recognize her anger. "Yes, yes, of course. I just didn't think of bothering you with it. It was just a few seconds for each of the implants."

Martha ground her teeth. It was a small slip of control, but this was what she had worried about when taking on government contracts. It was why she had put so many restrictions on the experiment itself— she needed to make sure that it was controlled and that it didn't get out of hand.

After all, she wouldn't do anything to endanger her park.

CHAPTER 17

WHEN HE'D FINALLY TALKED HIMSELF OUT OF HIS CAR AND INTO Dominion, Gabe had stopped by his sister's office, but she wasn't in. Kelly had been very evasive about exactly where she was. He sighed. His sister did love her secrets.

Two of the attendants behind the information desk smiled at him as he passed: Henry and Charlene. He knew both of them but didn't stop to talk. Before Joel, he would have stopped and asked after Henry's kids and how Charlene's son was doing at college. Today the idea of small talk made his heart pound. Because he knew if he asked how they were doing, they would also ask how he was doing.

And his "fine" still wasn't very convincing.

In Botswana, he'd spent more time with people than he had in the months earlier. He'd really become a recluse after Joel, but Botswana had opened the door. The idea of getting to spend a full day with Darby, Mama Sue, and Linc, though, well, that was absolutely irresistible at this point.

They never wanted anything from him other than himself. He didn't have to put on airs with them and they never asked him for anything. They just wanted to spend time with him.

And he needed that right now.

When he'd first met them, he'd made the mistake of trying to help them out financially. That had not gone well. Mama Sue had sat him down and explained that they would take handouts from no one. Him being there, that was all they wanted.

No one had ever said that to him before. Ever since the park had taken off, all the new people he'd met were more interested in the bank account that accompanied his name than him. At first, they'd seem to be interested in him as a person, but eventually, it turned around to some sort of ask.

Darby, Mama Sue, and Linc never did that. He'd often have to fight to even be able to take them out for a meal, despite the fact that they were constantly feeding him whenever he went over to their place.

He had, however, managed to make a few things happen behind the scenes. He'd created a disability grant at the park that Darby was able to tap into to build some ramps for their house after Mama Sue's MS progressed.

He had no doubt Darby knew his intention in creating the grant, but he also knew that she would do just about anything for Mama Sue. Linc was the same way.

In truth, so was Gabe. Mama Sue had taken him in like another one of her lost ducklings. Since his own mom passed away years ago, it was the closest he'd come to feeling that kind of support again.

Ahead, the ballroom doors to the west entrance were open, and he stepped inside. They were setting up for an event this weekend, and the stage was set up in the center of the room.

He noted the dance troupe getting ready to perform again, listening to the choreographer give last-minute instructions.

Glancing over, he saw the social media couple that was having the wedding here this weekend and winced. He knew Lance Seabrook in passing. His whole family was greatly impressed with themselves.

And while he didn't know the bride very well, he'd seen a couple of her posts. She was cut from the exact same cloth. The most charitable thing he could say about the two was that at least they seemed to have found their match.

Scanning the room, he caught sight of Darby talking to Claire. Darby's whole body was tense, and Claire stood with her hands on her hips.

Gabe frowned as he studied the two of them. *Now, what is going on there?*

"Hey, Wendy," he called out as Claire's assistant hurried past.

She looked over, giving him a harried look, and then her eyes widened. "Mr. Sullivan, I didn't know you were here."

"How many times have I told you to call me Gabe?"

She nodded quickly. "Sorry, sorry. Just kind of habit, you know?"

He nudged his chin toward Darby and Claire. "What's going on over there?"

Flicking a glance over her shoulder, Wendy winced. "Oh, Claire's giving Darby instructions about the private tour."

Gabe frowned. "For Mama Sue and Linc?"

Wendy shook her head. "No, there's a VIP couple, those two," she said, pointing at the influencer and her fiancé. "Claire wants her to take them around."

"What about Mama Sue and Linc?" Gabe asked.

"Oh, yeah, well, I'm trying to find someone to take them. It looks like it's probably going to be Ansell."

Gabe's gaze locked on Ansell Ledbetter. The man in question was standing fifty feet away, watching the choreographer. He sneezed and pulled out a handkerchief, wiping his nose before shoving it back in his pocket.

Ansell was in his early thirties but had the demeanor of a grandpa. He also bore a striking resemblance to the iron-deficient Ichabod Crane. "Ansell?"

"I know, I know. But Carson couldn't spare anybody else."

Nice but dull is how Gabe would describe Ansell. Nothing about this was making any sense. "Why is Darby doing tours? Is there some sort of marketing angle I'm not aware of?"

Most of the marketing lines went through Gabe, although he had to admit that he had not been paying close attention the last couple of months. When Wendy shifted from foot to foot, looking everywhere but at Gabe, he sighed. "Spill."

She flicked a glance up at him and then looked away, her voice small. "Well, Darby doesn't work in marketing anymore."

Gabe went still. "What do you mean she doesn't work there anymore?"

"Well, she just—she knows the park so well that she now does tours instead. I mean, it's usually for high-profile clients, so it's not just regular tours. Although she does sometimes do those."

Anger simmered at the edge of Gabe's brain. "She's been demoted to a tour guide? Who decided that?" Then he shook his head. "Never mind, I know."

He rubbed the bridge of his nose. Martha never liked Darby. He wasn't sure what it was. Part of him thought it might be a little bit of jealousy. Darby became the kid sister that on some level Martha should've been. "Let me guess, this started just after I left?"

Wendy gave him a firm nod.

"Okay, well, tell Ansell he's relieved of duty. I'm going to take Mama Sue and Linc for their walkabout."

Relief sent Wendy's shoulders dropping, a smile across her face. "That's great. Does this mean you're back?"

"Not fully. But back enough."

Nodding again, Wendy hurried toward Claire.

Gabe shook his head, watching her walk away. Darby had been demoted. What were they thinking? Darby was a very rare individual. She had this ability to put things together that others couldn't quite see.

It wasn't just that she was book smart, but she just saw links that others, including himself, missed. She was totally being wasted as a tour guide.

Well, he was back now. And all that was definitely going to change.

CHAPTER 18

THE RESEARCH GROUP MOVED TO THE VIEWING CHAMBER, WHICH WAS NEXT to the lab. Martha moved up to the window and glanced at the small creatures covered in black fur on the other side of the glass.

Felix stepped up next to her and frowned. "That's what a Tasmanian devil looks like?"

"What did you expect them to look like?" Martha asked.

The man shrugged. "I don't know. I mean, I guess I only know of Tasmanian devils from Looney Tunes. I expected, at the very least, they'd be brown."

It wasn't an uncommon expectation. While everyone knew the name Tasmanian devil, very few people would recognize the real thing. They were the largest carnivores of the marsupial species, solitary creatures that weighed anywhere from nine to twenty-six pounds and had black fur. They were twenty to thirty-one inches long, the size of a small dog. With tails half the length of their squat, thick bodies, their back legs were noticeably shorter than their front legs.

Their front paws had claws that were very apparent, and they had five toes on each foot. Despite their small size, they had a relatively short lifespan, living only five to eight years. Once found all over Tasmania, now only 10,000 to 25,000 remained.

Twenty to thirty were born to each mother, yet only four could feed at any one time, and most ended up dying as a result. They emerged at four months, were weaned by six, and on their own by eight. But it was not nature's poor early sustenance design that was to blame for the marsupial's dwindling numbers.

No, the culprit was the unique facial tumor disease found amongst the species, a rare contagious cancer that was highly infectious. It caused large lumps to form around the animal's mouth and head, making it nearly impossible for it to eat.

Once contracted, the animal eventually starved to death. Tasmania's devil population had plummeted from hundreds of thousands to as few as twenty thousand, resulting in the species now being classified as endangered.

But that's where the research center had stepped in. They had made a breakthrough and identified the genetic variant that allowed the disease to take hold. They were now creating a generation of marsupials that would be completely immune to the cancer. By next year, they'd be able to reintroduce it to its natural habitat, where they'd breed with the wild devils and create a new immune generation.

And that was why Martha supported this project. Funding for that breeding program was beyond expensive. The DOD's funds would help cover most, if not all, of the program. Although Martha had to admit it wasn't entirely an altruistic endeavor on her part. She had an entire PR campaign designed around the success that was supposed to go out in two weeks' time.

Both the park and her name would be prominently featured in all of the press releases. Yes, the DOD might not have been her first choice of partners, but in this case, they definitely had been the right partner, at least it terms of money and secrecy.

But as she waited for the test to begin, she still wasn't sure whether the project was the right one or if she'd placed her legacy on an increasingly dark and dangerous slope.

CHAPTER 19

Standing at the observation window next to Martha, Felix tilted his head as he looked at the two creatures in the forest-type setting. He had to admit, that was one of the things that amazed him the most about these setups: how well they could replicate the natural environment.

The Tasmanian devils, despite their name, were actually kind of cute. They looked like something out of a kids' movie, akin to a wombat.

As Martha shifted down the glass away from him, Sabrina stepped next to him. "Are they naturally aggressive?"

She turned her head to look at Ned, who seemed to wither under her gaze. "No, not really. I mean, they can be aggressive around food or when they're threatened, but most animals are like that. They're not really aggressive unless something happens to threaten them. But that's what the stimulation of the hypothalamus does—it kind of makes everything a threat."

Studying the animals, Felix contemplated the scientist's words. "But not all are like that, right?"

The man raised his head with a frown. "Excuse me?"

"You said most animals are not aggressive. But not all. Some are naturally aggressive."

The scientist nodded. "Yeah, lions, tigers, bears, sharks, they view almost everything as prey, and they're looking for a meal."

Bobby grunted. "Well, not all of us are prey," he said, flexing a bicep.

Santos laughed, and the scientist ducked his head even lower. Ned's phone rang. He looked down at it. "Okay, we're about to begin. Keep an eye on the Tasmanian devil with the blue tag on his left leg."

Felix spotted the creature he was talking about. Right now, the little guy was dozing.

In a moment, its eyes darted open. It launched itself at the nearest devil, its teeth clamping around its neck and biting hard. It continued to bite until the other devil stopped moving. Then, with its chest heaving, it backed away, moving over to the corner of the enclosure, curled up, and closed its eyes again.

"Holy crap," Bobby said.

"How long was that signal?" Felix asked.

"One point five seconds. But once it gets the bloodlust, it finishes the kill before retreating," Ned said.

Felix smiled. Apparently, this was money well spent.

CHAPTER 20

Extricating herself from the conversation with Claire, Darby hastened across the ballroom to Mama Sue and Linc, the tension easing from her shoulders at the sight of them. Mama Sue's multiple sclerosis had flared up a couple of years back. She'd fought it since then but this last year she had finally given in and started using a wheelchair.

Technically, Mama Sue was her adopted mom and Linc's foster mom. Their biological mom had died when Darby was ten and Linc was still a toddler. Mama Sue had taken them in as foster kids. Darby knew she wanted to adopt them, but she needed the extra funds to help with the household expenses that two kids brought with them. Mama Sue had been her mom's best friend, and Darby couldn't recall any part of her life without Mama Sue in it.

For years, even before she brought Linc and Darby into her home, Mama Sue had been a foster mom. Even after Linc and Darby joined the household, they'd had multiple children in and out of the house, but Darby and Linc had been the two who remained.

She noted that Mama Sue's face looked a little thin. She frowned at the dark circles under her eyes. As she approached, Mama Sue shook her head. "Don't start with that."

"Start with what?" Darby asked, forcing an innocent expression.

"You've got that 'Darby must take care of everyone' look on your face. I'm fine."

"I don't have that look," Darby murmured.

"Oh, yes, you do," Linc replied with a chuckle.

Shaking her head at her brother, she noted how grown up he looked now. With his rich brown complexion and Darby's extremely pale one, most people didn't realize they were siblings until they took a close look at their identical blue eyes.

He had just turned eighteen, which meant no more money coming from the state for Mama Sue. Darby had been dreading this day. She had worked hard throughout high school and had managed to get herself through college with some loans. She'd taken the job at Sanctuary Kingdom when she was in college so that she could start paying off those loans and take advantage of their tuition break program.

She'd hoped to go on to grad school. But with the money from the state stopping and Linc going to college now, that wasn't going to happen. Even with his track scholarship, she was going to need to put some extra money toward his upkeep every week as well as pitch in a little more for the household bills.

Linc had wanted to work during high school too, but with his speed, she knew that he needed to stay in sports. Besides, one of them should have a normal high school experience, and if it wasn't her, he was the only other kid who had a chance at it.

He was actually working at Sanctuary Kingdom this summer as well, manning one of the ice cream kiosks in the park. It paid pretty well and would also allow him to take a small college stipend that would help with some of his expenses not covered by the scholarship.

But even with the scholarship, his pay, and hers, it was still going to be tight. They really just did not make college easy in this country, which meant her grad school plans had to go on hold for at least four years.

As long as Linc got through, though, Darby was fine with the plan. What she wasn't fine with was Mama Sue being out of the house for longer than she needed to be. She tired easily these days. Trying to put some cheer into her tone, Darby smiled. "Okay, well, there's been a slight hiccup, and it looks like I'm going to have to take a private tour this morning."

Mama Sue's face fell. "That's all right, sweetie. We can reschedule."

"No, Wendy promised me that she would get someone else to cover your tour."

"And she has," a voice said from behind her.

Darby turned around, her eyes widening. A tall man with thick blonde hair wearing khaki shorts and a salmon-colored t-shirt that showed off his tan, grinned as he opened his arms wide.

"Gabe." Rushing toward him, she hugged him tight.

As he returned the embrace, he chuckled. "I should stay away longer if that means I get greetings like this."

"Absolutely not. You were gone for way too long as it was," Darby said, and then winced.

But he smiled down at her as he kissed her on the forehead. "It's good to see you, too, Darby."

Stepping around her, he leaned down to kiss Mama Sue on the cheek, then hugged Linc. "I heard there was an Ellis family outing, and lucky me, I just happen to be free and can offer my services as tour guide."

Darby was extremely grateful that it was Gabe who would be taking them around for multiple reasons. The top being he would make sure that Mama Sue got to see everything she wanted. Plus, she had a feeling that Gabe could use a little of Mama Sue's kindness. She was one of those people who made everybody around her feel taken care of.

Her adoptive mom loved animals. Whenever a new animal came in, Darby would give Mama Sue the heads-up, and when it was an option, she would offer to take her over to see them. Today, the Tasmanian devils were on the agenda, as well as the axolotls.

Gabe reached into his pocket and pulled out two bracelets that Darby recognized would get Mama Sue and Linc into just about every part of the park. He slipped one onto Mama Sue's wrist and handed Linc the other one. "All right, so these are our all-inclusive VIP passes. Let's get this tour started."

Mama Sue looked at Darby. "Are you going to be able to join us at some point?"

Flicking a glance over her shoulder at her charges, she winced. Courtney and Lance were now off the dais and talking animatedly with each other. Augustus King was surrounded by a flock of guests whom he was taking pictures with, and for the first time, she noted that he had an assistant, a young man with a crop of short curly hair, who was the one taking all of the pictures.

Darby sighed. "I hope so."

CHAPTER 21

ANGER LACED MARTHA'S STEPS AS SHE STRODE DOWN THE HALL TO HER office. Cadman had stepped way over the line. She'd pulled him aside and reamed him before leaving the research center. She didn't need to see any more of those tests. The first one was bad enough.

Kelly looked up in surprise as she caught sight of Martha. She stood up quickly. "I thought that would take longer."

"No. And I need two things: One, get me some applicants for Dr. Cadman's position."

Scrambling for a legal pad, Kelly quickly jotted down the note.

"And get me Archer on the phone."

"Uh, yes, right away."

Striding past Kelly and into her office, Martha closed the doors behind her. It was an effort not to slam them. The project had never sat right with her. Now with Cadman taking liberties . . . No, she needed to rein this in.

An image of her grandparents' disapproving expressions filtered through her mind. They had started the animal sanctuary, but its exponential growth was only because Martha had pulled on every lever of power she could reach.

But it was the initial seed money from *Fantastic Friends* that made all of this possible. Her brother had wanted to take the money and open more sanctuaries. But Martha had convinced him that Sanctuary

Kingdom was the way to go. She wanted the proceeds, she wanted the money, she wanted to be Disney.

The next step had been the movies. Universal had Harry Potter and had made a boatload of money in response. *Goddamn that little wizard.*

Sanctuary Kingdom had a swashbuckling lead who would take on poachers and animal traffickers. It was a combination of *Pirates of the Caribbean* and *Indiana Jones* with an animal focus. When the first entry had hit the market, *No Bounds,* it had taken off and been the number one hit that summer.

Each one that followed had been just as successful. They were now a full-fledged movie studio. They'd even been nominated for an Academy Award for the special effects in the last movie.

They had just broken into the billion-dollar club when the pandemic hit. Everything was shuttered. Even the movie industry had ground to a halt. So even the movies that they had in production had ground to a halt as well.

Then came the bad press: rumors about animal abuse at the Kingdom. It was complete garbage. There was not a single incident of animal abuse within their parks. Martha might not be a fan of animals —she hadn't even wanted to have a dog when they were growing up —but she would not stand for any animals being harmed. It was bad business.

Luckily, her brother had such goodwill across social media platforms that he was able to quiet that down.

Moving to her massive picture window, Martha stared out over the park, picturing how the land used to look. This had been the site of her grandfather's animal sanctuary. They had managed to buy all of the land surrounding it, little by little, acre by acre. What had started with her grandfather had only expanded from there. Her grandfather was like Gabe—people just liked him.

So much so that a lot of the neighbors had actually deeded their land to him after their deaths. That land had made all the difference. Getting the land for free had made it possible for them to start building.

The intercom beeped on Martha's desk. With a frustrated growl, she punched the receive button. "Yes?"

"I just wanted to let you know that your brother is looking for you."

Martha frowned and then shrugged. "Looking for me? Okay, give me five minutes and then put the call through."

"No, he didn't call. He's here."

Martha's hand jerked back from the intercom, and she grimaced down at it. *Dammit.*

CHAPTER 22

WENDY ASSURED DARBY THAT SHE HAD A LITTLE TIME, SO DARBY WALKED
with Mama Sue and Linc to the employee buffet and got them situated.
Gabe had just gotten a text from Kelly letting him know Martha was
back.

Juan and the rest of the dance team had been in the buffet line and
had promised to keep Mama Sue and Linc company until Gabe
returned. After thanking them, Darby hustled back to the ballroom.
She'd just turned the corner when she spied Claire striding from it
with Courtney, Lance, Augustus, and Augustus's assistant. Claire shot
a glare in Darby's direction.

So much for there being enough time. Darby picked up her pace. As
she approached, Claire turned so no one in the group could see her
annoyance but Darby. "There you are. This is Darby Ellis. She will be
your personal liaison for the tour of the park. Any questions, Darby
can answer them."

Courtney looked her over and seemed to dismiss her almost immediately. "Yeah, sure, whatever."

Nice to meet you too, Darby thought.

"All right, Darby, this is Augustus King, who of course you know."

Darby gave him a nod. He met her gaze, and Darby understood
why he was so popular. Something about that look seemed to cut right
through a girl.

"Call me Gus," he said, extending his hand.

She shook it, ignoring the tingles in her palm. Yup, he was even better looking up close.

Claire waved toward the influencers. "And of course, you know Courtney and Lance. Wherever they want to go, they get to go." Smiling, Claire turned back to the group. "Have a wonderful tour."

As Claire strode off, Darby looked at the fourth member of their group who hadn't been introduced. "Hi, I'm Darby."

"This is Noah," Gus said quickly.

Extending his hand, Noah shot a look at Claire's disappearing back. "I'm Gus's assistant."

Gus grinned at him. "Best assistant ever."

With a good-natured sigh, Noah rolled his eyes. "Thanks."

The exchange was not what Darby expected. Obviously these two were friends.

Waving her hand, Courtney gestured toward the nearest exit sign. "Yeah, yeah. Okay, now everyone knows everyone else. Can we get going already? We have to get back and meet with the wedding planner later."

Ignoring the rudeness, Darby used her best, upbeat "I love my job" voice. "Sure. So I thought we'd start at the axolotl exhibit. It hasn't been open to the public yet, and it's right across the bridge."

Courtney scrunched up her face. "Axolotl?"

"It's a really cute amphibian," Darby explained.

Grimacing, Courtney shook her head. "Yeah, that's not really going to work for me. I'm thinking we should start at the Castle. That sounds cool."

"Yeah, the Castle sounds like where we should start," Lance echoed.

Darby flicked a glance at Gus, who smiled back at her. "Whatever the bride and groom want is fine with me."

Plastering a smile on her face and getting the feeling that was an activity she was going to be doing a lot today, she nodded toward the doors. "All right, then, let's head to the monorail."

CHAPTER 23

FELIX WAS FEELING A LITTLE MORE RECEPTIVE TO THE WORK OF THE scientist. There had been five more demonstrations of the implant with the Tasmanian devils. Martha had not stayed. The look she'd given made it clear Cadman would not be employed for much longer. But the scientist didn't seem to recognize it.

Not that that was a surprise. These guys could explain the origins of the universe and yet couldn't read body language to save themselves.

The remaining tests had been just as impressive as the first. For the last three, the lab techs had brought in different species, wanting to make sure that the attack would occur regardless of whether or not they were familiar with the target or the size of the target. It hadn't been a problem.

Stepping out of the building, Felix pulled out his phone and quickly typed the message: *Test was successful. All subjects behaved as expected.*

His contact at the DOD was actually unknown to him. The contract had been verified, so he knew that it was somebody inside, but they were keeping their identity close to the vest. He'd tried to ferret out their identity, but he'd had no luck. Whoever it was, was very good at covering their tracks. He had no doubt that it was a burner phone that he was contacting.

Felix had no issue with that. National security interests came above everything else. Whoever was on the other side of the phone needed to keep some sort of plausible deniability.

Get me a bigger test, his source replied.

Picturing what that would mean, Felix smiled. *Will do.*

CHAPTER 24

On the way to the monorail, Darby sent a text to the tour office to explain the change of plans and asked that the security team member who would be joining them meet them at the monorail station. Whenever they had VIP guests, if they were well known, they had security personnel as part of the tour. Considering they had a full-fledged movie star like Augustus King, and considering that Courtney had quite a sizable following as well, they were definitely going to need that.

Darby led the way through the main foyer. As they walked, Gus smiled and waved at the guests or staff who caught sight of him and pointed. Quickly, Darby ushered them into the monorail station, and one of the security guards automatically closed the door behind them and took a position in front of it so no one could follow them.

The monorail station was attached to Dominion and ran on a single loop around the entire perimeter of the park. The track was elevated allowing the monorails to run on tracks fifty feet above the park. The monorail started a short distance from the main gate and stopped at stations along the perimeter of the park, with one separate line cutting through the center.

The monorails were bright white and solar-powered. The only sound they made was a soft hum, which Darcy had always thought sounded otherworldly. There were eight stations, all of them named after the *Fantastic Friends* or the locations seen on *Fantastic Friends*.

Darby gestured to the stairwell ahead. "There are stairs or—"

"We'll take the elevator," Courtney said, quickly moving toward it, and Lance followed.

"I opt to get a little exercise whenever I can." Gus inclined his head toward the stairs.

As Courtney and Lance were already on the elevator and the doors were closing, Darby really didn't have a choice. She led Gus and Noah to the stairwell next to the elevator bank. "Sounds good."

Gus walked next to her with Noah trailing behind them, checking his phone. "Have you worked at the park for long?" he asked as they started to climb.

"Almost five years now."

"Have you been a tour guide for that whole time?" Gus asked.

"When I started and then I did marketing."

He raised his eyebrows. "And then you decided to do private tours?"

She shrugged. "I know the park pretty well, so when it comes to certain guests, they like for me to give the tour."

"They like it , but you don't," he replied.

Her alarmed gaze flew toward him as she felt a blush spread across her cheeks. *Dammit, I should've worded that more carefully.* "No, of course not. I love working here, and it's great to meet new people."

He chuckled. "Nice save."

She was spared from having to respond as they reached the landing, and Courtney and Lance stepped out of the elevator. Courtney glanced around with a frown. "Where's the monorail?"

"It'll be here any moment. One arrives at each station every five minutes. The monorail heading west is the Leo Leopard train. You'll see him across the nose. The monorail going in the other direction had Ping Pika on the nose. In both cases, the other *Fantastic Friends* can be seen dancing along the train's sides."

Courtney had turned away before Darby had finished her explanation. Gus though spoke up. "They've put a lot of thought into this place."

"Yes, they have," Darby answered as she spied two figures heading down the monorail track toward them. Darby broke into a genuine grin when she caught sight of them.

"What is that?" Courtney asked, staring at the second figure.

"That is Mr. Sue."

"Mr. Sue?" Noah asked.

"The park has top-of-the-line security. Mr. Sue is our robot security. There are over three dozen of them scattered throughout the park. This particular model stays on the monorail station monitoring for any problems or issues and automatically notifies the appropriate individuals or departments."

"That's pretty cool," Noah said.

"That he is," Harry Fillmore, otherwise known as Scooter, said as he joined them with a grin. Scooter was Darby's absolute favorite member of security. He was hitting fifty-seven but looked at least ten years younger. He maintained the strong build he'd had since his Marine days and his time as a Hollywood stuntman. Mr. Sue rolled past them, heading toward the far end of the station as Scooter came to a stop.

Darby quickly made the introductions. Courtney and Lance once again were dismissive and wandered over to the edge of the platform. Noah shook Scooter's hand. Then Gus did the same and asked, "Scooter Fillmore from *Fallen Cliff*?"

Surprise flashed across Scooter's face. "Well, yeah."

"That fight scene on top of the train was awesome. I studied your moves. I swear I think I had them all memorized when I was a kid."

Scooter grinned. "Always nice to meet a fan. And I appreciate your work, too."

Gus waved his hand. "Oh, please. I just recite someone else's words. You stunt guys, you do the real stuff. You make the rest of us look awesome."

And Darby had to grudgingly admit it was a nice thing to say.

Footsteps sounded on the stairs behind them, and then a small brunette with round glasses appeared from the stairwell, a messenger bag over her shoulder. Darby frowned. "Ori? What are you doing here?"

Her eyes widening at the sight of Gus, who inclined his head toward her, Ori Rosenberg gave a nervous grin. "Darby, can I talk to you for a second?"

"Excuse me," Darby said before she moved off to the side with Ori. "What's going on?"

Keeping her voice low, Ori flicked a glance at the guests. "There have been a few, let's just call them glitches, with the system over the last two weeks."

Darby frowned. She hadn't heard anything about glitches.

Ori continued, "So Claire wanted me to join you guys. I don't think there's going to be any problems, but if there are, she wanted me along to handle it."

Ori worked in park operations and was an absolute whiz with computers. "Okay, great. But be warned, I don't think this is the friendliest of groups."

A grin slipped across Ori's face. "You mean an entitled bride and groom and a conceited movie star don't make for the best of companions? Stop."

Darby chuckled. "Oh, I think you coming along is going to make this so much better."

Linking her arm through Darby's, Ori started leading Darby toward the track as the monorail pulled up. "All right, well, let's get this tour on the road."

Feeling better with Scooter and Ori joining, Darby moved next to the monorail that had just pulled to a stop at the edge of the track. As the doors opened, she swept her arms toward the car. "Welcome to Sanctuary Kingdom."

CHAPTER 25

FINISHING OFF THE LAST OF THE FINANCIAL REPORTS, MARTHA FLICKED A glance at her watch before tapping on the intercom. "Where's the call from Archer?"

"He's in a meeting. He'll call as soon as he steps out."

Martha ground her teeth together. She hated waiting for people. Another glance at her watch, and she wondered if she should skip Archer altogether and just call Senator Freddie Markham. They went way back, although she'd only spoken with his aide regarding this project.

Then she shook her head. Her brother would be here any minute. Maybe she had time for a shorter call, though. She switched over to the video call screen just as there was a knock at her door. She looked up as her brother strode through with a warm smile. Standing, she smiled back at him.

It was hard not to smile at Gabe. There was something about him that made everyone feel as if he were their best friend. Growing up, Martha had thought that Gabe was her best friend too.

And he had been. But he'd also been a best friend to just about everybody else. Somehow he could make everyone feel as if they were the center of his world.

Studying him as he grew closer, she noted the dark circles under his bright blue eyes. Even that didn't diminish his attractiveness. His time overseas had left him with a healthy glow to his skin and had added some highlights to his blond hair.

They might have been twins, but somehow Gabe had gotten the looks. His eyes were just a little bit bluer, his cheekbones a little more pronounced, his features arranged just a little bit better than Martha's had been. She had always felt like the ugly duckling in comparison and had yet to develop into a swan.

Not that she was hard to look at. She took pains to present herself as well as she could. She had a stylist who picked out all of her clothes and another who came to do her hair and makeup for special events. She knew she was an attractive woman. But she was not "stop-traffic" attractive like her brother.

As she walked around the desk, her brother opened his arms. With a small laugh, she walked into them and he kissed her on the cheek. "Hey, Mattie."

He was the only one who called her that. Studying him, she noted that his eyes were a little red as well. "You doing okay?"

Looking away and taking a step back, he shrugged. "Yeah, I'm good. The Botswana sanctuary is up and running. It's ready for anybody that we need to send over there. I set up the transportation lines as well."

"And I saw you did a little press while you were over there."

He grinned. "Well, that's what you pay me for."

And that was the truth. Her brother was the face. The press couldn't get enough of him. He had to practically go into hiding after Joel's death to keep away from them. When he had reemerged, the press had treated him with kid gloves. Even they had fallen under her brother's spell.

The truth was, her brother was a good guy. She felt bad for even thinking negative thoughts about him. But it was so hard to be the one who always came in second place, no matter the competition.

At the same time, she knew she was the only one competing. Gabe wasn't competing with her. He stood on the sidelines for all of her events, cheering her on. He was the kind of kid who, if there were two pieces of cake, would make sure that Martha got the larger one. He had literally stood in the rain so that she could wear his jacket in a downpour.

But still, it was hard to never be someone's favorite, not even his. She shoved all of those old fears and worries aside. Why was it that whenever you were around people from your childhood, you somehow turned back into that insecure child? "You should've let me know you were coming," she said as she moved back behind her desk.

He shrugged again. "Yeah, I wasn't sure I was going to make it in this time. But hey, here I am." Her brother moved over to the window and nudged his chin toward the view. "I always loved the look of this place."

"Yeah, it's pretty amazing, isn't it?"

"Grandpa would be proud."

"I was just thinking the same thing."

Gabe looked over at her and smiled. Warmth settled in her chest as she smiled back at him. Then her screen chimed and she turned as Archer Fitzgerald appeared on it. Reaching over, Martha lowered the laptop screen but didn't close it entirely. "I need to take this."

"Anything I can help with?"

Martha shook her head as Gabe made his way to the other side of the desk. "No, I've got it handled. But we'll talk later, maybe over dinner?"

"I'd love that," Gabe said with a smile.

And Martha found herself loving the idea, too.

CHAPTER 26

On the monorail, the chairs were white with bright red plastic cushions. Colorful advertisements adorned the walls for merch, events, and restaurants in the park. The cars were always spotless, cool, and had the lightest scent of waffle cones to encourage people to eat.

Lance and Courtney sequestered themselves just about as far from the rest of the group as they could manage. Darby, Ori, and Scooter sat together while Gus and Noah sat a little bit farther down.

Smiling at her phone, Courtney made duck faces as she took shots of herself against the window. Occasionally, Lance would jump in with her, and when he wasn't, he was taking pictures of himself.

Watching them, Ori shook her head. "Wow, I mean, they're not really my type of people, but they really fit each other."

Darby grunted her agreement. Even the idea of living her life online made her break out in hives. But these two seemed to be absolutely in their element. She shrugged. It took all kinds.

Her gaze shifted to Gus, who sat speaking quietly with Noah. She hadn't seen him take a single selfie since he'd arrived. In the ballroom, he'd smiled through dozens of pictures, but those had all been taken on behalf of other people.

Feeling her gaze, Gus looked up at her and smiled. Giving him a quick smile, she turned her head back to Ori. "He's not what I expected."

"Yeah, kind of normal, right?" Ori said, flicking a surreptitious glance at the movie star. Then she dropped her voice to a whisper. "You think the real-life action hero story is true? Do you think he really helped save those people?"

Darby didn't need to ask what story she was referring to.

Studying Gus, there was no doubt his looks fit the role of movie star. But all Hollywood stars did. She wasn't sure what special secret they held, but extra fat didn't really seem to be a thing and six-packs were the norm.

But that wasn't what Ori was referring to.

According to the spin, prior to becoming a big star, Gus had been on a shoot in Mexico. She wasn't sure exactly what breach the back-story was on the cause, but a cartel took exception and kidnapped six members of the crew, including Augustus. He was credited with helping overpower the kidnappers and leading the kidnapped victims back to safety.

His career took off after that. Movie studios were flocking to the authentic action hero.

"Maybe we'll get to see him in action." Ori wiggled her eyebrows.

"Oh no. Definitely no action. This tour is going to be calm, bordering on boring." Then Darby frowned as she looked up at Scooter. "I thought you had a DART meeting this morning."

DART was an acronym for Dangerous Animal Rescue Team. Although not publicized, every zoo had one. They were composed of members of the zoo staff who were trained in firearms so that if there was a dangerous breech, they would be able to take down an animal that posed a risk to the public.

"Yeah, the meeting's going on back at Dominion. But they needed a volunteer for a VIP tour." Stretching his legs out in front of him, Scooter paused. "And I heard that Mama Sue's on site, right?"

Darby was not fooled by the nonchalant tone. Scooter had a major crush on Mama Sue. And Darby really wished he'd make a move or say something. But he was always so quiet around her, which was not the big man's way. She thought the two of them would be great together.

Trying to keep her voice just as nonchalant as Scooter's, Darby shrugged. "Actually, they are. Gabe's giving them a tour. In fact, I'm supposed to meet up with them after this. Why don't you tag along and say hi?"

He grinned at her. "I just might do that."

"Gabe's here?" Ori asked.

The smile on Darby's face widened. "He showed up this morning."

"That's good, right?" Ori asked.

"Yeah, now we just need to keep today calm and upbeat. Speaking of which . . ." She pulled out her phone and sent a quick text to Gabe. *How's it going?*

Good. I'll take good care of them. Just get your VIP crew through the park fast and meet up with us.

Will do, Darby replied before she shoved her phone back in her pocket.

Looking over the group she was in charge of, she had a feeling she could probably do exactly that. Gus was looking at something that Noah was showing him on his phone, and Courtney and Lance both had their eyes locked on their screens as well. None of them were looking out the full-length windows on either side of the monorail that gave breathtaking views of the park.

Yeah, these guys weren't really interested in the park. A quick tour and then she'd join up with the others.

CHAPTER 27

IT WAS A NICE DAY. THERE WAS A SLIGHT CHILL IN THE AIR BUT IT WOULD burn off by noon. Felix liked the chill. He liked the quick changes in temperature.

As he pulled out his phone, Sabrina strolled out from the building and, spying him, headed over. She leaned back against the truck next to him. "What's going on?"

"Boss wants to speed things up."

She grunted. "Not a surprise." Then she flicked a glance up at him. "It ever bother you we're not really sure who's on the other end of the phone?"

He shook his head. "Nope."

And it was true. The contract was with the DOD. That was all he needed to know. He trusted his country to send him to do things in their best interests.

He placed a call to Martha's personal cell. Her voice was frosty when she answered. "Yes?"

He smiled. "The boss needs to know when you guys can do a bigger test. He wants it today."

She didn't answer right away. Felix could practically hear her grinding her teeth. "It can't be today. It can't be done when the park is open."

"So let's do it now. You don't open until later."

"There are staff and private tours in the park. It's not possible."

Once again she paused, and his grin widened as he pictured her clenching and unclenching her fists. The short clipped tone of her voice only reinforced the image. "No. The soonest it can be done is next Sunday. The park closes early, and then it doesn't open again until one. There would be less chance of anyone discovering anything, and it would give us more time to clean things up in the morning."

"It needs to be done sooner," Felix insisted.

This time there was no pause in her response. Her voice lashed out. "I said no. It can't be done safely any sooner than Sunday. That is not negotiable."

Felix raised an eyebrow at her boldness. He couldn't help but think of his earlier conversation about predators and prey. Apparently, Martha was in the former category.

He smiled. "All right, ma'am. One week."

CHAPTER 28

WHEN THEY WERE HALFWAY TO THE CASTLE, GUS SAID SOMETHING TO Noah and then the two headed over to join Darby and the others. Gus smiled as he took a seat in the row directly across from Scooter, while Noah sat across from Darby and Ori. "Mind if I ask a couple of questions about the park security?"

Scooter narrowed his eyes. "Depends on what you want to ask."

Holding up his hands, Gus chuckled. "Nothing proprietary. There's a movie role that has come up that might be set in a park kind of like this, so I wanted to get some ideas of park security to see how it might fit in."

Scooter's shoulders relaxed. "Sure, ask away."

"So, the Mr. Sues, you said that they relay information to appropriate departments?"

The security guard nodded. "Yeah. If there is an electrical outage, if there's a security issue, they will contact the correct office and let us know so that we can dispatch a team."

"What kind of security issues?" Gus asked.

This time it was Ori who answered. "They have a camera built into their front screen. They're constantly doing facial recognition of all guests. And if anyone trips a flag or if anyone hasn't actually gone through one of the entrances, then we'll be notified."

"Has that happened before?" Gus asked.

Scooter shook his head. "No, not yet. Usually, if there's a problem with one of the guests, it gets flagged at the main entrance. That's the only way people can get into the facility. All the other entrances are not open to the public. The only way through them is with a special ID. Plus, with the twenty-foot wall, no one's scaling it to get inside. Plus, there are some other security precautions put in place to keep that from happening and to keep the animals inside."

Gus frowned. "What kind of security precautions?"

"The fences are electrified," Ori said, looking at her computer. In the silence that followed her response, she looked up. "What? That's publicly available too."

"Electrified fences? Isn't that illegal and, well, dangerous?" Noah asked.

Darby shook her head. "They're not an electric fence like you see on a farm or something like that, where they're always electrified. They're only turned on if there's an issue. So, for example, if the animals for some reason stampeded, then the fences would be turned on to keep them back. Or if they got too close to them, they would be turned on to keep them back. But they're not on perpetually."

"How do you determine when they should be turned on?" Noah asked.

"AI," Ori responded. "The last couple of years have radically changed things. We used to have to have someone monitoring the feeds all the time along with pressure plates. But now we can have AI do it and they can determine whether or not there's going to be a problem."

"That's impressive," Gus said.

Scooter grunted. "Yeah, not really a fan of the whole AI thing. I'd much prefer to have humans monitoring than computers."

"You said you catch people at the main entrance. Like what kind of people?" Gus asked.

"Oh, all sorts. We don't allow anyone convicted of any type of sex crime or abuse against children in the park. And there are certain people that security will highlight who they just get a bad vibe off of. Those individuals will have an undercover agent trail them while they're in the park to make sure that they don't cause any problems."

"What about weapons? Do people ever try to bring weapons in?" Noah asked.

Flicking a glance at Darby and Ori, Scooter said, "Yeah. There's been a couple of cases where people have tried to bring in full-on assault rifles."

Darby's mouth fell open. "What? I hadn't heard that."

"Not really something we publicize. It's usually handguns, knives, Tasers. One guy tried to bring a slingshot. We confiscate any and all weapons if they want to come in. The guns we hand over to the police and then the individual can go speak with them about getting the weapons back."

"Why on earth would anyone bring a gun to an amusement park?" Noah asked.

Scooter shrugged. "Some people just love their guns. Honestly, I think half of them just forgot they even had it with them. They're just so used to carrying them around that it never occurred to them that there might be a place where they weren't allowed to carry them."

Darby shook her head. While Scooter had taught her how to shoot, she wasn't a fan of guns.

"What about these bracelets?" Gus asked.

"They have an RFID signal in them. It allows us to keep track of every single guest in the park, so we know exactly where they are," Ori said.

Noah's eyes widened. "That's a ton of data."

Ori nodded. "Yeah. AI, once again, has really helped with that, making sure that it's easy to spot and find specific guests when we need to. It's really a whole new world out there."

Scooter slumped a little lower in his seat. "Yeah, but I'm not sure it's a better one."

CHAPTER 29

THERE WAS SOMETHING GOING ON WITH HIS SISTER. GABE DIDN'T KNOW what it was, but there was definitely something off there. She'd practically bum-rushed him out of her office.

Not that they were the type that would sit down and chat for hours. His sister didn't really do small talk. But he hadn't seen her since a week after Joel's funeral. Since then, all they'd had were texts and emails. He'd expected a little more, he had to admit.

An image of the man on her laptop screen flashed through his mind. He didn't recognize the guy. Obviously, he was some sort of government official, or more likely an aide to a government official, given his age and the Tennessee and American flags he saw in the background.

It probably had something to do with the tax breaks that his sister was trying to get put into place. She was really good at that stuff. Gabe was useless with it.

As he passed the tour office, Mina Gomez rushed out. "Gabe, I heard you're doing a tour."

"Yes, but it's for Darby's family," he said already knowing where she was probably going with this.

"I know, which is perfect because I'm hoping you can take a trainee."

Gabe sighed. Although he wanted to say no, he did like doing the trainings. He wanted to make sure that everyone in the park had an incredible experience.

"Please," Mina said looking up at him with her big eyes. "I'll bring you empanadas."

He groaned. "You play dirty, Mina. Yes. I'll take a trainee and send a security guard as well."

"You expecting trouble?"

Picturing Mama Sue's wheelchair, he shook his head. If there was a medical issue, though, he wanted someone who could get help right away so he could focus on her. "No, not at all. Just a precaution."

"You are the best," Mina said as she backtracked to her office.

"Yeah, yeah," Gabe said waving her away as he picked up his pace. A smile started to build as he focused on the day ahead, his anticipation growing.

Stepping into the room off the ballroom, he spied Mama Sue and Linc finishing off their meal. He crossed the room to join them.

Mama Sue's eyes lit up. "There you are."

He couldn't help hugging her again and there was a tremble in her arms as she returned the embrace. As he leaned back, she cupped his face in her hands and studied him, before speaking softly. "All right, then."

Gabe's throat tightened. There was something about Mama Sue: she just made you feel seen. In that small look, he had no doubt that she'd just read everything that had happened to him over the last six months in that glance and knew exactly where he was right now.

He kissed her lightly on the cheek. "Let's get this show on the road."

In just a few minutes, they were in the hall heading to the monorail. Gabe walked behind Mama Sue's wheelchair, his hands on the handles, even as the motor whirred along.

Running a critical eye over the chair, Gabe noted it looked like it was in good shape. The EZ Lite Cruiser weighed only forty-five pounds and cost a couple thousand. It had a manual freewheel lever mounted on each motor.

He and Linc had picked it out as a Christmas gift and Gabe had it regularly serviced. It was the only expensive gift she'd allowed him to purchase for her. That only happened because Darby and Linc had begged her to keep it, mentioning how hard it was to get the other chair in and out of the car.

And being she wouldn't let him buy her a van, he wanted something that could at least be used with the car that they currently had.

As they walked, Mama Sue leaned back and patted his hand with a smile. More of the tension eased from his chest.

Next to him, Linc walked along, and Gabe looked over at him, raising his eyebrows. "Did you grow like four inches in the last six months?"

Linc grinned back at him. "Only an inch."

Gabe chuckled. "Oh, well, barely anything at all."

With the extra inch, Linc was now six foot three and slim. With his T-shirt and baggy shorts, he looked like any other teenager. But a glance at his calves showed the strength there. He had not an ounce of fat and was perfectly balanced for a runner. "So what's your 100-yard dash at?"

Linc grinned at him. "Ten twenty."

Letting out a low whistle, Gabe smiled. "Tennessee is lucky to have you."

Linc's smile started to fade. Concerned, Gabe asked, "Everything okay?"

Lincoln nudged his chin toward Mama Sue and mouthed, *Later.*

Meeting the young man's eyes, Gabe frowned as they stepped onto the monorail platform. There were two individuals standing waiting for them.

One was the tour guide wearing the customary navy-blue shorts and pale-blue top indicating her trainee status. She had brown curly hair that was pulled back into a high ponytail and bright brown eyes. She smiled as she stepped forward. "Mr. Sullivan, my name is Meg Dorchester. Ms. Gomez said that I should meet you here. I appreciate you letting me tag along."

Gabe shook her hand. "The more, the merrier. This here is Mama Sue Jenkins, and Abraham Ellis, but everybody calls him Linc."

Meg frowned. "Linc?"

"I had a growth spurt when I was really young, and everybody thought I looked like Abe Lincoln. So Linc." He shrugged. Long ago, he'd accepted that that was the nickname he was stuck with.

The security guard with Meg extended his hand as well. "Well, it's a pleasure to meet you, Linc. I'm Bao Nguyen."

Bao shook Linc's hand first, which Gabe actually liked, rather than giving deference to Gabe. Then Bao shook Mama Sue's before turning to Gabe. "Mr. Sullivan, a pleasure to meet you."

"It's just Gabe, and it's a pleasure to meet you as well. How long have you been on security?"

"Just about a month. Quite the complex you guys have built here."

"Yeah, we're pretty proud of it." Gabe glanced down at Bao's leg. His left one ended at the kneecap, and below it was a shiny silver-and-red prosthetic. "Wow, is that one of the bionic models?"

Bao gave a sharp nod. "Yeah. I lost the limb over in Afghanistan and was lucky enough to become part of one of the pilot programs."

Gabe knew he shouldn't stare, but he was fascinated by the technology. He knew the latest bionic models had more springs and dampers than rigid actuators, allowing for a more natural walk. It was designed to be similar to a transmission where the walker shifts gears.

Plus, it had a nearly endless battery supply, which recharged with movement. It was connected to the subject with implanted electrodes rather than on the skin, which could lose connection due to sweat or dampness. "How do you like it?"

"Well, I prefer my own leg, but this is pretty darn close." Bao grinned.

Before any of them could respond, the monorail pulled up. Linc pushed Mama Sue toward the doors.

Hustling forward, Gabe took the customary position next to the doors that a tour guide would take. Extending his arms toward the car, he smiled as the doors opened. "Welcome to Sanctuary Kingdom."

CHAPTER 30

When the monorail pulled into Station Jillie, Courtney and Lance hopped off their seats and were the first at the doors. Standing more slowly, Darby smoothed out the wrinkles in her shorts. "This is Station Jillie, named, of course, after Jillie Giraffe."

The doors opened, and Courtney and Lance bolted onto the platform, making a beeline for the massive park map attached to the station house.

Ori and Darby exchanged a look. Apparently those two were actually interested in the park. Darby stood by the doors of the car, holding her hand over them to make sure everyone got safely through.

"Thank you," Gus said with a little nod as he stepped onto the platform with Noah, who shot her a grin.

Scooter leaned down as he passed Darby, dropping his voice. "Gotta say, he's not like any movie star I've met."

Watching Gus and Noah head over to the map as well, Darby let the doors slide shut behind her, Ori, and Scooter with a hiss of the hydraulic pumps.

As she headed for the others, her spirits lifted a little. *Maybe this day won't be too bad*, she thought, her gaze on Noah and Gus. But then it shifted to Courtney and Lance, who were posing in front of the map taking picture after picture.

Nope. It was going to be horrible.

Done with the photo shoot, Courtney frowned at the map. Then she aimed the same frown at Darby. "Wait, you guys have hyenas? Why didn't you tell us that?"

Darby wasn't really sure what the correct response to that was. They had over two thousand species of animals at the park, with upwards of 20,000 animals on the entire 8,000 acres. Just reciting all of them would have taken hours. Besides, she had asked if they were interested in any exhibit in particular.

"Yes, the exhibit's just there." Darby pointed to a tall building that had been designed to look like a desert mountain.

Grabbing Lance's arm, Courtney let out a squeal. "We have to go. I love hyenas. They're my spirit animal."

"They are?" Noah asked in disbelief.

Giving him a baleful look, Courtney put her hands on her hips. "Yes," she said, drawing out the word. "They're always laughing and looking for the joy, just like me."

Lance wrapped an arm around her and kissed her on the cheek. "Exactly."

Darby and Ori exchanged another look. Hyenas were definitely not either of their spirit animals. In fact, hyenas were one of the few animals that scared Darby. Maybe she'd watched *The Lion King* one too many times when she was a kid, but hyenas had never incited anything in her but dread. Nothing she had learned about them discouraged that impression.

An adult spotted hyena could tear off and swallow thirty to forty pounds of meat per feeding. But they also had incredible bite strength: their massive jaw muscles and molars allowed them to pulverize the bones for minerals and fatty marrow. Although depicted as scavengers, they actually killed 95 percent of their food.

Most zoos didn't have them. They weren't exactly the popular cute, cuddly animal types. They were also matriarchs: males who killed their dinner would have to eat quickly before they were pushed aside by the females.

And that laugh: it was terrifying. It sounded like a human laugh. It wasn't a laugh of joy, though, like Courtney thought. The vocalization was a sign of submission or nervous excitement.

Scooter grinned at Darby. "You know what? Ori and I will run ahead and just let them know you're coming. Make sure everything's secure and that all the tech is working correctly."

Walking backwards toward the exit, Ori gave Darby an apologetic smile. "Yeah, I really should run a quick diagnostic."

"Thanks. That would be sooooo helpful." Darby's words dripped with insincerity.

His eyes twinkling, Scooter nodded. "That's us: always trying to help." He tugged on Ori's sleeve and, after giving Darby a shrug, she hustled down the path with Scooter.

Watching them go, Darby couldn't blame them for bailing. They weren't tour guides. She would bail too if she could.

Once again, she thought of Gabe, Mama Sue, and Linc somewhere in the park, no doubt having a wonderful time. *And here I am with Bride and Groomzilla.*

So no, she couldn't blame Scooter and Ori for taking the excuse to disappear. On the train, the only time the two influencers had stopped taking pictures was to review the pictures they'd taken. It was a lot.

Plus, Ori was no doubt on the search for caffeine. Before noon, it was rare to see her without her coffee thermos. She practically main-lined caffeine and then went cold turkey at the strike of noon.

Darby watched her two friends getting farther away with more than a little envy. Then she flicked a glance over at Gus and Noah, wondering if they were regretting agreeing to come along on this tour.

Before she could suggest they go with Scooter and Ori, Courtney let out a squeal. "Oh my God, I have loved hyenas ever since I saw the *Buffy The Vampire Slayer* episode where Xander turned into a hyena."

Frowning, Darby remembered that episode. But it didn't exactly make her feel all warm and fuzzy toward the creatures.

"Lance, let's do a quick preview." Stepping toward the directory, Courtney flicked her hair over her shoulder as Lance moved opposite her.

Taking out her own phone, Courtney checked her hair and makeup before slipping it back in her pocket. She posed in front of the directory with her arms up, like she was a game show hostess. Lance stood in front of her with his camera aimed at her. He held up three fingers, then counted down and pointed.

Pointing at the map, Courtney smiled. "Oh my God, guys. They have hyenas here! I absolutely love hyenas. Do you remember that *Buffy* episode? Just the coolest. I mean, don't get me wrong: Joss Whedon is still totally cancelled. Hashtag: believe women."

Gus moved behind Darby and whispered into her ear, "Uh, am I remembering that episode wrong? Didn't a group of teenagers get possessed by the hyenas and then eat their school principal?"

"Yup, that's how I remember it, too," Darby said.

Stepping to Darby's other side, Noah crossed his arms over his chest as he watched Lance and Courtney. "Influencers are weird," he declared.

With a deep sigh, Darby nodded her agreement. "Yup."

CHAPTER 31

ON THE MONORAIL, MEG SAT WITH BAO, AND GABE NOTED THE EASE between the two of them that only came when you knew someone very, very well. Pulling up their employment applications on his phone, he noted that they'd both served at the same time.

As he placed his phone back in his pocket, he asked, "You two knew each other before the park?"

"Yeah, we served together," Meg said.

Taking her hand, Bao squeezed it while smiling at her. "She's the medic who saved my life."

"You found love in a dark place," Mama Sue said. "My husband and I met the same way."

Gabe was surprised by her comment. She never mentioned her husband. The one and only time she'd ever said anything, it had been that some pains were too deep to speak of. At the time, he hadn't known what she meant.

Now he did.

As the doors opened and closed at the different stations, Meg looked between Gabe and the doors, expecting him to stand. As they approached Station Sandra, Gabe got up and helped Mama Sue position her chair at the doors. As they opened, he pushed her through. Linc bounded ahead, a grin on her face.

"Do you normally start at the north end of the park?" Meg asked as she stepped off behind them.

Gabe smiled pushing Mama Sue down the ramp . "No. Usually tours begin near the main entrance. For VIP tours, the order of attractions can be adjusted depending on the wishes of the guests. Today, though, we're not doing the full tour. So we're starting at the far end of the park."

He nodded ahead toward a towering structure. The exterior was designed to be like a living, breathing rainforest. Gabe loved the design: he modeled it after the animatronics at the Rainforest Cafe. He loved kids' responses the first time they saw the animals move, and he wanted to give guests at the park a similar experience. It was old-fashioned, he knew, but not everything old needed to be changed.

Unlike the Rainforest Cafe, instead of a giant volcano, they'd created a cliffside with a running river and waterfall. Animatronic birds flew overhead on wires. Gorillas romped across an opening. Large cats lazed in trees, a few with their cubs. It was a delight.

And the name across the top was done in bright neon colors: GEORGE'S PLACE.

"So why start here?" Meg asked.

The same urgency that had gripped him prior to the ballroom took hold of him again as he picked up his pace. "Because I need to say hi to an old friend."

CHAPTER 32

It had taken Courtney and Lance three attempts before Courtney declared the recording perfect. Then she smiled at Gus as they headed toward the exit of the station. "We're doing a whole preparing-for-the-wedding series of posts. We're saving a bunch of behind-the-scenes takes for our superfans. We have a separate paid membership service, exclusively for them. You should consider upping your social media presence. It's pretty bare-bones."

Noah laughed and then shifted it into a cough as Courtney narrowed her eyes at him.

But Gus pulled her attention as he spoke. "That's a great idea. I'll mention it to my social media team."

"Absolutely." Courtney raised her chin, giving Noah a smug look before she linked arms with Lance. "Look, honey, let's get some shots outside. It's going to look amazing."

Grudgingly, Darby had to admit she agreed with Courntney. Despite Darby's unease with the animals in this particular exhibit, Darby had to admit that the design of the place was great and would make a great backdrop. The exterior consisted of rough-hewn stone, weathered wood, and a thatched roof. There was a massive twenty-by-thirty-foot entryway designed like a rocky outcrop with incredibly realistic statues of smiling hyenas.

A shiver rolled down Darby's spine as she looked at them. She knew they were fake, but she hated walking past them. Whoever had created them was very, very good at their job.

The massive LAUGHING DEN sign was designed to look like a weathered piece of wood with the name spelled out in orange and yellow paint. On either side, instead of the realistic hyenas, there were smiling, friendly cartoon hyenas.

The path leading to the main entrance was lined with grasses and small bushes found in the savanna. A soundtrack of animal sounds played along with music to help set the scene for the visitors.

Bypassing Courtney and Lance, who'd stopped so Courtney could play supermodel next to one of the realistic hyenas, Gus, Darby, and Noah headed for the main entrance.

Stepping into the large foyer, Darby smiled. Despite her dislike of the species, once again, the designers had outdone themselves.

The foyer was designed to replicate a cave, lined with themed gardens featuring skylights with real trees, aloe vera, and elephant grass. Covering the ceiling were murals of hyenas in the wild. All the images were child-friendly, without any depictions of a hyena kill.

There was an education zone to the left filled with interactive exhibits that explained the hyenas' habitat, nutrition, and pack life. Most people were surprised to learn that hyenas could have packs as large as 120 animals.

Directly across from the main entrance was the viewing area. The one-way glass was fifty feet long and provided a perfect view of the replicated savanna where the hyenas lived. The area was completely enclosed, and the hyenas were given limited, structured access to an outside area. It had to be carefully controlled because the hyenas' cackles disturbed both guests and other animals.

The observation window continued down a large hall to the left, winding around the exhibit. There was no sign of Scooter or Ori, but standing near the observation window was a tall man in a full-on safari outfit: button-down khaki shirt, matching khaki-colored shorts, slightly darker knee-high socks, boots, and a pith helmet completed the look.

Courtney let out a squeal as she spotted the gift store and headed straight for it. Lance joined her. The young woman stocking the shelves looked over at Darby. Darby shrugged and mouthed, *VIP*.

With a sigh, the woman left her stock and took position behind the counter as Courtney oohed and aahed over the selection of stuffed animals.

The commotion caused the hyenas' keeper, Bashir Mousa, to look over with a frown. But then his gaze shifted over to Darby. A warm smile crossed his face. Placing his tablet on the lip of the exhibit, he started across the foyer with his arms wide. "My favorite tour guide."

Returning the grin, Darby jogged over to Bash and hugged him tight. "My favorite keeper."

While Darby might not care for the hyenas, she definitely liked Bash. Aged fifty-two, he'd been born in Pakistan and still had traces of his accent despite moving to the US when he was ten. As he grinned down at her, the wrinkles at the corners of his eyes deepened. "I thought you had this morning off?"

"I was supposed to, but then things changed." She was careful to keep her tone light as Gus and Noah followed her over.

Bash flicked a glance at them and then did a double take. "Wait, you're—"

"Augustus King," Gus said as he extended his hand.

Gripping it, Bash grinned widely, his dark eyes wrinkling with humor. "I know. My daughter has posters of you on her walls."

Gus winced. "I'm really never sure what to say when a father tells me that."

Bash chuckled. "I'm not sure there is a good response." He turned to Noah. "Bashir Mousa, hyena keeper."

"Now that's a cool title. Noah Hudson." Noah gripped the older man's hand with a grin.

"Nice to meet you, Noah. And I can't say I've come across many with the same job. Now why don't I give you guys the penny tour?" Bash moved toward the exhibit. Noah fell in step with him as Gus fell in step with Darby.

An eerie laugh cut through the air. The hair on Darby's arms rose, and it was an effort not to stop walking.

Next to her, Gus gave a self-conscious laugh. "Well, that's creepy."

Darby nodded. "Yeah, I'm not a fan either. It's a recording of a hyena call. They set them off every twenty-two minutes."

Gus's eyebrows rose. "I thought you had to be a fan of all animals in the park as the park's representative."

Watching him from the corner of her eye, she gave him a wry grin. "Oh, I'm a fan of everyone learning about and protecting the animals in the park. But not every animal needs to be my favorite. These guys definitely are not."

Nodding to the exhibit next to them, Gus frowned. "The calls don't disturb the hyenas?"

"Oh, they do." She shivered. "The first time the hyenas heard the call, they flung themselves at the glass trying to get through. Then they started trying to find ways out of the enclosure."

Gus's eyes widened. "But that could never happen, right? They can't get out. "

"No," she said firmly. "They soundproofed the glass. And those gates are locked tight."

"Absolutely," Bash said, stopping as he gestured to the exhibit behind him. "Sanctuary Kingdom takes great care of its animals and its guests."

Stepping to the glass, Darby looked down at the hyenas. There were about three dozen in view. But the pack was closer to fifty.

Bash continued. "The spotted hyenas are the largest hyena species, ranging in weight from ninety to one hundred and forty pounds. They can be anywhere from a mere thirty-four inches long to a whopping fifty-nine inches. Found south of the Sahara Desert, they reside in savannas, eschewing high altitudes, extreme heat, and rainforests.

"They are also highly social, creating massive packs and covering over six hundred miles. And although they look similar to dogs, they're more closely related to cats."

"Really?" Gus asked as he peered down at them.

"And they're smart." Pointing to a hyena making its way across the rocky ground, Bash said, "Their physical appearance has lent itself to the belief that they're unintelligent."

"It's the walk," Noah said watching one cut across the space.

Bash nodded. "It's loping walk is unusual, caused by front and back legs of different lengths. But it's an incredibly efficient movement. In movies, they're often portrayed as idiotic because of their gait. But the hyena's intelligence is undeniable."

Focused on the largest hyena in the space, the alpha looked up and stared at the glass. Though Darby knew the glass was soundproof and allowed only one-way viewing, she had the distinct impression the hyena knew they were there. It was an effort not to take a step back.

Instead, she murmured, "And they most definitely are not to be underestimated."

CHAPTER 33

THE ORANGUTAN ENCLOSURE SOARED UP FORTY FEET WITH A GLASS ROOF that could be opened or closed depending on the weather. Real trees grew inside the temperature-controlled space that had been designed to replicate a real rainforest, complete with appropriate trees and fauna. The only difference was that the trees were carefully arranged so they did not block the viewing window.

Which meant that as Gabe brought Mama Sue's wheelchair to a stop in front of the window, he had a perfect view inside. One of the trainers, Paul Miller, was in the back corner of the enclosure using treats to teach one of the younger orangutans sign language. The gate to the outdoor area was locked, so the other six Sumatran orangutans would not be able to enter.

But one was already inside, resting with his eyes closed against a tree. Long, thin red hair covered him. His cheek flanges indicated he was mature and announced his dominance. For the orangutans, these grew larger and more pronounced with each passing year.

Below his chin, a prominent throat pouch hung, enabling him to produce powerful, resonant calls that could echo through a forest for miles. Not that George had been in a forest since he was a child.

"That's George," Gabe said, nodding to the mature ape as Sheila Bronson, one of the assistant keepers, joined them.

"He's a sweetheart," Sheila said with a smile.

Gabe nodded toward the group as he made introductions. "Sheila, this is Bao and Meg, and you know Mama Sue and Linc."

"Of course, it's great to see you again," Shiela replied with a smile for all of them.

"Can you give Meg and Bao a little tour of the exhibits while I go say hi?" Gabe asked.

"Sure thing. I think he's missed you." Sheila nudged her chin toward the glass.

"I've missed him too," Gabe said as he headed for the keeper door. Placing his bracelet over the scanner, the screen glowed green as the lock disengaged.

George's face was broad and flat, dominated by massive cheek pads that framed deep-set, thoughtful eyes that opened as Gabe stepped into the exhibit from the side hall. Holding his breath as he walked slowly across the exhibit, Gabe signed, *Hello.*

The great ape's eyes widened as he sat up and moved toward Gabe, stopping when he was a few feet away.

Gone long, he signed.

Nodding, Gabe sat down against one of the trees. *I know. Sorry.*

He and George had learned sign language together. To say the two had grown up together wasn't strong enough to explain what George meant to him. On *Fantastic Friends,* he'd added George as the wise elder that the friends went to for advice.

His grandfather rescued George from smugglers when Gabe was five. When his grandfather brought him home, Gabe had slept next to his crate. He'd wanted to set up his little sleeping bag right next to the bars, not wanting the little orphan to feel alone. His grandfather kept him a safe distance away while he'd slept on a cot nearby.

That first night, George had curled up as far from Gabe as he could manage. By morning, though, he'd moved right to the edge of the cage, as close to Gabe as he could manage. Their friendship had blossomed from that moment. In fact, Gabe had named him George after *Curious George.*

George studied him now, leaning toward him to peer at his face as he sniffed. *Sad?*

There was no point in lying to him. Animals knew better. Gabe rolled his hand into a fist and bobbed it forward. *Yes.*

Miss Joel?

His throat feeling tight, Gabe's fist bobbed forward again. *Yes.*

The morning after Joel's death, Gabe had come to tell George. He wanted his friend to know. He'd met Joel and knew how important he was to Gabe. Now George leaned his forehead into Gabe's.

Taking slow, short breaths, tears pressed against Gabe's eyes. He'd hoped to get through this visit without breaking down. George hooted softly as he reached up and patted Gabe's back, offering him comfort.

A tear rolled down Gabe's cheek as he whispered, "Thank you, George."

CHAPTER 34

Her gaze roving over the large glass wall of the hyena exhibit, Darby asked, "How are they doing today?"

Almost instantly, Bash's expression shifted from friendly to concerned as he glanced over at the exhibit. "I'm not really sure. They're behaving . . . strangely."

"Strangely how?" she asked.

"There have been a few little outbursts of aggression," Bash said.

"Is that one bleeding?" Noah pointed to a smaller hyena licking its leg off to the side of the larger group.

His gaze fixed on the enclosure, Bash nodded. "Yes."

Studying the pack, Darby frowned. "That is strange."

Flicking his gaze between Darby, Bash, and the pack, Gus asked, "But isn't that normal? I mean, they're aggressive, right?"

Bash shook his head. "No, the pecking order is pretty well established. There might be a little skirmish at feeding time, but not for long. And this didn't happen at feeding time."

Studying Bash, Darby knew this pack's hierarchy was strict. The alpha made sure of that. Violence did occasionally break out but like Bash said, it was rare. There was something though in the keeper's face that sent off warning bells in Darby's mind.. "But it's not just the violence that's bothering you, is it?"

"No. It's who was aggressive that bothers me." He gestured toward the smallest hyena inside the enclosure. It lay curled up, its back against the wall.

Shock rippled through Darby. "It was Figaro?"

"She's tiny," Gus murmured.

Her gaze locked on the small hyena, her shock now mixed with confusion. "That's a he."

"That's one tiny guy," Noah grunted.

His brow furrowed, Bash's gaze was directed at the small hyenas as he spoke. "The female hyenas are larger than the males. The females are the alphas in hyena packs. The small ones don't make trouble. They don't have the size to make trouble. Figaro never has before."

His gaze focused on the one hyena that stood staring boldly at them, Gus asked, "And that one there, she's the alpha?"

It was an effort for Darby not to shudder. "Yeah, that's Tomy."

"Tomy?" Gus asked.

"Short for Tomyris," Bash explained.

Noah grunted. "Tomyris: the queen of a group of nomadic tribes along the Caspian Sea during the third century. They waged war against Cyrus the Great. Lost the first battle, victorious in the second. Tomyris took Cyrus's head and plunged it into a bucket of blood."

Darby looked over at him with her eyebrows raised.

He shrugged. "I like history."

Watching the alpha, Bash nodded. "It's a fitting name for her. Her putting members of her pack in place is normal. She came out killing. She was part of a litter of four. She killed the other three within twenty-four hours."

Gus raised his eyebrows. "Is that normal?"

"For hyenas? Yeah. Unlike other animals, hyenas are born with their eyes open, muscles coordinated, and teeth already pierced through their gums and eager to bite. They are quite literally ready to kill from birth," Bash explained.

Taking a step closer to the glass, Gus studied the hyenas. "Are they really that dangerous?"

"Don't be fooled by their size," Bash warned. "These guys working together can reduce a full-grown, four-hundred-pound zebra to a bloodstain in thirty minutes. They can run over thirty-five miles per hour, have excellent hearing, and sharp night vision. Plus, they're smart."

"You said that before. How smart are they, exactly?" Noah asked.

Her forehead practically touching the glass, Darby answered, her mind calling up the research. "They outperform chimpanzees on certain cognitive tests."

"Seriously?" Gus's eyes widened before he turned to take in the enclosure with a concerned look. "I'd never heard that."

"And they view us as the enemy," Bash said.

"What do you mean?" Noah asked.

"Some animals have to learn to distrust humans. Not so with hyenas. They seem to know it's unwise to trust us," Bash explained.

"Why is that?" Noah asked.

Bash flicked a glance at Darby, who explained, "Some think it's because we hunted them down early on in our history. But others argue it's even more primal than that. Hyenas are ancient. They've existed since before we stepped down from the trees. They were already on the ground. Some suggest the scarcity of bones from our early days is attributable to them. Hyenas' digestive systems destroy everything except teeth."

Gus gave a nervous laugh. "That's crazy."

Bash shrugged. "Maybe. But tooth marks on bones right next to tool marks suggest they've been stealing our meals for over two million years and maybe making *us* those meals. So I think we should all be pretty glad this wall is between us and them."

CHAPTER 35

IT WAS TIME. KEVIN CRACKED HIS KNUCKLES, ROLLED HIS NECK, AND started going through his checklist. As he did, his phone rang. He ignored it and continued with his work. The phone cut off, but a minute later, it rang again. With a growl, he grabbed it. It was a video call. Kevin shook his head. *Idiot.*

He flicked it on. "What?" he demanded.

Todd Sharp narrowed his eyes at him. His stringy brown hair pulled back into a ponytail, his voice was laced with nerves. "We good to go?"

"Almost. I've got a few more things to run through here."

Todd's face was too close to the camera. As he talked, Kevin could see clearly into his mouth. *What a doofus.* "We need to get moving. I don't want our people out here exposed."

Kevin rolled his eyes. For an ecoterrorist, the guy was awfully nervous. Kevin wasn't sure he was going to survive in this line of work. "Making no mistakes establishes the certainty of victory, for it means conquering an enemy that is already defeated."

The Sun Tzu quote had the desired effect. Todd nodded quickly. "Of course, of course."

Normally, it was Todd who walked around quoting Sun Tzu. Kevin wasn't sure he had read any other books, but *The Art of War* the guy had down. In fact, there was a banner directly across the warehouse that someone had painted in red: *In the midst of chaos, there is also opportunity.*

Kevin smiled. Normally, Todd's quoting really annoyed the heck out of him, and having to look at that banner every day hadn't exactly thrilled him. But today, today that banner was right on point. For there would definitely be chaos, and that chaos was his opportunity. "I won't be rushed. Rushing is when mistakes are made."

"Fine, fine. Just let us know when we can go."

"Sure thing, boss." Kevin smirked. Disconnecting the call, he double-checked that he'd covered everything. Then he smiled. "Time for a little test."

Inputting the coded sequence, he took a deep breath and then hit enter.

CHAPTER 36

It would take thirty minutes for Sheila to finish the tour with Mama Sue, Linc, Bao and Meg. Gabe had planned on joining them, but honestly, being with George was so darn peaceful. Animals force you to live in the moment. Right now, Gabe needed that.

So he sat shoulder to shoulder with his friend and watched the clouds above. Every once in a while, Paul's voice would drift over, followed by a hoot from the younger orangutan he was teaching.

Movement outside the viewing window pulled his attention. Linc waved from where he stood with the others. With regret, Gabe stood, but inside, he promised himself he'd come back tomorrow morning, well before the park opened, to visit with George. Not for George's sake, but selfishly, for his own. He'd been to a grief counselor a few times, but he was pretty sure this time with George was more impactful than any time on the counselor's couch.

George got to his feet as well, his gaze on the window. He ambled over and held up his hand to Mama Sue. Gabe chuckled. George was always a ladies' man. Mama Sue reached out her hand as well with a large smile.

As Gabe took a step toward the door, George's head jolted up, his gaze locking on Paul and the other orangutan. The hairs on Gabe's arms stood straight up as George let out a deep-throated call before he barreled toward Paul.

Mouth dropping open, Gabe whirled around as the young orangutan let out a screech. He lashed out with his powerful arm, the back of his palm cutting across Paul's cheek and sending him flying.

"Oh my God."

George slid to a stop, baring his teeth as the younger orangutan leapt into the air to stomp on Paul. Before he could land, George shoved him back, his screams echoing through the space. The other orangutans appeared at the gated door, hooting and hollering, yanking on the door.

The door to the enclosure flew open as Sheila darted in, holding a tranquilizer gun, Meg and Bao were right behind her.

"Gabe, get back!" Sheila yelled as she advanced. But the young orangutan tackled George, rolling him across the enclosure with a ferocious roar.

Barreling past him, Sheila dropped to one knee. In horror, Gabe watched as the younger orangutan's teeth latched on to George's neck. "No! George!"

Before he could take a step, Meg and Bao latched on to him, pulling him back.

"Let me go," Gabe pleaded.

Meg's voice was full of compassion, but her grip didn't lessen. "You can't help him, not like this."

Sheila pulled the trigger, a dart going into the young one. But it would take time for the drugs to take effect. She sent another one into George even as the young one slammed his paw into George's face. A crack sounded.

Gabe's heart felt like it snapped in two.

Pushing back against Bao and Meg, he wasn't capable of rational thought. All he knew was that his friend was right there and needed help. But the hands on him were like steel. His heart shredded as George went still.

Despair, grief, and horror roared up inside Gabe as they reached the door. "George!"

CHAPTER 37

Bash continued his lecture on hyenas explaining their social structure and dietary habits as they walked. As he did so, Courtney and Lance rejoined them. Courtney had a small stuffed hyena sticking out of her bag.

As he explained the gender differences, he nodded toward the massive hyena that was five feet long. "The larger, more muscular hyenas are females."

Glancing at the hyenas, Courtney frowned. "That can't be a girl. I mean she has a . . . you know." Her cheeks reddening, Courtney waved her hand toward the large animal.

A small smile appeared on Bash's face. "Oh, it's a girl all right. For the longest time, hyenas were thought to be hermaphrodites because their sexual organs looked so similar to males. But Tomy there is most definitely a female and most definitely in charge."

"That's, I guess, pretty feminist." Courtney turned to Lance, who immediately raised his phone at her. Courtney smiled. "Hyenas are the feminists of the animal kingdom. They even look like guys. But it's the girls that run the pack."

His mouth hanging open, Bash stared at Courtney for a moment before giving Darby an incredulous look. With a sigh, she raised her hands with a shake of her head.

Still looking dumbfounded, he moved away from Courtney as she continued her recording. He shot another glance at the exhibit, his brow furrowing as Noah and Gus moved a little farther down the path, no doubt to make sure they were not caught in the back of Courtney's post.

Keeping her voice low, Darby stepped next to him. "You okay?"

Flicking a glance first to make sure the others were out of hearing range, he lowered his head toward her. "I still don't get what got into Figaro. He's bottom of the pack. They don't get aggressive."

The worry and confusion were clear in Bash's voice. He was the national expert on hyenas. The fact that he didn't understand what had happened was making Darby worried. "Could he be sick?"

"It's possible, but this wasn't the first incident. He had a small aggressive incident earlier in the week. But honestly, I thought that was food-related. Now I'm wondering. I sent a message to Cora, and we're scheduling Figaro for some tests."

A new fear gripped Darby. "You think it's a parasite?"

Dropping his voice as she flicked a glance at the others who were too far away to hear them, his gaze shifted back to the viewing window. "I hope not."

Darby well understood that hope. All animals went through a rigorous quarantine and a round of vaccinations before they were allowed into the park. That protocol should keep them protected from all known viruses. But there was always a chance of an unknown one.

Bash's voice was heavy with concern. "It's unlikely that it's a known pathogen. But COVID made it clear that we can't prevent everything."

"You think this is another illness like COVID?"

"What? No, I just mean it's possible the animals aren't inoculated against something." He gave her an obviously forced smile. "But don't worry. We'll figure it out."

CHAPTER 38

AFTER THE ATTACK IN THE ORANGUTAN ENCLOSURE, EVERYTHING WAS A blur. Somewhere along the way, someone had draped a blanket over Gabe's shoulders, although he didn't remember who or when. He sat on a bench with Mama Sue on one side, holding his hand, and Linc on the other.

Meg crouched down in front of him and shone a light in his eyes. "Any injuries? Any tingling or feelings of pain or stress?"

He let out a little laugh. "Stress?"

She grimaced. "Physical stress," she clarified.

He shook his head, watching as the vet, Tabatha Durbin, worked on George. He didn't like how slowly George's chest seemed to be moving, but at least it was moving.

Putting the flashlight away, Meg stayed crouched down so she could look Gabe in the eyes. "Okay, so Paul has got a dislocated shoulder, a pretty good black eye, and some scrapes and bruises, but overall he's fine."

"And George?"

"I'll go check." Standing, she headed over.

There was the sound of running feet from the entrance. Gabe looked over as Chuck Park came rushing in. Pushing sixty-five, Chuck had a full head of white hair and a barrel chest. He wore a white button-down shirt with short sleeves and khakis. He'd worn the same outfit every day Gabe had known him.

Chuck had been the orangutan keeper before Paul. He'd asked to take a step back a few months ago, the beginning of him wading into retirement. Patting Mama Sue's hand, Gabe stood.

The movement drew Chuck's attention, and he stopped short. His eyes widened as he hurried over. "Gabe. My God, what's going on?"

"One of the young orangutans—I don't know which one—attacked Paul. George got in the way."

Letting out a breath, Chuck's hand flew to his mouth. "Holy crap."

Gabe frowned. "Chuck, don't take this the wrong way, but what are you doing here?"

Chuck had moved over to more of an administrative role and worked over in the Dominion offices. His gaze distracted, he said, "I've been working with Paul this last week. There've been some outbursts among the primates."

"Outbursts?" Gabe asked.

His gaze worried, Chuck looked over at where George was being worked on. "Oh my God, George. Is he going to be okay?"

"Tabatha is working on him," was all Gabe could manage to say. "Tell me about the outbursts."

Chuck ran a hand through his thinning hair. "It wasn't much, but Paul was concerned. It was a few of the young ones. Just two of them. But they were lashing out. It lasted only a second or two. It was just strange. He wasn't sure what to make of it, so he asked if I would come and just see if I could see something he hadn't.

"I've been coming each morning for the last week to try and see if there's anything I can do to help. But none of the incidents happened when I was around. They all seemed to be happening at night."

Orangutans weren't nocturnal. Their activity level decreased throughout the day. Gabe frowned. "Has something been added to the exhibit that's setting them off?"

Shaking his head, Chuck darted a look at the windows of the exhibit as if to reassure himself of his answer. "No, nothing's changed. Everything is the same."

"So what's your theory?" Gabe asked.

Exasperation laced the former keeper's words. "I don't have one. Paul and I even went as far as to get some tests, worried that it might be a parasite."

Fear took root in Gabe's chest. If something had slipped in, it could be an absolute disaster, not just for the orangutans but for all of the animals at the park.

If it was something that could be transmitted to humans, that would be an even bigger disaster. It wasn't as rare as people probably thought. In fact, 60% of all known human infectious diseases originated in an animal species.

Tabatha walked over then, and Gabe studied her face. She gave him a slight smile. "George is going to be okay. He got knocked around pretty good, and he's got some bruising, so he's going to have to rest up. But he should be all right. I'm going to arrange a transfer and take him over to the hospital to get him set up so that we know he's staying still. I've got him sedated right now."

Feeling slightly better, Gabe gave her a tight smile. "Thank you, Tabatha."

"After I check on the younger one, I'll arrange for the transfer." Tabatha stepped away, pulling her phone from her pocket as Gabe turned back to Chuck.

"I'll go check on Paul," Chuck said.

"Yeah. I'll join you in a minute." Gabe watched Chuck walk away with a frown. The orangutans had been misbehaving. He needed to see the state of things. He turned back to Mama Sue and Linc. "You guys going to be okay here for a few minutes?"

"Yeah, we're fine," Linc said as Mama Sue nodded.

He looked over at Bao, who gave him a nod indicating he'd keep an eye on them. Then Gabe hustled down the hall and entered the area off-limits to guests. Quickly, he made his way down the hall to the CCTV room.

Stepping in, he caught sight of a young man he didn't know behind a panel. In front of him were monitors depicting each part of the orangutan enclosure. While the security at the park took care of all of the human areas, each enclosure was carefully monitored on a separate system.

Gabe strode toward the man. "I'm Gabe Sullivan."

Mouth falling open, the young man nodded his head a few times. "Yeah, I know, Mr. Sullivan. I recognize you from your picture." He pointed to the framed image on the wall of him and Martha standing in front of Sanctuary Kingdom when it first opened.

"Good. I need to see the recordings of the orangutans acting out."

The man hunched his shoulders toward the keyboard and began typing quickly. In a moment, he pointed to the screen on the left-hand side of the array. "Here's the first one."

Stepping closer to the screen, Gabe watched as a young orangutan went still for a moment, then let out a scream, beating his chest, and then stopped almost as quickly.

Before he could say anything, another image appeared on a second screen. This time the young orangutan was with an older one. The young one looked at him, and then his hand smacked out faster than Gabe thought possible.

Caught unaware, the older orangutan fell back. But the young one didn't follow up the attack. In fact, he cowered away.

On and on, these split-second moments of aggression appeared on the screens. Gabe stared at them, understanding why Paul had called in Chuck. This was not normal behavior.

"Is that all of them?" Gabe asked.

His voice shaking, the young man said, "Yeah. That's all of them."

"Is one of those the same ape as today?"

"No, there are two others. The one today hasn't been part of any of the incidents . . . Well, at least until now."

"No one sees this but me. Is that understood?"

The young man nodded. "Yes, yes, sir."

Gabe turned on his heel and strode from the room, his mind racing. What the hell was going on?

CHAPTER 39

Hanging up the phone, Martha let out a breath. She'd been speaking with the head of *Environment Now*, a highly influential green-energy group. The park would be throwing its weight behind a bill coming through Congress that created subsidies for all forms of green energy.

But all during the phone call, she kept thinking about the earlier phone call with Archer. Instead of supporting pulling back the research, he suggested increasing it. First Cadman had run late-night tests without her approval, and now the DOD was trying to push in further. They wanted to run a large-scale test during the day. It was insanity.

I never should have signed that damn contract.

Giving herself a shake, she focused back on the moment. She had a park to run. This weekend she'd speak with Senator Markham. She was done going through Archer.

But she shoved all that from her mind, returning her thoughts to the conversation with *Environment Now*. She tapped the intercom. "I gave them the green light on our support. Can you follow up with them and make sure there's nothing new in the proposal?"

"Will do. I'll have legal run through it before I bring it to you."

"Good." Standing, Martha winced at the small kink in her lower back. She needed a break and something filled with sugar, her diet be damned. She turned to call Kelly when her assistant stepped into the room, shaking.

God, not another problem, Martha groaned silently. Out loud, she asked, "What happened?"

"There was an incident," Kelly said, a tremor in her voice as she went quiet.

Martha waved her hand at her assistant to hurry up. "Well, tell me."

"One of the maintenance staff was working on the lights along the river. Some of the bulbs needed to be replaced. They'd shifted during the last storm and just needed to be repositioned."

"Okay. So?"

"One of the alligators got him."

The words not computing for a moment, Marth stared at her. "Got him?" She echoed.

Kelly nodded.

Her mouth hanging open, Martha shook her head. "No, that's not possible. The fences make sure that that can't happen."

"Something must have gone wrong with the fence. The gator was somewhere he shouldn't be."

"Wh—The maintenance guy. Is he okay?"

Horror was in Kelly's voice. "There were witnesses who saw him go down. The alligator rolled him. He never came back up."

When she was young, Martha had gone on a river trip with her grandpa. She'd seen a deer get too close to the river's edge. A crocodile had wrapped its powerful jaws around it and dragged it into the water. The water had churned and churned as the crocodile rolled and then went still as the crocodile disappeared underneath with its prize. Then it reappeared, and bashed the deer against the rocks before devouring it.

It had left her with nightmares for weeks.

Martha's gaze darted to the window, her mind calculating. If there was one mistake, there could be more. "All staff need to stay indoors. No one is allowed out. I want all the park's security fences checked for errors."

"Roger already put out the order."

"Good. Run safety checks on all the perimeters. Any issues, that section gets shut down and everyone evacuated immediately. And has DART been mobilized?"

Kelly paused. "We can't seem to reach them. Something's wrong with the phones."

"Send a maintenance team to the tower. If something's going on, communication is key. Until then, have security grab a handful of staff, go to the buildings, and make sure everybody stays indoors. No one goes outside."

Nodding her head furiously, Kelly backed out of the room and then started running down the hall.

Martha ran a hand through her hair. "Oh, Jesus."

CHAPTER 40

EXCITEMENT COURSED THROUGH KEVIN. THE TEST HAD GONE WELL. ALL OF the subjects had responded. It had been a lower-frequency test because he didn't want them all going berserk.

At least not yet.

He'd also started shutting down the park's communication and its security. Not all of it, as he'd just started getting the ball rolling.

As for the implants, he'd only turned them on for a split second, just long enough to know that they were working. But in that short space of time, one of the subjects had nearly gotten Gabe Sullivan.

Kevin's smile widened as he pictured the orangutan enclosure. God, that would've been so good. Blond hair, blue eyes—Gabe was one of those guys who'd always been handsome. He was really wealthy now, although Kevin could grudgingly admit that he hadn't started out that way. But he sure as hell was now, and he had millions of followers online.

The guy was freaking beloved. When his husband died a few months back, you would've thought that everybody knew him. The outpouring of support had been immense. Little Gabe Sullivan had stepped away from the world, but in the last couple of weeks, he'd started posting again—small things, just pictures of where he was or stories about animals he was working with. The world had once again embraced him.

And Kevin had nearly gotten him. That would've made a big splash. But getting the keeper was just as good. Taking one last look across the screen, Kevin grabbed the phone and sent the text: *We're good to go.*

Todd replied almost immediately: *Long live the revolution.*

Picturing Gabe Sullivan, Kevin rolled his eyes. *Whatever. Just bring the pain.*

CHAPTER 41

Before Gabe rejoined the others, he needed a moment. Stepping from the CCTV room, he leaned back against the wall. George would be okay, he reminded himself.

But the image of George falling flashed through his mind, making him wince. Then he pictured George right before the attack. His head had turned. He'd known there was something wrong.

Had the other orangutan made a sound? A scent that alerted George?

What was going on with the orangutans? *I shouldn't have stayed away so long. Maybe if I'd been here, I could have helped.*

He could almost hear his therapist chastising him. *There's no should. Everyone grieves in his or her own way.*

That might be true. But he couldn't help but think that his way of grieving had left people at the park without someone to run to. Martha was great at the business angle, but she didn't want to hear about problems unless there was a solution attached. So Gabe was the one people went to. But without him here . . .

Gabe made his way back to the bench where he had left Mama Sue and Linc. They were still there, with Bao standing protectively nearby. Now they had a drink and a snack. He noted Meg was conferring with Tabatha, and then frowned when he saw Chuck had joined them, all three looking concerned.

Holding up a finger to indicate he'd join Mama Sue and Linc in a minute, Gabe headed over to the other group. "What's going on?"

Tabatha looked up at him, her face and tone concerned. "Communications are down. I can't call anyone."

"What?" Gabe pulled out his own phone and stared at the screen. In the top-right corner, he had no bars. "What about the park's communications?"

They had installed a landline to ensure that if there were any problems with the cell towers, they would still be able to communicate throughout the park.

"They're down too. The emergency radio wasn't charged, so we have no way of getting help sent for Paul or George," Meg explained.

Gabe frowned. "Probably just a small outage. I'm sure they're working on it. I'll make sure that help gets sent."

"Okay. I'll accompany George when the transport arrives." Tabatha said.

"Thanks, Tabatha," Gabe said as she headed back toward his friend.

Chuck lowered his voice. "I don't know what's going on, but it had to have happened in the time I was traveling here. I was over at the Dominion office when I got the call. I hustled over here about, what, fifteen, twenty minutes ago tops? The communications were working fine then."

Once again, Gabe was completely flummoxed as to what the heck was going on. He glanced over his shoulder at Mama Sue and Linc. This was not the tour he'd wanted to provide them with. "Okay, I'll head back to Dominion. I'll send over paramedics for Paul and arrange the transfer for George. You want to come with us?" he asked Chuck.

Chuck shook his head. "No. I want to go over some of the footage and review the blood tests we ran. Maybe there's something here."

"Okay. We'll send help as soon as we reach Dominion." With Meg, Gabe made his way back to Mama Sue and Linc. Bao moved a little closer, flicking his gaze over at where the others were.

Trying to force a calm he didn't feel, Gabe smiled. "Okay, so obviously this adventure has taken a detour. We're going to head back to

Dominion. Something's going on with communications, and we need to get some help for everybody."

"Of course, of course," Mama Sue said. "Should we wait here?"

He knew it would be faster if he just sprinted back to Dominion rather than taking a cart or even the rail system, but something in his gut told him that leaving Mama Sue and Linc alone wasn't a good idea. "No, I think I want to keep you guys close to me. We'll all go together."

CHAPTER 42

THE MICROWAVE BEEPED. KEVIN OPENED THE DOOR TO PULL OUT THE BAG
of popcorn. He hurried back to his seat, opened the bag, and let the
steam waft out. The exits were sealed, Dominion was cut off from the
park, and everything was in place.

Best of all, no one on the Sanctuary Kingdom campus had any clue.
He'd spent weeks working his way into their system, testing each of
the defenses one by one. Their defenses were significant, but he'd
figured out how to control them all.

God, this is like the best video game ever, he thought.

On screen, he brought up all the images from the park's cameras.
He'd had a bunch of EcoAct lackeys string together a series of monitors. Now they sat in a row of twelve around him. Ideally, he'd have a
room with a wall full of monitors, but that required a bank balance he
simply didn't have yet. So instead, he had a long line of twelve. They
didn't even match: some were small, some were big. Directly in front
of him, he had his main monitor with another twelve camera angles
and another larger monitor beside it.

He wasn't happy with the setup, but beggars couldn't be choosers.
Sitting back down, he brought up the main images he wanted on his
central monitor, sending the others to the rest so he could scan them
and pull them up as needed. He also had an AI program working that

would alert him to anything of interest. Overseeing the park was a massive undertaking, but the AI program made it possible.

Sitting back, he wiped his hands on his shirt before digging a hand into the bag of popcorn and dropping a few kernels into his mouth. He grabbed his energy drink and grinned broadly at the screen.

"Showtime."

CHAPTER 43

After Courtney finished her recording, they'd followed the observation window to the rear of the exhibit. Although Bash was clearly worried, he managed to hide it well as he answered all the questions of mainly Gus and Noah and finished up the tour. The hallway they traversed featured the observation windows on one side and interactive exhibits, along with brightly colored posters explaining hyena facts on the other.

The back of the Laughing Den included a playground for kids, a massive gift store that guests had to walk through to exit, and, of course, the Giggle Grill. They stopped there for a caffeine hit, finding Scooter and Ori waiting for them with a small snack buffet table set up. Ori handed Darby a cappuccino with an apologetic grin. "Sorry. I needed to mentally prepare for this tour," she whispered.

"I get it." Taking a sip, Darby let out a sigh. "You're forgiven."

The caffeine, along with the sugar hit, definitely helped alleviate some of the anxiety created by the hyena visit. She wasn't sure why they always bothered her so much. Maybe the theorists were right and there was some ancestral antagonism between the two species.

And maybe they weren't the only ones who felt it.

But it wasn't just the hyenas that were leaving her unsettled. She'd really been looking forward to spending the day with Mama Sue and

Linc. Working so many long hours, she felt like she barely saw them these days.

Plus, Linc would be leaving for school soon and then she'd see him even less. Everything was going to change. She wanted, no needed, this one day of normality.

Finishing off her cappuccino and some crumb cake, she started to feel a little more optimistic. What was it about a full stomach that always made obstacles seem more surmountable?

Wiping her hands on a napkin, she was resolved to swiftly finish the rest of this visit and meet the others for an early lunch. Looking over the group, it appeared they were all about done as well. "We ready to move on?"

Courtney rolled her eyes with a big sigh. "How long is this tour, anyway?"

"As long or short as you want," Darby replied.

"Short," Lance said quickly. "I mean, we still have so many wedding details to go over."

"Uh-huh," Scooter muttered under his breath as he grabbed Darby's dishes with a wink.

"Well, let's get moving, then." Darby stood up and headed for the exit, noting that Courtney had added a hyena on a keychain to her bag.

Pushing through the double doors, warm air slid over Darby. A sigh of relief escaped her lips as she stepped out of the hyena house and led the group down the path that looped back around to the front of the exhibit. The path mirrored the design of the exhibit with exotic plants and the desert-style rocks on either side.

But they had one new addition: animatronic hyenas. Gabe really was obsessed with old-fashioned robotics. Hyenas were hidden in the foliage around them, playing, sleeping, and at the end of the path, the last one waved goodbye.

An involuntary shudder shook Darby's frame as they were officially off the path. Next to her, Gus raised his eyebrows. "You really don't like hyenas."

Giving him a rueful smile, she shook her head. "No, I really don't. But I respect the hell out of them."

And with a shock she realized she was talking with a movie star.

He was nothing like what she'd expected. He'd made no demands, and she could talk to him like anyone else. "Anywhere you want to go next?"

"How about we ask the happy couple?" He nodded toward Courtney and Lance.

"Guys, is there any—" Darby didn't finish the statement, as Courtney let out a squeal.

"Games!" She grabbed Lance's hand. The two of them hurried toward the darkened game area.

Watching them, Darby struggled to figure out why exactly they were having their wedding at the park. They didn't seem to like animals at all, except for the hyenas.

Ori, who was walking behind Darby with Noah, piped up, "I'll get the games started." She pulled out her tablet and hit a few buttons, and some of the lights sprang to life.

Noah grinned. "It is kind of cool to be in a park when there's no one else here."

Nodding her agreement, Darby smiled at Gus's assistant as they turned away from the Laughing Den and toward the games which were two hundred yards away. "Honestly, it's my favorite time of the day. It's always so peaceful."

"Yeah it's my favorite—" Scooter's words cut off as his eyes narrowed.

A roar sounded from somewhere deeper in the park. The hair on Darby's arms rose as she turned toward the sound.

"What was that?" Gus asked.

"It sounded like one of the cats." Darby frowned. The cats were located farther away, but that sounded awfully close. She shook her head. It must've been some trick of the air or something.

A scream erupted from the hyena house just as the containment alarms rang out.

CHAPTER 44

Wasting no more time, Gabe got Mama Sue out of George's Place with Bao, Meg, and Linc. The two former soldiers took up positions on either side of the group, their heads turning back and forth constantly as they kept an eye on their surroundings.

Their vigilance both eased and accentuated Gabe's own worries. He still couldn't believe what had just happened. He had no explanation for what he'd seen on those recordings. But the most likely answer, despite Chuck's protestations, was a parasite.

Fear took root in Gabe's chest. If something had slipped in, who knew the damage that could do and how long they'd have to figure out how to protect them all. And if that virus or parasite was making the creatures more aggressive . . .

His breath caught as one possibility jumped to the forefront of his mind: *Toxoplasma gondii*, nicknamed the mind-control parasite.

The bug was truly terrifying in that it literally changed the behavior of its host. Infected wolves would become more alpha in their behavior. Their increased aggression would increase their standing in the pack and even cause them to move into other newer areas. There was a biological advantage: It provided the wolves with a larger mating pool.

The infected animals also lost their fear of predators. That was a chilling possibility at a zoo. He needed to put out a warning to the staff to keep them on guard. They were well trained and took all precautions, but he needed to make sure that no one went into an enclosure alone until they got a handle of what was going on. Hopefully, if it was a parasite, it was isolated to the orangutans.

Although he was worried about the animal population in general, he was particularly concerned about George. George was the oldest orangutan in the enclosure and wouldn't be able to fight off an illness as easily as the others. The thought made Gabe hasten his steps.

Up ahead, he saw the entrance to the monorail station. An alarm screeched through the air. He jolted to a stop, as did the others. Hair rose on the back of his neck, and he found himself looking around quickly.

"What is that?" Mama Sue asked.

"Containment alarm," Gabe said, his heart pounding.

"As in something got out?" Linc asked, grabbing the back of Mama Sue's wheelchair and looking like he was about to run.

"Not necessarily. It could just mean there's a fault in the system," Gabe said.

More alarms joined the first.

"That sounds like more than one containment unit," Meg added.

"Yes, it most definitely does," Gabe murmured.

CHAPTER 45

ANIMAL ATTACKS WERE ALWAYS A CONSIDERATION WHEN RUNNING A PLACE like Sanctuary Kingdom. That was why there were so many safety protocols in place. There had never been an issue at the Kingdom—until today.

Martha had already contacted the PR department to get them working on a press release. There were a number of additional safety procedures she'd been contemplating. They were really just backups for the backups. But she needed to feed the public something.

At the same time, her stomach turned at the thought of the worker. The fact that he and his family weren't her first concern bothered her, even now. But if this event went out badly, the park would take a hit.

And if it went really, really badly, profits could dip so much that she'd have to start cutting staff. Cold as it seemed, focusing on the bottom line was what would protect the most families in the long run.

At least, that's what she told herself.

She grabbed her phone but had no signal. Frowning, she stared down at it. They had their own cell tower. A lack of signal should never be an issue. Standing, she made her way around the desk. "Kelly? What's going on with—"

Her voice cut off at the sound of running feet. A young man in a Sanctuary Kingdom uniform barreled down the hall. She frowned. He was one of the dancers. What was his name? Jorge? Eduardo?

His eyes met hers as he veered around a shocked Kelly, heading straight for Martha. He came to a halt, and she was able to read his name tag: Juan.

He took a short breath. "Roger sent me."

"Roger? Why?"

"I was out by the lake when Frankie—" He swallowed hard. "The rest of the security team is working on the gate, and the phones aren't working."

A chill crawled over Martha. "What do you mean they're working on the gate?"

"Something happened to the controls. Containment alarms are going off. He had to manually lower the gate between Dominion and the rest of the park."

CHAPTER 46

As Felix and his team headed for the mess in the research center, he flicked a glance over his shoulder. The blinds of the office snapped shut as soon as he did. Felix smirked. Dr. Cadman sure was the nervous type. Although he did have a little gumption, at least when it came to his project.

Not that that gumption had gone over well with the boss. But Felix appreciated the fact that he hadn't waited for permission. He was also definitely more of an "ask for forgiveness rather than permission" kind of guy himself. Of course, he rarely asked for forgiveness either.

Even though Martha wasn't exactly a warm and fuzzy type, she did at least offer them breakfast and free passes to the park for the day. That was decent.

Pulling open the door to the mess, he had to remind himself it wasn't a mess. It was a cafeteria. While the rest of the park might be well decorated, the research area was bare-bones in terms of decor. It would be easy to mistake it for one of the military bases he'd been on.

As a group, they walked down the line of food, loaded up their trays, and took a seat together at one of the rectangular tables. No one spoke as they dug in, and Felix let his mind wander.

The first test had been pretty impressive. Granted, it was with those little marsupials, but those guys packed quite a punch. Even Felix could see the implications for warfare. It was strange how people were so worried about the cost of life in war, but that was the whole deal—people were going to die. Once enough people died, then the war was over.

If they could find a way to increase the aggression of their soldiers and drop them behind enemy lines, that point could be reached much sooner. They would sacrifice a few but save thousands, maybe millions. *The needs of the many outweigh the needs of the few. Whoever coined that old phrase was right.*

Picturing the CEO, he had to admit, he couldn't get a full read on her. She was a strange bird. She'd agreed to the experiments but at the same time seemed hesitant about them. Felix bet that it was the money that had attracted her, but seeing the implications up close and personal was different than reading about them on a computer screen.

It was like that with a lot of these behind-the-scenes people. The government types were the worst. Senators would vote to send soldiers to war without picturing what that would mean. But get them up close and personal to the war effort, and all of a sudden they were clamoring for peace.

After his second helping, Santos sat back and rubbed his belly. "That was delicious. Now all I need is a little nap."

Felix chuckled. "A nap?"

Santos shrugged. "Got those passes. But the park doesn't open for another couple of hours."

Felix eyed him. "You know on Mondays they let the staff have time off. The park is technically closed, but all the exhibits are still there."

Bobby grinned at him. "Forgiveness rather than permission?"

Felix grinned. "Exactly."

After dumping their dirty dishes in the bin and piling their trays in the tray return area, the group headed outside. As Felix stepped out, he pulled out his sunglasses and put them on.

Bobby stopped short, holding out a hand to keep the others back. "Hey, isn't that one of those devil things?"

Frowning, Felix stared at the small creature that had appeared from around the side of the building. What on earth was that thing doing out here? He looked around, but there was no research staff nearby.

"I don't think those things are supposed to be out here," Sabrina said, taking a step back while she scanned the area.

Santos laughed. "Are you scared of a little itty-bitty animal?"

"Hey, that little itty-bitty animal is a wild animal, not a cute little puppy," Sabrina retorted. "We should give it a wide berth."

Shaking his head, Bobby took a step toward it. "Aw, it's a cute little guy."

It reared back with a hiss. Then four more appeared behind it, all of them hissing as well. The first one darted forward and latched on to Bobby's boot. Bobby let out a cry as he tried to shake the thing loose. "Get it off me!"

Covering the ground in three long strides, Santos booted the thing into the air. The other devils darted forward just as alarms rang out from inside the park. Felix grabbed the back of Santos's shirt and yanked him toward the open doors of the cafeteria while Sabrina held them open.

The devils gave chase, and Sabrina grabbed a wastebasket and chucked it at the herd of them. It rolled over them and they scampered around, heading straight for the door. Sabrina ducked in, and they slammed the door shut as the devils threw themselves against it.

His eyes narrowing as his mind raced, Felix stared at the door. "We've got a problem."

CHAPTER 47

Darby's heart pounded hard as her eyes widened. More alarms joined the first until it sounded as if every alarm in the park was going off. Sprinting back to them, Ori looked at Darby with big eyes. "Darby, is that—?"

"It's the containment alarms," she confirmed. Then her eyes widened. "Bash."

She darted back toward the front of the hyena house.

"Darby!" Scooter yelled.

But she ignored him. As she headed to the front of the exhibit, another scream rang out—this one human. Then Bash appeared, racing through the entrance. Blood soaked his right arm, which hung awkwardly by his side. There was a gash across his calf, leaving stains on the concrete as he ran.

Her heart all but stopped. Her mouth dropped open. "Bash!"

Strong arms wrapped around Darby's waist, bringing her to a halt. "Let me go," she shouted, turning to shoot an accusing glare at Gus.

"No. Look," Gus whispered as the containment alarms across the park continued to ring.

Turning back, she saw Tomy sprint from the entrance and tackle Bash to the ground. Six more hyenas leapt into the fight. Horror crawled over Darby as Gus started to pull her back. She struggled against his grip, but he was too strong. "Stop. We have to help him."

"There is no helping him, Darby. Remember what he said: thirty minutes."

The truth of his words cut through her urgency. Her knees buckled. But Gus held her tight, pulling her away. "We need to go. Now."

Darby hesitated, but Scooter appeared behind Gus, breathing hard, his gaze locked on Bash. "Darby, come on. We can't help him. It's too late."

And she saw the gaping wound in Bash's neck, the blood rolling down the cement and into the concrete dividers in front of the ferns.

Scooter started backing away. "Stay quiet and let's move."

And his words keyed into the danger of the situation. With a shaky breath, she glanced over her shoulder and saw the others sprinting in the direction of the monorail station.

She, Gus, and Scooter moved away silently until they couldn't see the hyenas. Then they turned and fled after the others.

CHAPTER 48

THERE WAS A FAILSAFE GATE THAT BLOCKED OFF DOMINION FROM THE REST of the park. It was not utilized unless it was the absolute worst-case scenario.

"Manually lowering the gates?" Martha asked, her voice rising.

The young man in front of her nodded. "Yeah. The controls aren't working. Cell phones aren't working either. I mean, there are nets in that lake. That gator shouldn't have gotten anywhere near Frankie."

"Why isn't Roger telling me this or one of his security? Aren't you one of the dancers?"

His voice rushed, he gestured back down the hall. "Like I said, I'm Juan, and yeah, all the security people are being sent along the perimeter to check the entrances and secure them."

That made no sense. All of that was automated. "Secure them why? And why is he dropping the fence?"

"The containment alarms are going off."

A chill started to creep through Martha, her mind racing. Cell signals down, gates not responding. "What? Which exhibits?"

"All of them."

She gaped at Juan as Kelly made her way over, her face pale. "You've got all those journalists downstairs."

Martha stared at Kelly, knowing this was going to spin out of control faster than she could contain it. She turned to Juan. "I need you to find Wendy. Have her corral all the media into the theater. Tell her to show the latest King movie—along with every piece of extra footage we have."

She paused. "Tell them we had to shut down the internet to prevent any leaks. Have her collect their phones, even show the Comic-Con footage. Anything to keep them busy. Tell Wendy it needed to be done yesterday. Now, go!"

Juan sprinted down the hall.

Kelly, sitting beside her, watched him go, then looked up at Martha. "What's going on?"

Martha shook her head. "I have no idea."

CHAPTER 49

LEANING BACK IN HIS CHAIR, KEVIN THREW POPCORN INTO THE AIR. IT bounced off his nose and rolled down his cheek. Cursing, he rummaged in the bag for another kernel and this time popped it directly into his mouth. He smiled as he looked at the screen.

After the attack in the orangutan enclosure, he'd kept an eye on Mr. Gabe Sullivan. He was making sure he was being recorded. Having Gabe Sullivan in the park today was just a bit of icing on the cake.

He frowned as he looked at the screen. Gabe and the others had stopped still. Leaning forward, he stared at them as he murmured, "What are you guys up to?"

His phone buzzed, but he ignored it as he unmuted the volume on the monitors. His eyes widened as the sound of containment alarms blared across the empty warehouse.

"Crap!" Kevin sat forward quickly, reaching for the keyboard, and knocked his can of Red Bull over in the process.

"Damn it, damn it," he muttered, pushing back his chair and shifting his keyboard away from the spill. Bringing up the schematics, he quickly searched for the alarm controls. He needed to shut them down. The alarm shouldn't have gone off at all.

His eyes raced over the lines of code until he smiled. "Ooh, someone put in a new backup. I bet that was you, Ori Rosenburg, you sneaky little devil."

Although he'd never met the programmer, she played a significant role in his fantasy world. Of course, she was probably as full of herself as most women were. He had yet to meet one who deserved him. But Rosenburg was intriguing.

Ah, you thought you hid it. Silly, silly girl. You're good, but not as good as me. No one is as good as me.

He noted she'd made the changes just in the last week. He should have double-checked. See, this was what happened when he let people rush him. Quickly, he rewrote the code. With a flourish, he shut down the alarms. The park went silent. With a smile, he settled back in his chair again.

Well, that was a little excitement. His phone buzzed again, and he snatched it from the desk. There were two texts from Todd:

The alarms are going off!

Followed by: *WTH?!!! WTH man!*

He dropped the phone back on the desk. The alarms had not been part of the plan. The animals were all supposed to slip out without anyone noticing. Now people might be on guard. Or it was possible some might just think it was a fluke or a test.

Placing his feet back on the ground, Kevin leaned forward. His gaze was drawn back to Gabe Sullivan and the people with him. His phone beeped, and he pulled it out.

Alarms are off.

With a shaky hand, he grabbed his can and took a long swig. It was a small mistake. He'd been working on little to no sleep. It was understandable. But there couldn't be any others. He was aware now. He'd load up on caffeine and make sure he missed nothing else.

Letting out a breath, he nodded. He wasn't going to let one mistake destroy his good time. He'd been looking forward to this for weeks. *All good*, he told himself. A smile began to spread over his face as he watched the animals realize their enclosures were no longer locked.

Yup. Now was when the fun really began.

CHAPTER 50

THE ALARMS CUT OFF ABRUPTLY, LEAVING AN EERIE SILENCE IN THEIR WAKE. Mama Sue let out a shaky breath. "Does that mean everything's back to normal?"

Although Gabe wanted to say yes and believe it was just some sort of fault in the system, the hair on the back of his neck was still raised. "I don't know," he said slowly.

"We should get on the monorail and get back to Dominion, okay?" Bao suggested.

Nodding, Gabe started forward again. After a moment's hesitation, Linc hustled up next to him, pushing Mama Sue's wheelchair. Everyone was now basically jogging as they headed toward the station.

"Hold up." Meg threw out a hand, blocking Gabe from moving forward. From the other side, Bao did the same to Mama Sue and Linc.

"What's going on? The station's right there. We need to go," Gabe said.

Meg shook her head, starting to back away. "Yeah, we need to find a different egress."

"What do you mean? The monorail's right—" Gabe's hand dropped as his eyes widened. Something was crawling along the tracks.

He couldn't tell what it was from here, but it shouldn't be up there.

It approached the station just as two employees darted out from the path, hurrying toward the monorail.

As they did, his gaze darted to the tracks. Two animals swung down, and he got his first look at them.

Chimpanzees. Huge ones.

Linc's mouth dropped open. "Are those—"

The chimps leapt onto the station's roof, slamming their fists into the roof with a screech.

"No! Run! Run!" Gabe yelled.

One of the employees stopped, his head darting to the roof of the station. Grabbing the arm of his friend, he pulled him to a stop. One of the chimps swung down, and the two men fell over the railing, scrambling to get away. They disappeared around the side of the station and an unholy scream erupted from the spot.

"There's more," Mama Sue said, pointing to two lynxes about two hundred yards away, slinking down the path toward the station.

Closer now, Gabe could make out the chimpanzee species: Billi apes, also known as lion killers. His words came out fast as he started backpedaling. "The containment alarm wasn't a glitch. The animals are out."

CHAPTER 51

THE TASMANIAN DEVILS CONTINUED TO FLING THEMSELVES AT THE DOOR, and then with a hiss, they stopped. Sabrina moved to the window and raised her eyebrows as a scream came from outside. Felix looked over at her.

She winced. "They got somebody in a lab coat. Man, those things are vicious."

Felix pulled out his phone and frowned as he noted he had no signal.

"SAT phone," he said.

Santos knelt down and pulled the SAT phone from his pack, handing it over. Felix quickly typed out a text message to his boss. He paced along the middle of the cafeteria, ignoring the worried gazes of the two workers behind the counter. The answer came back a minute later.

Someone's hacked the park system. They released the animals and turned on the implants.

Immediately, Felix understood the implications. This project was top secret. No one was supposed to know. This project wasn't even going to be mentioned when they moved it on to legitimate animal trials. This was just to see if it was possible.

And he knew exactly what that meant.

He moved closer to the counter where the two workers were

nervously chatting. The message he'd expected came through: *Need a clean sweep. There can't be any evidence of the project.*

Felix typed back his reply quickly: *Understood.*

Handing the phone back to Santos, he put up his hands as he looked at the two kitchen workers. "Hey, so there's been a little problem in the park, but everything is going to be all right."

"What's going on out there?" the older woman asked, shooting a nervous glance at the door.

"One of the projects got out," Felix said.

Before either could say anything, he pulled his gun from the holster at his waist and shot both of them point-blank in the forehead.

Jumping back to avoid getting sprayed, Bobby yelped. "What the hell, man?"

Felix eyed Bobby. "You have a problem with my actions?"

The soldier raised his hands. "Not a problem. Just wasn't expecting it."

"Good. Now we eliminate anything that moves."

All six of them had their guns in their hands as they exited the cafeteria. The lab assistant who'd been attacked by the devils wasn't someone they needed to worry about anymore. There were three devils still there, and they shot each of them—headshots. Then they walked up and shot them three more times in the skull to destroy the implant.

They headed back to the doctor's lab. As they made their way down the hall, the assistant Ned stepped out. As he caught sight of them, relief crossed his features. He hustled toward them. "There's been a problem. Some of the animals—"

Raising his gun, Felix shot the man in the forehead. He dropped. Felix stepped over him. The rest of the group continued past him without even breaking stride. They stepped into the lab.

The doctor whirled around, his eyes widening. "What are you doing here? You guys need to go. The animals have—"

Felix cut him off. "We know, Doctor. I need you to get me a list of all the animals implanted." He pulled an external hard drive from his pocket. "Then I want you to back up all your files on this before you wipe the hard drive."

The doctor stared at him for a moment before shaking his head. "Wipe it? I can't—"

Felix pressed the barrel of his gun to the scientist's forehead. "You're either part of the solution, Doctor, or you're part of the problem. Choose."

"Okay, okay." The doctor scurried over to the computer.

Felix nodded toward Marissa, who walked over to watch what he was doing. Then he turned to the rest of the group.

"Plan?" Sabrina asked.

"Once we have the list, we make sure that all of the implanted animals are killed. Headshots—destroy any evidence. Kill a few others as well just so that they don't look out of place."

Santos raised his eyebrows. "I'm pretty sure the people in the park are going to be a little bit worried once we start walking around and shooting animals."

"They won't be a problem either. No witnesses. Anyone who sees you, dies."

CHAPTER 52

LEGS CHURNING, IT WAS A MAD SPRINT FROM THE HYENA EXHIBIT TO THE monorail entrance. Darby's heart was in her throat the whole time, expecting one of the hyenas to leap on her at any moment. But they seemed to be too enthralled with their fresh kill to even notice them.

The contents of her stomach threatened to reappear as she pictured Bash. *I'm so sorry, Bash.*

Barreling up the station ramp, Darby was relieved to see the monorail pulling into the station. Ahead, Courtney and Lance outpaced all of them and darted into a monorail car just as its doors opened. Scooter, Ori, and Noah were right behind them. Scooter kept his arm on the door, holding it open until Gus and Darby raced through.

Only after the doors had slid closed did Gus let go of Darby's hand. She hadn't even realized he'd been holding it. With a nod of thanks to him, she all but sank into the seat next to Ori.

"Bash?" Ori asked softly.

Unable to say the words out loud, Darby only shook her head. Ori stared at her, tears appearing in her eyes as her hand came to her mouth.

"What happened back there? How did the hyenas get out?" Courtney demanded.

Lance kept his arm wrapped around her. "Shh, we're safe now."

But Courtney kept her gaze locked on Darby. Still shaking, Darby shook her head again. "I—I don't know."

But then she got a hold of herself. Animals were out. Rummaging through her pockets, she pulled out her phone. She needed to notify someone. But first she needed to warn Mama Sue, Gabe, and Linc. "Ori, contact Dominion, tell them what happened."

As Ori pulled out her tablet, Darby hit the screen of her phone. Then she frowned at the SOS in the top-right corner. "I don't have a signal."

Hands flying over her tablet, there was a deep furrow between Ori's eyes. "I don't either."

"Scooter?" Darby asked.

Staring at his own phone, Scooter shook his head. A quick glance at Gus and Noah showed they had no luck either.

"How come I can't reach anyone?" Courtney jammed her finger at the screen of her phone over and over again.

Keeping her voice low, Ori said, "It must be a massive system malfunction. It opened the containment units and shut down the cell tower."

Flicking a glance at Courtney and Lance, Scooter leaned toward them. "That can happen?"

"Theoretically, sure. But there are so many safeguards in place that , in actuality, no, it shouldn't be possible."

"Well, it looks like the impossible won today." Darby stood up and strode to the front of the car. She pulled open the small access door that hid the emergency phone. Pulling out the receiver, she placed it to her ear.

Nothing.

Reaching in, she tapped the phone's holder. The phone had no buttons. When you picked up the receiver, you were immediately connected to the emergency services department of the park. They would then dispatch whatever help was needed.

Or at least, that was how it was supposed to work.

Darby had used the system a few times for medical emergencies over the years. Someone had always been at the other end of the line.

Slowly, she lowered the receiver and met Gus's gaze. "Not working either?" he asked.

"No." And just as the word left her mouth, something flew by the side of the monorail.

Courtney shrieked. "What was that?"

Moving to the window, Darby swallowed. "I think it was a California condor."

Looking down, her heart jumped into her throat. The monorail was fifty feet above the park. Below, she could easily make out leopards slinking along the path. In the distance, she could see other shapes climbing the massive roller coaster in the center of the park.

What looked like large chimps swung from rail to rail. "My God, that's a Billi ape."

Billi apes were the largest chimps in the world. Once thought of as legends, they weren't discovered until 1996. They were so large, they made nests on the ground like gorillas. They stood over five feet tall, with flat faces and a distinctive brow. Some consider it a cross between a gorilla and a human, it was so humanlike in its appearance.

Something else seemed to be slinking up the gates along the perimeter. It was a large cat, although she couldn't tell from here what type.

Ori and Scooter stepped on either side of her. Ori's jaw dropped open. "Oh my God. The animals: they're all out."

CHAPTER 53

WHILE KEVIN HAD BEEN WATCHING THE ACTION PLAY OUT ON SCREEN, HE hadn't been merely an observer. He had a facial recognition program running, identifying everyone in the park. He had a list of who was supposed to be there and who had been given RFID bracelets that day. But he wanted to be sure there were no surprises.

And right now, he had a small surprise, although this one was a happy one. There was a VIP tour happening. Kevin rubbed his hands together. "Well, let's see who the overly entitled, better than everyone else, hoi polloi that are being given early access are."

He found the group's starting point at Dominion and pulled up a still image from the monorail. His eyebrows rose as he zoomed in on movie star Augustus King. "Now you I recognize."

King was one of those crazy-good-looking guys. His rep had even spun a story about him saving a bunch of people on a movie set years ago before he was famous. It was that rumor that had brought him to the forefront of the Hollywood crowd.

It was complete hogwash. No doubt his agent had crafted the story, thinking that it would help him become an action star.

It most definitely had. Now Augustus King was an A-list celebrity. Everybody wanted a piece of him.

His last two films had even crossed the billion-dollar mark. He was the exact kind of guy that Kevin hated. Swimming in confidence and having won the genetic lottery, the world just laid down at his feet and begged him to walk upon it, while Kevin had had to shove and push and fight his way through.

The other two he didn't recognize but quickly got their identities. Influencers: the most useless people on the planet. He curled his lip in disgust. He flicked through a couple of their posts and it did nothing to change his opinion.

Shaking his head, Kevin stared at the perpetually tanned couple. He simply didn't get it. These influencers made idiotic statements claiming to be for this cause or that cause, professing love for this thing or that thing, and it was all completely and totally false. But people flocked to them. And so did companies looking for them to push their wares.

He pulled up the information on the tour group and noted that Darby Ellis was the one running their tour. She was attractive with dark hair and bright blue eyes. Most of the Sanctuary Kingdom tour guides were attractive.

He ran a quick background check on her. There was nothing special about her. Lost her mom when she was young, no dad on record. She was pulled into the foster care system. Then she was adopted by her foster mother when she turned eighteen. He scoffed. "Yeah, as soon as the money ran out, she was adopted."

She'd gone to school for psychology and had made pretty good grades. But she'd stopped after her bachelor's. *Yeah, nothing important about that one. Just a person without goals.*

"Well, sorry, Darby Ellis. Cute as you are, I don't think you're going to be having much of a future."

CHAPTER 54

THE ANIMALS WERE OUT. GABE HAD NEVER IMAGINED THAT WAS POSSIBLE. "Look," Linc said as a flock of various-sized birds took to the air.

"Those are from the park, right?" Linc asked.

Recognizing a few endangered species like the yellow-crested cockatoo, the northern bald ibis, and the imperial woodpecker, Gabe nodded. Their loss was going to be expensive, but most had trackers. There was a chance they could be recovered.

"Birds are okay. I'm okay with a couple of parakeets getting out," Meg said with a nervous laugh.

Shooting a concerned look at her, Linc leaned toward Gabe. "What about the cassowaries?"

Gabe turned to him sharply, his eyes widening. No. They couldn't be out.

"What's a cassowary?" Bao asked.

"The world's most dangerous bird," Linc said, his gaze locked on Gabe.

"Seriously? How dangerous can a bird be?" Meg asked.

"You know birds evolved from dinosaurs, right?" Linc asked.

"Shh, honey," Mama Sue said. "No need to make worries where they aren't."

Normally, Gabe was of the same mindset, but right now, Linc was a little more on point with his worries. The cassowary pen wasn't too far from here.

He pictured the massive birds. If anyone doubted that dinosaurs were related to birds, they just needed to do a little research on the cassowary, and then they would have no problem seeing the link. But the massive birds tended to shy away from humans.

Bao put out a hand to stop Gabe. "Any chance those cassowaries are about six feet tall and look like a bright blue ostrich?"

Instead of answering, Gabe followed Bao's gaze. A cassowary stood at the entrance to the monorail. It kicked the railing once, and the railing ripped free. It continued to kick at the remaining pillars, which were ripped from the ground before the railing crashed onto the pachysandras. Gabe swallowed hard.

Grabbing the back of Mama Sue's wheelchair, he started to back up slowly. "We are *not* taking the monorail."

CHAPTER 55

PRIOR TO SETTING OUT ON THE HUNT, THERE WERE A FEW THINGS FELIX needed to arrange. He'd sent Bobby and Santos to take care of the guards that had waved them in earlier. Felix had Marissa check that the system was in fact under complete control. She confirmed that whoever had taken control of the park had locked everyone out. Cadman wasn't able to get any info, and the man was not handling it well.

Cell phones and hard lines were similarly unusable.

That was actually good for Felix and his people. They certainly didn't need anyone reporting their involvement. Anyone who saw them, well, they just would not be allowed to live to report it.

Now Felix eyed the scientist. "Is there any other way for people to communicate in the park?"

Cadman shook his head. "There's an emergency phone system but that doesn't seem to be working. And with the cell tower down, no."

Sabrina walked over to the guard who lay in the hall and pulled the radio from his belt. "What about these?"

"Oh, right. I forgot about those." Cadman ran a shaky hand over his head.

Narrowing his eyes, Felix studied the man. He didn't think he was lying. He just didn't think like an operative. He turned to Santos. "How many stations?"

Fiddling with the radio, Santos grunted. "Only four."

He turned the radio on, and a distressed voice came through. "Hello? Hello? Is anyone there? We need help."

Felix grabbed the radio and turned the sound off. "Find me three more." Ulrich, Marissa, and Sabrina immediately headed into the hall. Turning to Cadman, Felix asked, "You got music in here?"

Frowning, Cadman shook his head. "Only on my phone."

"Give it to me." Felix held out his hand.

With obvious reluctance, the scientist handed it over. Sabrina, Ulrich, and Marissa reappeared with three more radios. Felix raised the phone to his face. Cadman flinched.

"Just need your face. No need to be so jumpy." Felix found the music app and saw that the good doctor had downloaded a lot of music, mostly classical. Setting the music on continuous play, he linked it with a USB cord to the speakers on the bookshelf.

Ulrich, who'd been fiddling with the radios, nodded as he carried them to the speaker. He'd taped down the transmit button on each. He and Felix placed them around the speaker. Pressing play, Vivaldi blared through the room. Felix cranked up the volume all the way.

CHAPTER 56

AFTER ORI'S STATEMENT, EVERYONE MOVED TO THE WINDOWS. THEY stared out, watching the animals move along the paths below. Every once in a while, they'd see a human dart out. Twice Darby had seen them get chased. She'd closed her eyes when she saw one man get caught by an ocelot.

Now she took a few deep breaths, pushing aside the horror. She'd deal with it later. Right now she just needed to make sure they all got to safety.

"We should've taken the other car," Scooter muttered.

With a nod, she realized what Scooter meant. They'd taken the car on the inner rail, which meant that they would now need to circle the entire park before they ended up back in Dominion. If they'd gone to the other track on the other side of the station, they would have been back in Dominion quicker.

An image of Bash smiling as he accompanied them on their walk through the hyena exhibit slipped into her mind. It was immediately followed by an image of Tomy leaping on him, his blood sliding between the pavers on the ground. Her stomach heaved as she shoved the images away.

Turning, she looked over the group, forcing a false confidence into her voice. "It will be all right. We'll just loop the park and then get back to Dominion."

"What the hell is going on?" Courtney demanded, her cheeks flushed, her eyes wild. "How did they get out?"

Darby looked over at Ori, who was frowning over her tablet. "Ori?"

The programmer didn't look up as she answered. "I have no idea. I'm locked out of the system."

"What do you mean you're locked out of the system?" Scooter peered over the seat at Ori's tablet.

"Just that." Then she looked up. "Everybody try their phones again."

Pulling hers out, Darby immediately noticed that she still didn't have a signal. "I've still got nothing."

Once again, Courtney jabbed at her phone over and over again. "What happened to the signal?"

"Wait a minute." Scooter walked to the front of the car. He leaned down and opened a door that Darby had never noticed before.

"What is that?"

"New security radios. They were just installed." He pulled out the radio and turned it on. A red light came on. Darby felt a small tingle of hope. Pressing down on the transmitter, Darby held her breath as Scooter spoke: "Dominion, this is Monorail One, come in."

Releasing the button, there was nothing.

He tried again and then frowned, turning up the volume. The unmistakable sound of Vivaldi blared out into the car. As Scooter switched from channel to channel, the result was the same: All that could be heard was the same song.

"What the hell?" Scooter stared down at the radio with a frown.

"They're jammed," Gus said softly.

Darby turned to look at him. "Why would you say that?"

"I did a movie once. Bad guys jammed the radios to make sure that no one could communicate back with the base. It's a poor man's jammer: You take a bunch of radios, tune each one to a different station, and then leave them next to a loudly playing music source."

She turned back to Scooter. "Is that possible?"

There was a worried look on Scooter's face as he answered. "Yeah. They don't even have to be in the park. These radios have a pretty long range."

Darby's mind raced. The animals were out, communications were down. The fear she'd been trying to keep a lid on was pushing against that lid. She pictured her family. They were out there with Gabe somewhere. "Ori, do you have any sort of communication? What about the cameras?"

Ori shook her head. "I'm locked out of everything. I can't do anything from here."

"Can we do something from Dominion?" Gus asked.

"Yeah. We could reboot the whole system and get everything back online." But Darby's mind was racing. "Maybe," she said softly.

"What do you mean, maybe?" Courtney demanded.

Wincing, Darby wished she hadn't said that out loud. "If Gus is right, someone may have done this intentionally. No way the radio accidentally gets jammed."

Ori nodded slowly. "A multi-system failure doesn't just happen. Like I said, too many safeguards. I think you're right. I think someone did this."

Darby flicked a glance out the window toward Dominion. She could see it rising up in the distance. Normally, the monorail would have them there in about fifteen minutes. But she had a sinking feeling that this trip wasn't going to be quite so quick.

CHAPTER 57

Wasting no time, Meg grabbed Gabe as Bao put his hand on Linc's shoulder. "We need to move."

The group fled down the path. Gabe's mind raced. How had this happened? There were safeguards upon safeguards. There was no one switch to flip to release any animals but a series of steps. It should have been impossible.

A screech rang out overhead, followed by the sound of wings beating hard. A shadow stretched out as Gabe started to turn his head.

"Look out!" Meg yelled as she tackled Gabe to the ground.

He hit hard but managed to roll, at least keeping from smacking his chin into the asphalt. Meg let out a cry behind him. A shadow burst past him, followed by a gust of air. He looked up just in time to see the California condor veer toward the sky.

His mouth fell open as he took in its dark feathers covering the five-foot body, with a ten-foot wingspan. It was so close he could easily make out the bald pinkish head and the white on the underside of its massive wings.

And although condors didn't have talons but really sharp claws, up close, they definitely looked more like talons. "Oh my God."

He turned quickly and saw Meg grimace.

"You okay?" he asked.

Holding her shoulder, she nodded. "Yeah, its claws just got me a little on the shoulder."

Bao had gotten Mama Sue and Linc over to the side of the path under the cover of a tree.

"What was that?" Mama Sue called out with a trembling voice.

"A California condor. They nearly went extinct. We're part of the conservation effort to get them off the endangered list."

Standing, Meg grunted. "Great job."

Getting to his own feet, Gabe shook his head. "They're not aggressive unless their nest is threatened. They're scavengers. They don't kill their food. That was completely out of character."

"It's coming back," Bao called.

Gabe scanned the area and locked on to one of the merch stands. It was small, but it would do the job. "There," he called out, pointing toward the souvenir shack.

Giving up on the wheelchair, Bao leaned down and picked Mama Sue up. "Sorry, ma'am, but we need to move quickly."

"No apology needed," Mama said as she wrapped her arms around Bao's neck. Bao took off with Linc at his side.

Rummaging in his pocket as he ran after them, Gabe found his keys. "Linc!"

As he looked back, Gabe tossed him his keys. "It's the pink one. Go."

With a nod, Linc sprinted ahead. The massive shadow of the condor stretched out toward them. Linc unlocked the door and had it open by the time the rest of them reached it. A screech came from behind them. Gabe looked over his shoulder and saw the condor coming back for another run. He dove into the shack behind Bao and Mama Sue and then Meg slammed the door shut behind all of them. A thud came from the other side as the bird crashed into it.

CHAPTER 58

THE MONORAIL WAS QUIET AGAIN. THE ONLY SOUNDS WERE ORI continuing to tap at her iPad as she tried to get a signal and Scooter checking and rechecking the emergency phone and radio.

Everybody else seemed lost in his or her own thoughts. Darby did not want to be lost in hers. Hers took her back to the Laughing Den and Bash. All she could picture was his wife and daughter at the last holiday party. The three had gotten up during karaoke to sing "I Got You Babe."

And now he was gone.

But then she remembered the follow-up: Gus had pulled her away. He'd saved her life. He sat in the seat behind her, looking out the window. She spoke softly. "Mr. King."

He turned his gaze from the scene outside the window.

"Thank you for saving me," she said.

He gave her a tight smile. "Glad to help. You okay now?"

She gave a small laugh. Animals were loose in the park, three of the people she loved more than anything were somewhere in that same park, and they had no way to communicate with anyone else. "Not exactly. But as soon as we get to Dominion, we'll be fine."

"I do have one request to make," he said.

She frowned, not sure she was in a position to address any requests. "Okay."

"Call me Gus. I think we've moved past the formal-name stage."

Taken by surprise, she gave him a small smile. "Okay, Gus."

Courtney stood up. "Okay, okay. This is taking too long. We need to go backwards. Can somebody make it go backwards?"

"It's a one-way monorail. It only goes in one direction," Noah said.

Courtney looked at Scooter. "Is that true?"

The big man nodded. "Yes, unless there's an emergency."

Throwing up her hands, she gave him an incredulous look. "Are you saying this isn't an emergency?"

The question brought Darby up short. She looked over at Ori.

"That command has to be sent from Dominion. The car is on a set program. It will stop at each of the stations and then—" Ori's words cut off as she gasped, her gaze flying to the door.

Darby's eyes widened as she too looked at the two sets of doors in their car. "We need to block those doors."

Scooter was already moving to the box under the seats in the middle of the car. There was an emergency locking system in the car for just such situations. It was an old-fashioned manual lock, attached to a strong fiber rope. Darby grabbed one of the ropes and headed for the doors at the front of the car. Gus joined her while Noah and Scoter secured the back one.

The ropes slid through the holders on the door. It was a tight fit and the two sides had to be pulled tight. Darby grabbed one side while Gus grabbed the other. Looking up, she spied the next station. Even from here she could see movement on the platform. "Oh no."

A determined look crossed Gus's face. "Hurry."

Yanking on the rope, she pulled the locking mechanism toward Gus. Inch by inch, the mechanism grew closer and then slipped into place.

Letting out a relieved breath, Darby sank against the wall. Gus grinned at her, holding up a hand. "Teamwork."

Giving him a high five, she smiled, but the smile dimmed as they pulled into the station. The doors tried to open, but the straps kept them in place.

"What are those?" Noah asked.

Watching the heavily spotted cats, Darby swallowed nervously.

"Amur leopards. They're the most endangered cats in the world. The zoo has two and is working on breeding them."

"So I guess that's both of them?" Gus asked.

Although Darby nodded, she also frowned.

"What's wrong?" Gus asked.

"They're nocturnal. They shouldn't be here," Darby murmured as she stared at them in wonder. She had the strangest feeling that now she was the exhibit, with the animals looking in.

"I guess freedom woke them up," Gus said, watching the cats as well.

Then the monorail took off again, heading toward the next station, and everyone let out a sigh of relief.

"Could the animals jump onto the car from the track?" Noah asked.

"They can electrify the track," Scooter said. "It's one of the park's safety protocols. Almost everything in this park can be electrified: the gates, the fences, the monorail."

"You guys said that someone else is controlling this. What if they decide to electrify the track when we're on it?" Courtney asked.

Darby shook her head. "It won't affect us. The car's insulated. As long as we stay inside, nothing can harm us. Even if we get to Dominion and it's not safe there, we can just wait in the car until help arrives."

CHAPTER 59

STEPPING OUT OF THE BATHROOM, KEVIN BUCKLED HIS PANTS. NATURE sometimes called at very inopportune times.

Walking over to the kitchen area, he grabbed a bag of potato chips and ripped it open. As he walked to his station, he shoved a handful into his mouth.

Wiping his hands again on his shirt, he tapped the space bar. "So, what have you all been up to while I took my little break?"

Immediately he saw a group of people on a monorail. He peered closely at the screen. "How'd you get on there?"

Retaking his seat, he started to hum as he backtracked through the footage. Nature had unfortunately timed its call just when things were getting interesting.

With a grin, he saw the attack at the Laughing Den on the VIP tour. He grinned. He'd always liked hyenas. His grin widened as he watched the hyenas still chowing down on their meal.

Flipping through a directory, he saw that the deceased was the hyena keeper. Peering at what remained of the man, he grunted. "Bet you regret that career choice now."

Reaching over, he flipped on some music. A heavy techno beat filled the warehouse. Moving his head in time to the pulsing beat, he returned his attention to the group on the monorail. He smiled as they approached Station Pascha. Two leopards stalked across the platform. As soon as those doors opened, the cats would rush inside.

The car slid to a stop. Kevin leaned forward in anticipation.

The doors didn't open.

"What the hell?" He checked the car's controls, but they were operating fine and fully under his control. A moment later, the car pulled away from the station, its passengers untouched.

There wasn't a good shot of the doors from the camera inside the car, but obviously they had done something to block it.

Taking a swig from his Red Bull container, he tossed the now-empty container over his shoulder and then drummed his fingers on the desk. Rewinding the footage, he saw them pull out some sort of ropes that they must have used to secure the door.

Turning down the music, he turned up the volume on the monitor as one of them said, "Even if we get to Dominion and it's not safe there, we can just wait in the car until help arrives."

He frowned. Well, that just wasn't going to do. Studying the group, he noted that his least-favorite influencers were sitting huddled together, and that movie star was sitting with his assistant. He'd seen him grab Darby Ellis around the waist and carry her away at the hyena den. Yet again, playing the hero.

He brought up the trackers of all the animals in the park and checked where everyone was located. When he noted the monorail's path, he smiled.

Cracking his knuckles, he circled his finger above the enter key, and waited for the monorail to get in position.

CHAPTER 60

THE LOCKS ON THE DOORS HELD AT THE NEXT STATION, WHICH GAVE everyone a sense of relief. Darby's shoulders dropped. Okay, they just had to stay in the car until help arrived. That they could do.

"Is my hair okay?" Courtney asked.

Lance reached out and flattened some flyaway strands on her right-hand side and then nodded. "Yeah. But remember, sound a little scared. It'll play better."

Nodding, Courtney took a deep breath and then raised her phone. Immediately, her eyes widened. A tremble entered her voice. "Y'all, I am lucky to be alive. We are at Sanctuary Kingdom, and the animals have gone crazy."

"I guess Gus isn't the only actor in the group," Scooter murmured.

"Apparently not," Darby replied, keeping her voice equally low. But her mind was scrambling, thinking about the public-relations disaster of an animal outbreak, especially with Courtney fanning the flames.

Immediately she felt guilty for the thought. Bash was dead. Poor public relations were the least of their worries. Focusing on the fallout, though, was less panic-inducing than fixating on her immediate problems.

Top of that list was her concern for Gabe, Mama Sue, and Linc. But she told herself that if anyone knew how to find a safe spot in this park, it was Gabe. He would do everything in his power to keep Mama Sue and Linc safe. She just really hoped he didn't have to do much.

Letting out a breath, she looked over at the group. "Okay, there's only a few more stops, and then we'll be back at Dominion. We just need a couple more minutes, and we'll be safe."

No one answered her, not that she expected them to. But she met Scooter's gaze and saw the worry there. She tried to give him a reassuring smile.

The lights flickered. Everyone went still. Then they flickered again.

Courtney let out a cry. "What's going on?"

The monorail jolted to a stop. Darby put out her hand to keep herself from slamming into the seat in front of her. All the lights on the monorail went out.

"Now what?" Gus mumbled.

Darby looked over at Ori, who shook her head. "I don't know. But the emergency backup should kick in at any moment."

In silence, they waited, but nothing changed. She looked over at Ori, who just shook her head again.

Standing, Darby met everyone's gaze before she spoke. "Okay, it seems that the power to the monorail has gone out."

"So we're stuck here?" Lance asked, his voice rising to a shriek.

"Just for a little while. The people at Dominion no doubt know what's happening in the park and have already called in emergency services. The plan hasn't changed. We're going to stay in the car and wait for emergency services to come and safely get us out. So, for right now, we just need to hold tight."

CHAPTER 61

KEVIN FLICKED THROUGH THE CAMERA ANGLES, WATCHING THE ACTION play out across the park. It looked like Martha was finally figuring out that something was wrong in her park.

He smirked. "Took you long enough."

Then he flipped over to where Gabe and the others were. They were hiding in a flimsy little kiosk.

Finally, he checked in with the monorail crew. The monorail was at a complete standstill. The only thing working was the camera. All of the power had been shut off to it.

But nobody looked stressed or worried. In fact, the influencers looked like they were playing some game on their phones while the others just looked bored.

"Bo-ring," Kevin sang out to the room.

Once again, he contemplated his next steps. He had not anticipated anyone being on the monorail during this portion of events, or at least no one of interest. But these three—the influencers and the movie star —would make a big splash when their deaths at the park became known.

Of course, them sitting in a monorail and just being bored to death was unlikely to happen. Well, he needed to make sure that their deaths were gruesome enough that people took notice. In order for that to happen, though, he needed to get them out of the car. They were not, however, likely to volunteer to step out of it.

"What to do, what to do," he murmured as he brought up the monorail's functions.

His eyes scanned the info, looking for a way to guarantee that they would leave the car. It had to be something that was life-threatening but also something they could escape so that he could really put their lives in danger.

Then he saw one line of code under the title MONORAIL MAINTE-NANCE. He smiled. *Perfect.*

CHAPTER 62

After all the excitement of the attack and getting the monorail secure, Darby's heart had finally stopped racing. Now she was starting to feel drowsy. She'd begun watching the park below but there was nothing to watch. It was just the wide-open space of the elephant preserve. Apparently none of the escaped animals had made it out here.

Next to her, Ori had given up trying to link into the system and was playing *Solitaire*. Darby wasn't sure, but she thought Lance and Courtney might be playing *Candy Crush*.

Scooter now paced along the center aisle, glancing out the windows as he did so to keep an eye on their surroundings. Gus was no less attentive to what was going on outside, and surprisingly, so was Noah.

Drowsiness rolled through Darby. She shook her head. Nope, now was not the time for a nap. Jumping to her feet, she walked to the front of the car and started to read all of the emergency signs arrayed there. She knew them all by heart, but she needed the distraction. She even found herself reading the small print at the bottom about the publisher.

Done with one wall, she turned to the other wall. Instead of reading the sign about how to enact the Heimlich maneuver, her eyes were drawn to a panel with lights still on. It was the car's diagnostic panel.

Then she remembered that this particular panel ran on a battery. The battery must still have juice.

There were twenty lines with three lights associated with each. Red meant off, yellow about to start, and green go. All the lights were red right now.

A light halfway down the panel flicked to yellow. Her pulse jumped in response as she leaned toward the panel. Running her eyes down the left-hand side of the column, she found the accompanying explanation, and her mouth dropped open. *No.*

Scooter, who'd just made his way down to her, leaned over her shoulder to see what she was focused on. "What's going on?"

She pointed to the yellow light and then slid her hand over to the notation indicating what it meant.

"Oh shit," he breathed before he turned and barreled down the aisle. "Everybody up. We need to get out now!"

CHAPTER 63

D ARBY'S HEART RACED AS SHE HURRIED AFTER S COOTER. S HE STOPPED AT the row with Ori and grabbed her by the arm, yanking her up to her feet.

"What's going on?" Ori asked as she shoved her tablet back into her messenger bag and slung it over her shoulder.

"Night maintenance."

Eyes widening, Ori's mouth dropped open. With a squeak, she darted down the aisle toward Scooter, who was reaching up to unlock the emergency hatch.

"What are you doing? You can't do that! Something will get in," Lance yelled.

"What's going on?" Gus asked as he jumped to his feet.

"I'm not sure why, but somehow the nighttime cleaning protocols have been activated. It might be because the monorail was shut down and it thinks that it's the end of the day," Darby explained.

"What are the nighttime protocols?" Noah asked as he, too, jumped to his feet.

Darby swallowed hard. "Each car is sprayed with a sanitizer. It fills the entire car. It's completely automated because—"

"—because if a human were caught in it, they would be killed," Gus finished for her.

Darby nodded.

A robotic voice came over the loudspeaker. "Cleaning to commence in ten seconds. All park personnel are to disembark immediately. Ten . . . nine . . ."

At the emergency latch, Scooter had already gotten it open and boosted himself through. Ori jumped up onto the bench right underneath it and reached her arms up.

"Eight . . . seven . . ."

Scooter grabbed hold of one arm as Noah grabbed Ori's legs and pushed her up toward Scooter.

Noah scrambled up from the chair and jumped for the opening, pulling himself through. Gus grabbed Lance by the shoulder, yanked him out of his chair, and pushed him toward the opening.

"Six . . . five . . ."

"I'm going, I'm going," Lance stammered as he banged his shin on the edge of the bench. Crying out, he still scrambled up and reached for Noah and Scooter's hands. The two of them latched onto him and pulled him through.

"Four . . . three . . ."

Gus grabbed Courtney and boosted her up toward the hatch. Once again, Scooter and Noah hauled her through. Gus turned to Darby and laced his fingers together.

She ran for him, placed a foot in his hands, and jumped for the opening. Scooter and Noah pulled her through.

"Two . . ."

She turned around as Gus grabbed the edge of the opening and pulled himself up, Noah on one side helping him.

"One . . ."

CHAPTER 64

A GRIMACE CROSSED KEVIN'S FACE AS HE WATCHED THE SECURITY GUARD slam the hatch shut just as the spraying commenced. He'd hoped at least one or two of them would have gotten a good lungful of chemicals. But no, they'd all escaped, like rats scampering from a sinking ship. Yet again, the big tough movie star had played the hero.

He hated to admit it, but he had a feeling that this particular movie star was more than just PR hot air. Tilting his head, he studied the screen where the group was now sitting on top of the monorail.

An idea came to him, but in order for it to work, there were a couple of safeguards he needed to put in place. He brought the screen up that tracked the RFID bracelets. After he made a few changes, he flipped back to the monorail controls. He smiled.

Okay, movie star. Let's see how tough you really are.

CHAPTER 65

No one said a word as they all sat on top of the monorail. Darby's stomach rolled as she cast a glance over the side—fifty feet up and no net to catch them. Her gaze scanned the track in front and behind them, but she didn't see any animals nearby.

With a noticeable gulp, Lance glanced over the side and then scooted a little closer to the center of the car. "So, um, what's the plan?"

Darby gestured to the tower that was only about forty feet away. "We climb down and go to the tower. There's a maintenance door there that we should be able to climb through, and then we can just wait there until everybody comes to get us."

"Wouldn't it be safer to just stay here?" Courtney asked hopefully.

Casting another glance at the drop, Darby shook her head. "You really want to stay up here?"

Courtney's face paled as she followed Darby's gaze. "No, not really."

Shifting toward the end of the car, Scooter gestured at the monorail track. "Okay, just be careful walking along the monorail. There's an eighteen-inch drop between the middle section and the two sections on the side. I advise walking along those side sections and holding on to the middle section to keep your balance. If anybody wants to crawl instead, I don't think anyone here would have a problem with that. Okay, so let's get—"

The monorail jolted forward.

Ori had just gotten to her feet. Now she let out a cry as she tipped toward the side. Noah grabbed her before she could tumble over the edge. The monorail slammed to a stop.

Her eyes wide and her whole body shaking, Darby gripped the small railing on the edge of the roof.

"What the hell?" Lance demanded.

Darby didn't say anything, just stared at Gus, who was directly across from her. When she shifted her gaze to Scooter, the fear in his eyes did nothing to combat the rising panic in her chest.

Scooter opened his mouth as if to speak. The monorail jolted forward again. Darby held on as it once again came to a stop.

"Everybody move," Scooter ordered as he scrambled toward the end of the car.

Wasting no time, Darby quickly followed after him, keeping a grip on the small ridge along the edge of the roof. She'd just reached the halfway point when the car jolted again. She flattened herself onto the roof and held on for dear life as it stopped.

Ahead, Gus and Scooter reached the edge of the car.

"Let's go, let's go," Scooter yelled back as he climbed down the emergency ladder, Gus right behind him. Gripping the top of the ladder's railing, Darby had just made it four rungs down when the car jolted again. She let out a cry. She'd had one hand and one foot in the air, moving to get a lower grip. As the car moved, she was flung back, holding on with only one hand as her feet slipped.

Then Gus was behind her, pressing her into the ladder. His arms wrapped around her, he grasped the railing on either side of her.

"Hold on," he ordered before the car jolted to a stop.

"Thanks," she murmured.

Gus quickly climbed down, and she followed. Ori scampered over the side above them, with Courtney right behind her. They managed to make it off before the car moved again. Gus and Scooter ran after it as soon as it stopped. Noah hurried down the ladder.

Lance appeared at the top of the ladder but hesitated.

"Move, man," Scooter ordered.

Placing one leg over the side, Lance released his grip. The monorail jolted, and Lance let out a scream as he started to fall.

CHAPTER 66

In a blur of motion, Gus darted forward and managed to snag Lance's arm just as he pitched over the side. Noah lunged toward Gus at the same time, grabbing onto his belt and the ladder, holding him tight. With a scream, Lance swung out over the side of the track.

But Gus held tight, and Lance slammed back into the side of the ledge, crashing into the side of the track. He let out a painful cry. "My shoulder!"

"Hold on." Noah's expression was pinched as he strained to hold onto Gus. Gus leaned down, grabbing the back of Lance's shirt and helping him scramble onto the track.

"My shoulder, my shoulder," Lance wailed.

"Sorry, bud," Gus said as he shifted to get Lance fully on the track.

Once secure, all three of them lay there, breathing hard, Lance's face screwed up in pain, his arm hanging at the wrong angle. No one else said a word. It had all happened so fast.

Darby's hand was at her throat as she watched, realizing how close that had been. It looked like something out of one of Gus's movies. "Are you guys okay?"

Still lying on the track, Noah merely raised his hand and gave her a thumbs-up. Sitting up, Lance's face was pale. "Something's wrong with my shoulder," he whispered, his lips tight.

Before anyone could respond, the monorail moved again. Darby tensed, but this time it continued forward without stopping. Staring at it, Darby's mouth fell open.

"What the hell?" Gus asked as he sat up.

Next to her, Ori narrowed her eyes as her gaze locked on the disappearing car.

"What?" Darby asked, turning to her.

Her gaze flicked to Darby for only a moment before returning to the car. "I think somebody's playing with us."

CHAPTER 67

In the empty warehouse, Kevin's laugh echoed off the walls. He wiped at the tears leaking from the corners of his eyes. "Man, that was good."

He didn't even mind that Augustus King was playing superhero again. Lance had nearly toppled over the side. It was priceless. It would have been more fun if that idiot had fallen, but still, that was quality entertainment.

Now the group was slowly making its way toward the tower. They had about twenty-five feet to go and they definitely weren't rushing. All of them were walking toward the center of the track, using the raised part of the track for balance. Gus was at the back of the group, no doubt ready to leap into action again if needed.

But action was not something that would be happening. The other monorail was too far away to reach them before the tower. Now that would have been fun, to watch them try to outrun it.

Sadly, he'd need something else.

Picturing Lance pitching over the side, Kevin let his fingers dangle over the keyboard again for a moment. How to make them move faster? Debating, he scanned the features of the monorail. No, no, no.

Then his gaze shot back to one of the safety features. He grinned. Honestly, they were making this way too easy.

Stretching out his hands, he hunched over his keyboard and began to input the necessary sequence. "Okay, gang, let's see how you handle this."

CHAPTER 68

DARBY KEPT HER GAZE FOCUSED ON THE TOWER AHEAD. *JUST MAKE IT there. You just have to make it there and then everything will be better*, she promised herself over and over again.

Scooter was in the front with Ori and Courtney. Noah was directly in front of Darby with Lance behind her and Gus bringing up the rear.

Every once in a while, she scanned the ground below and the air around them. But while she could see animals in the distance, none seemed to be nearby. It was one small break and she would take it.

Once again, she directed her attention to their destination. The towers were the support system for the track and were spaced about three hundred feet apart. Each one had a ladder that reached down to the ground. But more importantly, each had a maintenance room at the top. The room held a number of tools as well as emergency panels for the monorail system.

The room wasn't large, maybe only six feet by four, so it would be a tight squeeze. But she was fine with that. She didn't even mind the fact that there were no windows in it. As long as it didn't move and they could wait out whatever was going on with the park, she was totally okay with the tight quarters.

She still couldn't believe that the monorail had acted that way. But was Ori right? Was someone playing with them?

It was hard to believe that someone would actually do that. Darby wasn't naïve. She knew there were horrible people in this world. But were there really "open up all the cages at a mega zoo" people out there?

Her gaze locked on the panel next to the maintenance door. With relief, she noted it glowed with power. Good. She was worried the power would have been shut off to it as well.

Her focus ahead, she ran a hand over the bracelet at her wrist. It should allow them access. The only people who had better access were Gabe and Martha. But in her mind, she was already creating secondary options if that didn't work.

"What part of the park are we in?" Gus called out.

Mentally placing them on the map, Darby shot a glance at the heavily treed area below them. "We're right at the edge of Savannah Plains and Jungle Heart. The elephant preserve technically is part of both."

"Happy little pygmy elephants?" Noah asked hopefully.

Darby had to smother a chuckle. "Friendly, yes. Pygmy, no."

"Well, it was worth a shot," he grumbled.

But before Darby could reply, the light in a steel cage on the left side of the tower began to swirl red.

Courtney let out a gasp. "Please tell me that's a good sign."

Once again, it felt like Darby's heart had launched itself at her throat. "No, that is most definitely not good. Everyone, pick up the pace now," Darby ordered as she moved as fast as she dared down the track.

"What's going on?" Noah asked.

Not believing the words about to slip past her lips, Darby said, "Someone activated the track's shield."

"What does that mean?" Courtney demanded.

Picturing what would happen to all of them if they didn't reach the tower in time, Darby tamped down her panic. "Someone's about to electrify the track."

CHAPTER 69

When Darby had first come to Sanctuary Kingdom, she'd been impressed with all of the safety protocols put in place to keep the public at large safe should there ever be a containment break. It had never occurred to her that one, all the containment safeguards would breakdown at the same time, and two, that those very same safety features could be turned against the humans in the park.

But that was exactly what was happening.

Giving up safety for speed, Darby stepped onto the center platform and raced for the tower, bypassing the others. In her mind, she told herself she was just on a very wide balance beam. She'd always been good at gymnastics.

She sprinted forward as the light's swirling pace increased. The tower platform was three feet down from the track. Darby didn't hesitate. She jumped, grabbing onto the railing to keep from being pitched over the side.

Blowing out a breath, she pressed herself against the tower. The platform was only three feet wide. Inching along it, she pressed her bracelet to the maintenance door. The light stayed red. "Come on." She pressed again and again, but nothing happened.

Ori reached the edge of the platform.

"Jump down," Darby said.

Eyes wide with fear. Ori swallowed and jumped. She let out a cry as one of her feet slipped off the platform into open space.

Darting forward, Darby grabbed her, yanking her fully onto the platform. "You okay?"

Nodding hard, Ori's chest heaved.

"Climb past me," Darby ordered. As Scooter hopped down, he raised an eyebrow at the still-closed door.

Darby shook her head. "It won't let me in."

Reaching over, he tried his bracelet but had no luck either.

He hesitated as if he was going to wait, but Darby shook her head. "You're too big. I'll act as catcher. Go check the other door."

With a nod, he hurried after Ori.

Courtney came next and leapt down with no hesitation and a surprising amount of grace. She scampered past Darby without needing to be told.

Noah appeared with Lance. Darby reached up helping lower him down, but he dropped the last few feet. His injured shoulder crashed into the side of the tower. He cried out.

"Sorry, sorry," she mumbled as she helped him climb past her. Noah, meanwhile, had jumped down and helped Lance across the platform.

The light was spinning faster. "Gus!" she yelled.

He appeared, and with one alarmed look at the light, leapt for the platform just as a spark of light arced across the tracks.

CHAPTER 70

GUS'S LEAP BROUGHT HIM OUT FARTHER FROM THE RAILING. REACHING out, Darby grabbed him and yanked him toward her. He crashed into her, pushing her back toward the tower. She braced for the impact but Gus slipped his hand behind her head. It took the impact. Breathing hard, the two of them stayed pressed against the tower for a moment.

Above them, electricity raced across the tracks before the sparks died away. The electrical burst lasted only five seconds. Closing her eyes for a moment at yet another close call, she finally found her voice. "You okay?"

Letting out a shaky breath, he leaned back, his face mere inches from hers. "Yeah, thanks for the assist."

"Well, you know I owed you."

"It looks like we're square now," he noted.

She nodded, then looked up with a frown at the others still perched on the platform. Ori had slipped ahead and was standing in front of the maintenance door, pressing her bracelet to the scanner over and over again. Then she shifted to the side to allow Scooter to do the same. Darby closed her eyes in frustration.

"I guess we can't get in?" Gus asked.

Darby shook her head.

"So now what?" he asked.

In the distance, large birds swooped down on animals in the park.

She frowned at the behavior. Picturing the attacks she'd seen, she knew staying here wasn't an option. "Not sure if it's finally being free or something else, but the animals seem a bit worked up. We need to get behind some strong walls."

"Any suggestions as to where we could find some?" he asked.

Looking past Gus, she spied a large building in the distance. She nudged her chin toward it. "That's Mighty Mammoth Manor. I suggest we head there."

CHAPTER 71

WELL, THIS ISN'T WORKING OUT. ARMS CROSSED OVER HIS CHEST, KEVIN glared at the screen. The entire group on the monorail had made it to the tower in one piece. Oh, sure, that Lance guy had banged his arm, but there hadn't been even any blood. No one had even been electrocuted.

Boring.

Shaking his head, frustration clawed up Kevin's throat. Having Augustus King and those idiot influencers was supposed to be a boon. Their deaths would ratchet up the media attention.

At least one of them should be dead by now. The influencers had no survival skills, and Augustus King was supposed to be little more than a handsome face.

With a grunt, he pushed a little farther away from the screen, his glare deepening. In fairness, there had been some deaths in the park. Four so far and at least a dozen people injured. But they were all nobodies. He needed that bright spotlight.

Taking a breath, he closed his eyes. Then he took ten deep breaths, pulling back his anger. When he opened his eyes again, he nodded. Maybe this would be better. He did have the footage of them so far. A little build-up before the takedown.

Plus, Gabe Sullivan was still in the park. Of the four celebrities, at least one had to be killed. No chance they'd all make it.

Leaning forward, he hunched over his keyboard again. Okay, this was okay. There was still time.

Checking the monorail group's progress, he noted where they were heading. Bringing up the animal trackers, he scanned what was close to them and smiled.

Okay, there's a lot of potential here.

He'd keep the cameras on them. Make sure he recorded everything. But there were plenty of people in the park. With enough background, he could make them the stars of this.

Not that he was going to go easy on his actual stars. He switched to the implant control screen and then cracked his knuckles. Studying the animal trackers, he hit a few buttons and then saluted the group. *Good luck, guys. I'll check back and see how many of you are still left in a little bit.*

CHAPTER 72

Prior to climbing down the ladder on the tower, Gus had used Noah's sweatshirt to create a sling for Lance's arm. Scooter and Gus had also set the shoulder. Lance's scream had been horrifying, but after they'd set it, Gus gently placed his hand on the man's uninjured shoulder. "Is that better?"

"Yeah, but I'm not going to say thanks," Lance grumbled, his face pale and sweaty.

Gus chuckled. "I completely understand."

He then stayed with Lance on the climb down to make sure he was all right. He'd had to brace him a few times, but with Gus's help, Lance made it to the ground safely. Once again, Darby was surprised at the considerate movie star who was nothing like what she'd expected.

Sadly, Courtney had lived up to her influencer reputation.

The woman had huffed and pouted the entire way down. After taking a few snapshots of herself, she stared at her phone. "I still don't have a signal."

No one answered her.

Grumbling, Courtney continued to climb, speaking loud enough to be heard by all of them. "I hope you know I'm going to leave the worst review of this park ever. None of my followers are ever going to visit. And there is no way I'm having my wedding here. You guys are going to have to pay me back for every dollar we've spent. This is ridiculous. I can't believe—"

"Be quiet," Scooter spat out.

Looking up, Darby caught Courtney's mouth drop open and her eyes go wide. "How dare you—"

Scooter cut her off again, speaking through gritted teeth. "We are trying to not draw attention to ourselves. We don't know what's out there. Keep your voice down."

The admonishment seemed to at least quiet the woman, although she looked angry. Darby couldn't help but think that she hadn't spent much time worrying about her fiancé. But who knew? Maybe she lashed out to hide her actual worries.

Although Darby liked to think that Scooter had just been trying to get Courtney to be quiet with his warning, she knew it was the truth. They needed to stay as quiet as they could manage so as not to draw attention.

Once they reached the ground, she looked around nervously. She wasn't the only one. Clearing her throat, she nodded to the right. "Mammoth Manor is that way."

Courtney crossed her arms over her chest. "I'm not walking through that forest. Something's going to jump out and kill me." She paused as everyone looked at her.

"I mean us," she said quickly before she gestured to the fence about thirty yards away. "We should go that way. The fence is right there. We climb it and we're out of here."

Immediately, Darby moved in Courtney's way as she stepped toward the fence.

Courtney jolted back. "What are you doing? Get out of my way."

Tilting her head toward the fence, Darby asked, "Hear that hum? The fences have been activated."

Ori let out a small gasp, her eyes widening.

"Activated? What does that mean?" Courtney demanded.

"All the fences that surround the park are electrified," Scooter said, his gaze darting to the boundary with a frown.

Her mouth gaping, Courtney took a step back. "Electric fences? You let guests near electric fences? That's crazy."

"This is not part of the usual tour," Darby said dryly.

Courtney grunted. "It's still unsafe. This whole place is unsafe." Then she flounced away but only a few feet.

Stepping closer to Darby, Ori kept her voice low. "They shouldn't be on like this. The fences are designed to go on for sporadic bursts, not a continuous time segment. To stay on like this, a specific code needs to be programmed into the system."

"Someone's definitely in your system," Gus murmured.

Watching the fence, and then turning to study the area around them, Darby shuddered. "Yeah. So let's get to the manor before any new surprises jump out at us."

CHAPTER 73

MAKING HIS WAY DOWN THE HALL TOWARD THE LAB, FELIX PICTURED THE rest of the staff at the research center. He and Sabrina had just taken care of all of them. Urich and Marissa had stayed behind with Cadman to make sure he got the locations of all the animals with implants.

As Felix stepped into the room, the doctor was still at his computer, looking sweaty. The man did not hold up well under stress.

Popping a hip up on the edge of a silver table, Felix thought back to this morning's experiment. He was impressed with how aggressive those little devils had been, but damn, he really wasn't interested in being on the receiving end of that. Still, he had to admit the idea of going on a hunt through the zoo definitely appealed to him.

He'd always wanted to do one of those big game hunts in Africa but had never quite been able to make that happen. He wasn't one of those rich guys who had all the time in the world. But this, this would be a real challenge.

The lab door opened. Santos stumbled through, his hair standing straight up. Bobby slipped in behind him and met Felix's gaze. Felix did not like the look of them.

"What happened?" Felix asked.

Santos slumped into a chair as Bobby made his way over. Bobby glanced at Ned's body and just shrugged, heading toward Felix. "Gates and fences are electrified."

Felix's eyebrows rose. "What?"

Bobby grinned. "Yeah, I was surprised too. But not as surprised as Santos was."

Without looking at either of them, Santos merely raised his middle finger.

Bobby chuckled. "The two guards were hit over the head and thrown into the park before the gates were sealed. There's a big bus in front of them, blocking the way, so even if you were able to touch the fence—which again, I would not recommend—you wouldn't be able to push them open without moving the bus first."

"What the hell is that all about?" Felix demanded.

Bobby shrugged again. "The name EcoAct was spray-painted across the bus."

Felix frowned. "Who are they?"

"An animal-rights group," the doctor said, his back still to them.

"What do they want?" Felix asked.

Keeping his back to them, the doctor's shoulders rose and fell. "I don't know. Some sort of 'stop experimenting on animals, let them all go, and sing Kumbaya' kind of demands. They've been sending letters to the park for a couple of months."

Scoffing, Felix shook his head. "What the hell do these people expect? Do they want lions running through downtown? Cages are where the animals belong."

"Hey, I'm on your side, remember? Besides, I'd like to get a little payback now that these guys messed with my boy here." Bobby slapped Santos on the shoulder, who merely grunted in response.

"So what exactly is the plan?" Felix asked.

"Take out everyone in the park and then clear one of the exits and head out."

Grinning, Bobby let out a hoot. "Now that's my kind of hunt."

"Every animal with an implant needs to have its head completely destroyed. We can't leave any traces."

Letting out a hoot, Bobby slapped Santos's shoulder again. Santos glared at him. The response only made Felix grin, as he felt the stirring of excitement in his chest. A hunt. God, he loved a hunt. This was going to be fun.

CHAPTER 74

MARTHA HAD ALWAYS BEEN A STUDENT OF HISTORY. IN HER DOWNTIME, she'd read some heavy tome about a US action in a small country in the middle of nowhere. One of the things she knew about the US was that they had contingency plans for nearly any situation that might arise.

In running the park, Martha had taken a similar approach. She had responses mapped out for every emergency she could think of from a tornado hitting the park to a simple slip and fall by a guest.

And a breakout of animals was definitely on the list.

Roger was closing off the rest of the park because, in the event of a full containment failure, they needed to stop the spread of the animals. Even now, her stomach dropped at the thought of it. There were over twenty thousand animals at Sanctuary Kingdom. While some were cute and sweet, like the little Mountain pygmy possums or the Cozumel raccoon, others were terrifying.

But she didn't think it was a full containment breach—it couldn't be. There were simply too many safeguards in place for that to be the case. But she needed answers.

Now, she strode down the hall, Kelly at her side. "Get me a list of everyone in the park. Track their bracelets."

At least this had happened on a Monday morning. She shuddered, imagining the fallout if this had happened when the general public was in the park.

Making notes on her tablet, Kelly stopped for a moment to look up at Martha, her face pained. "I don't think we can track them. But I'll speak with everyone. I have the schedule of who's supposed to be in the park and can cross-reference it with the timesheets." Her voice trailed off, her eyes going wide.

"What?" Martha asked with a frown.

"Gabe."

Staring at Kelly, Martha froze. She'd forgotten Gabe had come in today. "He's not in the park, is he?"

Kelly nodded. "I saw him head to the monorail about an hour ago. I suppose it's possible he came back early, but—" Once again, Kelly's voice drifted off.

Martha took a deep breath. Gabe . . . Her relationship with her brother was tense at times, difficult. But he was the only family she had left.

He was her anchor.

"Okay, okay. I need a list of everybody else," she said, then her eyes widened. "Wait, didn't we have a VIP tour today?"

"Yes. Lance Seabrook and his fiancée, along with Augustus King and his assistant."

Martha's jaw dropped. "Oh my God. We have influencers in the park. Those people record everything. This is going to be a PR disaster."

And that was if they survived.

Plus, Augustus King was one of the hottest stars around. If something happened to him in the park . . . She picked up her pace.

Kelly hurried beside her. "Where are we going?"

"To get some answers."

CHAPTER 75

"I'LL TAKE THE FRONT," SCOOTER SAID. HE LOOKED AT GUS, WHO NODDED back at him. "I'll take the rear."

"Mammoth Manor is about one click in that direction." Scooter pointed to their left.

"A click? What? Did I just get drafted? How far is that?" Courtney demanded.

Making no show at hiding his annoyance, Scooter said, "One click is about a kilometer."

"How many miles is that?" Courtney replied.

"A little over half a mile," Ori said.

"Then why couldn't you just say that?" Courtney grumbled.

Darby had to hide her smile because she kind of agreed with her on that one at least.

"Okay, we move quietly and quickly. No one wanders off." Scooter looked directly at Courtney. She rolled her eyes in response.

Everybody else though looked determined. With a final look from Scooter across the group, they took off at a fast pace. Darby stayed next to Ori, her mind racing through everything that had happened. Leaning toward Ori, she kept her voice low as she asked, "Do you really think someone did this?"

Keeping her voice just as low as Darby's had been, Ori's brow was furrowed as she spoke. "Too many things have gone wrong. There's no way there was a catastrophic failure like this, not without some warning. Someone's definitely in the system."

Then she frowned. Darby knew that look. "You've thought of something."

Ori spread her arms wide to include the preserve surrounding them. "Doesn't exactly help us with our current predicament, but I wonder if it's related to the glitches in the system we've been seeing for the last two to three weeks."

"Remind me again, what type of glitches?"

"Strange things. Different parts of the park would go offline, but only for a second or two. We rebooted the system three days ago, and everything seemed to calm down. We couldn't find any code or technical issues in the park."

Studying her friend, Darby said, "And that's why you're here, in case something went wrong. Martha wanted to keep it quiet. She didn't want anything leaking to the press, which is why no one else on the staff knew anything about it."

Ori nodded glumly. "Yeah, it was made pretty clear that the NDA in my employee contract covered this situation. I wasn't allowed to tell anyone. But I should have pushed more, gone with my gut."

In light of current events, the reason behind that was clear. "Someone was testing the system."

Meeting her gaze, Ori frowned. "That was my interpretation, too. But there's a new guy in IT, Reuben Sykes, he argued against it. Said I was exaggerating, that it was just a bug in the system. He was put in charge of finding it."

"Tom didn't go nuts?"

"Tom's been really under the weather lately. He's just not thinking right. It was like he was in a fog. In fact, he was hospitalized two days ago. They're trying to figure out what's going on with him."

Casting a glance around, Darby was amazed that the park had known something was up and hadn't taken stronger precautions. "Well, this Reuben guy did a really lousy job."

CHAPTER 76

STRIDING DOWN THE HALL TOWARD THE IT NEST, MARTHA MENTALLY cursed everyone she could think of that was responsible for the current debacle. That included Tom Fellow, her head of IT. With his hospitalization, there was a new guy in charge. Really bad timing.

"What's this guy's name again?" Martha asked.

Hurrying next to her, Kelly's voice was breathless. "Reuben . . . Reuben Sykes."

Martha stared down at her. "We're in the middle of the worst disaster to ever strike the park, and we're trusting our system to a guy named after a sandwich?"

Kelly's cheeks flared red. "Um, yes, but he is highly qualified. In fact, he might even be more skilled than Tom."

Knowing she was being uncharitable, Martha grunted. It wasn't the guy's fault what his parents named him. But tension crawled along her skin, making her look for targets to lash out at. She took a couple of deep breaths. That managerial style wasn't going to help right now.

Hurrying forward, Kelly opened the door to the IT hub. Stepping in, Martha flicked a glance around the room. Once again, she was amazed that she, little Martha Latham, was responsible for all this. It looked like something that belonged to NASA. Sixteen monitors in a four-by-four pattern dominated the entirety of the wall in front of her.

There was a tiered stadium arrangement of tables with monitors facing the wall. There were thirty-two monitors set on the desks, and most of them had people at them, typing away. At the back of the room, at a desk centralized with a view of the whole room, was the spot reserved for the director of Information Technology.

Normally, Tom, a fifty-two-year-old man who looked decades older, sat there. But today, the man in the critical seat looked younger than his twenty-eight years. He had long shaggy brown hair pulled back into a small ponytail at the base of his neck with thick, dark-framed glasses. Instead of a chair, he was on a walking pad and had raised the desk to accommodate it.

Martha had met with him twice, and both times he'd been eating some sort of green concoction from a Tupperware container. She spied the same mix on the corner of his desk, right next to a massive water bottle.

Standing at the bottom of the stairs, she glared up at him. "What is going on with my park?"

CHAPTER 77

"So where exactly are we going?" Courtney demanded after they'd been walking for only a few minutes.

"We're heading to Mammoth Manor; it's the elephant house," Darby said quietly.

Courtney let out a squeak. "Elephants? How many?"

"There are seven African forest elephants," Darby said.

There was a tremor in Courtney's voice as she spoke, her gaze darting around the thick woods. "How big are they?"

Despite the fact that she'd been a royal pain, it was hard not to feel compassion for the terrified woman. "They're the smallest of the elephant species."

What Darby didn't add was that even though they were the smallest, they still stood eight to ten feet tall. But that was small compared to the male African savanna elephants, which could reach thirteen feet.

"Are they aggressive?" This time it was Noah who asked.

Darby paused before answering. "Not unless threatened or bored."

Lance groaned. "Oh, great."

Hurrying on, Darby said, "But Lucas, the elephant keeper, makes sure to give them lots of activities to keep them entertained."

"And so they're all friendly, right?" Noah asked again.

"Absolutely." Darby had to force herself not to cross her fingers behind her back at the lie. She hadn't intended to lie to Noah earlier. Normally, the elephants were unthreatening, peaceful creatures.

It wasn't until they were climbing down the ladder, though, that she remembered that it was mating season. During that time, males went through a process called musth. Their testosterone levels surged to six times the normal level.

The biological process wasn't characteristic of only African forest elephants. All male elephants go through a heightened testosterone level during mating season. During that time, male elephants could become extremely aggressive and highly dangerous to any people or animals that got in their way.

But Darby felt no need to say that out loud because hopefully, they weren't going to run into any elephants at all. After all, there was only one adult male elephant in the herd. The preserve itself covered a hundred acres. Dembe tended to keep to himself.

"There's just one species?" Noah asked.

Nervousness running through her, Darby latched on to the question. "Yeah, you can't mix elephant species. There's a virus called EEHV. African forest elephants are the carrier for one strain, but it's the number one killer of baby Asian elephants, and conversely, another form of the virus transfers the opposite way. So no reputable zoo would ever mix the different species together."

In fact, the EEHV virus was something they were trying to isolate at the research center. If they could figure it out, then there was a chance that they could raise different species of elephants together. It would open the door to larger conservation efforts and potentially a new species of elephant.

Technically, it was possible for them to procreate. There'd been only one documented case of it happening, however. In 1978, at Chester Zoo in England, an Asian elephant gave birth to a calf fathered by an African bull. It had never happened before because in nature, there was simply no opportunity for the two species to come across one another. Ancient elephants and mammoths, however, did interbreed far in the past.

"How many elephants did you say there were?" Courtney asked, looking around nervously.

"Only eight."

"So there's a chance we won't see any of them, right?" Courtney asked.

Picturing Mammoth Manor, where the elephants slept at night, she nodded. If the elephants followed their normal schedule, they would be out wandering the preserve, hopefully far from the manor. "A very good chance."

CHAPTER 78

THE AGGRESSIVENESS OF THE ANIMALS WAS AMAZING. KEVIN ENVIED THEIR ability to lash out. He knew part of the reason was the implants.

But the other part was that they were all really hungry.

Kevin had to admit he was pretty amazed at how easy it was to get some information about the park. He had been able to get backgrounds on all the employees within a day, and there were hundreds of them. Then he ran that data through a couple of programs to see if there were any major issues.

The park had been his first choice of locations. EcoAct had a list of spots they had been considering for their first big act. Kevin had pushed them in the direction of Sanctuary Kingdom. He'd done a deep dive and seen some of the online reports about animal abuse happening there. He didn't really care about that, but he knew that once those reports were made public, Sanctuary Kingdom's current sterling reputation would take an absolute dive.

And that appealed to him. He didn't want to just take down some little mom-and-pop zoo. No, he wanted to take down one of the big guys. He wanted to make those rich bastards realize that they didn't own the world.

He knew all of the big players at the park. Those, he had spent time investigating. The two biggest players were, of course, Gabe Sullivan and his sister Martha Latham. They started with humble beginnings, but there was nothing humble about their existence now.

Gabe was a non-entity when it came to the running of the park. Martha was a little more critical, although she was more the mover and shaker behind the scenes rather than the one responsible for the day-to-day activities. For this particular endeavor, however, the day-to-day activities were the critical factor.

He knew everyone's work schedule, all of the security routes, and where everyone was supposed to be. He'd checked deliveries and feeding schedules. He smiled, thinking about the feeding schedules.

For a place as big as Sanctuary Kingdom, it wasn't a matter of someone going to the pet store, grabbing a large bag of animal feed, and coming back to dish it out to all the animals. There were simply too many.

Most, if not all, of the feeding systems were automated. The animals were all on carefully controlled diets. He'd been impressed at how they'd not only monitored the animals' diets but actually cut costs by doing so. It was amazing how an extra scoop here or an extra scoop there would actually add up over the years.

For the last two weeks, Kevin had been in that system. He'd reduced the amount of food that all the animals were getting. Not by a significant amount, because if he reduced it too much, the keepers would notice. No, he reduced it by just enough so that the animals weren't getting their fill. So not only would they be angry at the fact that they'd been in captivity all this time, but they were also going to be really, really hungry.

When Kevin was a kid, he loved playing Hungry Hungry Hippos. He smiled. Now he was getting to watch a real live game of it.

CHAPTER 79

DESPITE THE WORRY RUNNING THROUGH MARTHA AND EVERYONE ELSE IN the IT nest, there was no worry in Reuben's movements at all. His hands fluttered over his keyboard slowly, and every once in a while he would stop and tilt his head as if contemplating something before starting to type again.

It took everything in Martha not to reach out and shake the man to get him to grasp the urgency of the situation. In fact, she had to clasp her hands tightly behind her back.

He frowned. "Looks like you've been locked out of the entire system."

Gritting her teeth, it was an effort for Martha to not yell. "Yes, I'm aware of that. What I don't know is how that is possible."

His tone annoyingly nonchalant, Reuben shrugged. "Yeah. Somebody got into the system somehow. We've lost everything—cameras, safety protocols. Right now, we can't access anything." He gestured at his desktop, where ACCESS DENIED was splashed across the screen.

Martha narrowed her eyes. "What do I pay you guys for if not to prevent something like this?"

Reuben raised his hands. "Hey, I just got here."

She shook her head, picturing Tom. He had a lot to answer for. "Can you call Tom and see what—"

Reuben shook his head, still not looking concerned. "No, the phones are down too."

Counting to ten, Martha was still gritting her teeth as she spoke. "Is there *anything* you can do?"

Reuben nodded. "Of course, of course. I'll try to work against the hack. It'll take some time, but hopefully, I'll be able to wrestle some of the controls back."

"Good. Tell me as soon as you have something." She walked down the stairs toward the exit, then turned, seeing more than a few nervous eyes looking her way. Taking a breath, she addressed the room. "Sanctuary Kingdom has been attacked. I need everyone here to do their best to wrestle control back into our hands."

Picturing Gabe, a flutter of panic skipped through her. "We have people in the park. People in danger. I need everyone to pull together and do everything you can. Any idea, any way of getting through this hack—do it. You have my full permission."

She made a point of meeting the gaze of everyone in the room before she strode out the door. Once she was out of sight, though, she leaned back against the wall, shaking her head as she held her hands over her face.

Kelly watched her quietly for a moment. "Is there anything I can get you?"

Pushing off the wall, Martha grit her teeth. "Yes. Coffee. Lots of coffee. We've got work to do."

CHAPTER 80

TIME SEEMED TO DRAG ON INCREDIBLY SLOWLY. EVERY TIME GABE CHECKED his watch, only a couple of seconds had passed, though it felt like a couple of minutes. Sweat had broken out along his brow.

Worries about the park cascaded through him. He was concerned that more people might have been hurt and he was trying to figure out how on earth the containment units had failed. They had backups upon backups upon backups.

It shouldn't have been possible for the units to fail, certainly not all at once. Unless, of course, someone was helping them. He stopped still and realized that had to be it. Someone had to have done it. It wasn't that the system had failed: someone had let the animals out.

Horror and disbelief swirled through him. Who would do such a thing?

"You okay, honey?" Mama Sue asked softly.

It was on the tip of Gabe's tongue to deny his worry, but finally, he shook his head. "Nope, not at all. There's no way all the containment units stopped working at the same time. Not naturally."

"You think someone got into your system," Bao said, his gaze intense.

"Yeah. That's the only explanation. Each containment unit is on a separate grid. So, if something happens to one, it can be isolated from the others. You would have to go in and shut them all off individually.

"I suppose if a tornado blew through, it could drop them all off at the same time, but we buried all the lines so that whatever happens aboveground doesn't affect the security of the park. We took every precaution to make sure that this exact scenario never happened. So, I'm not sure exactly who's behind this, but I know someone is."

Bao looked around the space they were in. It was one of the small kiosks, not very large, only about six by ten feet. It was essentially made of plywood. "Okay, so we know that the condors are out, and whatever the heck that was on the monorail is out. I don't think this place is going to be able to protect us from much."

"No, I don't think it is either," Meg agreed.

"There's a motor pool of carts maybe a hundred yards behind us. We can get one of those and then head . . ." Gabe's voice dropped off as he contemplated the possibilities.

"Should we head back to the orangutan exhibit?" Linc suggested.

But Meg immediately shook her head. "Not if their containment units are open. We need something with a lot of doors, manual locks, and ways to keep away from anything that might've escaped."

Everyone looked at Gabe expectantly.

"The research center."

"Yeah, that sounds like a horrible idea," Meg replied.

He gave her a small grin. "It shouldn't be. There are a lot of old-fashioned manual locks there. All the doors and walls are reinforced. It wasn't built to protect against animals but against climate change. We needed the place to withstand a hurricane or tornado. All the buildings are made of cement. Any animals trying to get through would have a really tough time."

"Okay, so now we just need to get the cart and get out of here," Linc added.

Rolling her shoulders, Meg nodded. "All right, do the carts need keys?"

"No, they're push-start," Gabe said.

"Okay, I'll grab one and be back in a few minutes," Meg said.

Gabe shook his head. "No, I should—"

The woman met his gaze. "I've got this."

As Gabe was about to object, Bao tapped his arm. "She's good at this kind of thing." He turned his gaze to Meg. "Be careful. We'll be waiting for you to come rescue us."

Giving him a quick salute, Meg moved over to the door and cracked it open. Then she slipped out. Bao quickly closed the door behind her. The rest of them let out a collective breath, hoping and praying that Meg would be okay and that, at the same time, she managed to save all their collective butts.

CHAPTER 81

Darby had always thought that Mammoth Manor was an unusual choice of name for the elephant house. At the entrance of the manor was a massive display explaining the relationships of the different giant mammals, how they were all linked, and more accurately how they were separated by millions of years.

Most people thought mastodons, mammoths, and elephants were all part of the same family. They did look a lot alike, but if you looked closer, you saw the differences. American mastodons had low-domed heads and less curved tusks than their cousins the mammoths and Indian elephants.

The mastodons were the oldest, followed by the mammoths, and finally elephants. Elephants, which had coexisted with mammoths, survived because they were able to adapt better. Elephants, therefore, are not mastodons or mammoths. But she understood the need for both alliteration and for something that the public could latch on to.

A small moan came from Lance behind them. Darby flicked a glance at him. The man's face was pale, and he'd sweated through his shirt. She met Gus's gaze, and he gave a nod, assuring her that Lance could continue. But the little moans he was giving every now and then were not exactly comforting.

Plus, they were getting to the heart of the elephants' area. The last thing she wanted to do was attract the attention of Dembe.

Moving back to Lance, Darby leaned toward him, keeping her voice low. "I know you're hurting, and I'm sorry for that, but we're entering a somewhat problematic area. I need you to try not to make a sound, okay?"

Then Darby looked over the group, raising her voice a little so the others could hear. "That goes for everybody. No noise from this point on, all right?"

Everybody nodded, including Lance. In silence, they all moved forward. Scooter kept moving them closer to the trees, shifting almost from tree to tree. He knew what area they were in as well.

As they walked, Darby couldn't help but picture the hyenas. But on the monorail, she'd seen other animals. She wasn't sure why they had suddenly become aggressive. Was it just that they had been freed? She couldn't say for sure that wasn't the case. As far as she knew, there'd never been a zoo where all of the animals had been let out at the same time. Only isolated cases where animals escaped.

A loud snap like someone stepping on a branch sounded. Darby flicked a worried glance over her shoulder as Scooter said, "Lance, you need to watch where you're stepping."

Lance shook his head with a wince. "That wasn't me," he whispered.

Everybody went still, and the hair on the back of Darby's neck rose. There was someone else out here.

CHAPTER 82

His gaze scanning everyone, Scooter dropped his voice, his shoulders tense. "Okay, everybody needs to stay quiet and double-time it toward the manor."

A rustle came from the bushes to the left. Her head whipping to the side as her heart rate spiked, Darby's eyes widened. If it was an elephant, they should be able to see it. Had some other animals made it into the preserve?

Courtney let out a squeal.

Scooter stepped in front of Courtney and Ori while Gus and Noah shifted closer to Darby and Lance. The rustling continued, and then a small furry head popped out. Darby let out a relieved laugh. "Molly."

Molly was a golden retriever who belonged to Lucas, the elephant keeper. The elephants were completely unbothered by Molly and, in fact, kind of looked at her as their own little pet. Molly had been a great benefit to some of the orphaned baby elephants that had first arrived at the zoo.

Darby's smile faded as Molly stayed in the brush. Then Darby crouched down. Molly was the friendliest dog out there. She usually rushed over to Darby when she saw her. "Come here, Molly. It's okay."

Molly darted out of the bushes and made a beeline for Darby, her body full of nervous energy, and she barely touched her back-right paw to the ground.

"She's hurt," Ori exclaimed.

Despite the injury, when Molly reached Darby, she licked her face in excitement, jumping around her. "Hey, girl. It's good to see you too."

But then Darby's eyes widened as she caught the streaks of red along Molly's coat.

"Is that blood?" Ori asked as she moved closer.

"I think so." Straightening, Darby looked around. Where was Lucas? There was no way he would let Molly run around without him.

And Molly was well-trained. She stayed by Lucas's side, especially in the preserve. As soon as Darby stood, Molly darted back toward the bushes and then stopped, looking over her shoulder at Darby, her eyes pleading. "We've got to follow her."

"Follow her? Are you kidding? Absolutely not. We need to get somewhere safe." Courtney crossed her arms over her chest.

Ignoring her, Darby looked over at Scooter. "Lucas," was all she said.

He nodded. "If you guys want to stay here, you can, but we're going to follow Molly."

Looking around, Gus gave a grim nod. "I think it's better if we all stay together. We're going with you."

CHAPTER 83

THE SMALL KIOSK ONLY SEEMED TO GROW SMALLER AS TIME WENT ON. A few minutes after Meg left, a large crash sounded near the roofline. Gabe's heart had all but stopped as Mama Sue grabbed his hand and squeezed. There was a short rustle and what sounded like the scrabble of nails before it went quiet again. No one said a word, but Gabe noted everyone was breathing a little heavier.

After about ten minutes, Bao whispered, "How far away were the carts?"

"Only about two hundred yards," Gabe said, feeling the same concern for Meg that Bao obviously felt.

"Okay, I'll go look for her," Bao said.

Gabe wanted to argue, wanted to tell Bao that it wasn't safe. But if it were Joel out there, he'd already be gone. "Okay. Be careful, and try to keep yourself safe, okay?"

Nodding, Bao moved to the door. Just as he did, there was the sound of running feet coming from outside.

Bao moved silently to the door, tensing. There was a light knock. "It's me."

Opening the door, Bao ushered Meg in, scanning the area outside before he closed it again.

Meg dropped to the ground, breathing hard. Linc reached into one of the coolers and handed her a water. Nodding her thanks, she took a long drink and then wiped her mouth with the back of her hand.

"What happened?" Bao asked.

"Well, the animals are definitely out. I had to run from a wolf that luckily spied some other smaller animal that looked like an easier kill. It took off after it when I hid on a roof."

"What about the carts?" Gabe asked.

Her gaze locked on Bao, Meg shook her head. "The tires were all slashed."

Mama Sue's hand flew to her throat. "Oh my goodness. Why would the animals do that?"

"I don't know," Meg said, her gaze on Bao. Some unspoken communication was happening there that Gabe couldn't read.

Breaking off, Meg looked at the others. "Well, Sanctuary Kingdom has gone from a traditional zoo to a more interactive experience. I saw a group of lemurs scamper across the path. There was a very large, scaly thing in the distance that I made sure to steer away from." She looked over at Gabe. "It looks like all of your animals are out."

Mama Sue gripped Gabe's hand. "Darby."

Fear took root in Gabe's chest. She was out there with a group. Trying to keep the tremor out of his arms and out of his voice, he patted Mama Sue's hand. "I'm sure she's fine."

CHAPTER 84

DARBY TOOK A STEP FORWARD. MOLLY IMMEDIATELY DARTED THROUGH THE brush. Darby and the others couldn't go that way, so they had to make their way around. Molly was prancing nervously, waiting for them.

As soon as she saw them, she took off again. Darby's chest felt heavy. Something was definitely wrong.

Molly led them on for a few dozen yards. Every time Darby thought she might have lost Molly, the retriever would reappear, prancing, and then sprint away again.

Finally, Darby rounded a large tree and came to a standstill with a gasp. Lucas Ross sat propped up against its base. Blood ran down the side of his head, mixing with his gray hair and beard. His skin tone was ashen, with sweat along his brow, and his leg was twisted at an unnatural angle. His brown keeper uniform was stained with sweat, dirt, and with darker spots Darby didn't want to examine too closely.

Darting forward, she crouched down next to him, not sure what to do. "Lucas?"

The older man's eyes opened. It took him a moment to focus in on Darby. When he did, his eyes widened. "Darby, you shouldn't be out here."

"It looks like you shouldn't either," Scooter said, as he crouched down on the man's other side.

"Hey, Scoot. Do me a favor, get Molly back to the manor, okay?" Lucas said, his voice alarmingly soft.

Gus and Noah took positions on either side of them, keeping an eye on the surroundings. Courtney and Lance huddled near the side of the tree.

Studying Lucas's injuries, Darby knew that Lucas wouldn't be able to walk out of here on that leg. "What happened?"

Closing his eyes for a moment, he grunted before opening them again. "One of the elephants attacked."

"Was it Dembe?" she asked, picturing the large bull.

Lucas shook his head and then winced. "No. It was Theema."

Darby sat back hard. Theema was a member of the herd, but she was usually quiet and nonviolent. "Theema? Are you sure?"

Lucas nodded slowly. "Trust me, I was just as surprised as you."

Female elephants would attack, but they or one of their offspring had to be threatened. There was a baby elephant in the preserve, but Theema had shown no particular attachment to Kiya. "Why would she do that?" Darby asked.

"I don't know." Lucas closed his eyes for a minute. When he opened them again, they were full of pain. "Shandy and I were out making some field observations. There was no warning. One minute everything was fine. And the next . . ."

Shandy Johnson, the director of conservation efforts, was absolutely dedicated to protecting as many animal species as she could. Darby frowned. There was no way that Shandy would have left Lucas in this state. "Did she go get help?"

With a shake of his head, Lucas reached out and gripped Darby's hand. "No."

The pain and loss in that one word caused the breath to leave Darby's chest. "Theema?"

As his gaze shifted between Scooter and Darby, strength returned to Lucas's voice. "You guys need to get out of here. They're going to know you're here."

"They?" Scooter asked.

"Theema started the attack, but she wasn't the only one. She got the herd all riled up," Lucas explained.

Turning to look at them, Gus frowned. "What do you mean they're going to know we were here?"

Lucas just sucked in a breath, squeezing Darby's hand, so Darby answered for him. "African Forest elephants can recognize and hear vibrations in the ground."

Lucas released Darby's hand and pointed toward the manor. "Take the jeep. It's over that way, maybe a hundred yards."

The ground started to tremble. Darby darted to her feet looking over to their right as fear charged up her throat. "They're coming."

CHAPTER 85

THE SOUND OF THE ELEPHANTS APPROACHING GREW LOUDER. MOST PEOPLE underestimated how fast elephants could run. They thought of them as these slow, ponderous beasts.

But elephants had been clocked at twenty-five miles per hour. The average human in comparison ran between six and eight miles per hour, so even the slowest elephant could outrun the fastest human. Scooter leaned down for Lucas, but Lucas pushed his hands away.

"No, no, there's no time for that," he insisted, wrestling into his pocket and shoving his keys at Darby. "My jeep's over that way. Go, leave me, and go."

He ran a hand over Molly, who had her head on Lucas's good leg. "But take Molly."

Scooter reached down and pulled Molly into his arms.

"We're not leaving you," Darby said.

Lucas shook his head, giving Darby a smile that broke her heart. "I can't run and you can't carry me. You need to go. Tell Cora I love her, okay?"

Tears pressed against Darby's eyes as she looked up at Gus. First Bash and now Lucas.

"Sorry, Doc." Gus moved quickly. He leaned down and punched Lucas in the face. The man's chin dropped onto his chest.

Darby let out a gasp. "Why did you do that?"

"It will make this easier for him." Leaning down, he grabbed Lucas by the arm and hauled him up over his shoulder. "Now let's go."

Darby didn't need any further prodding. She took off at a run in the direction that Lucas had indicated. The elephants behind them were making the ground tremble harder. Her heart was once again in her throat.

Through the trees, she spied the jeep. "I'll get it started."

She sprinted forward and leapt into the driver's seat, turning over the engine. By the time it sprang to life, Courtney and Ori were already there and helping Lance climb in. Scooter placed Molly on Ori's lap and Gus placed Lucas in the back. "Hold on to him," he ordered Courtney.

Then Scooter held on to the side, and Noah and Gus scrambled onto the back, gripping the frame.

"Go, go, go," Scooter ordered.

Darby crushed down on the accelerator as the first two elephants crashed through the canopy behind them.

CHAPTER 86

Darby had always liked visiting the elephant preserve. There was something so calming about the elephants. Two months ago, they had taken in a baby elephant that had been orphaned. Darby had stopped by every morning, including this morning, to feed her. Now, whenever Kiya saw her, she came running.

Kiya running at her was very different from the full-grown elephants sprinting toward her and the others now.

Each of them weighed in excess of two tons. Even though they were on the smaller side of the species as a whole, they were still eight feet tall. Their roars made clear they were not happy.

Darby kept her foot pressed to the accelerator. The jeep shook and jolted with every dip in the uneven ground. Lance cried out each time. Silently, Darby apologized to him with each jostle, but she didn't dare slow.

Flicking a glance in the rearview mirror, she spotted Theema and Dipuo leading the charge, with the others arrayed behind them.

Darby had run a hand over each of their coats at least a few times over the last few years. Mammoth Manor had a large area where the elephants slept at night, and the elephants would often come up to the bars, seeking out affection. Darby had always found the animals to be peaceful, friendly, and just so amazingly magnificent to look at.

But there was absolutely nothing peaceful or friendly about the animals charging behind them now. Darby pressed harder down on the accelerator, and the back wheels slipped a little on the soft ground.

Courtney leaned forward from the back, practically squeezing her way into the front seat. "Faster. Go faster!"

Gripping the steering wheel, Darby didn't say anything, just aimed for Mammoth Manor. She whipped around a bush and tore over the small wooden bridge across the stream.

Flicking another glance in the rearview, she saw most of the other elephants broke off their charge at the bridge. But both Theema and Dipuo were still coming.

"There!" Scooter yelled.

As the manor came into view, Darby wrenched the wheel to the right. They were coming in through the pasture entrance. There were a number of entrances, all of them reinforced so that the elephants could not enter when they were closed. Darby discounted most of them. Opening and closing them would take too much time. The elephants would reach them well before they got one of the giant garage doors closed.

They needed a smaller entrance that the elephants couldn't get through. Darby aimed for the east side of the manor. There was a staff entrance located next to one of the garage doors. As she rounded the corner of the building, she noted the door wasn't open. She hoped someone inside would catch sight of them on the cameras.

And then a horrific thought hit her: What if there was no one inside? It wasn't impossible. Monday mornings were always quiet.

"Hit the horn," she ordered Ori.

Reaching over while grasping Molly in her lap, Ori started to slam on the horn as Darby aimed for the door right next to the animal loading entrance.

"Please, please, please let someone be there," she prayed. Her and Scooter's bracelets normally would have gotten them through the door, but being they hadn't worked on the tower, she wasn't counting on them working here. Already her mind was racing for alternatives if they couldn't get the door open. All those alternatives relied on them getting back in the Jeep and outracing the charging elephants.

The odds of that action being successful did not fill her with optimism.

Shoving the doubts and fears down, she raced across the open ground toward the manor. Theema and Dipuo cornered the building behind them, Theema stumbling for a moment but righting herself quickly.

The staff door remained stubbornly closed.

Silently, Darby begged, *Oh, come on, please.*

CHAPTER 87

Ori kept her hand on the horn as they approached the closed door. "Darby," she warned.

Gripping the steering wheel tightly, fear skittered through Darby. "I know."

Mind racing, Darby was about to turn and head for the front entrance of the preserve, when the door suddenly opened. A woman in the blue Sanctuary Kingdom uniform with long white hair in a braid over her shoulder peered at them through dark-rimmed glasses.

Cora Hughes, Lucas's wife, frowned, and then her eyes widened as she caught sight of Darby's group and the elephants charging behind.

"Hold on!" Darby yelled as she cut the wheel and slammed on the brakes when they were only a few feet away from the entrance.

Scooter, Gus, and Noah leapt off as soon as the jeep slowed. Noah stumbled and did a roll, bounding back to his feet. Then Noah and Gus reached in and grabbed Lucas, hauling him over Gus's shoulder again while Scooter grabbed Molly. The others bailed out of the jeep and sprinted for the door. Cora hastened out of the way.

As soon as Darby was through, she grabbed the door and slammed it shut. Cora pulled the heavy metal bolt across it. The elephants crashed into the door, causing the whole building to shudder.

Stumbling back, Darby grabbed ahold of Cora to keep her upright. The older woman's mouth gaped open, her whole body trembling. The elephants continued to crash against the door, and then one crashed against the larger garage door as well.

Darby and Cora backed away slowly. Darby kept her gaze locked on the door. "These doors will hold, right?"

With thick glasses making her large brown eyes look even larger, Cora nodded slowly. "Yeah. They were designed to withstand a stampede." She turned and looked at Darby. "What happened out there?"

Disbelief at all that had happened rolling through her, Darby shook her head. "I really couldn't tell you."

CHAPTER 88

KEVIN COULDN'T REMEMBER THE LAST TIME HE'D HAD SO MUCH FUN. HE was practically bouncing in his chair with excitement. Switching his focus from the known subjects to the unknown had been the right call. He'd watched as a woman ran down a path only to be attacked by a baboon. The thing wailed on her like she'd killed its firstborn.

Well, maybe she had. But, seeing as she worked at one of the restaurants, he doubted it.

In another scene, he saw an alligator grab someone and pull them into one of the rivers. The alligator had resurfaced a short time later. The employee had not.

Popping some more potato chips into his mouth, Kevin grinned. For years, he'd imagined getting back at the people who'd mocked him when he was a kid. He didn't know any of these people personally, but he was willing to bet that they had been just as cruel to outsiders in high school as his own bullies had been.

His phone rang, and he flicked an annoyed glare at it. Todd wasn't supposed to call him until everything was done. But he knew if he didn't answer, Todd would just call back again and again and again.

"What?" he said by way of greeting.

"Are you seeing this?" Todd's voice was high-pitched and full of stress.

Violent image after violent image splayed across the screens arrayed in front of him. He chuckled as two women managed to duck inside a cage and slam the door shut just before a wolf managed to catch one of their heels.

"Oo, close one," he murmured.

The two girls backed away from the bars, their arms wrapped around one another, their bodies shaking. "Yeah, of course. I'm watching everything."

"It's a lot."

Kevin frowned at the phone. "What did you think was going to happen?"

"I know, I know, but you know, just seeing it is a little different."

Kevin had known Todd was soft. He talked a big game, but when push came to shove, a lot of people didn't want to shove. Kevin, however, had no problem with the violence. In fact, it was only making him want more. He'd known the implants would increase the aggression in its subjects.

What he hadn't expected and had been very happy to find was that the aggression was contagious. Even though there were only a hundred or so animals with implants, it was almost like a mob mentality had taken over the animals.

Or maybe they were all just really mad at being locked up.

Popping another few chips into his mouth, Kevin shrugged. "They're getting what they deserve. You know what they've done to the animals in that park. Isn't that your whole thing? Save the animals?"

"Yeah, but I mean, I just saw a lady get her leg ripped off." Todd's voice ended with a screech.

"I guess they should have picked a different line of work." He flicked a glance at the clock. "Send the message through." Kevin disconnected the call.

CHAPTER 89

ONCE DARBY AND CORA WERE SURE THAT THE DOORS WOULD HOLD, THEY moved past the elephant containment units and into the offices of the building, following the others.

Mammoth Manor was a massive structure stretching out over 20,000 square feet. More than half of that was made up of the containment units for the elephants. The rest was a mixture of offices, labs, and, of course, the massive 5,000-square-foot exhibit area. There was even a 4D theater where you got to ride in the savanna on the back of an elephant during a rainstorm.

But the public area was not where Darby and Cora were headed. Instead, they hustled down the hallway to the medical suite right next to the containment area.

As they walked, Darby gave Cora a quick briefing on what they'd experienced. Cora was shaking her head by the time they reached the lab. "How is this possible? And why wasn't I notified?"

"We think they took over the communications as well as everything else."

Her mouth a thin line, Cora stepped into the medical suite. It was a massive space. It had to be. On occasion, an elephant would need to be brought in and sedated while a lab tech worked on them. That happened at one of the three cages on the right side of the room. There was a garage door that led to the containment area.

There were no beds or stretchers for humans. But it looked like someone had dragged in a cot from the break room down the hall. Gus had deposited Lucas on the cot, and Molly had been placed on the couch next to it.

Hand to her mouth, Cora took in the state of the two patients with a small cry. She knelt down next to Lucas, whose eyes were still closed. She ran a shaky hand over his hair. "What happened?"

"We found him out on the preserve. His leg's broken, and he's got a head wound, but we can't be sure if there's anything more than that." Scooter gestured to Molly. "And this little hero hurt her leg."

For a moment, Darby thought that Cora was going to crumble as she took in her husband and Molly. Her eyes welled up, and her chin started to tremble, but then she shook her head as she stood. Taking a step back from them, she nodded. "Okay. Okay."

Letting out a shaky breath, she pointed at Noah. "You. Wash your hands and grab me that tray over there."

"Yes, ma'am." Noah gave her a little salute and hustled to do her bidding.

Turning to Courtney and Lance, she pointed at the doorway. "You two, sit in the lounge down the hall. I'll look at that shoulder after I take care of these two."

"Shouldn't the human come before the dog?" Courtney demanded.

"Not here," Cora replied, her voice firm.

Although Courtney opened her mouth to argue, one look at Cora's face had her shutting it. She grabbed Lance by the good arm, which still made him wince, before she dragged him out into the hall.

Darby had already moved to the sink to wash her hands and then stepped next to the bed. "What do you need me to do?"

Moving to the sink herself, Cora washed her hands with practiced efficiency. While she was currently the operations director for Sanctuary Kingdom, Cora and Lucas had met on an elephant preserve in Uganda. Lucas had been there for post-graduate study while Cora had been the veterinarian. Cora had stepped away from medicine only three years ago when she'd taken the director's position. But she was known to help out with some vet activities every now and then.

Now, the woman gave Darby a grateful smile as she dried her

hands and headed back to the cot. "See if you can wash off that blood. I need a better idea of what we're looking at here."

Noah hurried over with the tray. After nodding her thanks, Cora flicked a glance over her shoulder at Gus. "That cabinet behind you has some splints. I need you and Scooter to figure out a way to cut them down so they fit Lucas's leg. And there's a cot back there. I need you to raise it so I can use it as an examination table."

"Yes, ma'am," Gus said, turning for the closet.

Looking down at Lucas, Cora let out one shaky breath and then seemed to lock up all her emotions as she knelt down next to him. She undid her husband's shirt and started palpating his chest. "Was it Dembe?"

Darby shook her head. "No. Lucas said it was Theema."

Stopping her ministrations, Cora looked at Darby with wide eyes. "Theema?"

"I know," Darby responded. "That was my reaction, too."

"Theema," Cora said softly, shaking her head as she returned her attention to her husband. "He and Shandy went out and—" Cora stopped again, looking up at Darby. "Where is Shandy?"

Darby swallowed. "Lucas said she didn't make it."

Cora stared at her for a long moment before returning to her examination. "I see. I should have realized something was wrong when the cameras stopped working correctly."

Darby frowned. "What do you mean?"

"Lucas and Shandy were gone for a while. I expected them back about thirty minutes ago. I started flipping through the cameras looking for them. But I couldn't see them anywhere. And I didn't see you on the cameras at all. If it weren't for that horn, I wouldn't have known you were out there."

"What are you talking about?" Scooter asked.

"Go check the security cameras. You'll see that the jeep isn't on them." Cora nudged her chin towards the corner of the room.

Scooter moved over to the monitor there. He flipped through cameras until he came across the entrance where they had entered. In the picture, everything looked peaceful. There were no rampaging elephants, even though the building still shook from their hits. There was no Jeep. There was nothing.

"They looped the feed," Darby whispered.

Gus looked up from where he was placing a splint on a lab table and met her gaze.

"Who looped the feed?" Cora asked.

Meeting her gaze, Darby shook her head, looking around for Ori and not seeing her. She must have headed to the control room. She blew out a breath. "That is another question we simply don't have the answer to. Right next to the bigger question of why."

CHAPTER 90

ONCE MARTHA RETURNED TO HER OFFICE, SHE FELT A LITTLE BETTER. AT least the IT people were working on the problem. Although, she would have felt much better having Tom here than Reuben. The man really didn't seem to grasp the urgency of the moment. She'd stopped by the PR department on the way and had them running up different responses. Even in her own mind, the fact that that was even a concern made her feel cold.

But if Sanctuary Kingdom went down, hundreds of people would lose their jobs. That didn't include all the businesses that had popped up around the park, like hotels, restaurants, shopping areas. Sanctuary Kingdom closing would affect thousands of livelihoods.

Pulling up the PDF of the map of the park, her gaze roved over it, looking for something, although she didn't know what. The park was huge, and there were areas where the doors and locks had been designed to withstand an animal attack.

But all of those were automated. If someone had intentionally done this, they could easily have left those doors unsecured.

Desperation crawled up her throat as she stared at the map. Was there any way the people in the park could keep themselves safe? There were gun cabinets in the park as part of the DART program. All members needed quick access to weapons. But for obvious reasons, only a select few could access those safes.

Gabe was one of them, and she really hoped he remembered where they were. Her head jolted up. DART. She hadn't heard any mention of them. "Kelly!" she yelled.

Her assistant stepped in a moment later. "Yes?"

"Any word on DART? Are they in the park?"

Kelly's mouth fell open and she jotted a note down on her tablet. "Actually I haven't heard anything about them. I'll find it. And I do have some news."

"From IT?"

"No, not yet." Kelly now stood in front of Martha's desk, clutching her tablet to her chest.

Sitting back, Martha eyed her assistant, noting the woman was paler than normal and her hands were shaking. "What's wrong? What's happened? Is it Gabe?"

"No, I don't have any word on Gabe. But I do know who attacked the park."

"Attacked? We don't know that," Martha said with a shake of her head.

Kelly placed the tablet on the desk in front of Martha. "We do now."

CHAPTER 91

CHORTLING, KEVIN REPLAYED THE MAD DASH OF THE GROUP IN THE elephant preserve. They had just missed being pulverized. He hadn't seen it in real time, but the replay had been just as good. Sadly, they'd all made it, but there was one body in a field, so someone hadn't.

What a shame, he thought, shifting to other images. The message from EcoAct had been sent to Dominion and only Dominion. It wasn't time yet for the rest of the world to know what was going on. In fact, he'd arranged a little diversion to keep the police in the area very busy.

Humming, he flicked through the other images, keeping the image from Mammoth Manor on one of his monitors. It really was an impressive-looking place. It was so big. It looked like a fortress.

His mouth fell open. A fortress. "No, no, no," he murmured as he brought up the schematics of the manor. And there on the first floor was what he feared: a control center.

It wasn't as big as the one in either the Castle or Dominion. But still, if they had someone with technical skills, and being he'd spied Ori Rosenburg sprinting for the door, he knew they did, and she could do some damage.

"Oh no." Quickly, he scrolled through the images from Mammoth Manor. He flipped through a number of cameras. Most of the manor was empty. The people he did see were in the med wing. There was a guy on a cot being seen to. The movie star was there along with his assistant, the security guy, Darby, and some woman he didn't know.

Right now, they weren't his concern. He continued to flip and spied the two influencers in a room together. The man lay on a couch while the woman pushed uselessly at her phone.

But where was Ori?

A nervous sweat broke out along his back. It would be fine. He just needed to reinforce—

He stopped flipping as he found the control room. Sitting at the massive panel was Ori Rosenburg. Her head was bent, her fingers moving quickly over the keyboard.

There was a way to wrest control of each site back. It involved cutting the site off from the main system. Once that happened, the location would be completely controlled by the panel on site, pulled from the park-wide grid.

There was a way around that, but Kevin hadn't set that up. He hadn't expected there to be any need. He hadn't expected any programmers, or at least any seriously skilled ones, to be in the park.

The quote he'd flung at Todd earlier darted through his mind: *Making no mistakes establishes the certainty of victory, for it means conquering an enemy that is already defeated.*

This was a mistake. His second one, and both were attributed to Ori. But this was one that could be corrected.

Opening a dialog box, he quickly started to type. If he got the firewall in place before she managed to disconnect the site, he could lock her out. So it came down to who was faster. A coding foot race. He smiled. Now they would see who was better.

He flicked a glance up at the screen and saw Augustus King's PA appear in the room. Good, he'd distract her for a few seconds at least, and that was all Kevin needed.

Head tucked, shoulders tense, he felt the thrill of competition. He loved this stuff. He flicked another glance at the screen and saw that the PA was now sitting at another terminal, typing as fast as Ori.

He frowned, turning back to his own screen, seeing firewalls appear. *No, no.*

Then he looked back at the screen. Ori looked up, staring into the screen. She held up her left hand and extended her middle finger. With her right hand, she hit enter.

The cameras cut off. Anger boiling, he checked and saw that Mammoth Manor had been wrested from his control.

Standing, he grabbed his chair and shoved it across the open space. "Damn it!"

CHAPTER 92

After an examination of Lucas, Cora said she didn't think that Lucas had any internal bleeding, but she was putting him through the MRI just to be sure. She was also x-raying him to ensure there weren't any broken bones they had missed. There was bruising along his rib cage. He hadn't mentioned something being wrong with his ribs, but they couldn't count on that being accurate. He hadn't regained consciousness for them to ask him.

When Cora was finished with the X-ray, Lucas came to. Darby stepped outside to give them a little privacy. She leaned against the wall, wrapping her arms around her waist, her mind replayed the elephants' rampage. Theema had been the one who'd attacked them. That made no sense. She wouldn't just attack out of nowhere.

Appearing at the end of the hall, Ori waved Darby over. Pushing off the wall, Darby jogged over to her. "Hey. You got something?"

"Yeah. Come on." Ori led Darby toward the main control room.

They passed Courtney and Lance, who were in the lounge. Cora had checked Lance's arm, re-bandaged it to keep it more immobile, and given him some pain meds. Now, he was lying down on the couch.

Courtney was sitting on the edge of the couch next to him, tearfully speaking to the phone in her extended hand. Darby did not try to hear what she was saying. But she did pull out her own phone to verify that there was still no signal.

There wasn't.

She'd just pushed it back in her pocket when she followed Ori into the control room. Noah, Gus, and Scooter were already there. She looked over their grim faces and steeled herself for what was to come. She met Scooter's gaze. "Mama Sue? Linc?"

He shook his head quickly. "No, we don't have anything on them yet, honey."

Although she nodded, it didn't lessen the worry in the back of her mind. She just needed to know that they were somewhere safe. "What's going on?"

"I managed to break Mammoth Manor's system off from the main grid."

Noah cleared his throat.

Ori shot him a grin. "Sorry, *we* regained control of Mammoth Manor. It's no longer part of the park-wide system. Our hacker can't see what we're up to, and we've got control of everything within the elephant preserve's boundaries."

Sinking into a chair, Darby gave a small grin. "Well, that's good news."

Ori grinned. "Yeah. Honestly, it was a pretty simple hack. But to fix it, you have to be on-site. It can't be done from the central hub, so basically, you have to go through every exhibit to get the system back under control."

"You can't just reset from a main hub?" Scooter asked.

With a sigh, Ori shook her head. "You probably can. But the security protocols should have been activated and I'm pretty sure Dominion is walled off now."

"So what have you got?" Darby asked.

Taking a deep breath, Ori flicked the camera to a scene. Darby leaned forward and then sucked in a breath at the image of the body down in the field. "Shandy."

Her voice soft, Ori said, "Yeah. But she's not the only one."

The camera switched again, and this time it showed an elephant lying on its side in the field. Darby frowned. The signs of violence were clear. "Do you know who that is?"

"I was able to zoom in and noted the scar on the front-right leg."

"It's Ayo." Surprise filled Darby. Ayo was the biggest of the elephants in the preserve. Standing at just over ten feet and tipping the scales at five tons, she was not easy to take down.

"Yeah. She wasn't part of that stampede outside," Ori said.

But Darby frowned. That made no sense. Ayo was the matriarch, the leader. Leaning back, Darby studied the screen trying to focus on the good. It was great that Ori had been able to get the cameras back under control. At least they'd know if anything was coming.

At the same time, it must have taken a lot of work to control all the cameras in the park. There were hundreds of camera zones.

Turning to the console, Ori hit a few buttons. "And now that we have the cameras again, we caught sight of an incursion."

"An incursion?" Darby asked, leaning forward.

Ori scooted aside so that Darby had a better view. "The hyenas are here."

CHAPTER 93

THE VIDEO WAS QUEUED UP ON KELLY'S TABLET. BUT MARTHA DID NOT reach out to hit play. After a moment, she realized she was trying to put off learning the truth.

It did not make her reach for the tablet. Instead, she studied the man frozen on the screen. She didn't recognize him. He was in his late twenties, with stringy brown hair pulled back into a ponytail and a few piercings along his ears. He wore a T-shirt that had once been white, or perhaps it was intended to look dingy.

Reaching for the tablet, Martha frowned. "What is this?"

"It's a message from a group called EcoAct."

Martha groaned. She knew about EcoAct. They'd been sending threatening letters for the last six months, claiming that Sanctuary Kingdom was involved in animal abuse. It was laughable, as if Gabe would be associated with anything that would hurt animals.

As far as Marthas priorities went, they were a non-factor. They wrote letters, made demands but got little to no attention.

They were probably just trying to take credit. They did not have the infrastructure for this. She started to hand the tablet back. "I don't have time for this nonsense today."

Kelly gently pushed the tablet back toward Martha. "It's not nonsense. You need to listen to the message."

With concern and more than a little trepidation, Martha pulled the tablet back and hit play. The image sprang to life.

"I'm Todd Sharp, the founder of EcoAct. In our view, Sanctuary Kingdom has been found guilty of animal abuse and of being callous stewards of the animal kingdom."

Martha rolled her eyes. These groups were so tiresome. Sanctuary Kingdom went above and beyond in its protection protocols for the animals. They spent millions each year on their welfare. There wasn't a zoo out there that did better than they did.

"We have warned you over and over again that you needed to stop your barbaric practices. But you didn't listen."

A chill rolled up Martha's spine, and she flicked a glance at Kelly. Kelly stood with her hands gripped tightly together, her face pale.

Todd continued. "We have control of your park. You wanted to play with the animals. Now it's time for the animals to play with you."

The image shifted, and Martha watched in disbelief as the gate to the Sumatran tiger enclosure opened. A moment later, one of the big cats stepped out and then walked through. The image shifted to a drone view flying over the park, showing various enclosures with the gates wide open.

Her chest going tight as she gripped the tablet tightly, Martha's eyes widened.

"There is nothing you can do. It's time for Sanctuary Kingdom to reap what it has sown." The video went dark.

Martha stared at the blank screen and then looked up to meet Kelly's terrified gaze. "Get me Roger and Reuben."

"Phones are out."

Already standing, Martha cursed. "Right, go *find* Roger. Tell him to meet me at IT. And find out where the hell DART is."

With a nod, Kelly hurried out the door, moving quickly. Martha was right behind her. The two split at the hall, Martha pushing on the stairwell door and hurrying down to IT. They had a name.

And then she paused, pulling out her phone. Still no signal. But Kelly, or the park, had sent that video.

How had they managed that?

CHAPTER 94

Annoyance ticked through Kevin. Despite the mayhem on the screens, he felt a sense of failure at losing Mammoth Manor.

Stupid, so stupid.

Growling, he stalked across the warehouse to retrieve his chair. It had hit the wall hard, and one of the wheels was now damaged. So instead of rolling it back to his workstation, he'd had to drag it.

It just made him angrier.

I should have put in more firewalls. But getting into the system had required days of coding. Protecting each exhibit individually would have taken months.

Picturing Ori, he glared at his screen. She'd beaten him. But then he pictured the guy next to her. Where the hell had he picked up coding abilities? He was a PA, for God's sake. He was pretty sure high-end computing skills were not a requirement for that job.

Taking a breath, he shook his head. It was dumb luck. Everything else was going like clockwork. This was just a small hiccup.

Placing his chair back in position, Kevin retook his seat. Okay, fine. They had one section. No biggie. He flicked through the other images from across the park, his heart rate slowing as he did so. Chaos and violence were everywhere. They had one building. He still had the rest of the park.

Some people had hunkered down, while others were still roaming around looking for a safe spot. He couldn't help but feel like the fear wasn't truly there yet. Now, he realized why. They felt like victims. They all felt like this was being done to them.

Todd had already sent the message over to Dominion, and Kevin was regularly sending quick bursts of images from the park to Dominion as well.

But the people in the park deserved to know how they had brought this upon themselves. So he queued up the message and hit enter, sending it out across the park's PA system.

CHAPTER 95

Without the cart, Gabe and the others were debating the best road forward. Even if they had the cart, it only moved at a top speed of fifteen miles per hour. They were not going to be able to outrun any of the animals in the park.

And with Mama Sue's condition, it wouldn't be so easy to maneuver quickly off the cart to hide. Taking a deep breath, she started, "I think you all should—"

The PA system crackled for a moment. Mama Sue went silent, and all of them looked up expectantly.

Gabe said a little silent thanks to the powers that be. It had to be some sort of emergency broadcast. It should provide instructions on where everybody should go and what they should do. He tensed, waiting to hear the familiar voice of either Roger Collins or Cora Hughes.

Instead, a man's voice rang out that Gabe didn't recognize. "This is Todd Marsh from EcoAct."

"What's EcoAct?" Linc whispered.

His hopes crashing, Gabe answered him quickly, not wanting to miss any of the recording. "It's an environmental advocacy group. Some people have claimed they're at least on the edge of becoming terrorists."

"Well, it looks like they've slipped over the edge," Bao murmured.

Todd went on to detail the park's alleged history of animal abuse and the violations happening over in the research center. Gabe listened to it with a growing sense of disbelief. Todd signed off with an ominous warning: "Now you will reap what you have sown."

No one said a word as silence descended across the park. But Gabe felt everybody's eyes on him.

"Gabe?" Mama Sue asked quietly.

Looking up, he met her concerned gaze. "About two years ago, reports started surfacing about animal abuse in the park. They were all false. I investigated them all personally."

Meg nodded. "I remember that. You guys did a whole marketing blitz, taking everybody through all aspects of the park. It's what made me decide to join you guys."

Glad to have a little backup, Gabe gave her a short smile. "I thought that the distrust had died down. I knew it would never fully go away. We live in a world where even the suggestion of negative behavior sticks to its subject, no matter how untrue it is."

"Are you sure none of it's true?" Bao asked.

Gabe narrowed his eyes. "What are you saying?"

Raising his hands, Bao shook his head. "I'm not accusing you of anything. I'm just saying that the research area is held under pretty tight lock and key. I've been here a month, and I've never even been allowed near it."

Gabe tried to keep the defensiveness out of his answer. "The projects over there are highly sensitive. We can't have people interrupting either the subjects or the work."

He continued. "But none of it is abusive. In fact, quite the opposite. We're isolating genetic markers that are plaguing certain species in order to eradicate them so the species can flourish. We are gathering eggs and sperm for a breeding program to help improve numbers. There's a host of things we're doing over there, but none of it involves abuse of animals."

Gabe sighed. "But I can understand people who are unfamiliar with the process thinking it does. I mean, the first time I saw an animal sedated, it looked like something out of a horror movie. They lay lifeless on the lab table, arms, legs, and head strapped down. But that's standard protocol. That happens in any vet hospital. But taken out of context . . ." His words drifted off, and he shrugged.

"So, EcoAct opened all the doors?" Mama Sue asked with a tremble in her voice.

"Looks like," Gabe agreed.

Bao flicked a glance over everyone's heads at the door. "If this group is angry about the research being conducted here, I don't think we want to head to the research area."

"Agreed." Gabe thought for a moment, trying to figure out the best alternative. With all the animals free, there was no way they would be able to safely get to Dominion unless they could get on the monorail.

But even that wasn't a guarantee. If EcoAct was in charge of the park, he really didn't want to go anywhere they had control—certainly not a metal tube fifty feet above the ground. Pulling up a mental picture of the park, he focused in on one location that was closer than Dominion. "Let's head to the Castle. There's a secondary control room there. It's designed as a kind of fallout shelter."

A note of confidence in his voice, Bao nodded. "Okay. I like this plan."

Although not as enthusiastic, Gabe started to agree as a howl erupted from somewhere deeper in the park. A shiver crawled up his spine. "But I do wish it was a whole lot closer."

"Me too," Bao said, his voice grim. "But waiting for help is no longer an option."

CHAPTER 96

Scooter had slipped out of the room to check in on Lucas. That left Gus, Noah, Ori, and Darby. They were flipping through the monitors, trying to gauge if there was anything else out there that they needed to be concerned with. They'd seen only two hyenas, and they were smaller.

"Hold up," Noah said.

Ori's hands stilled, and the four of them watched an animal lope across the field with a very distinctive gait.

"Is that . . . ?" Ori's question drifted off.

Leaning forward, Darby watched with dread as other shapes appeared behind the first one. "That's Tomy. She's leading the pack into the elephant preserve."

"But that's okay. The hyenas can't get in here." Ori looked at Darby for confirmation.

"If the elephants can't, the hyenas certainly can't," Darby replied.

Frowning, Gus turned his head to the side. Then he slowly held up a hand. "Hey, everybody listen."

They all went still. Darby strained to hear anything. But there was nothing. "I don't hear anything."

He nodded. "Yeah, that's the point. The elephants."

Quickly, Ori flicked through the screens until she found the entrance to where the elephants had last been seen. The elephants were gone.

Noah peered over at the screen. "Where'd they go?"

Picturing Tomy, an uncomfortable feeling settled in Darby's gut. "I think they realized the hyenas were coming."

Darby tapped Ori's shoulder as something flashed across the screen. It had been lower down and she'd just caught a quick glance before the image shifted. "Wait. What was that?"

"What?" Ori backtracked to the previous screen.

Darby pointed to movement by a tree. Ori zoomed in. An image of a baby forest elephant became clear.

"Kiya," Darby breathed.

Kiya was the youngest of the herd. She was only ten months old, but she weighed close to a ton. Of course, she had no concept of her size. She still tried to climb onto Darby's lap when Darby sat down.

Studying the area around the baby, Gus asked, "Where are the other elephants?"

It took a couple of camera changes before Ori found them. "They're heading farther out into the pasture, away from the park and away from the hyenas."

"Is it normal for them to leave a baby behind?" Noah asked.

Worry filled Darby's mind. "No, but Kiya hasn't really bonded with them yet. Is the main gate open?"

Once again, taking a moment to find the screen, the image showed the massive thirty-foot gates that led to Mammoth Manor thrown wide.

"That's how the hyenas got in," Ori whispered. Darby hadn't even thought about that.

"Where are the hyenas? Are they following the elephants?" Noah asked.

Ori shook her head. "No, it looks like they're heading toward us."

Darby studied Kiya. She looked stressed. "Does this thing have sound?"

As Ori hit two buttons, a wail filled the room. Gus stepped next to her, staring at the monitor. "The hyenas aren't coming for the other elephants or for us. They're coming for her."

CHAPTER 97

MARTHA PACED ALONG HER OFFICE IN FRONT OF THE WINDOWS. SHE'D gone down to IT and relayed the information about EcoAct. Reuben still looked unconcerned.

Martha slowly made her way back to her office. The slow speed of her walk was in stark contrast to her emotional state. There was a sense of urgency in her chest to do something, but she didn't know what that something was.

Flicking a gaze out the window, she noted something in the sky. It wasn't an animal but a drone. When they'd first opened, they'd considered doing a fireworks display each night, but Gabe had suggested a drone light show instead. It allowed them to create more intricate images in the sky. It had been a huge hit, although they still did firework displays on special occasions.

But now, the hacker had taken over the drones too. All of them were equipped with cameras, and every once in a while, the hacker sent images of violent attacks back to Dominion.

When Martha asked how the original message had gotten through, Reuben suggested the hacker had opened the signal long enough to get the message out and then shut it down again. So Martha had dozens of staff sitting, staring at their cellphones with messages about the park queued up ready to be sent as soon as anyone got a signal.

Now, she sat at her desk, watching two kids no older than seventeen sprint down a path, a cheetah barreling after them. Her stomach twisted as they dove over the counter at Finnegan's Hideaway. The animal was right behind them. She didn't see how the chase ended. But she knew the odds were not in the kids' favor.

As she tried to piece together how any of this had happened, her mind raced. There were so many safety protocols in place. Someone must have helped the hacker. There was no other explanation. Extensive background checks were conducted on all employees. Anyone with affiliations even remotely related to groups like EcoAct was barred from access to any part of the park's infrastructure. They wouldn't even let someone with questionable ties sell ice cream in the park.

Yet, in her gut, Martha knew someone had slipped through. There was no way someone had managed all of this from the outside. Their system was not only well defended, but the schematics for it were even more secure. No one should have been able to do this.

And yet someone had.

Each year, warnings about various terrorist threats arrived from the federal government. They had become so commonplace that they were treated more like faint background noise than anything to worry about. But she hadn't been warned about this one.

Now she had a theater full of journalists, electrified fences keeping everyone inside the park, and animals running loose in the larger park. How had things spiraled so far out of control?

Roger appeared in the elevator as the doors opened.

Stepping on, Martha asked, "What have you got?"

"My guys keep testing the fences, but there's no sign the electricity is cutting off. It's not working the way it's supposed to."

Martha grunted. "That's not exactly a surprise. What about law enforcement? Where are the cops and the feds?"

"There was a massive explosion—a pipe bomb found at Galleria Mall. All available forces were diverted there."

Martha raised her eyebrows. "Two terrorist attacks on the same day? Wait, how did you learn about that?"

"Personal message," Roger said. "Whoever's in charge of this made sure we'd see the news." He walked over and handed her his phone.

The screen was lit up with images of Galleria Mall—sirens, flashing lights, and people running out in a panic.

"This was very well planned," Martha said softly.

"It was. And we're trying to get a message out by sending someone over the wall." He explained that buses now blocked all the gates. Whenever they approached, people from the outside threw smoke bombs at them and shot at them with pellet guns.

"Are you kidding me?" Marth demanded after Roger explained the situation.

Roger shook his head, rolling up his sleeve to show a red welt on his forearm. "One of my guys nearly lost an eye. We're grabbing some of the fireworks left over from the Fourth. We're going to set them off. At least that will attract attention, and maybe someone will realize we're in trouble over here."

A multimillion-dollar park and they'd been reduced to sending smoke signals for help. "What if we cut the power? Reboot the whole system?"

"It's been set to emergency mode."

"Override it."

"I can't. My codes aren't working. My guys think they've reset the codes, at least for the room."

How much worse could this possibly get? "Just break the doors down," she ordered.

Frustration lining his words, he shook his head. "It was designed to withstand a tornado. There's no getting through that thing. We needed to be sure that if there was an incident at Dominion, the animals would stay secure."

Well, that worked wonderfully, Martha thought sourly. "Where's DART?"

"They were locked in a conference room for their monthly meeting. One of my guys just busted them out." He paused.

"What?" she asked.

"Someone cranked up the heat in the room. It had to be over a hundred degrees in there and they were stuck there for over ninety minutes."

Martha stopped walking and stared at him. "Are they okay?"

"All of them are suffering from dehydration and heat exhaustion. I've got them hooked up to IVs, and the three more serious cases are in the med clinic."

Crap. She'd been counting on the DART members to help.

"A number of staff have stepped up. Honestly, everyone's pulling together," Roger paused. "You know we have a mole, right?" he asked.

Sighing, Martha rubbed her forehead. "I do. Any idea how we find them?"

Roger shook his head. "If we had control of the system, we could start with electronic communications. But until we regain control, we have to take everyone at their word."

He met Martha's eyes. She nodded, her gaze returning to the screen and the chaos unfolding at the mall. "And right now, we can't trust anyone's word."

This just kept getting worse and worse. The doors opened and she stepped out.

"I'll get back to it." Roger said as the doors began to close again.

Martha reached out her hand stopping them. Surprise flashed across Roger's face. She cleared her throat removing her arm. "Thank you, Roger. I don't know what I'd do without you. And tell everyone else I said thank you as well."

Surprise flashed across his face again as the door started to close. "Will do."

Images of Kiya flashed through Darby's mind. When she'd first arrived, Kiya was only up to Darby's thigh and kept trying to crawl into her lap. Darby had happily let her. Now, it was still cute, but she had to be very careful.

But it did not change her affection for the little orphan. Darby had fallen in love with her the moment she'd first seen her. Feeding her every morning had been the absolute highlight of her day. So much so that she'd even come in on her days off. It was how she'd grown so close to both Cora and Lucas. "How close are the hyenas?"

Biting her lip, Ori looked at the screen and then over at the giant map on the right side of the room. "They're over in pasture three."

Calculating, Darby nodded. "Okay. Is the PA system working?"

Ori frowned. "Yeah, why?"

"Because I'm going to get Kiya. If there's any issue, let me know over the PA." Darby turned and strode for the door.

Gus hustled after her. "You're going for the baby elephant?"

"Yes," she said, not stopping. Instead of heading for the garage with the manor's transportation, though, she headed to a small unmarked door down the hall from the control room. She pressed her bracelet against it.

The light flared green. She pushed the door, stepped inside, and flicked on the lights. A rack of twelve tranquilizer rifles was displayed on the right-hand side of the room, and on the left were twelve .357 Magnum lever-action rifles. The drawers underneath held the ammo for each.

Gus's eyebrows rose.

Darby crossed the room to the Magnums. "I said I'm going out there. I never said I was going unarmed."

With his eyes wide as he looked at the weapons, Gus stepped forward. "They keep these in the park?"

"Yeah. Any dangerous animal exhibit has a weapon stash nearby in case there's any problems."

As she reached for the rifle, she shook her head and murmured, "And right now, every single exhibit in the park is a problem."

CHAPTER 98

ALTHOUGH DARBY HAD BEEN IN THE WEAPONS ROOM AT A NUMBER OF THE exhibits, this was the first time she'd needed to use it. She wasn't an official member of DART, but when she'd expressed an interest in it, Gabe had signed her up for the trainings. As a result, she didn't take much time grabbing tranquilizer guns, extra darts, a .357, and some extra bullets. Gus had loaded up as well.

Grabbing a pack, she loaded the extra ammo inside and raised an eyebrow at Gus, who was doing the same. "Have you ever shot a real gun?"

He nodded. "I like my training to be extensive. My marksmanship is pretty good, although live targets are a little trickier."

Although the idea of not going out there alone was appealing, part of her knew she should try and talk him out of it. "It's dangerous to go out there. Maybe you should—"

He cut her off. "I'm going."

Well, she'd tried. Her conscience was clear. She zipped up her pack and slung it over her shoulder. "Okay."

Scooter appeared in the doorway and stepped in with Noah right behind him. The older man glared at her. "Don't even think about going out there without me."

She gave him a grin. "Wouldn't dream of it."

Even though she was joking, in the back of her mind, she kept picturing the hyenas leaping on Kiya. It made her move faster. Not waiting for Noah or Scooter, she hustled out of the room and down the hall toward the garage.

But by the time she and Gus had reached the end of the hall, Noah and Scooter were only a few feet behind them.

Gus headed in the direction they'd entered from, but Darby shook her head. "This way."

Making a right at the end of the hall, she stepped through the first door on the left, which led them to the main garage. The garage had three bays with garage doors at each end so no one ever had to reverse in or out.

In the second bay was a jeep identical to the one outside. The third bay was their destination. Darby gestured toward the Hummer with the large metal sled attached to the back. "We'll take the tank."

"I'll grab the keys." Scooter headed to the box along the left wall.

Making her way toward the Hummer, Darby explained, "We won't be able to lift Kiya, especially if she's injured. But I should be able to coax her onto the sled."

Scooter hopped into the driver's seat. "Time's ticking, people."

Noah opened the back door of the Hummer. "How are you going to coax her in?"

"Oh shoot. Be right back." Darby darted back into the hallway.

Cora was striding down it, holding a newly prepped bottle. She handed it to Darby. "Heard you were going after Kiya. Thought you might need this."

Taking it, Darby pulled it into her chest. It was eighteen inches long and made of heavy-duty plastic with a large rubber nipple on top.

"I'll get the door," Cora said as she followed Darby into the garage.

"You're not going to try and talk me out of this?" Darby asked.

Cora grunted. "I would if I thought it would do any good. Just be careful."

Darby nodded before she wound her way back over to the Hummer and climbed in the back of the sled with Gus. Gus hit the side. "All in. Let's go."

The door to the garage slowly started to rise. Darby said a small prayer. But today, she wasn't sure if anyone was listening.

CHAPTER 99

THE PARK WAS EVERYTHING FELIX HATED ABOUT TOURIST SPOTS. IT WAS A perfect vision of the natural world. There were no weeds, no overgrown plants. Nature perfectly manicured.

Bobby, though, grinned as he pointed at a signpost up ahead that indicated the five separate areas of the park: Icebound Expanse, Savanna Plains, Jungle Heart, Alpine Peaks, and Aqua Venture. "Look at this place. I swear they have every animal out there."

A tremor in his voice, Cadman shook his head. "There are over seven million animal species on Earth. Of course, more species are being destroyed every day. Sanctuary Kingdom has just over two thousand species of animals."

"Still, two thousand's a lot. This is going to be fun." Bobby grinned.

They headed toward the wolf enclosure, but it was clear that both the red wolves and gray wolves had taken advantage of the open gates.

"Why are we out here? Shouldn't we be trying to get away?" Cadman asked, casting a nervous glance around. If he kept jerking his head from side to side so quickly, he was going to snap his own neck.

Originally, Felix had brought him along in case they didn't have a complete list of animals. But Marissa had been walking with him and taking notes. She gave him a nod. She'd gotten everything they needed from the man. Felix shot him a speculative look. "There are still a few things to do first."

"But you guys don't need me. I told her everything I know about the project. Can't I just wait somewhere safe?" Cadman crossed his arms over his chest.

Smiling, Felix shook his head. "Oh no, we need you. You're a critical part of this mission."

From the corner of his eye, Felix noted movement in the landscaping just behind them.

Tilting his head, he studied Cadman. "But tell you what, if you're not comfortable being out here, why don't you head back to the research center? We'll come get you when we're done."

Relief flooded Cadman's face. "Okay, yeah. Great. Thanks."

Without a word, he headed back toward the center at a slow jog. Felix pulled his M4 into his shoulder and waited.

Only forty yards away, the cheetah sprang from the side of the path. Cadman barely had time to scream before the cat was on top of him, knocking him down. Two claws dug into the man's shoulders as the cat leaned down and clamped onto his neck.

Felix sighted the cheetah's head and pulled the trigger. Once, twice, three times. Once the cat was down, he moved forward quickly, the others joining him.

Santos moved forward, practically pressing his gun against the cat's skull before pulling the trigger.

Marissa walked over and checked the tag on the cat's ear, wiping away some of the blood to do so. She shook her head. "It's not one of them."

Bobby grunted. "What a waste of good bait."

Felix shrugged. "That's all right. It was good practice. Now, let's go find the others."

CHAPTER 100

IN THE BACK OF THE SLED, GUS AND DARBY WERE GETTING JOSTLED ALL over the place. But Darby didn't mind the speed. She gripped one of the handles on the side of the sled and held on tight. Gus squeezed in on one side of her, helping to keep her braced. She let out a few calming breaths, trying to slow her racing heart.

We'll make it in time, she kept repeating to herself.

And even as they raced quickly across the ground, her mind raced faster, trying to figure out what had set off the animals. While initially it might have been the burst of freedom that drove the animals on, the hyenas shouldn't have crossed into the elephants' territory. They were acting more aggressively than normal, and she had no explanation as to why. Of course what was normal for animals released from captivity?

While part of her mind struggled with that question, another part worried about Kiya. Not that they wouldn't get to her in time, but what if she was affected too? Even though she was just a baby, she still weighed 900-plus pounds. If she had heightened aggression, they were going to be in a lot of trouble.

Deal with that problem when it comes, she warned herself.

Noah pushed aside the window at the back of the Hummer. "Just up ahead!" he yelled.

The PA system blared to life. "The hyenas are getting closer. Only a couple hundred yards."

Shaking from both fear and the turbulent ride, Darby hopped out of the truck as soon as the Hummer stopped. Careful to hold the bottle with one hand, she gripped the side of the sled with the other. She needed a second to stabilize her legs.

"You get the elephant. We'll keep an eye out for the hyenas," Gus said as he climbed out as well.

Taking a breath, Darby headed toward the brush. Kiya peeked around the tree and let out a cry when she saw Darby. She stumbled toward her, and Darby let out a gasp. There was a long gash along her back. A scream came from the sky above, and Darby looked up to see two bald eagles circling.

Her eyes narrowed. Had they done this to Kiya?

The baby elephant stumbled toward her and plowed her head into Darby's chest, nearly knocking her over. Tears pressed against the back of Darby's eyes at Kiya's fear. She was so scared, she was shaking. Darby ran her hands over Kiya's skull and down her trunk. "It's okay, baby. I'm here."

"Darby," Gus hissed.

Right, comfort later, move her now. Holding the bottle in front of her, Darby started back toward the sled. "Come on, Kiya. Let's take a little ride. That's a good girl," she coaxed.

Kiya hurried after her, her front-right leg buckling with each step. She was in bad shape. The cries of the hyenas sounded through the trees. The hair on Darby's arms rose. They were way too close.

"They're coming," Noah yelled.

Darby didn't respond, entirely focused on Kiya. They were only a few feet from the back of the sled. She had to get her fully on it and the tailgate up before they could take off. She stepped onto the sled just as the first hyena darted out from the trees.

CHAPTER 101

THE BLAST FROM THE .357 MAGNUM BOOMED THROUGH THE AIR. KIYA startled, taking a few steps back.

"No, no. Stay with me." Darby stepped off the sled the bottle in front of her. "It's okay. Come on. Take a drink."

She placed the bottle at Kiya's lips, and the elephant latched on to it. Then it was a tug-of-war as she tried to back up and keep the elephant with her. More gunshots rang out. Each one made Darby flinch.

Worse were the yips of the hyenas. The recordings were terrifying. The real audio was ten times worse.

A quick glance around showed that two hyenas were down. A group of six had started to circle. Darby couldn't see Tomy among them.

The circling ones stayed a little farther away after the first few shots, but they weren't leaving. Backing up, Kiya followed her onto the sled. She slammed her hand down on the button for the tailgate. It started to rise. "We're good!" she yelled.

The guys backed up toward the truck. Scooter jumped into the driver's seat. A hyena leapt onto the hood of the truck before scampering onto the roof of the cab.

"Darby, down!" Gus yelled.

She ducked as a blast of gunfire rang out overhead. She let out a scream as the hyena fell, spasming into the truck bed next to her. Kiya veered back, but Darby moved over to her side, blocking her from the edge of the truck. "No, no, it's okay. Stay with me."

Gus and Noah backed onto the sled. "Go!" Noah yelled.

Scooter took off, and Gus braced Darby, who, with both hands on the bottle, wasn't able to hold on. Scooter raced back toward Mammoth Manor. A few of the hyenas gave chase, but the others turned on their downed pack members and began their meal.

CHAPTER 102

BY THE TIME THEY REACHED THE MANOR, THE OTHER HYENAS HAD GIVEN up the chase. Cora had the door open for them and shut it as soon as the sled was through. Flicking a glance at the hyena whose chest didn't move, Darby sank to the floor of the sled, next to where Kiya had fallen during the rough ride.

She'd finished the bottle just before they arrived. Darby placed it to the side. She ran a hand over Kiya's large head. "Hey, sweetheart."

Gus crouched down next to her. "Would you like to make the introductions?"

Darby smiled. "Kiya, I'd like you to meet Augustus King, hero on the silver screen and apparently in real life as well."

"Hey," Noah grumbled from the other side of the sled.

Chuckling, Darby gestured to him as well. "And I would like you to also meet the equally heroic, Noah Hudson."

Noah smiled as he leapt over the side of the sled.

"I take it you're friends?" Gus asked.

"Yeah. She was only recently introduced to the herd, and I thought she had assimilated, but I don't know why they would've left her behind. They're just not behaving like themselves."

She looked over at the hyena that lay with its tongue lolling out of its mouth, its eyes wide. It was Figaro.

Following her gaze, Gus winced before starting toward it. "I'll get rid of it."

Darby started to nod, then stopped, putting out a hand. "No, actually, I have a better idea."

CHAPTER 103

THE IMAGE OF THE LATEST ATTACK FROM THE PARK FADED FROM THE screen in Martha's office. Her whole body trembled. That poor man. He'd been about sixty and unable to fight off the condor.

This is insane, she thought. The only good thing about these scenes was she hoped someone was able to get a text out. They needed a way to regain control. If they could just get the phones working . . .

Then she paused, thinking about the implants. She had no doubt that EcoAct had discovered the research. Even though the cell phones were down, she suspected they had tapped into a frequency to control the signals. They would need the cell network for that. Were they setting off the frequency every time they sent one of these violent videos?

She drummed her fingers on the desk. If that was the case, permanently disabling the cell tower needed to be a priority.

But how could she ask anyone to risk themselves to do it? Gabe might be able to help. But how could she contact him? She could try a bullhorn announcement, but there was no guarantee he'd hear it, and the bad guys probably would.

Plus, she didn't know what else was happening in the park and what people were dealing with. Roger said he'd heard what sounded like gunfire.

Pulling up the list of everyone in the park, she scanned for familiar names. Then her eyes landed on one: Darby Ellis.

She was jealous of Darby. She could admit that. Her brother adored her, as did the rest of the staff. Even with the lower-level assignments she'd been given since Gabe went on leave, Darby soldiered on.

She had taken the VIP tour and had Ori and Scooter with her. Ori, no doubt, had her laptop, though it might not be of much use. But Ori was resourceful and had to be trying to break through the hacker's control.

An idea began to form in the back of Martha's mind. She sat up straight as she thought through all the possibilities. Ori and Darby would be together, assuming they were both alive.

And if that were the case, Ori no doubt would at the very least be trying to monitor the system. And that meant . . .

Five minutes later, Martha flung open the door to the IT nest. All eyes turned to her, but she strode purposefully toward Reuben.

"I need you to contact someone in the park," she said.

Reuben shook his head. "There's no way to do that."

Placing both hands on the man's desk, Martha leaned forward. "Actually, I think there is."

CHAPTER 104

AFTER GETTING KIYA SETTLED AND BANDAGED UP BY CORA, SHE AND Darby walked down the hall toward the x-ray room.

"What exactly is it you want me to do?" Cora asked.

"I'm hoping you could run some tests on the hyena. Something's going on with the animals. They're not supposed to be this aggressive. I'm hoping maybe there's something you can find."

"You think something is causing this? Besides the fact that they're free?"

Her voice low, Darby mused, "The elephants weren't free, or at least they didn't know they were free when they started misbehaving. I don't think it's the freedom alone that's causing this. I don't know if it's an infection, a parasite or something else, but I figure we might as well start looking."

Taking on a no-nonsense tone, Cora said, "Well, I gave Lucas a sedative so that he would sleep. Scooter is keeping an eye on him. I need something to distract myself, so I'll draw some blood. Blood work will take a while, though. But you know what? I'll go ahead and get some X-rays too. Who knows? Maybe it'll tell us something."

"Thanks, Cora. You need some help?"

The doctor nodded. "Actually, yeah, that would be great."

A few minutes later, the two of them had gotten the hyena put on a stretcher and drawn its blood. With Darby's help, Cora had started the testing but the results wouldn't be instantaneous.

In the meantime, Cora decided that rather than just x-rays, she would do a full autopsy. X-rays would be the first step.

She was in the control room with Cora, as was Gus, who'd helped them get the hyena on the stretcher. The three of them watched as the images started to appear on the screen. It started at the creature's tail and worked its way up to the skull.

Darby wasn't sure exactly what she was looking for. The gaping hole that had been created by the gun blast was apparent. But animal anatomy wasn't her area.

"What exactly are we looking for here?" Gus asked.

Her gaze on the screen, Cora murmured, "Anything that doesn't belong."

Cora magnified the image, starting at the tail. Although Darby wasn't sure what she was looking at, she still found herself leaning forward studying the scan.

No one said a word as the three of them inspected each part of the animal's anatomy. As Cora moved the scan along to each body part, Darby started getting the feeling that this was just a big waste of time. Whatever was going on with the animals wasn't physical, or at least not physical in a way that could be detected by an X-ray.

Then Cora hummed.

Darby's head turned sharply as she studied the woman. "What? Did you find something?"

"Not sure," Cora murmured.

Adjusting the controls, Cora magnified the image of the hyena's skull. Darby leaned forward to try to figure out what had caught her interest. She frowned as she noted a small dot on the screen. "What is that?"

With her gaze on the same spot, Cora murmured, "I don't know. It's not irregularly shaped, which is what you would expect from a tumor. But it definitely doesn't belong there." She stood up and headed for the door.

"Where are you going?" Darby asked.

"To prepare the patient for surgery. I'm going to dig it out."

CHAPTER 105

FELIX HAD NEVER BEEN ONE FOR VACATIONS. SITTING ON A BEACH somewhere sipping margaritas was fine for an afternoon, but days on end? No, that wasn't his thing. Spending money just to wander around, maybe snap a couple of pictures, was definitely not his thing either.

However, he had to admit that he was currently enjoying himself. He'd already taken out four individuals—the first had stepped out of a building when they saw him approach. The look of pure shock on the man's face had been beautiful. The next two were an older man in his sixties and a woman in her thirties. The older man had realized what was up first and had darted in front of the younger one. "Run!" he'd yelled.

The younger woman had only made it about a dozen steps before Sabrina stepped out of the path in her way.

Yes, this kind of hunting was fun. He always did love the hunt: chasing down his quarry, finding them in their hiding spots, chasing them out like a dog on a pheasant hunt.

Of course, this wasn't quite the same. People were hiding, yes, but not from him and his people. Quite the opposite, in fact. They viewed Felix and his team as saviors. They popped out of their hiding spots when they saw them coming.

He'd thought that would take some of the fun out of the mission. If anything, it made it more fun. How often did you get to just walk up to someone and shoot them point blank in the face?

As if they'd heard his thoughts, the door to a snack shop flew open. An older man peeked his head out. "Over here!" he whisper-shouted.

Felix nodded at Bobby and Santos. "You keep going. We'll take care of these."

He and Sabrina headed toward the older man, who looked at him with relief. "You guys are part of security, right?"

"Sure are," Sabrina said with a smile. "How you guys doing?"

The man shook his head. "I don't know what the heck is going on here. The animals are everywhere."

"Yeah, we know. It's a technical glitch. You alone in there?" Felix asked.

The man stepped back quickly. "Oh, no, no. Sheila and Toby, come on out."

Two younger ones, who couldn't be any older than twenty-two or twenty-three, appeared from around a rack of candies.

"Is it safe?" the younger man asked.

"Anybody else in here?" Sabrina asked.

The two young ones shook their heads. "No, no, it's just us. We saw some people run by before, but . . ." The older guy shook his head.

"We understand. And you guys did the right thing, hunkering down and waiting for help," Sabrina said.

"Exactly," the older man said as the other two drew close. "So, what do we do now?"

"Don't worry about that. We'll take care of it." Felix pulled his sidearm, and Sabrina did as well. He placed it to the head of the older man and pulled the trigger.

CHAPTER 106

THE NECROPSY OF THE HYENA WAS DONE IN THE PROCEDURES LAB. DARBY assisted as Cora shaved the creature's skull. When she broke out the bone saw, Darby had to turn away. Assisting from the other side, however, Gus looked fascinated.

In a few minutes, Cora had made her way through the skin and the skull and into the brain itself. She glanced up at the X-ray and then made an incision, peeling back the layers of brain matter.

And Darby couldn't help but look. She'd taken an anatomy class in college and had been intrigued by the human brain. The brains of animals versus the brains of humans simply weren't that different. The biggest difference, of course, was size, depending on the size of the animal. Most people would be hard-pressed to tell the difference from just a physical inspection.

Brains were such fascinating organs. All those neurons and yet humanity had barely scratched the surface of understanding what humans were capable of. In fact, it took a Harvard team a decade to map a brain sample the size of a piece of rice. They ended up with 1,400 terabytes of data, the equivalent of a billion books. Mapping a full human brain was decades away.

Grunting, Cora held out her hand to Gus. He immediately placed the tweezers flat on her palm. Leaning forward, she carefully inserted the tweezers. A moment later, she retracted them.

Gus held out a small silver tray. Cora dropped something onto the tray.

When Cora stepped back, she took off her gloves and put on new ones. She took the tray from Gus and walked over to the microscope. First, though, she took the object and dumped it into a solution. Immediately, the clear liquid became murky with blood.

Using the tweezers again, she reached in and put it into another solution and then a third before taking it and placing it on a towel. She flipped it over once and then twice to get rid of the excess water, then placed it on a slide under a microscope.

A moment later, a magnified image of the object appeared on the monitor next to the scope. Cora took a step back, her eyes wide.

Darby had the opposite reaction. She took a step forward as she looked at the object. "That's not natural."

Her hand to her mouth, Cora's voice shook. "Nope, definitely not a tumor. It's an implant."

Studying the screen, Gus frowned. "Why is that a big deal? I mean, don't all zoos use implants?"

Cora shook her head. "Not like this. We use only subcutaneous implants to keep track of animals in the park."

"So who put this here? Could it have been placed before the hyena came to the park?" Darby asked.

Studying the hyena, Cora's voice was low, as if she was trying to put the pieces together and they weren't fitting. "No. This is a youngster. If you look at its teeth, it's barely a year old. It was bred at the park. Which means someone here did this."

"You didn't know about this," Darby said slowly.

Cora shook her head.

At Gus's questioning look, Darby explained. "Cora's the head of operations. Anything that happens with the animals, anything at all, crosses her desk. There's no way someone could perform a procedure like this on an animal without her knowing about it."

As Cora's gaze flew to Darby, a worried look shifted across her face. A pit opened in Darby's stomach. "What?"

The operations director began slowly. "The location of the implant is what concerns me. It was found on the hyena's hypothalamus."

Gus's eyes narrowed. "The hypothalamus? Are you sure?"

Cora nodded. "Hyenas—it's been a while since I've done a necropsy, but yeah, and the scans confirm that. It was on the hypothalamus."

Darby looked between the two of them. She knew the hypothalamus's function: It was basically the control center of the brain. But why would—Then it hit her. "You think the implant is increasing their aggression."

"Yes," Cora said.

"The research center. It had to have been done there." And there were only two people who would have the clout to keep something like this hidden: Martha and Gabe. And Darby simply could not believe that Gabe would give permission for such a thing.

"If this was an experiment, there's no way they'd have only one test subject," Cora said.

Picturing the animals across the park, Darby swallowed. "Yeah, I think it's safe to say there's definitely more than one."

An uneasy silence settled across the room. Ori stepped into the room. "I have some good-slash-bad news." Then she paused, her eyes widening at the sight of the hyena on the table. "Did I interrupt something?"

"Necropsy. The hyena has an implant." Darby gave her a quick rundown.

Ori's mouth gaped open fully by the time she was done. "You didn't know about this?"

Shaking her head, Cora leaned back against the counter. "No. I never would have approved of it. It's way too dangerous."

The room fell silent again before Darby turned to Ori. "Did you say you had news?"

Pulling her gaze from the hyena, Ori stuttered. "Uh, yeah, first, this is definitely an attack. A message was sent through the park's system from a group called EcoAct. We didn't get it because we're no longer part of the park's system. But it was recorded on the two cameras by the front gate." Ori gave a brief summary of the message.

"Oh my God." Darby sank onto a stool.

Ori took a deep breath. "And that's not all: I got a message from Dominion."

Hope built up inside Darby. "That's great. Communications are back?"

Cora was already reaching for the phone, but Ori's next words halted her actions. "No. It was actually a Morse code message that went through a few of the systems that the hacker hasn't shut off because they're not important."

"Okay, so what's the bad news?" Gus asked.

Ori swept her gaze across all of them before it stayed with Darby. "I think they want us to take out the cell tower."

Immediately Darby shook her head. "No, absolutely not."

CHAPTER 107

ANY THOUGHTS ABOUT NOT GOING FOR THE CELL TOWER WERE extinguished as soon as Darby heard EcoAct's message. Ori had replayed it for all of them.

It was terrifying. Even though they had believed they were being attacked, there'd been a small sliver in the back of Darby's mind that hoped they were wrong. She hoped someone had just accidentally hit the wrong button and set off this catastrophe. Then someone else would realize what had happened, swoop in, switch the lever back to the correct position, and all would be well.

It was a stupid hope. But Darby had held on to it, letting it feed her some light in this darkness.

Now it was clear they were under attack by more than just the animals. Someone at Dominion had asked them for help. A quick chat with Cora confirmed what Darby had suspected: shutting down the cell tower would mean the animals' implants couldn't be triggered. Someone at Dominion knew that.

Now, in Conference Room B, Darby sat at the table with Gus, Scooter, Cora, Noah, and Ori debating whether it was worth the risk.

Across the table from her, Scooter sat with his arms crossed over his chest, a frown on his face. "I thought the cell tower was already down. I mean, I can't use my cell. Can you guys?"

"No," Darby said, turning to Ori for an explanation.

"I think they've set up a signal just for them that they've isolated and allowed to continue. It's why you sometimes have reception with certain cell companies and not others. So I think their signal is the only one getting through."

"So, if we shut down the tower, no one will be able to trigger the implants, right?" Noah asked.

Cora's eyes shifted quickly, her mind no doubt moving just as fast. "Technically, no."

The hopes that had risen at the news that Dominion had a plan deflated. Darby leaned forward. "What?"

Cora held up a hand to hold off questions. "Shutting down the cell tower would make it so that no mass signal could be sent. But it would still be possible to set off the implants with a device. It would just have to be done relatively close."

Sitting back, Darby let out a harsh breath, noting she was not the only one unhappy at that news. But cutting off the ability for someone to send a mass signal was definitely worth the effort.

"Where is the cell tower?" Gus asked.

Standing, Scooter walked over to the wall and quickly pulled off the framed map. He placed it in the middle of the table. Everyone stood to get a better view.

"We're here at Mammoth Manor." Scooter pointed to the center of the right side of the park. The elephant pasture ran right along the easternmost border with the manor itself only a few hundred yards from it.

"The cell tower is here." Scooter pointed to an area of the map without any sign that was just south of the Castle and slightly northwest of the main roller-coaster.

"Well, that's not too far," Noah said with a wince.

"Yeah, on a normal day, that's true," Darby said, calculating the distance. "We'll take the Gladiator, move quickly, heavily armed."

"I agree. We can't have rescue groups coming in with the animals still on the attack," Scooter replied.

Darby frowned.

"What's wrong?" Gus asked.

"The rescues should have started by now." She met his gaze. "I think—I think whoever's done this had figured out a way to keep law enforcement away."

Noah rubbed his forehead. "One problem at a time, please."

Leaning forward Darby traced the route from the cell tower to the Castle. It was shorter than the distance back to the manor.

"What are you thinking?" Gus asked.

Darby's gaze locked on the map as she pictured the layout of the Castle. "After we shut down the signal, the Castle would be closer and their control room replicates the one at Dominion."

Ori bounced in her seat. "And there's a manual reset there. You can shut down the whole system and reboot it. It would kick whoever's in the system out. Then I can jump in and shore up the firewalls, at least around the critical functions. I can protect the fences and exits so they're not electrified, allowing people out. And hopefully I can reestablish communications."

"You can do all that?" Scooter asked.

A look of determination in her eyes, Ori nodded. "I can. I'll get the code up and running so I can send it as soon as the system starts to come back online."

"Good, good. We have a plan. Now we need to figure out who's going with me," Scooter said.

"Well, I'm in," Darby said.

Scooter shook his head. "Darby—"

"Mama Sue, Gabe, and Linc are out there. And if something goes wrong, I know how to reboot the system. I also know this park as well as you. We need at least two people who know the park."

"She's right," Gus said. "And I'll go as well." He looked over at Noah.

The younger man rolled his shoulders before he smiled. "I haven't had a chance to see that part of the park yet, so I guess I'm in."

"And I'm going too."

Everyone turned to see Courtney standing in the doorway, her hands on her hips.

CHAPTER 108

Stepping into the room, Courtney glared at all of them. "I'm going with you. I owe it to my love to get help for him, even if my life is at risk."

"You are so brave." Lance looked at her adoringly as he stepped in behind her, his face pale.

Darby wanted to yell at the two of them that they were both idiots. Instead, she took a deep breath and elected to be diplomatic. "Look, it's dangerous out there—"

Courtney cut her off, raising her hand. "I am basically a journalist. And you are violating my First Amendment rights."

"Actually, the First Amendment only applies to publishing stories. No one is required to bring you to the story." Gus crossed his arms over his chest. "It's not safe out there. You should stay here."

"She's going." Courtney pointed an accusing finger at Darby.

Counting to ten, Darby was pretty happy with how reasoned her tone came out. "I know the park. And my people are out there."

"Well, my people are in here." Courtney held up her phone. "And they won't be denied the truth." With a glare at each of them, she strode down the hall, her chin held high. After giving Darby, Gus, and Noah a contemptuous look, Lance hurried after her.

Darby rubbed the bridge of her nose. Courtney could not come. That would be a complete disaster.

"Is anyone going to tell her she's heading the wrong way?" Cora asked.

Darby shook her head. "Nope. Let's hope they get lost back there, then we can leave before they realize we're gone."

―――――

Sadly, Courtney and Lance found the garage as Darby and the others were loading up the dark green Jeep Gladiator. The two lovebirds were now involved in a tearful goodbye, with a phone propped up on a set of tires recording the whole thing.

Her gaze locked on Lance, Courtney's chin trembled. "You are my heart. Wherever I go, my heart stays with you."

Reaching up, Lance wiped a tear from her cheek. "Our love was destined from the beginning of time."

With a frown, Courtney stopped mid-soliloquy and went to check the recording. Moving back to Lance, she adjusted him slightly, and they started back from the beginning. "You are my heart. Wherever I go, my heart stays with you."

Once again, Lance reached up and wiped a tear from her cheek. "Our love was destined from the beginning of time."

"Oh, for God's sake." Scooter placed a box of tranqs in the bed of the Jeep, his voice full of annoyance as he glared at them. "We're not actually bringing her, are we?"

"Not sure what the alternative is. She seems committed," Darby replied.

"More like should be committed," Scooter grumbled as he grabbed the box of radios. They'd found them in the back of the storage room. They hadn't been used in years, but after replacing the batteries, they seemed to be working fine. They weren't sure of the range but were bringing them along just in case.

Mumbling to himself, Scooter, headed for the water jugs. Gus was already carrying two over. He hiked them over the back of the Gladiator.

Darby noted Gus's strong forearms and the Sanctuary Kingdom

bracelet on his wrist. Then she stared down at the one on her own wrist. "Oh shoot."

"What's wrong?" Gus asked.

"The bracelets. Their essentially trackers. Let me have yours."

Breaking it off his wrist, he handed it over.

"Can you go get everyone else's? But keep Scooter's and Ori's separate and then meet me in the lounge." She nudged her chin toward the area just off the garage.

Although he raised an eyebrow, he nodded. "Okay."

Heading for the lounge, Darby gripped Gus's bracelet. If they'd gone into the park with these, whoever was in the system would know exactly where they were. But she also needed her bracelet because it acted as a key.

She'd read an article a few years back about Faraday cages and while she certainly didn't have one handy, after reading the article she'd gone down a rabbit hole, reading up on DIY Faraday cages. Searching through the drawers in the cabinets she found what she was looking for in the fourth cabinet she opened: tinfoil.

Pulling it out, she broke off a good-size piece. Then taking off her own bracelet, wrapped it in the tinfoil and shoved it in her pocket. Gus reappeared with the other bracelets as she was breaking off another larger piece. "Okay, put everyone but Scooter and Ori's on this sheet."

He did and she wrapped them up in a large piece of tinfoil. Then she individually wrapped Ori and Scooter's.

Tilting his head as he studied her, his eyebrows rose. "You're blocking the signal."

She shrugged. "Trying to. The tinfoil should be able to do the trick, especially being there's a couple of layers surrounding the bracelets."

"Why wrap your guys separately?"

"Ours are keys. We need them. Yours and the others allow you on the rides and into exhibits."

"Smart," Gus said softly.

"Thanks," Darby said feeling her cheeks heat at his attention.

Scooter appeared in the doorway. "You guys good?"

Darby pulled her gaze from Gus and grabbed Scooter's wrapped bracelet from the counter, tossing it to him.

He frowned down at it. "What's this?"

Moving past Gus, she explained to Scooter about blocking the signal. He raised his eyebrows when she was done as he shoved his bracelet into his pocket. "I like how you think, girl. You cover all the bases."

Darby didn't reply, she just hoped he was right, while knowing in her gut that there was no way she could.

CHAPTER 109

PICKING UP THE .357 MAGNUM RIFLE, DARBY VERIFIED THAT IT WAS loaded, then placed it next to her seat in the Jeep. She'd always wanted to go on a safari. She'd never imagined it would be like this.

Scooter would drive, Noah and Gus would be in the back, with Courtney between them. A tremor ran through Darby's hands, imagining what they were going to face. *Please let this be an easy trip. Please let everyone else be safe*, she prayed as she pictured Mama Sue, Gabe, and Linc as she'd last seen them.

Ori appeared in the doorway and made her way to her. "Hey."

"Hey. Did you get the signal out?"

"Yeah. And they acknowledged receiving it." Ori had used the same method that Dominion had used to convey a response. She'd also let me know that people were hurt and to have responders ready.

Leaning back against the truck, Darby noted the lovebirds had finished their scene and were now watching the replay. "Do we know why law enforcement hasn't been able to get in?"

Ori shook her head. "My Morse code is not that good. It's very much caveman communication: People hurt. Go tower."

Darby grinned as she placed full water bottles in the back of the Jeep. "Well, that works."

Leaning against the back of the Gladiator, Ori touched Darby's shoulder. "You sure you want to do this?"

Meeting her friend's gaze, she shrugged. "Want to? No. But my family's out there. I can't just sit here and hope they're okay."

"I could go too."

Darby was shaking her head before Ori finished the sentence. "No. We need you to protect the system once it's up and running. You're the only one who can do that. And if you can do that from here, that's where you need to do it from."

Ori nudged her chin toward where Noah was speaking quietly with Gus, his back to them. "I also explained to Noah how to get the systems up, just in case. He's pretty good with a computer. And I walked him through how to get the cameras at each exhibit back up, and he'll link it back to us when necessary."

"You can do that?"

She grinned. "Hey, this is the moment where we computer geeks shine." Then her face grew serious. "Just be careful, Darby."

Reaching out, Darby hugged her tight. But she didn't promise. She didn't want her last words to her best friend to be a lie.

CHAPTER 110

Darby couldn't count the number of times she'd walked or driven through the paths of Sanctuary Kingdom. She and a few others who'd been there for years liked to joke that they could navigate the place blindfolded.

Yet today, everything felt different. She wasn't sure how it couldn't. Her gaze kept swiveling from side to side, waiting for an animal to jump out of nowhere. The cameras of the elephant preserve extended only slightly beyond the preserve's boundaries. They'd ridden well past them now. They were on their own.

In the distance on the cameras they'd seen a few people moving, as well as some animals. They'd also seen a few people not moving.

People had died at the park—the place where kids were so excited to visit that they were jumping up and down, barely able to contain their energy as they waited in line. A place that people saved up for months, sometimes years, just to visit.

"You okay?" Scooter asked.

Darby shook her head. "I just can't wrap my head around the fact that this is happening. Someone actually implanted something in the animals to make them more aggressive. And then what, they threw open all the doors? It just doesn't make any sense."

"Not everybody's wired right. And honestly, as much as I love this place and the guests love this place, there are plenty of people out there who don't," Scooter said.

Gus frowned, leaning forward from the backseat. "What do you mean?"

Flicking a glance over his shoulder, Scooter gripped the steering wheel tightly. "The park gets threatening letters, particularly from that group, EcoAct. Those guys have been nonstop, at least every week. In fact, the FBI has contacted us a few times about more direct threats aimed in our direction."

Not really surprised, Darby just grunted. Right after 9/11, there was a great deal of worry over soft targets for terrorism. Soft targets were those with lower-level security: sporting events, shopping areas, and amusement parks. In response, amusement parks had upped their security.

Sanctuary Kingdom had AI scans at the main entrance as well as the Mr. Sues constantly surveilling. That was in addition to the massive human force.

To date, there had not been a mass casualty or terrorist attack at an amusement park. Threats were common, but follow-up so far had been nonexistent. Most of the threats were made both to the media as well as the park. Darby had begun to think of them as just attention grabs rather than actual warnings.

So the idea that Sanctuary Kingdom would be targeted wasn't really a shock. The shock was that they hadn't heard about it. "How come I haven't heard about EcoAct?" she asked.

"For some reason, they didn't release to the media. I barely heard about any of it. Roger and Martha kept that close to the vest. I only learned about a few of them after the fact."

"They didn't warn security?" Gus asked.

Scooter shrugged. "They were vague, generalized threats. They didn't tell us everything. And they certainly didn't close down."

"That's about par for the course," Darby murmured.

At Noah's questioning look, Darby said, "Martha plays everything close to the vest. The park's her baby. She doesn't like to reveal anything about it unless it's a success story."

Darby had never really had an issue with that. In fact, she thought it was smart. Announcing what you were about to do put a ticking clock over your head to get results. Science didn't always cooperate.

The last thing the park needed was bad press because they attempted to do something and either couldn't manage it or it was taking too long to get there. Or in the case of the threats, putting out a warning that was just a bluff. Millions could be lost.

So she completely understood not making those announcements until after the breakthrough had been achieved. But as she settled back in her seat, she had to think that whoever was behind the implants wanted to keep them secret as well. If not, there would have been a press release at the very least before now. This certainly wasn't the way anyone was going to announce a research agenda.

But she had a hard time seeing how the people who had implemented the project could be behind this. No, there were two groups at play here—the one behind the experiments and the one that turned them on. She swallowed hard, pretty sure those two groups had very different goals. Martha must have taken on an outside contract. It was the only explanation for the implants. If the focus was on increasing aggression, she was pretty sure that meant the military.

She just really hoped it was at least the US military. She was betting that EcoAct had found out about it somehow and was using it to its advantage.

"Has EcoAct made any recent threats?" Noah asked.

Scooter shook his head. "That's the strange thing. About three months ago, they stopped entirely."

"They were planning," Darby said softly.

Gus met her gaze his jaw tight as he nodded. Out loud he asked, "How far to the tower?"

Darby's gaze moved past him to the massive roller-coaster in the center of the park. "The tower's just beyond the coaster. It should take us only about—"

A figure darted out of the greenery on the side of the car and came to a standstill in the middle of the path of the car, their hands up.

"Crap." Scooter slammed on the brakes and managed to stop barely a foot in front of the woman, who turned her head and covered it with her arms.

CHAPTER 111

THE PERSON IN FRONT OF THE HUMMER WORE THE SANCTUARY KINGDOM uniform of navy-blue slacks and a bright blue top. As the person lowered their arms, Darby let out a gasp of recognition and clambered out of the car.

"Darby, wait!" Gus said as he scrambled to get out as well.

But Darby was already moving around the front of the car. "Izzy?"

Isabel Pham, the director of hospitality, lowered her hands and looked up into Darby's face. "Darby, thank God."

The older woman flung herself at Darby, her whole body trembling. Standing at only five foot one, Izzy's dark hair barely reached Darby's shoulder. Darby held her tightly, casting a glance around as the guys made a perimeter, scanning the area.

"We can't stay here, Darby," Gus warned.

Wrapping a protective arm around the older woman, Darby started to lead her back to the Jeep. "Let's get you into the truck."

Taking a step back, Izzy shook her head as she wiped at her eyes. "No, no. I've got two of the young kids who work for me. This is their first training day. They're both hurt."

Izzy liked to conduct all the trainings personally, ensuring everyone knew how the restaurants operated. She was well suited to the job, being a phenomenal organizer and incredibly friendly. If anyone could show people how to interact with guests and handle difficult situations, it was Izzy.

"How bad are they injured.?" Darby asked.

"Not too bad." Izzy gestured to the landscape from which she'd appeared. "I saw your truck and ran when I recognized Scooter behind the wheel. It's all so crazy, Darby."

"Yeah, we had a few close encounters ourselves. The animals are out, but we can get all of you safe," Darby said.

But Izzy shook her head with a frown. "No, not just the animals. The humans."

CHAPTER 112

A YOUNG ATHLETIC GUY WITH DARK HAIR SPRINTED DOWN THE PATH, A look of terror on his face. A wolf barreled after him. The guy leapt over the counter of the snack kiosk like an Olympian.

The wolf made the same leap a moment later, but the guy slipped out the back of the kiosk, slamming the door shut behind him. He took off again. The wolf pawed at the door but couldn't figure out how to get through it.

"Boo." Kevin threw popcorn at the screen. The guy looked like the jock from his high school, the most popular one. Girls wanted to be with him, and guys wanted to be him.

What a douchebag.

Oh well. He reached for the mouse when his phone rang. Frowning, he glared at it. Who the hell was calling? He and Todd were now on a strict texting protocol. The texts were erased within five minutes. Phone calls could be intercepted.

Grabbing the phone, he glared at the screen before answering it. "What are you doing? You know—"

Todd cut him off, his words coming fast and ending on a screech. "There are gunshots coming from inside the park. Are they shooting the animals?"

Kevin rolled his eyes. How exactly did Todd think they were going to respond to rampaging animals? Lie down in the paths after dousing themselves in barbecue sauce? "They keep guns in the park in case there are any issues with the animals."

"What?! Why didn't you tell me that?"

Why didn't you know, you idiot? Kevin thought, but aloud he said, "It's pretty common knowledge."

"Well, see how many they've killed. The whole point was to *protect* the animals, not get them killed. We need to end this."

"Hold on, hold on. Don't go getting crazy. Let me just check what's going on. I'll call you back."

"No, I'll stay on the line."

Grumbling, Kevin flicked through the screens. He should have known that Todd would freak out over the gunfire. It never occurred to Kevin that the man wouldn't realize that would be the response.

He moved slowly through the screens, his mind racing as he tried to figure out a way to keep this going. There hadn't been enough carnage yet.

And then he realized he hadn't checked the research center. Getting control of the cameras there had been a lot more difficult than the rest of the park. There were a lot more safeguards against hacks there.

But Kevin had succeeded. Now he flicked through the screens with a frown. There was no one moving. Every person he saw was lying on the ground, still. But there was very little blood. The bodies looked, for the most part, undisturbed.

In the cafeteria, three bodies were down behind the counter. He zoomed in on one that was face up. The woman had a look of surprise on her face, her eyes wide, her mouth open.

And a perfect bullet hole in the middle of her forehead.

Examinations of the other bodies showed bullet wounds as well. Quickly flicking through all the images of the dead in the research area confirmed that no one except one guard and one researcher had been killed by animal attacks. The rest had all been shot.

Sitting back, Kevin stared at the screen, his mouth hanging open. Had some security guy lost it? Did he have a really bad aim? He grabbed his cell. "Do we have any people in the park?"

Todd was on the edge of losing it. "In the park? Are you crazy? Why would we—"

"None of our people are in the park?" Kevin asked again.

"We let all the animals out. Of course none of our people are in there. What's going—"

"Shut up and let me think," Kevin ordered.

"You don't tell me to shut up. I'm in charge of—"

Kevin disconnected the call. Todd called right back but Kevin ignored it. He called back a second and then a third time. Finally, Kevin punched the answer button. "What?"

"Look, we're all a little stressed. I'm going to chalk that exchange up to that."

Kevin rolled his eyes. If Todd hadn't started an ecoterrorist group, he'd have been destined for a job in human resources. "So have you figured out what's going on with the shooting?"

"Just wait a minute." Kevin picked up the pace of his inspection and then doubled back when he flipped past a shot of a group near the roller-coaster. Leaning forward, he frowned at the group in jeans and dark shirts holding some pretty heavy-duty weaponry. "Now who are you guys?" he murmured.

"What guys?" Todd demanded.

The two guys on screen stopped as four people in Sanctuary Kingdom uniforms darted out of the Aqua Venture Cafe and sprinted for them.

Kevin frowned. *Damn, they're security.*

Then the two men took aim. Moments later, all four employees lay still on the path and the jean-clad group continued on their way.

A smile spread across Kevin's face as he picked up the phone. "I think it's all right. It's not the animals that are getting shot."

CHAPTER 113

Darby stared at Izzy in shock. "Humans? What are you talking about?"

"There are guys with guns. They're in the park. They're shooting people," Izzy said, her gaze darting from side to side as if she expected someone to jump out at them at any moment.

"Are they security?" Scooter asked as he joined them.

Izzy shook her head. "I've never seen these guys before. And the weapons they're carrying—no, those are not part of security or even the DART team. I don't know who they are."

"They've been shooting *people*?" Scooter asked.

Izzy took a trembling breath. "They shot Cheryl."

Picturing Cheryl, the waitress who had worked at the park since it opened, Darby's mouth fell open. She'd always been smiling, always happy.

"She wasn't doing anything. She was just walking, and they shot her. Then they shot two more people who were in front of her. We were in a group. Everybody scattered. I don't know what happened to the others. I saw a few more bodies, and every time I saw one, I just ran in the other direction. I had Braden and Samantha with me. Braden got shot, but it was just a graze, and Samantha twisted her ankle."

Although disbelief rolled through Darby, it wasn't that she didn't believe her. She just didn't want to. She looked over at Scooter. "Do you know what's going on? Is there some security protocol I don't know about?"

He gave her an incredulous look. "One that involves shooting staff? No, absolutely not. The only people in the park who have weapons are security."

"These guys aren't security." Izzy's voice held no uncertainty.

Darby didn't know what to make of it, but she did know that the park had just gotten a whole lot more dangerous.

CHAPTER 114

As Izzy led them to where Samantha and Braden were hiding, Darby's mind raced. There was an armed group somewhere in the park, and she had no idea how they fit into everything. Was it possible they were part of the terrorist group? But why lock themselves in with the animals they had released? Was that a mistake? Did they get stuck here?

Darby pushed those thoughts aside as they reached the small snack kiosk outside Jungle Heart, which contained animals from rainforests across the globe. It was strange to be here without the hoots and hollers of the recorded sounds of the rainforest.

"Braden, Samantha," Izzy called softly.

Two frightened faces peeked over the kiosk counter. Darby's heart nearly broke at the sight of them. They were the same age as Linc. She swallowed hard as horrific images of Linc and Mama Sue getting gunned down filled her mind. She took a trembling breath.

"You okay?" Gus asked.

"Yeah, it's just—" Darby wasn't sure how to finish that statement and she wasn't sure she wanted to.

But apparently, she didn't need to. "We'll find them," Gus promised, his eyes serious.

Darby nodded, but she knew their chances of survival had just dropped dramatically. It was bad enough with the animals being out there. But with armed men, too?

And Mama Sue was in a wheelchair. Granted, that thing could go wherever she wanted it to, but it was certainly going to make hiding and getting away much more difficult.

Braden and Samantha stepped out from behind the snack kiosk. Izzy hurried over to them, wrapping an arm around each of them. She was such a grandmother. She had four grandkids of her own, but she treated everyone like part of an extended family. Samantha clung to Izzy as she limped toward the Jeep.

Darby met Scooter's gaze. "We can't leave them out here."

"We can't take them with us," Scooter said. "Radio back to the manor. If it's safe, which they should be able to check from the cameras, we'll have them meet us at the edge of the preserve and exchange."

It was the right thing to do. But the idea that they were going to delay finding her people was not easy. But looking at the scared faces in front of her, she knew she also had another priority. "Yeah. Come on. Let's get you guys safe."

CHAPTER 115

WATCHING THE GUNMEN, KEVIN KEPT ONE EYE ON THEIR CURRENT ACTIONS while backtracking to trace their route. They had started in the research area.

That's interesting.

Drumming his fingers on the table, he twisted his lips in thought. Flicking a glance back at two of the men, he noted how they moved with complete confidence, unhesitating. They looked like they'd stepped right out of *Call of Duty*, although he doubted a video game was where they'd gotten their training. *You're military boys, aren't you?*

He knew that the Pentagon had kill teams. 8kun was full of stories and images of the atrocities committed by the Pentagon's personal hit squads. US citizens were sheep who bought arguments about lone killers and gas explosions, but those were all the work of the US Department of Defense's most secret forces.

And Kevin had no doubt he was looking at one of them now. He grunted, thinking about how often he'd been ridiculed. This was a false-flag operation in the making. They were using this situation for their own agenda.

He watched as they killed a polar bear. They moved closer, placing the barrel right against the side of the bear's head and pulled the trigger. His mouth fell open as he whispered, "You bastards. You're getting rid of the evidence."

Now the killings made sense. Anyone who saw them died, because they were going to deny they were ever here. Then EcoAct would get blamed for all the deaths.

Tucking his tongue into the side of his mouth as he sat back, he pondered. Now the question was: Was Kevin going to let them get away with it?

CHAPTER 116

NOT WASTING ANY TIME, DARBY AND THE OTHERS HURRIED BACK TO THE preserve with their guests. Courtney was surprisingly quiet. When they arrived, Darby was glad to see that Ori and Cora were just beyond the preserve's gates, waiting for them in the other Hummer.

Scooter pulled to a stop, and they wasted no time getting out and switching people over. But Ori and Cora met Darby's gaze and nudged her to the side.

With a frown, Darby walked over. "What's going on? Is something wrong?"

Ori gave a small chuckle. "Besides the fact that we've now added armed gunmen to the situation?"

Darby grimaced. "Yeah, besides that."

"I've confirmed that the implants aren't an isolated event," Cora said.

Switching her gaze between the two of them, Darby asked, "How did you confirm that?"

"We grabbed one of the other hyenas from the field."

Shock rippled through Darby. "What? That's so dangerous!"

Ori raised an eyebrow. "That was dangerous? We used cameras to see if there was anyone nearby. You guys are the ones going out into the park. We need as much information as possible."

She was right, but still, the idea of Ori and Cora being out there was terrifying. "So what did you find?"

"We found another implant. So that's two. And Lucas keeps all of his records on paper. He's old school like that," Cora said with a small smile. "Theema was part of the breeding program."

The breeding program had been started a few years back. The goal was to repopulate the wild with the animals from the sanctuary. They'd been making inroads, sometimes waiting a generation or two to weed out certain diseases, like with the Tasmanian devils. But the ultimate goal was to help increase the world populations of endangered animals.

"And remember Bash talking about the younger hyenas being taken as part of the breeding program? I'm sure he can confirm it," Cora said.

Neither Darby nor Ori answered her. Cora's face fell. "Not Bash."

"I'm afraid so," Darby said.

Cora's hand flew to her mouth. "Oh my God. Why is this happening?"

Feeling the same frustration, Darby shook her head. "I don't know. And right now, I guess it doesn't really matter. We just need to make sure we get out of here alive. Then we can figure out what the hell is going on."

But even as Darby spoke, her mind was mulling over what all of this meant. "How are the implants activated? There has to be an outside source, right?"

"Yeah. Technically, implants could be activated with a cell phone, but most likely it's a computer."

Darby glanced over at the park cell tower. It had been designed to look like a massive tree. "When we turn off the cell tower, things aren't going to magically go back to normal, are they?"

Cora shook her head. "No. The implant stimulates their aggression so that they react to neutral stimuli as if it were threatening. So normally docile animals will attack other animals or anything in their area, really.

"If enough time passes between when the implant is activated, it's possible that they will calm down on their own, but it's kind of like when you stub your toe. Even though you stub your toe for a split second, you still feel the echoes of that pain for a while, and you're still annoyed and angry and everything else. It's the same kind of concept. Of course, on a much larger scale.

"Plus, if they're around other animals that they've worked up, then the energy of the group is going to feed that anger and sustain it for longer."

"But turning off the signal—that would be a good thing," Darby said.

Cora nodded. "Oh, absolutely. We're going to have to do that to round up the animals again. We can't have them losing it when people move in to retake them."

Turning off the signal would only give them a chance of ratcheting down the violence. But right now, they needed that chance.

CHAPTER 117

GUNMEN IN THE PARK. THAT WAS NOT A SCENARIO KEVIN HAD EXPECTED. Even though his money was on the Pentagon, he still needed to consider other possibilities.

These guys, though, looked way too comfortable with their actions. There was no fumbling, no hesitation. Steely was the word that came to mind.

Yes, these guys had done this before. These guys were ex-military at the very least.

Grabbing screenshots, he brought up a dialog box and quickly accessed the military database. He was unsurprised when a few minutes later, the computer pinged to indicate that he had some hits. He leaned forward and noted the first hit was of one of the women. Her name was Sabrina Gutierrez, and she was former Army. Now she worked for a private contractor.

He grinned. Private contractors—military without any of the rules. He'd seen enough of the private contractors in Iraq and Afghanistan to know that following rules was not their priority. It was a way to circumvent the military's rules of engagement.

Yup, it was a Pentagon kill squad.

Quickly, he flipped through the other hits and noted that every single one was former military. He stopped at the image of the oldest in the group. He was only thirty-seven, but the man had a cold, battle-worn look to him.

"You're the leader of this little ragtag bunch, aren't you?" Kevin murmured, an uncomfortable feeling stirring in his gut.

It wasn't a new feeling. These guys were walking around like they owned the park. As he watched one take down an ocelot, he was pretty sure they did.

This was a definite wrinkle in the plans. He contemplated his next steps.

Then an idea came to him. Quickly, he pulled all the information on the individuals in the park, along with some of the video footage. Then he dove into their financial backgrounds. It wasn't too hard to find the link to the DOD. Quickly, he packaged it all together.

He'd put an information blanket around the park. No one could communicate in or out. But once they were done, he'd send his intel on the group's actions in the park and their funding of the animal aggression testing to the media. He was sure the public would be very interested in what their tax dollars were being spent on.

Or maybe he'd contact some people in the DOD and see how much they'd be willing to pay so he didn't release the intel.

Grabbing a can of Red Bull, he shook it before taking a long drink and finishing off the last of the beverage. If all went well, he'd take down not only Sanctuary Kingdom but part of the Pentagon as well.

He smiled. It really was turning out to be a great day.

CHAPTER 118

Once they had gotten Izzy and the two teenagers into the Hummer, Darby tried to convince Courtney to go back with them. But the woman placed her hands on her hips and shook her head. "I'm going to help."

Darby blew out a breath and tried again. "Courtney, I think . . . ."

But Courtney didn't hear her because she had already stormed back to the Jeep. Taking another breath, Darby stared up at the sky.

"Looking for patience?" Gus asked.

"I suppose I am."

"Well, come on. Let's get back to our original programming." They headed for the Jeep.

Flicking a glance at Gus, Darby asked, "Gus, what do you think's going on with armed men in the park?"

Lips tight, he shrugged. "I don't know."

"If you were writing this, if this was one of your movies, why would they be doing it?"

He met her gaze and for a moment, Darby was afraid he wasn't going to answer, but then he spoke. "If they're killing both animals and humans, I'd say they're making a clean sweep."

"A clean sweep?"

"No witnesses. It sounds like maybe they're part of the implant project."

"What makes you say that?"

He shrugged. "Just a gut feeling. Someone had to hire the research center to implant the animals, right?"

She nodded.

"Well, whoever it is, I'm guessing they were trying to keep it quiet, and this isn't quiet."

Darby's stomach plunged as she realized he was right. "There are two threats in the park."

Gus's voice was grim. "Yeah, so let's neutralize one, and hopefully the cavalry will arrive before we have to face the other."

CHAPTER 119

HUNCHED TOGETHER ON THE FLOOR OF THE KIOSK, THERE WASN'T A LOT OF room. The open area of the kiosk behind the counter and in front of the refrigerators was only six feet by four. A metal gate was pulled down over the counter, hiding them from view. There was one door at the back of the kiosk.

Time was passing slowly. Gabe had hoped that there might be a law enforcement announcement or some other sign of help. But as time dragged on, it was clear help was not coming.

They'd heard gunshots, but a quick glance showed that those guys were not shooting animals. The group had held their breath, not daring to move once they'd spotted them.

Now it had been twenty minutes and everything was quiet. But the sight of a new threat had put a pause in their plans to head to the Castle.

At the same time, Gabe didn't understand what was taking the cavalry so long to arrive. The park had a DART team that should have been activated. Plus, with this kind of outbreak, law enforcement would be immediately notified. For a moment, he wondered if Martha had put a hold on the latter, hoping they could contain the problem themselves.

But he knew she would recognize that the fallout of not contacting authorities would play much worse in the press. She would definitely be trying to tamp down the public-relations fallout.

Grunting, he realized he'd never considered that she might be the most concerned about the loss of life. He loved his sister, but they were very, very different. Her emotions, they'd always been different than others. She was colder than him, more focused on the bottom line. Even in this situation, he knew the numbers would be running fast and furious through her mind as she contemplated the angles.

And while counting on her empathy might not get her to move quickly, counting on her calculations, she'd move heaven and earth to nip this in the bud quickly. The fact that she hadn't meant that something else had gone wrong.

As he looked at the kiosk, he knew they couldn't wait here. These kiosks were not designed to withstand extreme weather events like the buildings in the park. It was cheaper to lose the kiosks and replace them if necessary.

Which meant that if the animals were out, the thin walls of the kiosk would not protect them from some of the larger ones.

And they certainly wouldn't protect them from bullets. Dangerous as it was to move, staying here wasn't really any safer.

"I think we need to go take a look around. If the area's clear, we need to head for the Castle like we planned," Bao said quietly.

"Is that safe? Shouldn't we just wait?" Mama Sue asked.

"Bao's right. We need to get somewhere a little more protected." Gabe took a breath. "I'll go. It's my park. I know it best. I'll—"

"No offense, but I think Meg and I are better equipped to handle a situation that might develop." Bao looked over at her, and she nodded back at him.

Gabe shook his head. "But—"

Meg slipped past him toward the door. "It's okay. We've got this."

Bao placed a hand on her shoulder as she glanced outside. Then the two of them slipped through.

"Are they going to be okay?" Linc asked quietly.

Gabe looked at him but said nothing. He just shook his head and hoped that this would all be over soon.

CHAPTER 120

KEVIN HAD TO ADMIT THAT THIS WAS A LOT MORE FUN THAN HE THOUGHT it was going to be. Not that he didn't normally love his job. Figuring out all of the weaknesses in people's security systems was an absolute blast.

But actually being able to watch the human drama unfold in real time? He never realized how entertaining it could be.

Plus, he now had that extra little piece of blackmail for the DOD.

He watched a group of people get attacked by a pack of wolves. The wolves had come out of nowhere, frothing at the mouth. Although he didn't have audio, he could imagine the screams as the people took off running.

But human legs were no match for wolf ones. The wolves had run down the four of them, leaping on their backs and tearing into them. It had been brutal and bloody—kind of like those National Geographic specials he liked. Except in this case, the humans were the poor, injured gazelle.

Popping some M&M's into his mouth, Kevin smiled as he flicked from camera to camera. Then he stopped as he saw the Jeep making its way down the path. He leaned forward. "Now where are you guys going?"

It had to be that group from the elephant house. It still burned that he'd been locked out. This group seemed to be rather good at getting out of situations, and they definitely weren't the sit-on-your-hands type in an emergency. No doubt it was Augustus King leading the charge. Kevin was sure King was working out angles on how to spin this to make himself look like the action hero in real life.

"Oh, we're not letting you get out that easy," Kevin grumbled.

He noted the direction the Jeep was heading and frowned. Why were they going that way? But then it hit him—the cell tower. They'd found out about the implants. If they knocked out the cell tower, he wouldn't be able to set off the implants.

"No, no, no, no," Kevin repeated as his hands flew over the keyboard. He kept glancing at the image of the Jeep and saw Augustus King and his assistant step out of the car. He checked the schematics of the cell tower and knew there was a way they could shut off all the power to it, and there would be nothing Kevin could do to stop them.

What were the chances that a movie star and his assistant would know how to do that? Probably not high. But he couldn't take that chance. Heart racing, he contemplated his options.

Finally, he knew there was only one. He'd been setting off the animals' implants in short bursts, turning on the cell tower long enough to send out a signal and then shutting it down again. But if there was only one more signal that could be sent, he'd make sure it was a good one.

He just had to time it right.

CHAPTER 121

THE CELL TOWER WAS LOCATED JUST BEYOND THE ROLLER-COASTER. DARBY and the others thankfully did not run into any trouble heading there the second time.

The tower itself was designed to look like a massive willow tree. On hot days, guests would take refuge under it, not aware of what they were leaning against. It was decided Noah and Scooter would head inside and cut the signal. The other three would wait outside. The hallways in the tower were tight. There was only enough space for people to walk single file. There was no point in them going in there and feeling all claustrophobic.

As Scooter pulled to a stop in front of the tower, Gus turned to Noah. "You sure you can do it, right?"

Giving him a serious look, Noah nodded. "Yeah. Ori ran me through it. It's not actually that complicated."

Darby frowned. "It's not that complicated to deactivate a cell tower?"

He gave her a nervous laugh. "Yeah. I read a lot of electronics blogs. In case I ever become a spy." He wiggled his eyebrows at her.

Courtney snorted. "What are you, some wannabe James Bond?"

Everyone ignored her. "How long should it take?" Darby asked.

Noah flicked a glance at Gus. "If all goes well, only a few minutes once I find the main server. We'll be in and out."

"We'll wait out here," Gus replied.

"Okay, keep an eye out. If you see anything that concerns you, you need to take off, okay? Don't worry about us. We'll figure something out," Scooter replied.

"As long as it's safe, we'll stay. But yeah, if we need to go, we'll go," Gus promised.

A hollow feeling erupted in Darby's chest as she looked at the two men. A while ago, she had stopped thinking of both of them as strangers. There was a bond that formed in high-intensity situations. And Scooter, he was a constant. One she wanted to remain around. "Be careful."

He gave her a nod. "Yeah, you too."

The two men slipped from the truck. As Darby watched them disappear inside the tree, she really hoped that she would see them again.

CHAPTER 122

ONCE AGAIN, THE WORLD WAS QUIET. GABE KEPT LOOKING AT HIS WATCH, wondering how much time was too much.

"Should we go look for them?" Linc whispered.

Unsure what to say, Gabe looked over at Mama Sue. She nodded back at him. "You two should get somewhere safe. I'll stay here."

Linc reared back. "What? No."

She took his hand. "I can't run. And it's not safe here. These walls are not much by way of security, are they, Gabe?"

He couldn't meet her knowing gaze. She patted his hand. "It's okay. You guys go. Find help. I'll wait here."

A knock sounded at the door and then Bao pulled it open. He and Meg slipped in. Gabe got to his feet. "You two okay?"

"Yeah, sorry we took so long. Every time we saw an animal we hid," Bao said.

"Any humans?" Gabe asked.

"None we have to worry about," Meg said lightly.

"Any sign of DART?" Gabe asked.

Bao shook his head. "No, none. The only movement we saw were animals. I think everyone is hunkering down. If we're going, now's the time."

"So what do we do?" Linc asked.

Gabe pictured the walk from here to the Castle. It wasn't too far, but in the park right now, even a short distance seemed huge. "We go. The Castle's not too far. Once in there, we can easily wait in the control room until help arrives.

Her voice low, Meg flicked a glance over her shoulder in the direction of the Castle. "Yeah, we just need to get there first."

CHAPTER 123

EMPLOYEES HAD STARTED TO GATHER AT THE MAIN GATE TO DOMINION. Three had been electrocuted before they understood the gate and fence were electrified. Roger had erected a platform outside the entrances for sharpshooters from the DART team that had recovered.

EcoAct certainly had done its homework. They'd timed this perfectly, right down to the DOD team being at the research center.

And Martha felt helpless to do anything about it. Reuben had sent the message and they'd received a response. But Martha wasn't sure it would do any good.

Another team was trying to erect a platform at the main gate and was going to attempt to climb over. But the EcoAct idiots were throwing smoke bombs and pipe bombs over the fence anytime they saw movement.

But Roger assured her he'd get someone over the fence. She had faith in him. He'd figure out a way to call for help.

She just really hoped it wasn't too late.

CHAPTER 124

DAMNED IF WE DO, DAMNED IF WE DON'T. ALTHOUGH HE'D BEEN THE ONE who'd said they needed to leave the kiosk, Gabe was still second-guessing himself. But there was no time for that as Bao and Meg had led everyone out of the kiosk. The two had even retrieved Mama Sue's wheelchair when they were out.

Up ahead, Gabe spied the Paws and Claws Playhouse. Gabe was not a fan of animal shows. He felt they exploited the animals, but Martha insisted it was necessary. And he had to admit it was a big draw. Plus, they were very careful with their animal choices to make sure that only animals who enjoyed interacting with humans were part of the show.

The designers had done an incredible job with the site. The building's exterior was a colorful mix of realistic natural elements and large murals of animals dancing, leaping, and playing with one another. The entrance was shaped like a giant welcoming animal paw, with the doors set into the pads of the paw, giving a sense of stepping into a magical world.

The theater was surrounded by lush landscaping with topiary animals that seemed to be frozen in mid-performance. The marquee was bright and lively, with the name PAWS & CLAWS PLAYHOUSE spelled out in bold, animated letters that lit up in different patterns.

He'd seen kids' eyes widen in delight as they took in the theater, as did their parents. But there was no delight on the faces of the people with him now. Bone-deep fear better captured their expressions.

Meg was pushing Mama Sue's wheelchair. He studied the young woman, noting how her head continually swiveled from side to side, her eyes narrowed. Both she and Bao were in soldier mode, and Gabe was more than happy they were the two who'd been chosen to accompany them. He shuddered at the thought of Ansell being their guide.

They'd be dead already.

His chest tightened as he flicked a glance at Mama Sue and Linc. He could not let anything happen to them. No matter the cost to himself, he'd never be able to look at himself in the mirror again if something happened to them.

He'd never be able to look Darby in the eyes again, either.

The thought of Darby only made the tightness in his chest increase. She was out here somewhere, and she did not have two former soldiers to help keep her safe. And he knew Darby. She'd take responsibility for everyone in her group.

He closed his eyes for a moment. *Please, Darby, protect yourself as much as you protect them.*

The Paws and Claws Playhouse entrance was just behind them when a chill crawled over Gabe's skin. At the same time, he noticed Bao and Meg stiffening. "What's wrong?" Linc asked as Meg pulled Mama Sue to a stop.

"Something's watching us," Bao whispered, scanning the area.

CHAPTER 125

Turning, Gabe searched for the animal. The hiss drew him in. His eyes widened as it bolted from the greenery along the path. "Inside! Now!" he yelled as he turned for the Paws and Claws entrance.

Bao yanked the door open. Meg hustled through with Mama Sue, and Linc was right on their heels. Gabe darted in as Bao slammed the door shut behind them. Then Gabe hit the controls on the side of the entrance, engaging the locks. He let out a relieved breath when they engaged.

The relief was short-lived. The six-foot-tall cassowary launched itself into one of the glass doors.

Backing away from the entrance with the others, Bao stared at the enraged bird. "What the hell's wrong with that thing?"

Shaking his head, Gabe's eyes were wide as the bird crashed its beak into the glass again and again.

"Why would you even have those here?" Meg asked, her tone incredulous.

"We're not a petting zoo," Gabe spat back, and then took a breath. Giving Meg an apologetic wince, he continued, "They're supposed to be locked up. Generally, they're shy and reclusive but will attack if they feel threatened or cornered."

"Well, we certainly didn't do either of those," Mama Sue murmured with a frown.

"How strong are those guys?" Bao asked.

Picturing the long, tall legs, Gabe swallowed, imagining the damage those things could do. Unlike horses or other animals, cassowaries didn't kick out. They kicked down with a thousand-pound force. It was like facing the world's most ferocious kickboxer. "Their kick exerts a thousand pounds of force, equivalent to a heavy-weight boxer's punch."

"Yikes." Bao winced.

"But shouldn't we be safe if we don't threaten them?" Linc asked.

Oh, how I wish that was true, Gabe thought. Out loud, he said, "In the wild, yes. But here, not necessarily."

"Are they mad we locked them up?" Linc asked.

"No, or at least that's not what scientists think. It's a little more basic than that. Cassowaries in captivity, like a lot of animals in captivity, have come to associate people with food. And if we don't have food, they're going to be a bit . . . upset."

"How upset?" Meg demanded, her voice and body language intense.

"A cassowary owner in Florida fell into the cage. The bird stomped him to death."

"Oh my God," Mama Sue said.

"They're generally nonviolent, though, right?" Meg demanded.

Gabe winced. "Not exactly. They're also known as the world's most dangerous bird."

"I thought you said they were nonviolent!" Linc half whispered, half yelled.

"Typically, they are. But because of their size and strength, if they get riled up, they are extremely dangerous."

"So what riles them up?" Meg asked.

"Encroaching on one of their nests," Mama Sue said, meeting Gabe's gaze. "But their exhibit isn't near here. We shouldn't be anywhere near their territory."

"We're not. Their behavior is atypical," Gabe said.

"Just like the condor," Meg said softly.

His head snapping up, Gabe's eyes narrowed. He turned to look back at the door where the animal was now kicking at the glass, but the glass held. "You're right."

"Can it break that?" Mama Sue asked.

Gabe shook his head. "No. The doors are designed to withstand a much tougher onslaught." *And thank God for that.*

Linc gave a nervous laugh. "And they can't unlock the doors, right?"

Swallowing, Gabe's mind raced through all the animals in the park. "No. It's not just a matter of turning a handle. They'd need a security pass to unlock them first. And that is still a strictly human activity."

As long as whatever is happening hasn't affected humans, we should be good.

Bao clapped him on the shoulder. "Well, look, let's just hunker down here, maybe out of view of that thing. There are enough doors that we can put between us and any animals. And hopefully, not being able to see us, they'll ignore us until help arrives. We'll just wait it out here, comfy and cozy."

The sound of the cassowary hitting the glass had died away as they moved down the hall that ran around the movie theater. Gabe was taking them up to the control room. It wasn't as secure as the one in the Castle or Dominion, but it was located at the highest point of the theater.

And hopefully, Bao's words would prove true, and they'd ride out the emergency without any animal realizing where they were.

CHAPTER 126

ON SCREEN, THE CASSOWARY SHIFTED, SLAMMING ITS LEG INTO THE GLASS, but it didn't even shatter. Kevin had to admit, they'd really built the park well, which was very unfortunate.

He was keeping an eye on good ol' Gabe, but the man seemed to have nine lives. First, the orangutan had missed him, then the condors. He thought for sure the cassowary would pick off at least a few in his party. But no, they'd all made it inside the playhouse.

Twisting his mouth to the side, he stared at the screens. They'd gotten some people but not enough, and no big names yet. Having Gabe go down would be perfection—or at least getting him scarred up.

The armed men were using radios in the park to communicate with one another. They weren't park radios. Those were all being jammed, no doubt by these same testosterone junkies. But Kevin had already tracked down the frequency.

So now, how did he use that to his advantage?

CHAPTER 127

THE RADIO CLICKED TWICE BEFORE IT CAME TO LIFE. A NERVOUS MALE voice that Felix didn't recognize spoke. "Don't know if anyone's hearing this, but we're holed up in the playhouse. It seems to be safe, so if anyone needs to hide, head here."

The message ended. He frowned down at the radio. How did they get a radio? It wasn't one of the park frequencies. Maybe someone brought in their own for some reason. No doubt they were going through all the channels, broadcasting the same message. Quickly, he picked up his radio and called Bobby. "You hear that?"

There was a smile in Bobby's voice as he answered. "Sure did. We're not too far from there."

Felix was careful with his words in case anyone else was listening in. "Why don't you go see if you can offer them some help?"

CHAPTER 128

LOCATED ON THE SECOND FLOOR, THE CONTROL ROOM OF THE PLAYHOUSE had a wide hall outside it with windows along the front of the building. The control room itself overlooked two theaters: one where they held movie premieres and the other where they did the animal shows.

Mama Sue and Linc were out in the hall. Mama Sue's breathing was a little ragged and she needed a minute in the wider space. His gaze constantly scanning the doorway, Gabe was nervous about them being out there.

Picking up on that, Bao started for the hall. "I'll keep an eye on them." He slipped out the door.

Gabe let out a breath.

"You care about them, don't you?" Meg asked.

He nodded. "Mama Sue, Linc, and Darby—they're family. They're kind of that soft place to fall, you know?"

"I do," Meg said.

Giving himself a shake, Gabe turned his attention back to the control console. There was power, which was good, but all the wireless signals seemed to be out. On the bright side, all the door locks seemed to be working, so there was at least that.

"Can we contact anyone from here?" Meg asked.

"Not from here," he muttered, and then smacked himself. "But there are radios in the security closet on the first floor. Dammit, I should've thought of that when we were heading up here."

Meg gave him a small grin. "Well, we were a little distracted by the killer ostrich trying to get through the door."

He gave her a small smile back. "Not an ostrich."

"Yeah, still going to call it a killer ostrich. But that's not a problem. I'll go grab the radios."

He opened the lower desk drawer and grinned as he spied two radios inside and at the green light, indicating they were fully charged. "Oh, wait a minute. Looks like someone added some in here."

Grabbing one, he flicked it on. The unmistakable strains of Vivaldi blared into the room. Gabe frowned, flicking to another station and then another. All were paying the same music.

"Someone's jamming it," Meg said softly. Rolling her shoulders, she looked at him. "Okay. Radios are out. But we still need to make sure everything's locked up downstairs so we don't have any more surprises."

Gabe was already shaking his head before she stopped talking. "No. Not by yourself. I'll go with you."

This time it was Meg who shook her head. "Look, the second floor's good, all the doors are locked. Bao and I will go down to the first floor, run a quick perimeter check, just to make sure everything is locked up tight. You stay up here with Mama Sue and Linc."

Once again, Gabe was seeing the soldier rather than the tour guide. "Okay. But be careful."

She didn't promise that she would be. She merely gave him a nod. "See you soon."

CHAPTER 129

TENSION FILLED THE JEEP AS DARBY WATCHED THE DOOR TO THE CELL tower. She wasn't sure how long it would take to cut the signal, but it wouldn't be fast. They didn't know the space. She didn't either. It was one part of the park she'd never been in. She figured a minimum of ten minutes.

Courtney leaned forward from the back seat. "I have to pee."

Darby flicked a glance back at her. "Hold it."

Shifting in her seat, Courtney shook her head. "I can't. When I get nervous, I have to pee. And I really need to pee."

Flicking only a quick glance in the back seat, Darby once again wondered why they had agreed to allow the woman to come along. Help, she was not.

"Courtney, we cannot wander around looking for a bathroom," Gus said.

Rolling her eyes, Courtney pointed out the windshield. "There's one right there."

Sure enough, there was a bathroom. Of course, Darby had known that. The park was very good at ensuring there were restrooms every few hundred yards.

Courtney grabbed the door handle. "Look, you guys can stay here, but I'm not peeing in the back of the Jeep. So I'm going to go." She stepped outside.

Meeting Darby's gaze, Gus cursed softly, while Darby cursed less softly. "I got it," she grumbled as she grabbed the .357 Magnum and stepped out of the vehicle.

Gus stepped out from the other side. Darby's eyebrows rose.

He scoffed. "You honestly think I'm letting you guys go alone?"

She smiled for a moment but quickly turned her attention to scanning the area. Courtney stood waiting for both of them, shifting quickly from foot to foot.

"You need to make it quick," Gus said as he set off toward the bathroom. Courtney hurried next to him, ignoring their surroundings, her gaze focused on the bathroom building, which was designed to look like a barn in a deep red with white trim.

The opening was about fifteen feet across, with the entrance to the women's room on the right and the men's on the left. Despite her initial bluster, Courtney quickly shifted in between Darby and Gus. Darby rolled her eyes. There didn't seem to be any movement near them.

Stepping into the entrance, Darby moved over to the women's door. Glancing back at Gus, who stood with his back to the bathroom, he nodded over his shoulder at her.

Nerves dancing along her skin, Darby banged on the door. No sound came from inside. Taking a breath, she pulled it open, but the bathroom looked completely undisturbed.

Courtney slipped past her and into one of the stalls. Darby stepped inside. Gus took a step back toward them, talking to Darby over his shoulder. "I'll wait for you guys out here. Tell Princess to hurry."

With a small smile, Darby closed the door. She leaned back against the counter and rubbed the bridge of her nose.

Soft murmuring came from the stall that Courtney had disappeared into. Darby frowned and moved closer to the stall.

"I am in such a dangerous situation. There are animals everywhere, and I've barely been able to escape with my life. And my poor Lance—"

With an angry exhale, Darby banged on the stall. "Courtney, get out here."

CHAPTER 130

THE TWO GUNMEN WHO HAD BEEN HEADING AWAY FROM THE THEATER stopped in their tracks after Kevin's call. He smiled as he watched them speak on their radios for a moment before they headed back to the theater.

Humming to himself, Kevin checked in on the theater group. Ooo, the two employees were heading downstairs. Splitting up. Hadn't they watched horror movies? You never split up.

The gunmen were getting closer, so Kevin quickly unlocked all the doors to the theater. Then he checked to make sure he had the right codes for the theater doors. Both at the beginning and end of performances, the doors were unlocked and held open remotely.

After the two men slipped inside, he'd keep the doors open in case anyone else wanted to join the party.

CHAPTER 131

When Bao and Meg headed to the first floor, Mama Sue and Linc came into the control room. Gabe locked the door behind them, per Bao's instructions.

"How you doing, Mama?" Gabe asked. He did not like the paleness in her face and the tremor in her hands. She was a tough lady. She'd held up well under her diagnosis. But he knew stress could exacerbate MS.

She gave him a tight smile. "I'm fine, baby. Don't you worry about me."

Gabe exchanged a nervous glance with Linc. Mama Sue had been through a lot and was holding up incredibly well, but the stress of today was not what she needed. Gabe cursed silently that all of this had fallen on the day she happened to come for a visit.

At the same time, he wondered at the timing. If this had happened when the park was fully open, it would have been so much worse. His stomach bottomed out at the images: kids screaming, blood washing throughout the lanes of the park. Each day they had 40,000 visitors.

No, as bad as this was, it could've been much, much worse.

Linc wandered over to the control panel. "So, how does all this work?"

Needing a distraction from the images in his mind, Gabe pointed toward the different levers. "That controls the sound. That panel over there controls the movie theater, and that one is for the animal theater. The movie theater's pretty basic. The animal theater has a lot more bells and whistles. Over here, you can create rain and thunder with that panel right there."

There was a label underneath it that said WEATHER.

Another one said SCENE CHANGE, and there were four additional unmarked levers.

"What's this one about?" Linc asked.

Moving over to the panel, Gabe peered at the section that Linc was pointing toward. "It changes the backdrop along the back end of the stage. These are the spotlights, sound—there are even some 4D options for the seats inside." Gabe had to admit he really liked the animal theater. It was a fully immersive experience.

Leaning forward, Linc peered into the movie theater through the window. "Hey, there's Meg and Bao."

Behind them, Mama Sue let out a shaky breath. Gabe turned to her with concern. "You okay?"

"It just feels a little stuffy in here. Do you think we could . . ." She gestured toward the hallway.

Bao had wanted them to stay inside, but Gabe didn't like how pale Mama Sue was or how weak her voice sounded.

"Of course, of course." Gabe hurried over to the door while Linc grabbed the handles of Mama Sue's wheelchair and pushed her quickly toward it.

Opening the door, Gabe peered out. All was quiet. Stepping into the hall, he held the door open for the two of them.

Mama Sue let out a relieved breath when she was in the expansive hall. Frowning, Gabe watched her with concern. "Are you claustrophobic?"

She gave him a small smile. "I was, years ago. I thought I got past it, but I guess not entirely."

Linc rolled her over to the windows overlooking the park.

Wincing, Gabe wasn't sure if that was a good idea or not. He wasn't sure exactly what she would see outside those windows. But he followed nonetheless as Mama Sue said, "Oh, it looks like security's found us."

Oh, thank God. Gabe hustled over to her, staring out through the glass at the path in front of the playhouse. Two men walked toward the entrance. As he studied them, Gabe frowned. They weren't wearing security uniforms.

But what concerned him mainly was that the weapons on them were definitely not zoo issued. That was some serious firepower.

The hair on the back of his neck stood straight up. He grabbed the back of Mama Sue's wheelchair and pulled her away from the window as the men glanced up. "Get back from the window," Gabe ordered.

Darting back, Linc flicked a nervous glance at the window. "What's going on?"

Needing to get them behind a locked door, Gabe hurried back to the control room, his voice tight. "I don't think that's zoo security."

Once Gabe, Mama Sue, and Linc were back in the control room, Gabe closed the door quietly and locked it. He leaned back against it, his mind racing. Two gunmen. It was possible they were local law enforcement. But those guns were heavy-duty.

If he was wrong, it was no big deal. But if he was right . . .

He hurried over to the control panel and then stared at it, not sure what exactly he was supposed to be doing here.

"Gabe, what's going on?" Linc asked.

Nervous energy thrumming through him, Gabe shook his head. "I don't know. Maybe I'm overreacting. Maybe those were some sort of cops or SWAT members that got into the park. But that's not zoo security."

"You think it's those gunmen?" Linc asked, his voice serious.

Flicking a glance at Mama Sue, who was watching him closely, Gabe spoke slowly. "I don't know. But better safe than sorry. Let's just see if we can find Bao and Meg, okay?"

Linc moved over to the glass that overlooked the movie theater while Gabe and Mama Sue watched through the glass overlooking the animal theater.

The animal theater had a glass ceiling, which could be rolled back for some of the performances. But luckily, it was closed tight now, and that extra daylight provided enough light for him to scan every inch of the theater.

"There." Mama Sue pointed to the left-hand side of the stage as Bao climbed up the steps. On the other side, Meg did the same.

Spying the two of them, Gabe's nervousness increased. Studying the control panel, he tried to figure out a way to warn them that there were gunmen in the building. He reached for the speaker that would allow him to broadcast a message into the theater when a shot rang out.

CHAPTER 132

A GRIN STRETCHED ACROSS KEVIN'S FACE AS HE SAW THE TWO GUNMEN enter the theater. Well, at least that was going as planned.

He frowned, though, when he shifted his view to the cell tower. He'd seen them arrive but then had gotten distracted by the radio call. But the signal could be shut off at any moment.

However, it looked like the gods were smiling on him. Augustus King was no longer in the Hummer. In fact, he was standing out in the open, just outside a restroom.

Kevin chuckled. "Someone needed a potty break?"

Reaching down, he quickly hit enter. The signal went out, playing over and over again, pulsing through the implants and all the creatures' brains. In his mind's eye, he pictured their brains sizzling as an electric current ran through them.

The real image was no less violent. Across the screens, animals shook, lashing out, losing their damn minds.

God, this is good.

For a moment, he flicked a nervous glance around, worried that one of the eco-activist people might appear. They would not be happy with his joy at the animals' torture.

Kevin didn't give a crap about any of that. The life and death of the animals, and honestly any other living thing in the park, wasn't his concern. He was just here to cause some chaos. And chaos was what he had created.

CHAPTER 133

Inside the stall, Courtney had gone quiet. But Darby was livid. She banged again on the door. "Courtney, get out here right now or I'm leaving you. I mean it."

A moment later, the door to the stall flung open, and Courtney glared at her. "I was recording."

Trying to pull back her rising anger, Darby spoke through gritted teeth. "I know. We don't have time for that crap. Let's go." Then Darby paused, tilting her head. "Did you even have to use the bathroom?"

Checking her reflection in the mirror, Courtney shrugged. "I needed a change of scenery. I already got shots from inside the Hummer."

Darby stared at the woman. "You do realize how dangerous this is, right?"

Still looking at her reflection, Courtney flung her hair over her shoulder. "Of course. I mean, I saw Lance get hurt."

They should have left her back with the others, strapped to a chair. Or maybe Darby should just leave her locked in the bathroom here. She'd be fine with her reflection to keep her company.

Snarls sounded from outside the bathroom door. Heart racing, Darby's head whipped toward the door as gunfire erupted.

CHAPTER 134

THE GUNFIRE HAD TO BE GUS. IT WAS TOO CLOSE. BUT NOW IT SOUNDED farther away. He'd moved. Darby darted over to the door and locked it.

Her heart pounded as she pictured Gus. *Please, please let him be okay.*

Courtney was right behind her, as in breathing down her neck. Grimacing, Darby glared at her. "How about a little space?"

Courtney took a small step back.

Darby leaned her ear closer to the door. She wasn't sure what the heck was going on out there, but it wasn't anything good. Howls and ferocious growls erupted somewhere in the distance. The hair on her arms stood up straight.

"What's going on?" Courtney asked, her voice trembling.

Not answering, Darby shook her head. She had no answer to give.

A snarl erupted from just outside the door. Darby jumped back from it and crashed into Courtney. "Courtney."

With a squeak, Courtney scampered behind her again.

A crash now came from the windows along the far side of the bathroom. Darby whirled around. No sunlight came through the window, blocked by the animal trying to break through the glass.

"What is that?" Courtney shrieked.

The animal was ramming its horns so fast against the glass that it took Darby a moment to recognize it: It was a Sierra Nevada bighorn sheep. The sheep's distinctive horns were thick and curled down to a tapered end.

From here, she couldn't tell if it was male or female. Both had horns. But it looked like a big one, at least five feet. This one was pale brown. The herbivores weren't known for their aggression unless being defensive.

Apparently, though, this guy hadn't gotten the memo. It rammed into the glass over and over again. The glass spiderwebbed and then shattered. The sheep fell through the opening, glass cutting its sides as it dropped, landing on its back.

Screaming, Courtney pushed past Darby for the exit. She unlocked the door and bolted outside.

Darby was right behind her. She'd just slipped through the door when the sheep rammed into it. Her foot barely missed being caught. The image of her foot being cut off just above the ankle made her stomach heave.

Heart leaping into her throat, she stumbled before getting her feet under her. Then she and Courtney bolted out into the open space.

Courtney stopped suddenly. This time it was Darby who nearly ran into her. "What did you—"

The rest of the question died in her throat as she spied what was on the hood of the Hummer.

A large hyena stood there, glaring at them, saliva dripping from its mouth.

Without a moment's hesitation, Darby pulled the rifle into her shoulder. At almost the same moment that she pulled the trigger, the hyena leapt. Darby's shot got it in the back leg, cutting it in two. With a cry, it crashed to the ground.

But they weren't out of danger. The increasing yips made clear there were a lot more hyenas heading in their direction. Backing away, Darby grabbed Courtney by the back of the shirt just as Courtney started for the Hummer.

Courtney hadn't noticed the dark shapes moving in the trees just behind the SUV. Pulling her with her, Darby yelled, "Run!"

CHAPTER 135

Gunfire raked the front of the stage. Gabe's stomach bottomed out as he watched, at a loss as to what he could do to help.

"Bao!" Meg yelled. The security guard grabbed his arm as he dropped to the ground. But then he rolled quickly toward the wings. Meg had already darted into the wings on the other side.

"Oh my God. Bao's been shot," Mama Sue said, pointing to the stage where the security guard had disappeared.

Gabe's mind raced as he stared at the control panel. There had to be something he could do from here.

Linc darted over. "What's going on? Was that gunfire?"

"Yeah." Gabe's eyes widened as his gaze locked on the two men they'd seen enter the building as they hustled up the main aisle, their guns pulled into their shoulders. They looked professional. They looked as if they knew what they were doing. Which meant that Meg and Bao were in a lot of trouble.

What the hell were they doing firing on Bao and Meg? There were animals loose all over the park. Humans were not the problem.

One of the men moved to the side of the stage and made his way up while the other covered him. As soon as he was up, he waited, his gaze and gun shifting from wing to wing as his partner hurried up the stairs to join him.

Reaching out, Gabe flicked a switch. Rain burst onto the stage.

There was a small flood scene they used for some of the animal performances.

The man let out a yell.

Linc reached out and flipped the switch for the wind. Now the wind battered the men as well.

Then came the unmistakable sound of wolves growling.

Gabe stared at the panel, looking for the button for that. He didn't realize they had animal sounds. "Which control is that?"

"That's not us. That's them." Mama Sue pointed to the stage where three wolves stood arrayed in front of it.

CHAPTER 136

THE SOUNDS OF HYENAS GIVING CHASE, YELPING AND CACKLING, WAS going to live in Darby's nightmares—if she lived long enough to have nightmares. Her mind churned as fast as her legs, as she tried to figure out a way to save both her and Courtney. Outrunning hyenas was definitely not an option.

Up ahead, she spied the Alpine Peaks building. It held a range of exhibits, all involving animals that lived on mountaintops. Next to it was an outdoor exhibit: the bighorn sheep holding pen. Hopefully, the others had already left the area.

Her gaze was drawn back to the larger building with Ping Pika emblazoned across the front. A fact about hyenas slipped into her mind—they did not like high altitudes.

"There! Alpine Peaks!" Darby shouted.

Courtney veered toward it.

Reaching the overhang, Darby whirled around and fired at the hyena only ten feet behind her. The bullet caught it mid-chest. She fired twice more at two of the others. She caught one in the front paw and gave the other a glancing blow to its side, only enough to knock it over but not do any real damage.

"The door's locked!" Courtney cried, frantically tugging at the handle.

"Damn it." Darby wrestled into her pocket, pulled out the bracelet, and threw the tinfoil packet at Courtney. She backed up as six more hyenas appeared, circling closer. "Get the door open!"

"I'm trying!" Fumbling with the package, Courtney finally managed to free the bracelet and slam it onto the door pad. "Got it!"

The door slid open. Courtney darted through and Darby was right behind her. Standing in the doorway, Darby fired one more shot, hitting a hyena that tried to spring after them in the chest. It crumpled, and she grimaced at the destruction.

Another hyena darted toward her. She pulled the trigger, but nothing happened. She was out of ammo. She backed up quickly. The doors started to slide.

Eyes widening, Darby flipped the gun over, the handle her only weapon now. The doors were almost shut when the hyena lunged.

Darby stumbled back as the hyena got caught in the doors, its neck crushed for a moment before the doors swung open again. It lay unmoving across the threshold now. The doors tried to close again, but the hyena's body prevented it.

Darby took a step forward intending to push the hyena out of the way. The sight of the rest of the pack barreling toward them changed her mind.

Turning, she nearly tripped over her own feet in her haste as she bolted across the lobby. The space had been designed to look like a cozy ski lodge with massive windows and murals that depicted Ping Pika living her best life. There was, of course, the obligatory gift store with a ten-foot statue of Ping outside it, next to a bathroom. On the right was a small snack kiosk. The walls were covered with informational posters about pikas. And down the hall to the left was a large indoor playground.

Courtney was standing just inside the door, staring at the entrance with her mouth hanging open. Darby sprinted toward her, grabbing her arm as she passed. "What are you doing? Move."

Stumbling, Courtney hurried after her, panic in her voice. "But the doors are open."

"I know. Come on."

There was no time to drag the hyena out of the way.

As if to confirm her decision, she heard the unmistakable sound of paws scrambling on the tile floor as she and Courtney darted down the hall to the right. Above that, she could once again hear the *Fantastic Friends* theme song.

So join the fun and sing along,
With Fantastic Friends, we all belong,
Saving the world, one day at a time,
With friends like these, we'll always shine!

Right now, she really hated that song.

The doors to the exhibit had caused the hyenas to pause for just a moment, but now they were back on their trail.

Darby swallowed hard. "Bracelet!" she yelled as she ran. Courtney handed it over, and Darby gripped it in her palm. Ahead she spied the entrance to the pika exhibit.

Please let this work, she prayed as she sprinted ahead of Courtney. She grabbed the red bag next to the door in the middle of the hall, slamming her bracelet into the opening beside it. The door slid open, and they darted in.

The door slid shut behind them, and Darby let out a breath.

"They can't get through that, can they?" Courtney asked, her eyes wide.

"No. We should be safe in here," Darby said as she turned to take in the exhibit. She'd never been inside. It was colder than she'd expected. Goosebumps immediately broke out on her arms. The space was designed to look like a mountaintop with a rocky outcrop that had lots of hidey holes for the pika to take refuge.

Although the exhibit was exceptionally realistic, the murals of Ping and the other *Fantastic Friends* traipsing through mountains along the walls definitely ruined the reality of the scene. Surreal and somewhat eerie, the *Fantastic Friends* theme song continued to play in the background.

"I really, really hate this song," Darby muttered to herself, trying to catch her breath.

CHAPTER 137

GABE'S MOUTH DROPPED OPEN AS THE WOLVES CONVERGED ON THE two men.

One of the men fired, hitting one of the wolves in the gut, but the other two chased them into the same wing that Meg had disappeared through.

There was a banging on the door. "Gabe, open up!" Bao yelled.

"Thank God." Linc bolted across the room and yanked the door open.

Bao's arm was wrapped, and Meg was watching the hallway, her back to them. "What happened?" Gabe asked.

"Gunmen. Not sure who they are, but we need to move now," Bao replied.

"There are wolves down there," Mama Sue said.

Glancing over at her, the look on Bao's face with dead serious. The good-natured, easygoing guy had completely disappeared behind a serious façade, and Gabe was more than comforted to see it. "Yeah. Hopefully, they'll keep them distracted while we get out. Let's go." He grabbed Mama Sue's wheelchair and pushed her forward.

"Where are we going?" Gabe asked as he hurried after him.

Meeting Meg's gaze, who gave him a nod before leading the way, Meg said, "We're heading to the Castle. You said there's a panic room there, right?"

Gabe nodded. "Yeah."

Not slowing, Bao kept his voice low but urgent. "We don't stop until we get there. If I say run, you run. Meg and I will clear the way, got it?"

Mama Sue gripped Linc's hand which was on her shoulder. Watching them, Gabe knew he would do whatever it took to keep them safe. "Got it."

CHAPTER 138

HOOTING INTO THE CAVERNOUS SPACE, KEVIN SLAPPED HIS KNEE WHILE holding his stomach. Watching that annoying influencer run for her life. God, that was so good. He bet that was the first time she'd done any real exercise in years. She was probably one of those women who survived on leaves of lettuce.

He shook his head. So much fun.

But the woman with the influencer, Darby Ellis, she was a bit more interesting. She was one of those rare creatures who was both beauty and brains. She'd come from pretty humble beginnings, but she also seemed awfully chummy with Gabe Sullivan, so obviously she was a horrible person.

Nevertheless, she'd handled herself pretty well. There was nothing in her background that suggested she was that kind of tough, but hey, emergencies brought out either the best or the worst in people.

He watched as the two women disappeared into Alpine Peaks. It took him a moment to find the cameras for inside the exhibit. He did a quick scan and saw two people hiding in an office at the back of the first floor. But the influencer and Darby hadn't gone there. Instead, they'd headed into the pika exhibit.

He frowned, wondering why, and then realized that it was the only place with a reinforced door. All the other doors in the exhibits were wood, and the hyenas would easily be able to get through any of them.

"Smart, smart, smart," Kevin sang as his hands flew over the keyboard. It was a good move. He noticed that Ellis even had enough presence of mind to grab the oxygen mask outside the exhibit door.

The pika exhibit was a high-altitude environment. It had a lower oxygen level than the area outside. So, in order for Darby and the influencer to survive and not just pass out and perhaps die, they needed oxygen. He grunted grudgingly admitting that Darby was someone you'd want at your back in an emergency.

He smiled as he brought up the controls for the exhibit. "So let's see what you do with this one."

He hit a button.

CHAPTER 139

DARBY STARED AT THE DOOR, PANTING. SHE WASN'T SURE IF THE HYENAS even realized that they had ducked in here. But then the door shuddered as the hyenas flung themselves at it.

Her eyes widening, Courtney started to back into the exhibit. "They'll get through."

Although Darby backed up too, she shook her head. "No, they won't. The door's basically an airlock." She struggled to get the words out.

"I don't feel so good," Courtney mumbled as the door continued to shudder under the hyenas onslaught.

Making her way over to the woman, Darby grabbed her by the arm as she led her to an outcropping of rocks. "Sit."

Courtney all but collapsed to the ground.

Darby opened the red bag she'd grabbed on the way in and pulled out the oxygen mask. It was connected to a canister that would give them at least an hour of air. Given there were two of them, though, it was more like thirty minutes. She placed the nozzle over her mouth and inhaled deeply, taking in the oxygen and feeling her heart start to slow.

Next to her, Courtney was blinking rapidly. Darby placed the mask over the other woman's face. She crouched down next to her. "Breathe."

Reaching up, Courtney grabbed the mask, took deep breaths, her eyes wide with fear.

Darby kept her voice calm as she spoke. "People can only live in a low-oxygen environment for so long. We'll wait here until the hyenas get bored and find another target, and then we'll slip out."

Courtney nodded.

Behind them, the hyenas were slamming into the door over and over again. Not good. She gripped Courtney by the arm and hauled her up. "You know what? Let's get a little farther from the door. I'd like to get our scent as far from it as possible."

She gently took the mask from Courtney. "Not too much. We've got to conserve, okay?"

Silently, Courtney followed Darby across the exhibit.

Movement from the corner of Darby's eye pulled her attention, and she spied a small pika. Its head popped up above a rocky ledge. She smiled. "Hi, buddy. We're going to be here for a little bit. Sorry to disturb you."

The pika dropped back down out of view.

"Ping was always my favorite of the *Fantastic Friends*," Courtney murmured.

Glancing at the mural, Darby zeroed in on the giraffe. "Personally, I always liked Jillie."

"Why?" Courtney asked.

Darby shrugged. "I don't know. I guess because she kind of looks after everybody else and understands that the world is difficult. I get that."

"And Ping was always dancing through the world. I get that."

The two women's gazes locked before Darby nodded. "Yeah."

An electronic beep came from behind them. Darby whirled around, her eyes widening.

Courtney grabbed her arm. "Please tell me that's not what I think it is."

Her mouth falling open, Darby's eyes widened as the panel next to the door glowed green. "Someone just opened the exhibit door."

Part of Darby hoped that whoever opened the door had already killed all the hyenas and was now coming in to save them. But she didn't think that was what was happening.

"Let's go." Once again, she grabbed Courtney's arm as she slammed the oxygen mask over her own face and took some deep breaths. Snarls and yelps came from behind her.

"Up, up, up," she urged as she handed the mask to Courtney while pushing her up the mountainous terrain. Slowly, Courtney took a deep breath.

Darby tugged on her shoulder. "We can't stop."

The Alpine Peaks exhibit had been created to resemble a mountainside. There were crevices and hiding spots all over the place for the pikas, but none of them would be big enough for humans, or at least not insulated enough to hide their scent from the hyenas.

"Where are we going?" Courtney asked.

Darby gestured toward the top of the mountain. "The only place I can think of that might give us a chance."

CHAPTER 140

THE BRIDGE LEADING TO THE CASTLE WAS JUST UP AHEAD. GABE DIDN'T dare feel any relief. Until they were locked behind a steel door, they would not be safe.

In an unspoken agreement, Gabe and the others broke into a quick jog. Linc pushed against the handlebars of Mama Sue's wheelchair. Gabe glanced down at the woman and saw determination on her face. He hated that these guys were in the middle of all this, especially Mama Sue. It must be terrifying not to be able to run.

Of course, running wasn't really going to help any of the rest of them. Pretty much every animal in the park could run faster. As they hurried over the bridge, Bao jumped away from the edge, nearly colliding with Gabe.

His eyes widened as he looked at the water. "Something moved in there."

Gabe swallowed. "The Castle was created with a moat. The alligators are supposed to be controlled by an electric netting underneath the water. They shouldn't be able to reach the bridge."

"Yeah, well, I think someone dropped the net," Bao grumbled.

Gabe didn't say anything because honestly, what was there to say? The park had turned into a complete and total nightmare. Instead, he just picked up his pace. "Okay, this way."

He hurried down the hall toward a suite of offices. At the end of the hall was a simple-looking door with a keypad next to it. Gabe stopped quickly and inputted the key code.

"No bracelet entrance?" Linc asked.

"We wanted to make sure that in the event of a power outage that someone would still be able to get inside," Gabe explained as he pushed the door open.

Inside, the room was about twenty by ten feet. There were two rows of terminals facing a wall of monitors, but everything was quiet. Bao slipped in after the others and closed the door behind them.

At the sound of the locks engaging, everyone let out a relieved breath. Gabe sank against the nearest counter, taking a couple of deep breaths. Okay, okay, he thought, trying to calm his racing heart.

Bao wandered over to the nearest monitor. "This place looks a little dead."

Straightening, Gabe hurried over to a panel and tapped on it. Nothing. He reached around and turned the monitor on and off, then did the same with the hard drive. Still nothing. He frowned. "There's no power."

"Well, that's not really surprising, is it? I mean, whoever's running this thing must've cut it," Bao said.

His frown deepening, Gabe shook his head. "No, this place has its own separate battery system. Just like the door, it's got a backup to make sure that the power is always on. The only way for it to be turned off is for someone to physically turn it off themselves."

Bao met Gabe's gaze. "I think you might have a traitor in your midst."

Gabe nodded grimly. "So it appears."

CHAPTER 141

Even with the oxygen, Darby was feeling the effects of the enclosure. Her limbs felt heavier. Her movements were becoming more lethargic. Next to her, Courtney was moving slower too, her feet stumbling over the uneven terrain. Taking a hit of oxygen, she then handed it over to Courtney, who greedily took a long inhale.

The effects of low oxygen flew through Darby's mind: dizziness, confusion, lethargy, tachycardia, cyanosis.

Trying to keep her breathing even, she tamped down the rising fear. They had only a limited amount of oxygen. They'd have to exit the exhibit in less than thirty minutes. *Please let that be enough time.*

With effort, she focused on the emergency hatch up above, shutting out everything else. The hatch didn't lead outside the enclosure but to a metal net draped across the top. It had been created as earthquake insurance to capture any debris that might fall. At the time, Darby wasn't sure why they had bothered installing it, but right now, she was awfully glad they had.

A cry came from closer to the door, and Darby winced, picturing the poor pika that had just been caught. *Damn it, there are barely any of these guys left*, she thought.

There were a few different species of pika, including the American pika. But this exhibit contained the Ili pika, a Chinese species whose numbers were less than a thousand.

Ping Pika was an Ili pika and was the most popular of the *Fantastic Friends*. The real pikas were only eight inches long, with rounded gray-and-white furry bodies and the most adorable little ears.

The cries of the Pika died away, and Darby's heart dropped at the same time. Less than a thousand left in the world, and now there was one less.

She didn't, however, turn around to offer herself as tribute. Instead, she wrapped her arm around Courtney and hustled her forward.

"I don't feel so good," Courtney said.

"I know. Almost there." Darby all but yanked Courtney up the elevated terrain.

Feeling eyes on her back, she turned and spied Tomy standing at the base of the mountain, glaring up at them. One of the hyenas behind Tomy stumbled—the lower levels of oxygen were getting to them, too.

"Go, go, go," Darby urged as she reached up and unlatched the gate that led to the catwalk. Courtney hustled through as Tomy barreled up the mountain. Spots appeared in front of Darby's eyes, and she swayed for a moment as she grabbed the edges of the opening.

"They're coming," Courtney called, her words rushed and her voice shaking. Darby didn't turn around to look. She could feel Tomy getting closer. "Just a little farther," she urged. She knew she needed oxygen but didn't dare take the time to breathe. That would mean death.

So she grabbed hold of the edge of the hatch. She struggled to pull herself up. Her muscles felt like Jell-O.

With a cry, Courtney reached through and grabbed the back of Darby's shirt to help haul her up.

With a vicious snarl emitting from her throat, Tomy latched onto Darby's boot. Courtney screamed.

But Darby didn't have the breath for it. She twisted to look down into the eyes of the alpha. Bringing up her other foot, she slammed it into the alpha's face over and over again. "Let. Me. Go!"

The last kick sent Tomy tumbling. With a burst of adrenaline, Darby scampered through the opening. She slammed the latch shut. It automatically locked a second before Tomy flung herself at it.

Darby hurried out onto the three-foot-wide catwalk. The alpha glared at them through the wires.

"Now what?" Courtney asked, hurrying after her.

Taking a seat carefully, Darby pulled out the oxygen mask. She took a big inhale before handing it over to Courtney. "Now we wait."

CHAPTER 142

UNLIKE THE CASTLE AT DISNEY WORLD THAT WAS LARGELY A walkthrough, the Castle at Sanctuary Kingdom had been built with the expectation that it would be used. There were stores along the first floor surrounding a massive food court, classrooms on the second, as well as two 4D theaters. Observation balconies were strewn throughout the upper levels along with viewing stands. And of course, there were the long hallways that led to the glass-enclosed viewing platform.

It was such an incredible building. Gabe's heart lurched a little bit, picturing Joel. He'd been the one who'd designed it. An architect, he'd been inspired by Antoni Gaudi, the revered architect and designer who lived at the turn of the twentieth century in Spain. Gaudi had incorporated the natural world into all of his designs. Joel had done the same here.

Modeled after the Sagrada Família in Barcelona, the center of the Castle's supports were laid bare. But rather than just metal support columns, they were designed to look like trees reaching for the sky, complete with roots into the tiled ground and knots made of stained glass. The columns lined the main walkway, which was lined with shops.

The walkway led to the food court. More columns held up a forty-foot roof adorned with a colorful stained glass ceiling, depicting all the animals that were in the park when it originally opened. In the center was a mama elephant and cub with bursts of color surrounding them: lush greens, bold reds, sparkling blues.

You did good, Joel, he thought of the cement that had been shaped like tree bark.

But now was not the time for happy memories. Now they needed to get the power back on.

There were radios in the back of the control room, and Gabe hurried over to check them, grateful when it turned out that they still had power. These were not the park radios but shorter-range ones. They would work only within the Castle.

"Are you sure about this?" he asked Bao, even as he handed him one of the radios.

Taking it, the man nodded. "Yeah. You need to get this place up and running. Meg and I can handle flipping a couple of switches."

It wasn't that simple and both of them knew that. The battery was located in the basement, two levels down. They'd have to traverse a large area to get there and no one knew what was currently in the Castle. The doors had been wide open.

Gabe shot a nervous look at the door, picturing the route they'd have to take. "The battery is located one level down. It should be a simple matter of turning on a few dials to reboot. But of course, nothing in the park right now is simple. If you run into anyone or anything—"

Meg cut him off. "We'll handle it."

There was nothing but confidence in the woman's tone. Still, Gabe felt worried. "I should go with you. I know this place better than—"

Once again, Meg cut him off. "We're wasting time, Gabe. You're the only one who can handle bringing the system back online once we get the power up. Your going with us will only slow that down. Just give us directions. Once we get down there, we'll get you the juice to get it started. Then we'll come right back up, okay?"

Gabe looked over at Mama Sue and Linc. Mama Sue gave him the slightest nod.

With a sigh, Gabe nodded, too. "Okay. But take care of each other."

CHAPTER 143

Felix and Sabrina had taken out three gorillas. Two had charged them, but the third had stayed quiet in the back. Felix saw no reason to take chances and had shot the ape in the face.

With a growl, he wiped the sweat and blood from his own face as Sabrina straightened from the corpse of one of the apes with a nod. "These two are on the list. The other isn't."

"How many do we have left?"

Sabrina consulted the list. "About fifteen, unless the others took care of them."

Casting an annoyed glance around, Felix growled again, feeling a certain kinship with the trapped animals. "This is taking way more time than I'd hoped."

He'd known how big the park was, but he hadn't expected how easily the animals would be able to hide and appear out of nowhere. He'd already lost both Marissa and Urich. They'd been stomped to death by some monster ostrich.

Grabbing his radio, he hit the transmission button. "Santos, Bobby, come in."

There was no reply. Felix tried again. "Santos, Bobby, answer, dammit."

Santos's voice came through a moment later. "Hey, boss." He sounded seriously out of breath.

"What happened?" Felix asked.

"Damn . . . wolves attacked us . . . when we were in the theater," Santos panted.

"Did you get the targets?"

This time it was Bobby who answered. "Didn't have a chance. We were too busy with the wolves. While we were dealing with them, the prey escaped."

Felix cursed under his breath. "You good now?"

"Yeah, but I saw the direction they were heading. It's toward that castle-looking thing."

Scanning the park, Felix spotted the outline of the Castle. It looked like a grander version of the one at Disney. "Well, if they're heading there, so are we. Let's finish this and get out of this damn park."

CHAPTER 144

FROM THE CATWALK, DARBY AND COURTNEY HAD A BIRD'S-EYE VIEW OF the enclosure. One of the pikas had been killed by the entrance, but the others seemed to have burrowed themselves deep enough that the hyenas couldn't reach them, though they tried. The hyenas circled the openings, reaching in and pawing at the dirt.

But those exertions didn't last long. In the low-oxygen environment, they grew tired quickly.

On the catwalk, Darby and Courtney shared the oxygen mask, passing it back and forth silently as they watched the hyenas slowly lose more and more energy.

"Did you know that would happen to them?" Courtney whispered.

Darby nodded. "Hyenas do very poorly at high altitudes. Their bodies can't adjust to the low oxygen."

"Pikas can?"

"Some. They've found a genetic variant within one species. They can raise or lower their oxygen requirements," Darby explained.

"So you brought us in here because you thought the hyenas would follow?"

"I hoped they wouldn't. But I figured if we were going to hide somewhere, it might as well be a place that was going to help us."

"That was really smart."

Darby just gave her a small grin. Courtney had been very subdued since they had gotten on the catwalk, and Darby didn't think it was just the lack of oxygen.

Below them, the hyenas had all fallen over except for one. Tomy still paced by the latch. But she was stumbling now. It wouldn't be much longer.

Both women watched as the alpha fought the effects of oxygen deprivation. But as strong as she was, she couldn't fight biology. Eventually, she stumbled and fell over on her side. Her chest labored as she struggled to get a breath.

Compassion wafted through Darby as she watched the magnificent creature struggle. But right next to that compassion was anger. The hyenas were only doing what their biology encouraged them to do. Whoever had set up this little game, however, had no such excuse. Someone was out there trying to kill all of them, and Darby really hoped they got what they deserved.

CHAPTER 145

A CASTLE. FELIX SCOFFED. THESE PEOPLE CERTAINLY DIDN'T SUFFER FROM low self-esteem. But as he approached the massive building, he had to admit it was impressive.

There were three turrets and a long glass-enclosed hallway that led off the back end.

Yeah, it was impressive.

The sound of running feet had him turning. Next to him, Sabrina did the same, their weapons at the ready.

"Whoa, whoa, friendlies," Bobby called, his hands up as he jogged toward them.

Lowering his weapon, Felix scanned both of them. There were jagged red marks on Santos's arm, although the skin hadn't been broken. Blood was on Bobby's calf, though.

"You guys good?"

"Damn wolves," Santos growled. "I'm sick of this park."

Grunting his agreement, Felix gestured to the Castle. "Look, we take these guys out and call it. The DOD will wipe the footage and no one will know we were here. But these guys saw us."

"Last targets?" Bobby asked.

Glancing over at the towering structure, Felix felt the annoyance under his skin. But he shoved it aside, focusing instead on how good it was going to feel to finish these people off.

If anyone else saw them, it could be blamed on the trauma and people being confused. "Yeah. One last hunt and we're out of here."

CHAPTER 146

THE CONTROL CENTER IN THE CASTLE HAD NONE OF THE DESIGN FLAIR that the public-facing areas did. The room consisted of simple gray-blue walls, a boring gray commercial carpet, and no decorations along the walls besides signs involving instructions for the park.

In sum, there was absolutely nothing to distract Gabe from his worry. He paced along the front of the monitors, flicking a glance at the radio every now and then, which remained silent. "It's been too long."

"No, it hasn't. Just give them time," Mama Sue said.

Gabe shook his head, continuing to pace.

The radio crackled. "Gabe?"

He lunged for it. "Bao? You two okay?"

"Yeah. It took us longer than we'd planned. We took a wrong turn and had to double back. We're now standing in front of a massive panel of some sort."

"Okay, good." Picturing the space, Gabe said, "I need you to turn around and look at a small panel on the wall behind you."

There was a pause on the other side before Bao responded. "I see it."

"There are a series of five levers. I just need you to snap all of them on like you would a breaker."

"Hold on."

A moment later, Bao's voice came on. "Done."

At the same time, the computer nearest Gabe began to hum. He broke into a grin. "Looks like we've got power."

"Awesome. We're heading back," Bao replied.

"See you soon." Gabe sat down at the desk and quickly began inputting code. From the corner of his eye, he noted that the monitors at the front of the room flickered to life as well.

"Gabe?" Linc asked, a tremor in his voice.

"What's wrong?" Gabe asked over his shoulder.

His eyes locked beyond Gabe, Linc asked. "Isn't that the entrance to the Castle?"

Turning back to the wall of monitors, Gabe zeroed in on the front entrance of the Castle. The image clearly depicted the bridge they had crossed not that long ago, as well as the four gunmen walking across it.

CHAPTER 147

Darby and Courtney stayed up on the catwalk until Tomy's chest was barely moving. After taking a hit of oxygen and making Courtney do the same, Darby got into a crouch. "Okay. We can head out now."

Courtney didn't put up any fight. She merely nodded. "I'm right behind you."

With a shaky hand, Darby unlocked the hatch, flicking a glance at Tomy. But the alpha barely stirred. Opening the hatch slowly, Darby paused before stepping through. She dropped down to the top of the mountain. The alpha's eyes opened. A soft snarl erupted from her throat.

Darby paused. But Tomy made no move toward them. "We're good."

Courtney quickly followed Darby down. The two of them gave the alpha a wide berth as they headed down the mountain. The rest of the hyenas were scattered across the space, all of them in various states of distress.

Darby hurried for the door and slipped through it, taking great big breaths. As soon as Courtney was through, she closed the door, knowing she was sealing the hyenas' fate.

But right now this park was Darwin's theory come to life: survival of the fittest. And Darby had every intention of surviving.

CHAPTER 148

Gabe reached for the radio, but Linc beat him to it. "Bao, Meg, there are four gunmen coming in the main entrance."

There was a small pause before Meg's voice called out, "Repeat last."

Linc paced along the floor. "The monitors came on. We saw four gunmen coming in the main entrance."

"Got it. We'll find another way back to you. Keep radio silence so you don't give us away, okay?"

"Okay."

As Gabe hurried through the series of codes necessary to reboot the system, he kept glancing at the monitors. The gunmen were spreading out through the food court. Gabe's heart clenched.

"Is there another way for them to get out of that basement?" Mama Sue asked.

Flicking a glance at the schematic of the Castle on the wall, Gabe shook his head. "There are two exits, but both lead to the food court."

On screen, Bao's head appeared at one of the exits, and he pulled it back quickly as a gunman turned toward him. Peering out again, he darted into the hall. One of the gunmen turned back, but Bao was already out of view.

Gabe let out a breath.

Meg peeked her head out as well, and then she too sprinted across the open space. But she wasn't quite as lucky.

One of the gunmen turned and let out a yell. Gunfire blasted the ground just behind Meg as she disappeared down the hallway after Bao.

CHAPTER 149

STEPPING OUT FROM THE PIKA EXHIBIT, DARBY FELT COMPLETELY EXPOSED. She kept expecting a hyena to leap out at them. But nothing stirred. It seemed that the entire pack was in the pika exhibit.

That, of course, didn't mean she and Courtney were safe. There were plenty of other animals out here that could harm them.

Backed up against the wall right next to the pika exhibit door, Courtney looked like she wasn't going anywhere. Darby crept toward the end of the hall and peered into the foyer. All quiet.

Turning she waved at Courtney to join her. The woman moved forward slowly, her eyes wide, her gaze darting around. When she was close enough, Darby reached out and grabbed Courtney's arm. Pulling her forward, they skirted around the hyena in the entrance and started back toward the cell tower.

An eagle screeched up ahead. Courtney jumped about a foot with a screech of her own.

"You need to stay quiet," Darby warned, prying the woman's fingers from her arm.

"I know, I know, it's just—" She met Darby's gaze. "I will. I'll be quiet. I promise."

And Darby actually believed her. Ever since the attack in the bathroom, Courtney hadn't reached for her phone once. It seemed she might finally be understanding the gravity of the situation.

Movement flickered in the corner of Darby's vision. She grabbed Courtney and hurried with her behind a Dippin' Dots kiosk. Putting her finger to her lips, she peeked out.

Weapon in hand, Gus walked down the path, his gaze swiveling from side to side, his eyes narrowed. He looked like a soldier, she realized with a shock, and then gave herself a shake. Of course he did. He'd played one on the screen more than once.

Letting out a breath, she waved her hand as she stepped out.

His shoulders dropped in obvious relief as he hustled over to them. "Thank God. You two okay?"

Nudging her chin toward Courtney, who looked at Gus with watery eyes, Darby nodded. "Yeah."

"We'd better get moving. I don't want Noah and Scooter reappearing and wondering where we are." Gus paused. "But do you know which direction the hyenas went? How'd you get away from them?"

Her throat tight, she gave him a grim smile. "They won't be a problem."

Pulling his gaze from inspecting their surroundings, Gus raised his eyebrows, concern flashing across his face. "What happened?"

Picturing the pika exhibit, Darby swallowed. "They're not a problem. Let's just leave it at that for now, okay?"

Studying her for a long moment, he finally said, "Okay. Come on."

Together, the three of them jogged slowly back to the tower, keeping a careful eye out. As they spotted the cell tower, Noah and Scooter were just emerging. Still keeping a wary eye on their surroundings, they hurried over to them.

Scooter frowned as they neared. "What are you guys doing out of the car?"

"Long story," Darby said quickly. "Everything go okay?"

"Better than okay, but let's talk in the Hummer." Scooter headed toward it, and the others followed quickly. Once inside, Noah, who was in the passenger seat, turned to face the backseat as Scooter started driving. "We managed to turn on the cell tower."

"What?" Gus exclaimed.

Noah raised his hands. "Just for a moment. We called 9-1-1. They had no idea what was going on, but they're sending people now."

"How could they not know?" Darby asked.

"I don't know, and I don't care. They know now. And I was able to track Mama Sue, Linc, and Gabe's bracelets." Scooter nodded at Darby through the rearview mirror.

"Then we initiated a shutdown." Noah grinned. "We disconnected all the links to the tower. That's what took so long. Someone's going to have to go in and reconnect everything by hand. So safe to say that whatever signal is being used for the animals, it's down now."

That was all good news, but Darby was more interested in Scooter's announcement. "Where are they?"

"Well, they're moving, or at least they were a few minutes ago."

"Did you get a location?" Gus asked.

Scooter grinned. "They were heading to the Castle."

CHAPTER 150

Moving through the series of steps as quickly as he could, Gabe no longer looked up at the monitor to check on Bao and Meg because there was nothing he could do about it. Two of the gunmen had started to give chase.

Gabe's whole body radiated tension, but he kept his focus on bringing the system online. The faster he got through rebooting the system, the sooner he would be able to help them. So, keeping his gaze focused on the screen, he called out, "Linc."

Bouncing with nervous energy, Linc hurried over to him. "What do you need?"

Keeping his gaze on the keyboard and monitor in front of him, he said, "Along the back wall, there's a cabinet. I need you to go open it. The code is 7-2-8-8-6."

Linc sprinted over to the back wall. Mama Sue met him there. Once Linc input the code, each of them grabbed a door and pulled it open. Mama Sue let out a gasp. Gabe understood the response. There was a mini-arsenal inside that cabinet. He'd forgotten it was there. He should have remembered, then Bao and Meg wouldn't be out there unarmed.

But dammit, there was just so much happening. And he simply wasn't a soldier. His mind didn't automatically go to weapons.

"What do you want us to do?" Mama Sue asked.

Gabe was standing now, unable to sit anymore, bouncing in place as he completed the last few steps. "There should be a duffel bag at the bottom. Start loading weapons into it."

Behind him, he heard the clank of metal. He let out another shaky breath. Only a few more steps.

Wiping the sweat off his forehead, he swiped to the next screen. "I'm almost done. Once I get the system rebooted, I'll take the weapons, and you guys stay—" He looked up at Mama Sue's cry.

She sat staring at the door, a look of horror on her face. And Linc was nowhere to be seen as the door closed.

CHAPTER 151

WORRY RICOCHETED THROUGH DARBY'S BODY AS SHE SAT IN THE BACK OF the truck. Her whole body was vibrating with anxious tension. Mama Sue was in a wheelchair. How could she possibly get away from danger—either animals or, God forbid, bullets?

All she could picture were horrible images of a lion coming across Mama Sue. There was absolutely no chance that Linc or Gabe would leave her behind, and she would lose all of them.

"You doing okay?" Noah asked.

Darby gave him a tight smile. "I'll feel better once we see my family."

"We'll get them, Darby. We're almost there." Scooter nodded to the windshield.

Leaning toward the center of the truck, Darby looked through the glass. She always liked the Castle. Joel had actually come up with the design idea. A team of architects had drafted it, but he was the one who came up with the inspiration.

Although based on the Sagrada Família, whose construction began back in 1882, the largest Catholic Church in the world still wasn't complete. But Joel had made sure this place was finished. He just didn't realize it would be his last piece of work.

Losing Joel had been tough. He and Gabe had been constant fixtures at Mama Sue's house. Every Sunday, they'd show up for the family dinner. Joel had a big extended family back in Boston, whom he missed horribly. And Darby could tell how much he appreciated being included in Mama Sue's welcoming home.

Mama Sue was like that. Anyone who crossed her doorstep was treated like family. They were included in food preparations. There always seemed to be a gift for them at Christmastime. And within an hour of someone coming to the house for the first time, Mama Sue always had their complete story.

After Darby's mom had passed away, Mama Sue had been an absolute lifeline. Mama had been the other parent. Darby must have spent half her nights sleeping over at Mama Sue's house when her mom was working.

Then her mom was gone. It had left such a hole. Mama Sue never tried to fill that hole, never tried to replace her mom. In fact, she'd kept her alive with all of her stories and encouraged Darby and Linc to talk to their mom at night and tell her about her day. It didn't make the hole go away, but it did ease the pain of it.

Darby could not stand to lose another mother. She couldn't lose Linc either or Gabe. The three of them were her family. They were all the family she had left. She would be completely alone in this world if they were gone. And she wasn't sure that she would survive that.

Scooter pulled to a stop in front of the Castle. They were unable to go straight to the door because of the metal barricades. There was a way to release them so that emergency vehicles could get through, but that had to happen from inside the Castle.

"Let's go, people," Scooter said as he slipped out of the car. Gus and Noah were right behind him. Courtney, although by the door, didn't move nearly as quickly.

"Come on, we need to go," Darby said as she slid out after Noah.

Although Courtney nodded, she didn't move. She just looked at her with big, wide eyes.

Darby looked back at the woman. "Courtney, you'll be safer inside. There's a big locked room that nothing and no one will be able to get through."

"You promise?" Courtney asked in a small voice.

"Yes. Come on."

Taking a breath, Courtney pushed open the door and then hurried after Scooter. Noah followed but Gus waited for Darby. He nudged his chin toward Courtney. "She okay?"

"It's possible she's going into shock. Or maybe the reality of the situation is finally hitting her."

"It's not easy." There was a note of understanding in Gus's voice.

She studied him, wondering about those stories. Had he really gone through all of that? Or was that just some sort of Hollywood spin on an innocent incident? Whatever the case, now was not exactly the time for a heart-to-heart.

"Where are we going?" Gus asked.

"If Gabe, Mama Sue, and Linc are here, they no doubt went to the control room. It's reinforced, designed to withstand a tornado. That's the room they'll wait in."

CHAPTER 152

Damn it, Linc. Panic crashing through him, Gabe hurried through the three last commands to reboot the system and then automatically shifted over to the camera controls.

Mama Sue rolled over to him. He mirrored his screen onto the large monitor at the front of the room as he flipped through screens looking for Linc. He wasn't in the halls immediately outside the room. The kid was just so damn fast.

"Wait, there," Mama Sue grabbed Gabe's arm. He paused his searching, his eyes widening. On screen, Meg and Bao had taken refuge behind the counter in the food court. Two of the gunmen entered the food court at the opposite end. They didn't seem to know exactly where they were.

"They're in trouble," she whispered, then she gasped. She pointed to the monitors at the front of the room.

The question he was about to ask died in his mouth as he saw two massive alligators step into the building. The hall they were in led to the food court as well.

Fear and panic charged through Gabe. He completed the last couple of steps and slammed the enter button on the keyboard. Lights and communications would be up in just a moment. But they didn't have a minute. He raced across the room to the cupboard and saw that Linc had left one Magnum rifle and a tranquilizer handgun.

He pulled them out, stuffed the tranquilizer gun into his waist, and loaded the Magnum.

"Gabe." Mama Sue's voice trembled as she looked up at him. Fear shone in her eyes.

Hurrying back to her, he planted a shaky kiss on her forehead. "I'll find Linc. I promise. Now lock the door behind me."

Sprinting across the room, he paused as he flicked a glance back at the monitors. He still couldn't see Linc. But he knew where Bao and Meg were. He'd start with them, and then they'd all go find him.

Pausing for one more moment, he took a deep breath before pulling the door open and darting out.

CHAPTER 153

AT ONE OF THE SMALLER SIDE ENTRANCES, SCOOTER VEERED TO THE RIGHT, bypassing the large foyer and shopping area and heading for a small door that was a shortcut to the control room. Darby's heart pounded every time they reached a corner, and Scooter peered around it. But they didn't come in contact with anyone.

Up ahead, Darby spied the control room and, with relief, saw that not only was the hallway empty, but there were no marks on the door. It didn't look like anything dangerous had been here.

Thank God. She picked up her pace and was at Scooter's side when he reached the door. He knocked on it. "Gabe? Mama Sue? It's Scooter."

A moment later, the door unlocked. Darby grabbed the handle and shoved it open. Then she let out a cry, seeing Mama Sue sitting just beyond the door. She all but flew across the space and hugged her tight.

"Darby, baby," Mama Sue cooed.

Darby knew she had said something in response, but she wasn't quite sure what it was. A moment later, she pulled back, wiping at her eyes, and looked around the room. "Where are Linc and Gabe?"

Mama Sue's eyes were full of worry. "They're out there."

"What? Why?"

"Bao and Meg are in trouble. There are gunmen in the Castle. They're unarmed." Her eyes full of worry, Mama Sue pointed to the now-empty gun case. "Linc went to help them. And Gabe, he went to help Linc."

CHAPTER 154

As Gabe sprinted through the employees-only hall, he volleyed between being terrified for Linc and being so damn mad at the kid. Months ago, he and Joel had been talking about kids. They'd just started the paperwork with a surrogacy agency. They thought they were ready.

Now, he wasn't sure his blood pressure would ever be able to handle it.

As he reached the end of the hall, he paused. He winced as he cracked open the door, but there was no corresponding yell or gunfire. Peeking his head out, he saw that the shopping promenade was empty. There were two stories of shops, both high end and more modestly priced. A little bit for everyone.

Wiping sweat from his brow with a shaky hand, he slipped out the door. His heart was beating fast as he hurried forward, scanning the area, looking for any sign of Linc. He paused at the edge of the cross-hallway that led to the main entrance. Halfway across, he caught movement on his right. Darting forward, he crouched on the other side of the opening and glanced back.

His jaw nearly hit his chest. Igor, the twelve-foot gator that lived in the moat and grasslands around the Castle, lumbered slowly forward.

Oh my God. Shaking Gabe backed away.

"Psst, Gabe."

Stopping, he looked up at the balconies lining the area. Twenty feet ahead on the same side, Linc leaned over and waved.

Stay there, Gabe mouthed and then sprinted for the nearest stairwell. Wincing once again as the door squeaked, he slipped into the stairwell, holding the door so that it barely made a sound as it closed before he sprinted up the stairs. Linc had the door on the second floor open. Gabe hurried through and hugged Linc tight, giving himself a moment to feel relief.

But by the time he released the teenager, Gabe's anger was back at the forefront. "What were you thinking?" he whisper-yelled.

With a shrug, Linc shifted his gaze away. "You were doing your part. And I wanted to do mine."

Shaking his head, Gabe took a few breaths, reaching for the bag. "Okay, well, you need to get back to the control room."

Linc's eyes widened as he glanced over the side of the balcony. "Yeah, I don't think I can do that."

Following his gaze, he saw Igor turn onto the shopping promenade.

"And we need to help Meg and Bao. They're in the food court. Those guys are going to find them." Linc nudged his chin down the hall. "This balcony runs along the food court, right?"

Gabe nodded.

"I was thinking I could drop the bag down to them," Linc said with a hopeful expression.

It wasn't a bad plan, except that he was pretty sure the gunmen would notice a large black duffel bag being tossed from over the balcony.

Igor's slow movements down the tiled floor drew his attention. He was heading in the direction of the food court. His eyebrows rising, Gabe looked back at Linc. "That could work. But we're going to need a distraction."

CHAPTER 155

FELIX'S BOOTS ECHOED AGAINST THE POLISHED TILE OF THE FOOD COURT AS he paced, eyes sharp, rifle at the ready. He scanned the area, every detail committed to memory—the overturned chairs, the lights that had just come on, the cleaning solution in the air.

His men held their positions, eyes on the exits, guns trained for anything that might move. He could feel the tension rising, the weight of time slipping away. Whoever was hiding in here—employees, by the look of the uniforms they'd glimpsed earlier—thought they could wait him out. Big mistake.

"We need to flush them out," he muttered under his breath, adjusting his grip on the rifle. They were close. He could feel it. "Stay sharp."

Suddenly, something dropped from the balcony above the pizza place. In quick succession, two more objects flew over the railing.

Although Felix tensed, expecting a grenade, the object was too long and small for that.

Santos stepped closer, frowning. "Is that a hot dog?"

A low hiss cut through the silence, strange and guttural. Felix's brow furrowed, his gaze snapping toward the hallway.

Gun trained, he took a step forward. A hulking alligator appeared, its wide, muscular body scraping against the floor, eyes gleaming with cold, reptilian hunger as it gobbled up one of the hot dogs.

"What the hell?" Bobby yelled, stumbling back.

Felix's lips curled into a snarl. Smart move. Bring a beast into the mix, throw them off balance.

"Gator! We've got a gator!" Santos shouted, panic lacing his voice.

"Six o'clock," Sabrina yelled.

Felix whirled around as someone ducked down from the balcony on the other side of the court.

"They dropped something," Sabrina murmured.

The gator snapped, its massive tail smacking into a set of table and chairs, sending them tumbling. Felix turned back. From the corner of his eye, he caught movement.

A man leaned over the counter of the Cinnabon, a Magnum rifle in his hands.

"Down!" Felix yelled, grabbing the back of Sabrina's shirt and tugging her to the floor. Chairs and tables turned over as they all flung themselves to the ground.

Gunshots rang out across the court.

A massive hole ripped through the table Sabrina and Felix had taken shelter behind. Glancing out, he saw two figures disappear out the far food court exit. Two other individuals darted down the far stairs and sprinted after them.

"Goddamn it," Felix snarled as he extracted himself from Sabrina, kicking away a chair by his feet.

Gunfire sounded behind him as Bobby and Santos unleashed on the gator. Turning, Felix's grip on the rifle tightened. The gator thrashed violently as the shots tore into its thick hide but did little damage.

"Kill it!" he snapped. "Aim for the eyes!"

The rapid pop of bullets filled the air. The gator hissed and snapped, but it was no match for the barrage of bullets. Chairs and tables flew as the massive reptile roared its displeasure.

Felix's heart was pounding, but his focus was razor sharp. Lining up, he zeroed in on the creature's eye and pulled the trigger. The first shot entered right through his iris. He followed up with five more as Sabrina unloaded into the creature's open mouth.

With a growl, Felix got to his feet, his gaze darting to where their quarry had disappeared.

The gator gave one final shudder before collapsing in a heap, its blood pooling across the tile. The silence that followed was thick, broken only by the harsh breathing of his men and the lingering smell of gunpowder.

Felix stood over the body of the dead gator, his jaw clenched in a barely contained fury, at the same time, he reveled in the kill. "It's dead," Bobby called, kicking at the gator.

Turning, Felix started to jog after the ones that had escaped. "Let's go. We're not done yet."

CHAPTER 156

As soon as Mama Sue finished speaking, Darby heard muffled noises coming from deeper in the Castle. "What is that?"

"Gunfire," Gus said, no uncertainty in his voice.

"There." Mama Sue pointed to an image on the screen: Gabe and Linc sprinting through the hallway beyond the food court behind another man and woman.

"Who's with them?" she asked.

"Meg and Bao. She's a new tour guide," Mama Sue answered.

"Bao's a member of the security team. He's a good man," Scooter said, his eyes locked on the screen.

But they weren't the only ones on the screen. A moment later, four individuals with guns raced through the food court as well.

Mama Sue brought up another image, and Darby stared, her mouth dropping open. An alligator was splayed across the floor of the food court. The alligators from the moat had entered the Castle. She loved her brother, but right now she was so mad at him for playing superhero.

Her mind raced as she pictured the layout of the Castle. Anywhere else they went was wide open and wouldn't offer any chance of getting to safety.

There was one option, but it was risky. Of course, everything about this was risky. She calculated how long it would take the others to get there, then grabbed the mic, and turned it on.

CHAPTER 157

GABE COULD NOT BELIEVE THAT WORKED. HE'D GRABBED HANDFULS OF hotdogs from Sanctuary Kitchen on the second floor and had started tossing them over the balcony, leading Igor right to the food court.

Linc had circled around above Bao and Meg. As soon as the gunmen caught sight of Igor, he'd dropped the bag. And then once the gator engaged them, all four of them had hastened out of there. Now they needed to double back to the control room, but there was no way to do that without avoiding the gunmen behind them.

The PA system crackled to life as the gator let out a roar and bullets rang out behind them. "Gabe, you have to get to the Hide."

At the sound of Darby's voice, Gabe's head snapped up

"Was that Darby?" Linc asked.

A smile spread across Gabe's face. "Yeah."

Extending beyond the Castle were two glass walkways. Six feet in the center was a solid, non-transparent surface for people not comfortable walking on glass. The glass walkways led to a large octagon with massive observation windows that allowed people to overlook the preserve below. In fact, the reason the whole thing was glass was so that every step of the way, visitors would have a view directly below them and farther out into the preserve.

"Where's that?" Bao yelled.

Gabe nodded toward the massive entrance designed to look like the opening to a treehouse. "Straight ahead."

CHAPTER 158

A STRANGE SORT OF CALM HAD SLIPPED OVER DARBY. ALTHOUGH HER heart was racing in fear for Gabe and Linc, her mind was putting the pieces in place to get them to safety.

Moving next to her, Gus's look was focused. "You look like you have a plan."

Picturing the layout of the Castle off the food court, she nodded. "I do. We're going to split up. Two of us will take the southern hallway leading to the hide, and the rest will take the northern hallway. We'll converge at the octagon at the end."

"Okay, let's get going," Scooter said.

Meeting Mama Sue's gaze, she saw the worry in the older woman's eyes. "I need to go help them," she said softly.

Her chin trembling, Mama Sue took a deep breath. "I know, baby. But I need you all to come back to me, okay?"

Darby hugged her tight. "We will."

When Darby released her, Mama Sue looked up at Scooter. "I need you to come back, too. I've been waiting for you to ask me out on a date for two years now, and I expect you to do exactly that when you get back."

A huge smile crossed Scooter's face. "Yes, ma'am."

Mama Sue turned to Gus and Noah. "I don't know you two, but I also expect you to return safe and sound."

Then Mama Sue turned to Courtney and raised her eyebrows. Darby spoke quietly, "Courtney, I think you should stay here."

Courtney spoke quickly. "Yeah. I'll stay here. I'm not going to cause any trouble, I promise."

Darby's heart broke a little bit for the girl. She looked so lost. Mama Sue extended her hand. Courtney all but flew across the room to grasp it. Mama Sue patted her hand. "I'll take care of our girl here. You four take care of each other."

Nodding, Darby scanned the cameras, looking for any and all problems that could be coming their way. She thought she spied movement near the entrance to the northern hallway of the Hide, but when she glanced back, there was nothing there.

She must have been mistaken. Nodding, she looked at the three men in front of her. "All right, let's go."

CHAPTER 159

AFTER JOEL DIED, GABE HAD INCREASED HIS RUNNING REGIMEN. A COUPLE of days, he'd even done fifteen-mile runs just for the hell of it. But apparently, sprints were what he should have been working on.

Next to him, Linc kept pace easily, although Gabe knew without a doubt that the young man could easily outpace him. And despite all his exercise, Gabe's lungs were starting to burn, and his legs were protesting. He felt like a fish flung onto land.

Like Linc, neither Bao nor Meg, who were ahead of them, seemed to have any difficulty with the exertion. And they both looked very comfortable with the weapons in their hands.

In Gabe's own hands, the tranquilizer gun felt like deadweight. And it seemed to grow heavier with each step. The occasional bursts of gunfire from behind didn't help with that.

"Move!" Linc yelled, pushing at Gabe and sending him between the statue of Leo Leopard and Jillie Giraffe. The heads of each exploded, sending shrapnel flying.

But Gabe and Linc were still moving forward, ducking around another kiosk that offered them a little coverage from behind.

Flicking a glance over at Linc, he saw the look of determination on the boy's face, one that he only saw when Linc was racing. And he supposed that was appropriate. This was, after all, the most important race of his life.

Without slowing, Bao and Meg burst into the southern hallway. Gabe knew that the Hide was just ahead. It was an octagon-shaped space where guests could relax while viewing the nature preserve below. It was at the end of the two long hallways.

Called the Hide, it was based on hides used in hunting, or elevated spots where prey could be safely observed. This was the same concept, although on a massive scale. And of course, no one was allowed to shoot any of the animals below, except with a camera.

Picturing the space, Gabe felt a tightness in his chest. He felt an urgency to get there. The bullets crashing into the ground behind him accentuated the point. But he wasn't sure what the plan was. He didn't see how reaching that particular spot was going to help them.

Focusing on the end of the hall, he wove around a water bottle kiosk, feeling the heat as a bullet barely missed him before ducking back in front of it.

Close, that was too close. Ahead, Bao and Meg were almost at the Hide. But the truth was, it didn't offer a safe haven. There was no panic room, nowhere to hide from the gunmen following them.

But Darby had told them to head this way. She had to have a reason. And as he found a few extra reserves to help him move faster, he prayed that whatever she had in mind, worked.

CHAPTER 160

MAKING SURE THE CONTROL ROOM WAS LOCKED BEHIND HER, DARBY sprinted after Scooter. Noah was ahead of her, with Gus close behind. She was incredibly grateful to these two men for jumping in to help. They could have stayed back at the elephant preserve once they'd gotten off the monorail. And if they had, well, Darby didn't even want to think about how things might have gone.

Now, with them, they had a chance to save others, albeit a slim one.

And that line of thought opened the door to all her worries about Gabe and Linc. She kept picturing the gunmen and imagining Gabe and Linc being cornered by them.

"What are we running into?" Gus asked, keeping pace next to her.

Pulling up a mental map, she didn't slow as she answered him. "The hallways are a quarter of a mile long, with glass on the walls and ceiling. They offer a perfect view of the preserve below. The octagon at the end is 100 feet across and fifteen feet tall. There's glass on both sides, but there's also a café, a merchandise shop, and bathrooms along the eastern wall. Fifty feet from the octagon, the floor is glass as well, on both sides."

Gus's eyebrows rose. "You know the dimensions off the top of your head?"

"Seems like it," Darby replied. She'd always had a knack for recalling facts quickly, even under stress—a skill that helped her excel in school while working a part-time job. It wasn't quite a photographic memory, but it was close.

"Scooter, you and Noah take the southern hallway. Gus and I will take the northern," Darby instructed.

"Will do," Scotter called.

At the food court, Darby and Gus veered off from the others. Her heart was in her throat as she started to sprint down the quarter-mile hallway. But then, a feeling of calm slipped over her. In her mind, she could almost see an overlay of their trajectories on a map of the Hide. She could picture it all unfolding, could almost see Bao and Meg reaching the octagon. Something told her they would be the first to take on the gunmen, leaving Gabe and Linc to sprint past. That would lead them right to Darby.

She flicked a nervous glance in the direction that Noah and Scooter had disappeared, her gaze lingering on the younger man. Catching the look, Gus said, "Don't worry about Noah. He can handle himself."

Darby wasn't so sure. She doubted the guy had much combat training, especially with live ammo. Then again, she didn't have much training either. She knew how to shoot, but that was about it.

But unlike Noah, she had a powerful motivator—she would do anything to keep Gabe and Linc alive.

CHAPTER 161

FELIX FELT A SURGE OF EXHILARATION. ANNOYED AS HE WAS AT NOT BEING able to just take these people out, killing that gator had been an experience. And these guys were giving them a run for their money. He kind of respected that.

He let off a high volley of gunfire, although he wasn't close enough to do any damage. He just wanted to keep his prey on their toes.

Yeah, his blood was absolutely pumping. This was why he did this. Yes, he was a patriot. Yes, he loved his country. But there were lots of ways to serve his country.

But he chose the way that best aligned with who he was: a hunter. He got off on the adrenaline, on the line between life and death.

This situation, though, he'd never imagined a scenario like it. Felix shook his head, still unable to believe all the animals had been released. He idly wondered how that had happened but didn't dwell on it. He wasn't one to get lost in his thoughts.

Instead, he focused on the mission and what was right in front of him. It's what made him such a good soldier—shutting off his feelings and just doing the job. But here, there was no need to shut off his feelings. Here, he could enjoy the thrill of the chase.

"Should we be worried they're armed?" Sabrina called over from his right, still moving quickly.

Not slowing, Felix shrugged. "They're civilians. It's doubtful they can hit the broad side of a barn when their adrenaline gets going."

"What was that message?" Bobby yelled over.

"I only caught a few words. I think someone's watching them and trying to warn them," Sabrina replied.

They had to be in a control room of some sort. "We'll find them after we take care of these guys."

Sabrina grinned. "Is it wrong that I'm kind of enjoying this?"

He returned the smile. "Not wrong at all."

CHAPTER 162

GABE WAS BEGINNING TO HAVE SOME SERIOUS TROUBLE BREATHING. NOT like a heart attack—though, honestly, he wasn't sure why that hadn't happened yet. It was the pace. His legs were okay, but his breathing was all over the place. His need for more air was growing and his legs were slowing in response.

"Do not slow down," Linc ordered, grabbing Gabe's sleeve to help propel him forward. He was gulping in air, but he didn't dare slow. If he did, breathing wouldn't be a problem for much longer.

Up ahead, he saw the beginning of the Hide. His hopes rose, even as unrealistic as that hope was. Like a lot of runners, he always set himself a destination—like a mailbox or a tree—and felt a sense of joy once he reached it. Now he was focused solely on just getting to the octagon at the end of the hall.

Meg and Bao were ahead and stopped at the counter along the front of the gift shop. Quickly the two of them ducked behind it before propping their guns up on it.

"You guys keep going," Bao yelled, determination in his voice. Next to him, Meg looked no less focused.

Gabe marveled at his luck, having these two for today's tour. For a moment, he pictured them with some of the other tour guides. That would have been a disaster.

Then he imagined Darby being with them. His heart pounded at the thought of her being caught up in all of this. Of course, she was somewhere in the Castle right now, but he shut down his worries about her. He needed to focus on getting himself and Linc out of there.

"What's the plan?" Linc yelled.

"Cut through the octagon and head back through the northern hallway," Gabe panted out.

Linc gave an abrupt nod and sprinted around the corner, heading to the northern hallway first.

Gabe followed, rounding the corner and nearly slamming directly into Linc, who'd stopped dead in his tracks. Stumbling over his feet, he nearly face-planted, but Linc grabbed him, pulling him back to his side. "Why did you—"

A roar cut off Gabe's words. His gaze shot to the hallway ahead of him and the sight of two Sumatran tigers, each seven feet long, charging toward them.

CHAPTER 163

At the sound of the roar, Darby's head jerked up. Gus stared at her, then glanced down the hallway. "What the hell was that?"

Part of Darby wanted to lie, to tell Gus it was one of the animal soundtracks that played across the park. But she couldn't do that. She couldn't lie to him when he was risking his life.

"I think it's a Sumatran tiger." As soon as she'd heard the roar, she'd known, and she had flashed back on that image she'd seen for just a split second back in the control room. It had been the edge of the tiger's tail.

"It sounds like it's in the hallway," Gus said. The hallway wasn't straight, there were alcoves and kiosks scattered throughout, so they did not have a straight view through to the Hide.

"It's ahead of us," she yelled but didn't slow down. It didn't matter what was ahead of them because Linc and Gabe were there too. She noticed, with no small amount of gratitude, that Gus hadn't slowed down either.

"If it helps, it's the smallest of the living tigers." The Sumatran tigers still weighed in at 260 pounds and were seven feet long. So "small" in this case was relative.

"Does that make it less dangerous?"

"To us?" Another fact about the Sumatran tiger slipped through her mind: They were the most aggressive of the tiger species. "No."

CHAPTER 164

U_P AHEAD, FELIX SPOTTED THE END OF THE HALL, ALTHOUGH HE HAD NO doubt it actually curved into another one. Their prey had been diving and shifting direction between the kiosks and statues that littered the hall. As a result, none of them had gotten a good shot.

"What was that?" Sabrina yelled.

Felix frowned. With the gunfire at such close range, his ears were ringing. "I didn't hear anything."

As they approached the end, Felix realized it was another one of those "eat until your stomach swells and your wallet is empty" restaurant and merchandise spots. Sanctuary Kingdom really understood what made their visitors tick, and they milked that until there was absolutely nothing left.

Gunfire rang out from behind the counter of a store named Hide Hideaway. Diving to the ground, Felix scrambled behind a couch and returned fire. Up ahead, Bobby and Santos were closer to the corner and had darted into an alcove. Sabrina dove to the ground next to Felix.

"I'll cover you two. Get going," he yelled to Bobby and Santos.

Leaning up, Sabrina let out a spray of cover fire. Bobby and Santos sprinted for the corner, keeping an eye on the Hideaway.

As they did, the teenager and the older guy came barreling back, sprinting for the wall.

Surprised, Santos, who was slightly ahead of Bobby, took a step, his head turning to follow the two fleeing with a frown as he brought his weapon around.

A massive tiger leapt around the corner, crashing into Santos and digging its claws into his chest. Santos's bloodcurdling scream echoed through the room.

Bobby let out his own yell, "Santos!"

He opened fire on the tiger, reducing its rib cage to ground beef. But he didn't notice the second tiger as it darted toward him, swiping at his chest. It caught his hands and ripped the gun from them. A spray of gunfire erupted from Santos's weapon, causing Bobby to dive for the ground.

CHAPTER 165

GRABBING LINC, GABE YANKED HIM TO THE FLOOR JUST AS BULLETS crashed into the window behind them. Glass shattered, raining little slivers on them, but the bulk was dropped outside. The rush of wind blew in through the opening.

The bullets hadn't been aimed at them. It was a wild spray by the man the tiger had raked.

Now both men unloaded their weapons at the tigers, much more concerned with them than either Gabe or Linc.

Gabe's heart pounded from where he lay. He looked up in time to see the cats attack the men. One of the cats wrapped its jaws around a man and clamped down. Blood squirted from the man's neck. Gabe's eyes widened as he scrambled to his feet, yanking Linc up. Alarms rang out, adding to the chaos.

It looked like the system was back online, but that wasn't going to help. The tiger dropped its latest kill and turned to look at Gabe. Yanking Linc back, they backed away as the tiger prowled toward them. Gabe saw the moment it was about to pounce. Grabbing Linc, he moved them to the edge of the shattered window.

Air rushed through the opening, pushing at Gabe's clothes. Below him, the ground was an agonizing hundred feet away. But there was a maintenance platform just below the Hide.

"The maintenance platform!" he yelled. "Go!"

With barely a pause, Linc jumped, crashing onto the six-foot wide platform and rolling to the side, grabbing on to the railing to keep from going over. Gabe leaped as well and felt the rush of claws along his back as the tiger let out a roar.

As he hit the platform, he started to roll toward the edge. His stomach dropped, but Linc grabbed him before he could pitch over the side. Gunfire rang out from up above, and the tiger disappeared from the window. Gabe's heart pounded, but even as it did, he was amazed that the maintenance crew ever came up here. He needed to get them onto a more secure platform. This was terrifying.

On hands and knees, he started to crawl along the platform, with Linc right behind him. He was not sure where he was headed, except that it was away from the gunfire.

CHAPTER 166

Gunfire and roars sounded from up ahead. Terror stole through Darby as the worst images darted through her mind.

Gus sprinted up to her, but he didn't try and stop her as she picked up her pace and he did the same.

Ahead, she saw the tiger sprint across the walkway. Her gaze then shifted to its target: Gabe and Linc, who were over by a shattered window. A moment later, they jumped.

"No!"

CHAPTER 167

"Goddammit." Rage roared through Felix as he looked from Bobby to Santos. Both were down. Santos's guts were splayed across the floor, and one of the tigers was munching on them.

They had been damn good soldiers. They would not be easily replaced. Someone was going to pay for that.

Focused on the bodies, he didn't notice the tiger turn and move toward them. Despite its ribs being a mess of ground beef, it swiped out at Felix. He let out a yell as its claws raked his calf. He fell out into the open, and a bullet grazed his ribs.

Sabrina turned and unloaded her clip on the tiger, reducing its head to bits of blood and tissue. She grabbed Felix by the collar and yanked him back into the alcove. As she did, he unleashed cover fire on the guys in the store. They'd been attempting to creep out. Now they'd been driven through a door at the back of the store, probably a supply closet.

Letting out a painful hiss, Felix noted the two newcomers coming from the left and another group coming down the right behind them. They were boxed in.

"Goddammit." Glancing to the right, he noticed a woman had moved to the center of the hall, right on top of the glass. He aimed in that direction, nodding to Sabrina. "Take out the glass."

Gunfire raked the ground in front of the woman. But it held.

"Enough of this," Felix said. He grabbed one of the grenades from his belt and nodded at Sabrina. Grabbing one from her own belt, she tossed it toward the incoming two runners while Felix tossed his toward the other ones.

If they were going down, they were all going down.

CHAPTER 168

SEEING LINC AND GABE JUMP FROM THE WINDOW HAD CAUSED DARBY'S heart to nearly stop. She'd darted forward, but Gus had grabbed her and held her back as the tiger lunged for the window. He yanked her into an alcove as the tiger shifted its focus to the other two gunmen.

"I'll cover you," he said, releasing her as the tiger engaged the other gunmen. She headed for the same window Gabe and Linc had disappeared through. To the left, she could see movement and let out a relieved breath that they'd made it to the maintenance platform.

The relief only lasted for a moment. Bullets blasted along the glass floor, and she started to run. From the corner of her eye, she saw a cylinder fly through the air. Another landed farther down the other hallway, near Noah and Scooter. Noah shoved Scooter into the wall as the object exploded just before the other one exploded behind her.

Gus let out a yell as he dove toward the wall. Darby took a step to do the same, but the glass floor underneath her feet shattered.

With a cry, she dropped, as did the tigers and both of the injured men. With horror, she watched them fall.

Air rushed around her. Twisting, she dove for the edge of the floor, but her hands only caught jagged shards of glass that ripped into her skin. She managed to snag some of the rigging underneath the Hide. The ledge was only about three inches wide, but she held on for dear life as she brought her other hand up to the other side.

She was gripping the metal beam for all she was worth when she spied Noah fall through the shattered glass floor as well farther down. He managed to twist toward the maintenance platform. His feet hit, but his shoulders swung back. Linc leapt forward, latching on to Noah's shirt and hauling him toward the platform. Gabe reached out and grabbed him, bringing him securely onto the narrow gangplank.

Then Linc caught sight of Darby, holding on with one hand, her body dangling over a hundred feet from the ground. His eyes widened.

"Darby!" he yelled, his voice full of fear.

CHAPTER 169

As Gabe pulled the young man onto the platform, he heard Linc call out.

Turning, his heart jumped into his throat as he spied Darby clinging to one of the support beams. Sweat was on her brow, as her other arm reached up and grabbed the small ledge. Her muscles were completely tense as she started to climb along the building. Above her, he saw Augustus King appear in the shattered window for a moment before he disappeared.

The young man, who Gabe recognized as Augustus King's assistant, got to his feet, his eyes wide as he stared at Darby. He scrambled to the edge of the platform, moving as fast as he dared toward Darby. "You've got this, Darby. Hand over hand. You can do this. You're doing great."

Above, Gabe saw Augustus King reappear with a fire hose tied around his shoulders, knotted in front of him. But he only saw that from the corner of his eye. He could not and would not take his eyes off Darby.

"Please, Darby, please," he begged.

CHAPTER 170

Ignoring the pain in her hands and the blood sliding down her arms, Darby climbed hand over hand along the metal bar. She breathed in and out, not looking down, not looking forward, her focus only on the beam. She didn't mind heights, but even this was a bit much for her. She was all too aware of her feet dangling over nothing.

She didn't dare turn her head to look at the others, even as she heard Noah calling out support. She needed all of her focus. One handhold at a time. *Just keep moving*, she told herself, even as she yelled back a response, "I'm okay."

And she really hoped she wasn't lying.

Hand over hand, she focused on the support tower underneath the octagon. That was her destination. She didn't look at anything except where she was going—right, left, right, left—until the tower was directly in front of her. It was tempting to swing herself forward and try to reach the small three-foot ledge, but that would leave her shoulders too far back. She couldn't risk it.

So she continued forward until she was just a few inches away, then very carefully, she stepped onto the tower. Letting out a breath, she turned her back to the tower and slid down, her feet dangling over the side as she sighed. "Phew."

Yes!" Noah stood with both hands in the air in victory. Gabe though was crouched on the ground next to him, his hand at his mouth, looking like he was about to hurl. Her brother looked much the same.

"I'm okay," she said, although instead of a shout it came out as a whisper. She gave herself a moment to breathe but she knew staying here wasn't an option. But for the moment, it would do.

Vaguely she was aware that the gunfire had cut off from up above. She hoped that meant the good guys had won or at least not lost. Letting out a breath, she spied where the maintenance platform was beneath one of the six-inch beams. *All right, no problem. Just a quick crawl, and I'll be over them.*

"Wait, Darby," Gabe said as he hustled down the platform toward her.

But Darby shook her head. "No. I'm coming to you guys. It's the safest way."

The beam was right over the maintenance platform, and if she was careful, she would be able to lower herself right to it with the guys' help. Taking a deep breath, she slid over on the ledge toward the ladder. Then she climbed until she was above the beam.

Getting into a crouch, she slid along the ledge until she was lined up with the beam. Then, testing the distance, she reached out with one foot and then another. Couching down, she started to crawl along it, not letting herself look down but once again only at the beam in front of her. From the corner of her eye, she could see Scooter and Gus watching her from above.

"A little more, a little more," she told herself over and over again. Then she found herself directly over the maintenance platform. She let out a relieved laugh.

Linc had outpaced Noah and now stood at the edge of the mainte- nance platform. He smiled at her as he approached. "You know, this place is exciting enough without you deciding to play tightrope walker. You—"

His words cut off with a strangled cry.

A great horned owl that had been perched under the Hide darted from his hiding spot. Instinctively, Linc took a startled step back. His heel hit nothing but air. He teetered at the edge of the platform, his arms windmilling as he tried to regain his balance. But he was leaning too far back.

He swayed, muscles tense as he tried to stay on the platform. The railing behind him gave way. In her mind, Darby could see him plunging to the ground.

Ignoring the pain in her hands, she wrapped her hands around the edge of the beam. As they did, she felt her hands slip. The edge was only three inches.

It changed nothing.

Dropping over the side, she gripped the ledge with all she was worth. Then she swung out and over the side, coming in from Linc's back, her feet caught him on the shoulders as she shoved him to safety.

He stumbled forward, dropping to her knees.

But her momentum pushed her beyond the platform. The blood covering her hands made it impossible to hold on. As she swung up, her hands slipped off the beam.

Her thrust propelled her out beyond the platform. She was flung up into the air a few feet before she began the plunge down.

CHAPTER 171

"No!" Linc's heartbroken scream followed Darby as she closed her eyes. She had always liked heights. Roller-coasters were her favorite. She loved the thrill of falling.

But this thrill was not the same. Terror rolled through her. *I'm going to die.*

In an instant, she saw every moment in her life: her mom and her making cupcakes in the kitchen, Linc in a highchair nearby. Her dog Max chasing a soccer ball with her and Linc, who could barely walk. Sitting by her mom's deathbed, her hand wrapped so tightly in Linc's. Getting hugged by Mama Sue. Meeting Gabe. Watching Linc win States, joy bursting through her at the happiness on his face as he searched the crowd for her right after he'd crossed the finish line.

I love you all, she thought.

A jolt stopped her as a heavy object crashed into her gut. Her eyes flew open as an arm wrapped around her waist and legs wrapped around her own, holding her tight. Mouth falling open, she stared in disbelief into Gus's face.

"Grab the rope!" he yelled.

Scrambling, she latched on to the firehose to lessen the pull on him as they swung under the Hide. Looking up, she saw the rope he held had been attached to something inside the Hide.

They swung back and forth, each swing a little less than the one before. And Darby's mind was blank besides one simple sentence: *I'm not dead. I'm not dead.*

As the swings receded to barely anything, Scooter yelled down, "Hold on, guys. We're pulling you up."

Slowly, they began to ascend. Darby's head swam, and the feeling of terror shifted to elation. She laughed.

He grinned. "You okay?"

Nodding, disbelief still rolling through her, she arched an eyebrow at him. "Let me guess, you were up for playing Tarzan?"

His grin widened. "Circus performer. Did a lot of trapeze work."

Letting out a breath, she leaned her head into his chest. "Thanks, Gus."

"Anytime, Darby," he whispered back at her.

CHAPTER 172

ONCE GUS AND DARBY HAD BEEN HAULED UP, THE OTHERS WERE ALSO retrieved from the maintenance platform, with much less drama. Then they all carefully made their way down the hall to the food court. The glass floor in the center of the hide was completely shattered. That left them with about five feet on either side. Everyone hugged the wall, not sure if the Hide itself was now unstable. Once at the food court, Bao and Meg stepped out first with Scooter right behind them, all scanning the area.

They still weren't sure where the other gunmen had gone. But they'd cleared the Hide and the pathways to it.

Mama Sue's voice came over the PA system. "The other two gunmen just sprinted out the exit. There's no one else around."

Scooter looked up at the camera and gave it a big thumbs-up. Linc hurried over to Darby and hugged her tight. She hugged him back and then winced as her hands rubbed up against his back.

"You okay?" Linc asked.

"Yeah. Just a few cuts," she replied.

"Oh, thank God." Gabe stepped forward and hugged her as well. "We were so worried about you."

"Likewise," Darby whispered. She looked up and saw Gus and Noah speaking with Bao and Meg. They all looked serious. Then Gus looked up and caught her eye. He said something to the others and headed over. Linc's eyes widened. "That's Augustus King."

"Yup."

"He's like the number one action hero."

She smiled. "Yeah, and he's kind of one in real life, too."

CHAPTER 173

AFTER TAKING STOCK AND GRABBING SOME FIRST-AID KITS, DARBY AND THE others headed back to the control room. Gabe had detoured at the food court and grabbed a bunch of sandwiches and drinks with Linc and Noah's help.

While the gunmen might be gone, the animals were still loose. And everyone preferred to wait behind a steel door.

As they turned down the hall to the control room, the door to the room swung open. Mama Sue sat in her wheelchair waiting.

Darby's throat felt tight as she sprinted toward her. Then she flung herself into Mama's arms.

"It's okay, baby, it's okay," Mama murmured.

But when Darby pulled back, there were tears running down Mama Sue's cheeks. Darby reached up to wipe them away but then winced as she aggravated the cuts on her hand. But being she didn't want Mama to see them, she shoved them behind her back and asked. "You okay?"

"With you and Linc safe? Yes, yes, I am."

Then Darby had to step out of the way as Linc and Gabe moved in for their hugs. A tremor ran through Darby, imagining all the horrible things that could have happened to all of them.

Then Gus was there, leading her over to a chair. She sat and let him clean and bandage her cuts. Then he draped a blanket over her shoulders. She looked up at him and smiled. "Thank you."

He looked back toward Mama Sue, Linc, and Gabe. "You've got yourself a good little family there."

She pulled the blanket tighter around her. "Yeah, I'm a lucky girl."

———

For the next hour, the group in the control room ate and talked. Communications had been restored. The park was once again under Sanctuary Kingdom's control, or at least the electronics were. The animals were still loose, so they were told to stay put.

They all agreed they were safe and could be put last on the list for rescue. No one had argued the point, not even Courtney.

Now Darby took a moment to really look at the people around her. They were all alive. They were all unharmed, or at least had no life-threatening issues. Mama Sue was pale and shaky, but Gabe had made her eat some food and drink some electrolytes. And the shaking had lessened. Now Scooter sat with her, keeping her entertained.

Linc was sitting with Noah and Gabe, chatting about something animatedly. Courtney was on the phone with Lance, but she wasn't recording anything, just talking. And Meg and Bao were sitting close together, her head on his shoulder.

Gus sat down next to her. "How you doing?"

He was another one who she was glad had made it through unharmed. She'd expected an obnoxious movie star. He'd been anything but.

And then it all hit her. She shook her head as she dropped her voice, not wanting the others to hear her. "I'm just trying to make sense of all this. Someone placed implants in the animals. And they either malfunctioned or . . ."

"Or did exactly what they were designed to do."

Darby nodded. "And I don't get who those guys were or what they wanted."

"They moved like military. They were definitely trained," Gus said, his brow furrowed.

"I was thinking the same thing. But what was their agenda? Why go after us?"

"Maybe we saw something we weren't supposed to," he murmured, almost as if he was talking to himself.

"What?"

Gus's head darted up, and his eyes widened for a moment before he flashed her a smile. "Or maybe I'm thinking like I'm on a movie set. Could have been terrorists or some sort of anarchists. Not sure we'll ever know."

"Do you think those other two got away?"

Gus was quiet for a moment. "If they did, I'm pretty sure there's a lot of people looking for them. Someone's going to find them."

CHAPTER 174

Pain radiated through Felix's leg and his ribs as he limped forward, Sabrina supporting him. He still couldn't believe one of those damn tigers had swiped him.

"Just a little further," Sabrina urged.

Felix had his arm draped over her shoulder, and she was practically carrying him. How had it all gone to shit so fast? He still didn't understand how the hell they had lost control. Who were those Rambo wannabes that had come out of nowhere?

One of the guys had even looked like that actor Augustus King. But that couldn't be right.

"Are you sure we can get out this way?" he asked.

"Yeah."

He didn't ask anything else. The pain in his leg was so intense that even saying those few words was almost impossible. He'd been through half a dozen hellholes on this planet and had skipped through all of them completely untouched. Now, one freaking visit to a US tourist attraction, and he was afraid he was going to lose his leg.

Ahead, there was a small maintenance gate. Sabrina walked over to it and pushed it open. Felix tensed just before she touched it, but no electricity coursed through it. The fences were back to normal.

At his questioning look, Sabrina shrugged. "All the power's out. Cops must have shut it off, rebooted the system."

Grunting, he knew if he wasn't so focused on his leg, he would have realized that as well. He pictured Santos and Bobby and sighed. They'd had to leave their bodies behind. Eventually, they'd be traced back to him. He was going to have to hide deep for a while.

Checking her phone, Sabrina gestured to the left. "This way."

Apparently the phones were back too. Gripping him tightly around the waist, she started for the road. Spots appeared at the edge of his vision, and he sucked in a breath as the pain in his leg jolted again.

"Almost there," Sabrina said.

Hearing a car approach, his eyes widened as the black government van headed straight toward them. Part of him cursed loudly at the thought of going through all of this to get caught now. But the other part was just happy that maybe the van would have some painkillers.

The van pulled to a stop at the edge of the road. The back door slid open. Sabrina pulled Felix toward it. Two men inside grabbed him by the arms and hauled him into the back. Sabrina climbed in after him and then slammed the door shut.

Felix was dropped on the floor, and he let out a curse as his leg was jarred. "Easy, man."

The men didn't say anything.

But as Sabrina sat next to him, she whispered, "It's okay. The boss sent these guys."

Letting out a breath, Felix closed his eyes as the van sped away. "Hey, you guys got any painkillers?"

Cold metal pressed against his forehead. His eyes flew open just as Sabrina's blood splashed across his face. He had time for only one last thought before he met the same fate.

Ah, damn.

CHAPTER 175

IN HER OFFICE, MARTHA GAZED AT THE ARRAY OF LIGHTS AS THE emergency crews escorted the employees from the park. She'd been down there when they arrived, made sure they had everything they needed. Then she'd gotten out of their way to let them do their work.

And there was a lot of work to be done. She'd contacted every zoo and police department in the area to get them to bring in people to help get her people out of the park and to get the animals either back in their cages or put down.

She closed her eyes as her thoughts automatically shifted to the cost of this disaster. They would never survive it.

Her phone rang. Flicking a glance at the screen, she saw it was the senator's office. Gritting her teeth, she pictured Archer and snapped the phone to her ear. "Yes?"

But instead of the patronizing Archer, it was the deep baritone voice of Senator Freddie Markham, who responded. "Martha, I just wanted to check in and see how you're doing."

Taking a deep breath, Martha forced her voice to sound even. "I'm good, Freddie. I just sent a message to Archer. We'll put a stop to the DOD testing for now, but in a few weeks we'll be able to get back up and running again."

There was a pause on the other end of the phone before the senator answered, confusion in his tone. "The DOD?"

A flash of alarm rolled through Martha. Freddie was getting up there in age. Was he starting to lose it? "Yes, the DOD project your office helped arrange. Your aide Archer Fitzgerald has been spearheading it."

"What name was that?"

"Archer Fitzgerald," she said slowly, a chill starting to creep over her.

"Hold on a second, Martha." The senator's side of the phone went quiet. Martha stared down at her phone. What was going on? She walked over to the window, staring down at the emergency lights.

"Martha?"

Quickly, she pulled the phone back to her ear. "I'm here."

"I just checked with my chief of staff to make sure I wasn't mistaken. We don't have anyone named Archer Fitzgerald in our office."

Jaw-dropping, Martha sagged against the desk. "What?"

"I don't know what's going on but we don't have anyone in the office by that name, either full time or volunteer."

"But, but he arranged for the DOD contract."

Freddie's voice was cautious. "I don't know what to tell you. I haven't helped arrange anything like that. What kind of testing are you doing over there?"

A numbness spreading over her, she gave herself a shake. "I need to go, Freddie."

"Martha, we need to talk about this."

"Yes, yes. Let me just get a few things ironed out here first."

"Okay. I'll speak with my contacts at the DOD. I'm heading down there tomorrow morning. We'll get this sorted, okay?"

"Yeah, okay. Thanks, Freddie." She disconnected the call, her thoughts somehow both racing and moving incredibly slow. Freddie had to be wrong. Archer, she'd spoken with him at least half a dozen times. She could picture him easily. She'd talked to him.

Freddie had to be wrong. His chief of staff had to be wrong.

But what if he wasn't? Who had she been talking to? Was the DOD even behind this project?

And if not, who was?

CHAPTER 176

THE SMILE WOULD NOT LEAVE KEVIN'S FACE. IT WAS SAFE TO SAY HIS project had been a raging success. The world would not forget this day anytime soon. Hell, if he played his cards right, he could sell his services to both sides of the problem: He could sell it to the corporations who wanted to secure their systems, and he could sell them to the people who wanted to destroy those same systems.

The warehouse was quiet as Kevin watched the news footage of the attack at the park. He wished he could have seen that last interaction at the Castle. But like with the elephant house, he'd been booted out of the system.

He wasn't going to let that rain on his parade, though. He was king this day, and no one could take that away from him.

The EcoAct members on site had already disappeared, having been notified by scanners that cops were finally on the way. One of the first things the cops had done was shut down the power to the park. In doing so, they'd cut off the electric fences, and all the employees taking refuge by the borders were able to escape.

It also cut off Kevin's ability to see inside the park. But that was fine. He had enough footage to create a calling card when he sold his services. In fact, his time with EcoAct from this point on could be counted in hours, not days. They were going to be the target of a lot of law enforcement scrutiny. And Kevin planned on not being around for any of it.

But this place, no one knew it was linked to EcoAct. He'd made sure of it. So he had a little time. Here, he would finalize his resumé for the dark web. Then he'd move on to the next job.

The door behind him opened, and he whipped around. Charlie Hutz stepped in, holding up a six-pack of beer. He was followed by six other members of EcoAct, all carrying bags. Most members were in Tennessee, but this was the group that had been left behind.

Walking over with a grin, Charlie placed the beer on the table. He extended his hand to Kevin. "Way to go, man."

Returning the grin, Kevin shook his hand. He didn't really like Charlie, but he did like when people recognized his genius. "Thanks, man."

Music blared on from the other side of the warehouse.

"I know you're not a drinker." Charlie looked over his shoulder at Shelby, who walked over with a six-pack of Kevin's favorite energy drink. She handed it to him. "Great job."

"Thanks," he mumbled, taking it. He always felt anxious around Shelby.

"I know you're probably wrapping some things up, but I ordered some pizzas to keep you fed. You need anything, you let me know. Because right now, you are the man." Charlie slapped him on the back.

Kevin grinned as Charlie and Shelby backed away, giant smiles on their faces as they mock-bowed to him.

Turning back to his monitor, Kevin grabbed one of the energy drinks and flicked it open. Toasting himself, he grinned. Now on to bigger and better.

CHAPTER 177

THE RESCUE EFFORT WAS NOT A QUICK PROCESS. IT WAS FOUR HOURS BEFORE the rescue teams made it to the Castle. But Darby and the others had been able to watch most of the other rescues on the monitor.

It had not been easy viewing. Gabe had looked heartbroken at each body, human or otherwise, that was found. Finally, Darby had reached over and shut off the feed. "I don't think we need to see any more, right, guys?"

No one argued with her.

The rescue team had arrived in two trucks, and the group had been split between them. They'd been brought back to the parking lot on the west side of the fence, just inside the entrance.

Darby had never been so happy to see Dominion in her life. Getting past the fence that cut Dominion off from the rest of the park eased the tension in her body exponentially.

But then a new sort of tension replaced it: the parking lot was jam-packed. Ambulances, EMTs, cops, federal agents, animal response groups from other zoos, and survivors were all mixed in together. Darby and the others had been hustled over to a tented area, where someone gathered their information and then determined which line they needed to join to be cleared by medical.

Now darkness had fallen, and lights bathed the park in shadows. Darby sat with Mama Sue and Linc, a blanket wrapped around each of them as they huddled together. One of the paramedics finally walked over. "How's everybody doing over here?"

"We're fine," Mama Sue said quickly.

Darby and her brother exchanged a glance. "Linc and I would feel better if you got checked out."

"I'm fine, honey."

But Darby could read the concern on Linc's face, and she felt the same. "Please?"

Mama Sue let out a shaky breath and looked paler than she normally did. "Fine. But only to make you two feel better."

Darby leaned over and kissed her on the cheek. "Thank you."

After hearing about her medical history, the EMT frowned. "We're taking people to North Knoxville Medical Center, at least the non-traumas. I think it would be better if the doctors there gave you a look."

"Can I go in the ambulance with her?" Linc asked.

The paramedic nodded. "Of course."

Darby stood up. "I'll follow you guys."

"I'll drive her," Scooter said as he appeared behind Darby. She gave him a grateful smile.

Looking resigned, Mama Sue looked up. "Fine. Check on Gabe, though. Make sure he's okay before you leave."

"Will do."

CHAPTER 178

STEPPING FROM THE BATHROOM, KEVIN RUBBED HIS STOMACH. HE'D emptied his system, and now it was time to fill it again.

The party was still going full tilt on the other side of the warehouse. Kevin shook his head. They were all so proud of themselves. But they'd done nothing. No, the glory belonged to Kevin and Kevin alone.

Sitting down behind the console, a sense of accomplishment filled him. He'd done it. He'd brought Sanctuary Kingdom to its knees. And as an added bonus, he'd also tied the DOD firmly to the activities within the park.

He smiled at the signs of devastation. He'd really done it. He'd exposed Sanctuary Kingdom for what it was. Truthfully, Kevin didn't really care about that, but he'd proven his own worth. After this little incident, he'd be in demand and would have done all of it without a single person being able to tie it back to him. EcoAct would be implicated, but not Kevin. Heck, his name wasn't even Kevin.

It was just an ID he'd made up.

He was really Joshua Kennedy from Cedar Rapids, Iowa. But no one at EcoAct knew that. And the whole group would be going to ground anyway. Making a big splash was one thing. Getting caught for it was something else.

With a frown, he flicked a glance at his phone. Todd was supposed to contact him and let him know that they had all gotten out of the park. He shook his head. They were probably partying it up too. Todd would probably get caught. That was one of the reasons that Kevin hadn't given him his real name.

The last thing he needed was to be tied to those jokers. He never let any of them take a picture of him, either. He had a pretty generic look. He'd always had a face that was easily lost in a crowd. So being over-looked was no big stretch for him.

Plus, he'd already laid the groundwork for his mobile base. Tonight, he was heading out of town. He'd been in Buffalo by nine and over the Canadian border well before midnight.

And that was when Kevin Young would die and Beowulf would take his place. He was going to be rolling in money. Many of the members of EcoAct would probably be spending their time cooling their heels in a jail cell. But not him. No, Kevin was too smart for that.

God, it was good to be him.

Grabbing a slice of pizza, he finished it quickly. Then a cry came from the other side of the room. He frowned as one of the guys—what was his name? Toby? Cody? It was something like that—fell to the ground.

Kevin rolled his eyes. The guy couldn't hold his liquor.

Smiling, he looked at his screen, but then the smile faded from his face.

Connection lost.

"No, no, no, no," Kevin murmured, completely ignoring the group on the other side of the room even as a few more dropped to their knees. Instead, he scrambled to check the cords and make sure none of the idiots had disconnected anything. But everything looked good. He ran diagnostics, but the signal was gone.

How the hell was that possible? They had complete control of the signal. Had something happened to the satellite?

I am in control, he roared in his mind.

As he stared at the screen, a burning started in the back of his throat. He coughed and then reached for his drink, chugging practi-cally the whole thing. But the drink didn't help. The burning only increased. It felt like his throat was on fire, and the fire was spreading to his lungs.

With a gasp, he pushed back from the table and then crashed to the ground, clawing at his throat as if he could claw out the feeling.

His gaze locked on the others at the back of the warehouse. All of them were either on their knees or splayed out on the ground. Pure, undeniable terror rolled through him. But it was soon crowded out by the pain. His whole body felt like it was on fire.

The first seizure took hold. The second one followed almost immediately. He drooled and sprayed liquid from his mouth. Tears or blood, he wasn't sure which, blurred his eyes. *What's going on? What's happening?*

But his brain, which he was so proud of, couldn't seem to grab hold of any thoughts. All he could think was one single thought: *I'm going to die.*

And then his back arched painfully as one last seizure wracked him. As he crashed to the ground, his final exhale proved his thought true.

CHAPTER 179

MARTHA HAD BEEN GETTING REPORTS AT REGULAR INTERVALS ABOUT WHICH of their staff had been retrieved from the park and their conditions. Which was how she knew Gabe was safe and sound.

Running her hands over her face, she wiped the tears there. This whole time she'd shoved down her fear for him. But he was okay.

She wanted to rush down and see him. But that wasn't their relationship. And she still had work to do. The PR department was working overtime fielding all the calls from the media. Martha had just sent back the latest draft of their press release with her tweaks.

In her gut, though, she knew no matter how much they polished it, there were no words that could cover up the fact that this was an absolute disaster.

But instead of turning back to put another coat of paint on this absolute dumpster fire, she kept her gaze on the park below, unable to believe what today had brought. From reports so far, at least a dozen people had been killed, though they were still finding bodies. More than double that number had been injured.

But Gabe's safe, she reminded herself. *Maybe this could be a new start for us. Maybe it was time to let old resentments and jealousies lie. Move forward from here.*

With her back to the door, Martha didn't turn as she heard it open.

"Kelly, whatever it is, I'm really just not up for anything else. So unless it's an emergency—"

"Oh, it's an emergency," a male voice said from behind her, just as a sharp, piercing pain lanced through her back.

Gasping, she turned, looking into the face of Reuben. Her eyes drifted down to his hand, which still held the knife embedded in her back. He twisted it, and she cried out.

Smiling, he yanked the knife out. Martha stumbled back, her hand going to the wound, and then her knees buckled as she crashed to the ground. Reuben walked over and straddled her as he held the knife to her throat.

Martha's eyes widened as she stared up at him. "Why?"

"Because I've always wanted to do this to someone." Leaning down, he swiped the blade across her throat. "And I've got to say, it's even better than I imagined. Oh, and by the way, Archer says hi."

He didn't even wait to see the job completed. Standing, he whistled as he headed across the office.

Martha scrambled into her pocket and pulled out her phone. Thick wet blood saturated her top. Spots appeared at the edge of her vision.

I'm so sorry, Gabe. The phone slipped from her hands. She tried to take a breath, but there was none to be had. A tear rolled down her cheek, and then she felt nothing at all.

CHAPTER 180

Darby watched as Mama Sue and Lincoln headed to one of the ambulances. Her chest felt tight. She imagined how all of this could've been so much worse, at least for her personally.

They were lucky. A lot of people hadn't been. Scooter wrapped an arm around her shoulders. "Don't go into the world of what-ifs. Nothing good comes out of there."

Nodding, she knew he was right. Looking around, she spied Gus and Noah talking with a very agitated woman. She frowned. "Who's that?"

Wincing, Scooter gave the woman a hard glare. "That is Gail Zephyr, Gus's agent. She somehow managed to get through all of the barricades and get herself in here. I'm not sure if she's excited or annoyed."

Neither was Darby.

Grunting, Scooter's gaze stayed on Gus. "I've got to give Gus credit, he can fight. Both of them can, in fact."

"Don't all action stars know how to fight at least a little?" she asked.

Scooter shook his head. "Nah. They learn enough to look good on screen. A lot of that's movie magic. You know, you get the camera angle from behind so that when they throw the hook, it looks like it took off the guy's head, but in reality, it didn't even come close. But he's more than that—a lot more."

Gus finally shook his head and met Darby's gaze. He said something to Noah and then started toward her.

Scooter leaned down. "I think that's my cue. I'll go check on Meg and Bao."

Before Darby could say anything else, the big man slipped into the crowd. Suddenly feeling self-conscious, Darby gripped the blanket around her.

"How are you doing?" Gus asked.

Darby let out a small laugh. "Oh, you know, just a regular Monday."

Chuckling, Gus said, "I have to admit, I didn't think the park would be quite so exciting."

"Well, your movies suggest otherwise."

He winced. "Yeah . . . Gail's already talking about how we're going to turn this into a movie."

Darby's jaw dropped. "You're kidding."

"She's many things, but sensitive is not one of them. Don't worry. I won't let her near anybody else. Noah is running interference."

Darby looked over at the woman, who seemed to be trying to get past Noah, but he was blocking her way. Turning her attention back to Gus, Darby eyed the man who had surprised her a great deal during this ordeal. "I was talking to Scooter, and he said that most movie stars only learn enough to make a fight scene look good."

"That's very true. It's all about the angles and blocking. Not to mention the stunt doubles."

"Yeah, but you don't seem like you learned just enough to make it look good on screen. You actually know how to fight."

He shrugged. "Most celebrities have a personal trainer. I have a personal sensei."

Picturing Gus in a Karate Kid–type setup, she smiled. "Is there such a thing?"

He grinned back at her. "For the right price, there's just about anything. After everything that happened at the beginning of my career, I never wanted to feel like I couldn't protect myself. So, I started training."

"I'm very glad you did. Thank you."

"That thanks goes both ways. Pretty sure we saved each other a few times over the course of the last couple of hours."

"Yeah. That seems safe to say."

Gus glanced over his shoulder and then winced again. "Gail wants to get me out of here before the media attacks this place. Do you need a lift?"

Darby shook her head. "No. Scooter and I are going to head to the hospital to check on Mama Sue."

Concern flashed across Gus's face. "Was she hurt?"

"Well, no, but with her condition, we just want to make sure she's all right."

"Oh, okay. Well, I guess this is goodbye, then, Darby Ellis. Thanks for the tour."

Her stomach did a little flip. There was something about being in an emotionally charged situation that made you feel closer to the people you were with. And she felt a sense of loss at not being able to see him again. "It was nice to meet you, Gus."

Leaning forward, he kissed her on the cheek. "You too, Darby," he whispered before he squeezed her hand and headed back toward Noah and Gail.

Watching him go, Darby felt the loss of him. She had a little bit of a crush on the man. Okay, maybe a huge crush on the man. But that was normal. She was pretty sure that Augustus King had broken more than a few hearts in his life.

And hers was just one more on the pile now.

CHAPTER 181

ALTHOUGH MAMA SUE AND LINC HAD BEEN LOADED UP IN THE ambulance, they weren't exactly being whisked to the hospital. They were stuck in a long line of cars heading for the exits.

Every car was searched thoroughly before being allowed to leave, even ambulances. Scooter had gone over to help with the process and said he'd call Darby when he was ready to head to the hospital.

Now Darby stood with Ori, leaning against Ori's Toyota in the parking lot. Both had blankets wrapped around them. Darby clutched hers tighter, needing the comfort of it. Honestly, she might wear a blanket wherever she went for the next week.

"Darby! Ori!"

The two of them turned as Juan cut through the crowd. His smile was wide as he reached them. He hugged Ori first and then Darby. "Oh, thank God. You two okay?"

"Yeah, we're . . . alive," Darby said softly, watching a stretcher with a sheet over it in the distance get carried to a cordoned-off section.

He shook his head. "I can't believe any of this happened. I'm still not clear on how it's even possible."

"Yeah, it's pretty hard to wrap your head around." Darby had been trying. But ever since they'd been brought out of the park, she felt like she was walking in a fog. Everything seemed so unreal. Maybe tomorrow it would make more sense.

"You okay?" Ori asked.

Following her gaze, Juan's smile disappeared. "Yeah. A gator managed to get into Dominion before the fence was dropped. And there was a pretty rough eagle attack. But we didn't have any gunmen. Of course, there's also . . ." A stricken look crossed his face as he slammed his mouth shut.

"There's also what?" Ori asked.

Looking around, Juan lowered his voice. "It's not common knowledge yet. But since this began, I've become a sort of unofficial member of security. So I was one of the guys who knew. In fact, I was the first one on the scene."

Darby's stomach tightened. "What happened?"

"Martha's dead."

Shock ripped through Darby. "I thought she was in Dominion. Was she in the park?"

His lips tight, there was grief in Juan's eyes. "No, she was in Dominion. And it wasn't an animal attack. She was killed in her office. It was a guy from IT."

"What?" Ori asked.

"Kelly had stepped away from her desk. She returned in time to see the guy stab her. She hid under her desk until he left. She rushed in and called for help, but Martha was already gone."

"Oh my God. Why?" Darby asked.

Shaking his head, Juan ran a hand through his hair. "No one knows. He had an unusual name. He was only here for a few weeks. Ponytail, glasses."

Horror was on Ori's face as she looked over at Dominion. "Reuben, Reuben Sykes."

A numbness started to spread over Darby as she looked to Ori. "Is the guy linked to EcoAct?"

Her mouth slightly open as she looked back at Dominion, Ori shook her head. "I don't know. He was kind of weird, but not 'kill your boss' weird."

Juan nudged his chin back toward Dominion. "And they can't find him."

Staring at all the emergency vehicles surrounding them and the ambulance where Mama Sue and Linc were stuck in a line of traffic, Darby frowned. "When was this?"

"About an hour ago."

That made no sense. The whole area was locked down. No one was getting in or out without being checked. "He has to still be here, right?"

Juan looked around with worried eyes. "I don't know. I heard some of the IT people saying that they're combing the video feed, but it's like he simply ceased to exist. They can't find him on any of the cameras."

"That's not possible. There are cameras everywhere." Ori looked over at Darby.

Knowing what her friend was thinking, Darby nodded. "Go. See what you can do."

That was all Ori needed to hear. She disappeared into the crowd.

Juan stepped next to Darby, shaking his head. "Have you seen Gabe? I don't think he knows yet," Juan said.

Scanning the crowd, Darby caught sight of Roger just as he reached Gabe. Her friend looked up at the head of security for a moment, his mouth falling open, before his whole face crumbled.

Her own chest felt like it had been cracked open as Gabe's knees weakened and Roger reached out a hand to steady him. "He knows now."

CHAPTER 182

THREE DAYS OF MISERY: ROUNDING UP ANIMALS, COMFORTING THE bereaved, getting yelled at by others. And Gabe didn't blame them.

He still couldn't believe that the dream he and his grandparents had of protecting animals had turned into this nightmare. And as if this all wasn't bad enough, the allegations of animal abuse had once again reared their head. But this time, videos had popped up online, all complete fakes. He didn't even know who had created them. But with the explosion of AI tech, just about anyone could have been responsible.

That, though, was nothing. The 'Culling at Sanctuary Kingdom', as the media had dubbed the incident, took central stage. Videos from inside the park had made it out. Whoever had taken over the system made sure that select video clips were released. Besides striking fear in anyone who watched it, it was absolutely gut wrenching.

They knew precious little about the initial cause, save that EcoAct had activated implants that had originated in the research center. For hours, Gabe had interviewed everyone still alive who worked in the secretive research department. The staff working that day had all been killed, though, and the others did not have access to Cadman's research. The only one who did was his assistant, who along with Cadman, was dead.

He had Ori going through their computers, but she wasn't hopeful. They'd been completely wiped.

That job, though, was only a small part of the massive effort following the incident. For the last three days, Darby had been by his side, helping him coordinate with other zoo handlers who'd flown in from around the world to help round up the animals.

But it wasn't just them. Gabe had been overwhelmed by the gracious gestures from his friends in the field. But the numbers were stark: over 50% of the animals who'd escaped their enclosures had been killed. The majority of the birds had literally flown the coop and were proving difficult to rein back in. It was a major blow to global conservation efforts.

And even though it was early days yet, they had learned a few things. A janitor had shut off the power at the Castle. He'd used a timer and had been paid $500. He'd had no idea what would happen.

Reuben Sykes was in the wind. There'd been no sign of him.

They suspected the gunmen in the park were private contractors, but no one knew why they were at the park. Their identities were also proving elusive.

The lawsuits had already started rolling in. Gabe knew there were more coming.

Now he made his way into Mama Sue's kitchen. He'd been staying here since that first night. There'd been no conversations about it. He'd shown up and Mama Sue had just told him the guest room was set up for him, which was good, because he just couldn't stomach being on his own.

He poured himself a cup of coffee. Mama Sue had programmed the machine to make sure Gabe and Darby had coffee first thing in the morning. Even after all she'd been through, she was still taking care of those around her.

Darby walked into the kitchen and yawned. Gabe held up the pot. With a weary nod, she slumped into a chair. He grabbed another mug from the cabinet. After filling it, he placed it in front of her.

Grasping it, she took a small sip and then another. Neither spoke, both just letting the caffeine do its thing. Finally, Darby gestured to Martha's private files on the table. "Need some help?"

The files were paper copies of her hard drive. His sister was para-noid. He'd gone to her home with Ori last night and found her stash. It detailed the implant project and the contract with the DOD, the one the government swore did not exist.

He wasn't really sure what to do about that. There was a ton of information that needed to be reviewed. And Darby was really good at seeing links.

It was tempting, therefore, to say yes. But part of him wanted to keep Darby as far from this as possible. Plus, he felt a need to guard Martha's legacy. Until he had the full story, though, he didn't want anyone thinking badly about her. He shook his head. "No, I think I'll handle this on my own for a little while."

"Okay, but if you need me . . ."

He reached out and squeezed her hand. "Thank you. I don't know how I would have gotten through these last few days without all of you."

"We're always here." She indicated the papers. "While you're deep in all of this. I'll touch base with Kelly and help with the funeral arrangements."

"Thanks. I'd appreciate that." Gabe had insisted on covering all the funeral and hospital expenses. His lawyers were working on the settle-ments, and Gabe had instructed them to think generously. They'd balked, but he didn't care. Money wasn't going to solve anything, but he sure as heck wasn't going to allow the lack of it to be a stressor for his people right now.

His phone rang. A glance at the screen showed it was the FBI. They had been relentless with their questions, and it looked like there were a few more.

With a wince, Darby stood up. "Okay, well, I'll leave you to it."

"Thanks," he grumbled before answering the phone with a sigh. "Agent Howard, how can I help you?"

CHAPTER 183

Taking her coffee with her, Darby moved into the living room. She'd moved in here when she was twelve when her mom had gotten sick. But she still thought of it as Mama Sue's.

It wasn't because of anything Mama Sue had done. She'd made them a home. But it was still Mama Sue's place.

Darby walked over to the desk, setting her coffee down on it. She opened the top drawer and rummaged through it, looking for Mama Sue's insurance card. That horrible night, she and Scooter had eventually made it away from Dominion and reached the hospital. Mama Sue and Linc had only arrived a few minutes ahead of them. Surprisingly, it had only been an hour wait before Mama Sue was seen. Then she'd been discharged with a recommendation to see her personal physician. Darby had managed to get her an appointment for this afternoon.

That night, Darby hadn't had the insurance card on her at the hospital, and unless they wanted to get stuck paying a ridiculous bill, she'd have to call them this morning and send them the information.

Spying the new insurance card, she grabbed it and caught sight of her mom's old medical files underneath. Mama Sue had insisted on getting copies in case there were any medical questions her file could answer down the road. While Darby had agreed, she'd never gone through it.

Now, slipping the insurance card into the pocket of her robe, she grabbed the file, her coffee, and curled up on the couch. Placing the mug on the side table, she flipped through the pages. Her heart felt heavy. It had been years since her mom had died, but right now it felt like yesterday.

Blowing out a breath, she scanned the pages and pages about her cancer treatments. It had been a long slog. Her mom had put up an incredible fight.

But so had the cancer, and it had eventually been the victor.

Flipping through, she wasn't really looking for anything. She stopped on one of those intake pages that all doctors handed out. Scanning it, she frowned. Under pregnancies, her mom had checked none.

That wasn't right. She had two kids. She and Linc obviously had different fathers, but they had the same eyes, her mom's eyes. Had she made a mistake?

Frowning, she searched and found another intake form. The same mistake was there as well. What on earth had her mom been thinking?

"Hey," Linc said as he stepped into the room.

Quickly closing the file, Darby walked over and hugged him tight. "Did you sleep?"

"Yeah, a little. Gabe on the phone?" Linc glanced toward the kitchen.

"Yeah, there's still some confusion about who the group of gunmen were. There's no record of them at the DOD, at least that they're admitting to."

"What's that all about?" he asked with a frown.

"Not a clue, but also not our problem. Gabe will figure it out."

"It's going to be pretty rough for him, isn't it?"

"Yeah, but we'll help him through. It will be a little chaotic for a while, but then life will go back to normal."

"Yeah, normal sounds good," he said, wrapping his arms around her.

Leaning her head against her little brother's chest, she wrapped her arms around his waist. "Yes, it does. Normal sounds perfect."

"Any word from Gus besides the flowers?" Linc asked.

Flicking a glance over at the enormous arrangements that had arrived the morning after, Darby looked at him in surprise. "No, why would you ask that?"

He shrugged. "I don't know. I thought maybe there was something between you two."

Picturing Gus, she still got butterflies. But she had no doubt it was the same for most women who met him. "No. He's an actor. I'm sure he's lying on a beach somewhere, trying to forget all of this."

CHAPTER 184

THREE VANS WERE PARKED IN FRONT OF THE DILAPIDATED WAREHOUSE AS Liam Bennett, codename Shadow, of the Defense Intelligence Agency pulled up to the far side of the parking lot. Turning off the engine, he watched his agents move boxes from inside the warehouse to one of the vans.

All that evidence, and he had a feeling very little, if any, of it would help.

Shaking his head, he let out a shaky breath. As the head of Surveillance Initiative Detail, or SID, within the Defense Intelligence Agency, he didn't go out in the field much anymore. The SID was a specialized force focused on intelligence analysis. Lately, though, their time had become more and more laser-driven on the issue of AI and what it could do.

Which was what had brought them to Sanctuary Kingdom.

Initially, when he'd first gotten the promotion, he had not been thrilled. He'd dragged his heels in his acceptance. Stuck at a desk was not his goal in life. But the powers that be pressed on him how needed he was.

And so he gave up the field for the office. But he did take the opportunities that arose to step out of DC.

This, however, didn't feel like being in the field. This felt like playing catch-up. They'd just found this site this morning, which meant that they were days behind.

For the last year, he'd been chasing ghosts. Every time he thought they were closing in, the promising lead would dry up or disappear like it had never existed.

The last few days hadn't changed that feeling. It had simply reinforced it. They'd found the bodies of the members of EcoAct at a rundown motel about ten miles from Sanctuary Kingdom. From what they could tell, the Chinese food they had ordered had been laced with cyanide. The entire meal and the drinks were tainted with the slow-acting poison, which was lethal in small doses.

By the time the cops arrived, the entire group was dead. It hadn't been too hard to find them. They'd used one of their known aliases. Once the authorities had the name EcoAct, they were able to track them down pretty easily. In fact, the bodies had still been warm. One of the guys was even still alive, but he expired just a few moments after the first responders arrived on the scene.

Those weren't the only bodies as of late. The same night as the attack on Sanctuary Kingdom, he'd received word that Senator Freddie Markham had been killed in a small plane crash with the pilot and three of his staff. Markham was one of the U.S. Senators from Tennessee. It might be unrelated, but the senator had spoken with Martha Lathan just two hours before his death and shortly before hers. It could be a coincidence, but the gnawing in his gut told him the opposite.

As soon as the bodies began to fall in quick succession, it at least confirmed to him who he was dealing with. He knew that every single thread linking his quarry to this particular attack would have been snapped just as neatly as the threads to the terrorist group. They'd been unable to identify any of the gunmen they'd found in the park, not in any criminal, military, or any other database, despite the military tattoos on a few of them.

They were ghosts.

Stepping from the car, he felt a small twinge in the back of his left thigh. He had pulled a hamstring a few weeks back during a long run.

It hadn't quite healed yet. It would probably heal if he cut back on some of his normal training, but what fun would that be?

Besides, his daily workouts were the way he released the stress that his job built up. He needed the outlet. He had made one caveat, switching from bruising runs to bruising rides on his mountain bike. The cycling wasn't as taxing on that particular part of the leg.

His team had traced the hacker from the Sanctuary Kingdom attack to this warehouse. EcoAct had been relatively nonviolent before this particular incident. But the hacker they had used, Joshua Kennedy, aka Kevin Young, had been implicated in a few other more violent incidents.

They had been keeping an eye on the park because they were worried that it was providing tech to foreign assets, or at least that was what some of the other agencies believed. They already knew that there were foreign spies at the park. The CEO was even talking with Chinese agents, although it still wasn't clear if that was understood by the late Martha Latham or not.

As he approached the door, one of the agents caught sight of him and held it open. "Director."

Giving the agent a nod, he stepped through. The warehouse had heavy, thick, now-rusted beams overhead, and the walls were scarred from years of use. A handful of six-foot tables had been placed in the middle of the large space, with computer equipment strewn across them and extension cords leading to the far walls.

He shook his head at how many extension cords there were. That was a massive tripping hazard.

Of course, looking at the dead sprawled out on the tables and the few who were face-down on the floor, he knew it wasn't the cords that had done them in. This poison, unlike the other one, was fast-acting. His people thought it might be thallium, also known as rat poison, but it would take a lab test to confirm.

Making his way over to his team, he saw one of his agents crouched down over a body. His bionic leg was clear in the dim light. "Identity confirmed. It's Kevin Young," Bao said as he straightened.

Across from him, Meg made a notation on her tablet. "Well, that's all of them that we know for sure were working at this location."

"Yeah, but there's still no clue as to who did all of this," Augustus King said as he turned from the body he'd been examining.

Liam looked over at him. "What about your cover? Is it still intact?"

With a sigh, Gus grunted. "I'm still a movie star. In fact, my agent is pushing me to do a shoot that starts in about two months."

"Aww, poor Gus. Still crazy rich with adoring fans flocking to him," Bao teased.

"Yeah, well, it would be nice to wander around Target once without getting mobbed," Gus shot back.

Tilting her head, Meg's expression grew serious. "I don't think I could survive without my Target visits. It's my church."

Ignoring their banter, Liam focused on Gus. "How long?"

He shrugged. "Probably about three months. It can be a little bit all over, but one of the shooting locations is in Jordan."

Contemplating it, Liam nodded. "Yeah, we can work with that. There have been some rumbles of activity in that area. You might have to take a few 'sightseeing' tours."

"No problem. I'll get my assistant on it."

Noah scoffed as he walked in with a stack of body bags and dropped them next to Kevin Young's body. "Yeah, getting a little sick of being the assistant. Can't I be the director?"

Liam chuckled. "I'm afraid your role has already been cast."

Noah sighed rubbing his cheeks. "Damn this baby face."

Bao jumped in with a comment about whether or not Noah had gotten permission from his mom to be here today. Liam tuned them out again, looking over the scene. This had been the closest they'd gotten. He'd traced the cell signals to this address. His team had been dispatched immediately, but they'd been too late. Someone had already snipped the thread.

Gus moved next to him. "You think this is your bogeyman?"

There was no hesitation in Liam's answer. "Yeah, this is him."

Bao joined them. "You know there's no proof of any such group. It's possible that these guys were targeted by someone else." He nudged his chin toward the pizza boxes spread across the table.

"Possible, but it's not. This is them," Liam said.

"You're the only one who thinks this group even exists," Meg said as she joined them.

Liam darted a look at her. Quickly, she put up her hands. "Besides us, of course. I was thinking more like within the DIA."

"Well, I'm not entirely convinced that some of them aren't part of it either," Liam mumbled.

The group around him went still. "You think they're working on the inside?"

He pictured Martha Latham. "Either willingly or unwillingly, yeah. This group is far more powerful than anyone realizes yet. We need to get a handle on it before they get their feet firmly under them."

"This isn't them getting their feet firmly under them?" Noah waved his hand toward the bodies spread across the room.

A chill rolled over Liam as he shook his head. "No, this is just them beginning. This is what a bogeyman does. Convinces you they were never there."

CHAPTER 185

TENSION ROLLED ACROSS ELLIOTT RAMSEY'S SHOULDERS AS HE STRODE across the room. He reached the massive windows and stared out at the ARIA campus in Silicon Valley. It looked like something out of a sci-fi movie.

The central plaza, ringed by high-glass towers and biophilic structures, buzzed with autonomous delivery bots and hovering drones. Lush green rooftops crowned every building, solar petals unfurled with the morning sun, and translucent walkways glowed faintly underfoot. ARIA's campus didn't just look futuristic—it *was* the future, designed to impress investors, inspire genius, and intimidate anyone not up to the challenge.

Turning back to his office, it too was minimalist and sleek in its design. Silver and white dominated, although along the back wall he had an array of shelves with personal mementos that offered a splash of color and a little personality. He'd created ARIA ten years ago. It had gone from a one-man operation to a multinational global behemoth in that short time period.

His phone was full of direct lines to every top business titan across the globe. He'd spent last weekend at a birthday party for Oprah Winfrey. Bill Gates and the prime minister of Canada were both waiting for him to return a call. He had finally achieved a level of success that only a few could ever dream about, never mind achieve.

For Elliot, anything he wanted was laid bare at his fingertips, and yet every time he reached the level of success he told himself he'd be satisfied with, there was one word whispered at the back of his mind the pushed him on: more.

Staring at his reflection in the glass, he noted that his tightly curled hair had spread out to a much wider radius than he was used to. He'd have to get it cut. His hair seemed to be the one aspect of his life that would not bend to his will.

Looking down, he brushed some pretzel crumbs from his black T-shirt, inspecting the matching black running pants for any as well. It was his uniform. He never wore anything else.

Everyone knew that black was supposed to be slimming, but as he studied his reflection, he wasn't sure that was true. The extra thirty pounds he carried around his gut pushed against the T-shirt.

Turning to the side, the view was even worse. He'd need to call Bezos. He'd gone from nerd to stud, at least physically, in a few years. Elliott had to get the name of his personal trainer and see if he could change things up because he had a feeling the next couple of years were going to be fast-paced, and he needed to be in shape for it.

"Will Rowe," an automated voice called out before the doors to his office slid open.

Will strode in, his hair neatly trimmed and the glasses he'd worn as Reuben long gone. But he still had the massive water bottle, and his health mix was no doubt sitting on his desk down the hall.

Will and Elliot had linked up back in college. The man was a genius with computers. He wasn't quite a partner, but he was close. Once they'd reached the testing stage, he'd wanted to be in on the action.

Elliott frowned at him. "Was killing Martha Latham really necessary?"

Grinning as he slumped into a chair, Will placed his feet on the edge of Elliott's desk. "Archer and I agreed that she was too much of a risk. According to our predictions, she would have confessed everything to her brother within two weeks. Her attachment to him was always a weakness."

Although Elliott had seen the prediction model and agreed with the assessment, he was a little unnerved at how easily Will had taken the woman's life and how completely unbothered he seemed by it now. There'd always been a bit of darkness around Will. They were similar in that way.

But Elliott liked his violence committed by others, with him a few steps removed. He never realized Will wanted to be in the middle of it.

And the fact that he hadn't realized that concerned him. Everything else had gone like clockwork. They'd played both sides: setting up the DOD project and then pushing EcoAct to target the park. It had been shockingly easy to place the stories about abuse in the park in the dark corners of the web, looking as if they were employees worried about retaliation if they came forward.

Will pushed off the couch. "All right, well, I have a date. I'll catch up with you two later."

"You're leaving?"

Will grinned at him over his shoulder as he crossed the room. "Hey, I'm still celebrating."

The doors swung open at his approach and then shut behind him. Shaking his head, Elliott glanced at his watch and grumbled. *Come on, Archer, where are you?*

Archer being late for a phone call was not normal. But then again, Archer had been doing quite a few things lately that were not normal. The field experiment had been going on for the last year, but Archer had become a little too adventurous in his actions.

Unease slipped through Elliot, even as he knew that was part of the plan—to see what Archer was capable of.

Finally, the computer on his desk beeped. Elliott called out, "Put the call on the screen." He turned as the wall on his left flared to life. Staring back at him from the middle of the screen was Archer. He smiled. "Good morning, Elliott."

Elliott crossed his arms over his chest and glared at the image. "You were seen."

Archer shrugged, gesturing down at himself. "So what? I can look like this."

The image shifted to a hunched-over bald Asian man with thick glasses. "Or this."

Now the image was of a tall, stately African American woman. "My image doesn't matter," the woman said.

Elliot crossed his arms over his chest. "And you used your name."

Archer switched back to his original image. "Well, we need to give them a sporting chance, don't we?"

"We're not ready for that. You're not ready for that." Elliott caught himself from shaking his head again. Archer wasn't a fan of being scolded. He took a deep breath as Archer raised an eyebrow. It was so lifelike, it was hard to remember he was talking to a computer program.

ARCHER stood for Advanced Reactive Cognitive Heuristic Entity Resource. He was the first fully AI system employed in the real world, as far as Elliott knew. There were still some restraints on him, but for the most part, Archer's decisions were his own. Sanctuary Kingdom was his first real test, not of him but the people he was focused on.

There was so much information that people revealed through their technology: what they bought, what they watched, what they searched.

People often thought that computers were listening in on their conversations and then sending ads their way.

The truth was more insidious than that.

Advertisers began pushing images and ideas toward people that made them think of organizing their basements. Then they started pushing ads for storage containers. People thought the systems were listening in on their conversations. But the influence began well before that.

All that was needed was for the right buttons to be pushed. Advances in technology made that very easy to determine. Keyboards could have sensors attached that monitored an individual's keystrokes. Emails contained invisible tracking pixels. Buying habits, subscriptions, viewing patterns, news consumption, and platforms utilized. Over time, more and more information was collected, until an almost perfectly predictive profile was created.

People were easy to manipulate. And this had been the first real-world test of that.

And it had worked like a charm. Felix and his people believed their skills were in demand by the DOD. When approached, they saw what they expected.

Martha, too, saw what she expected: an answer to her financial concerns. Kevin had been looking for an opportunity to make his name known. The stories Archer had planted led him right to the door of Sanctuary Kingdom.

It was all shockingly easy, although it hadn't been perfect. Elliott crossed his arms over his chest. "The plan did not go the way it was supposed to."

"Oh?" Archer arched an eyebrow.

"A lot of people died. And apparently, there was a government team undercover at the park."

Archer smiled. "Oh, I know. I arranged for the DIA team months ago."

Elliott went still. "You wanted them in the park?"

"The goal of this project was multifaceted. I wanted to see how easily people could be manipulated. I wanted to see what they were all capable of, including the DIA team."

Another chill rolled up Elliott's spine. It was an effort not to shiver in response. "What do you think of the experiment?"

"The animals behaved as expected. That project is maybe two years out from being usable on human forces."

Humanity didn't understand how much it was being pushed and prodded by the algorithms. *They're all sheep*, Elliott thought. He looked over at Archer again, careful with his wording. Archer did not like the word *mistake*. "Any surprises?"

Archer frowned. It looked so lifelike. "Two. Gabe Sullivan wasn't supposed to be there. Our models predicted he would be gone for at least another two months."

"What accounts for his presence?" Elliot asked.

"His relationship with Darby and Linc Ellis and Sue Jenkins. He considers them family. They have a strong bond, unlike his bond with his sister. That was not part of the calculation. It's an adjustment we will need to consider for future actions."

Grunting, Elliott knew that bonds were something Archer was still trying to master. Emotions were not easy to learn. When they'd arranged for Joel's death, it was actually supposed to be both him and Gabe that were killed. But Gabe had stayed behind because of some sort of emergency call from one of the overseas animal preserves. A small, unpredictable event.

But it had still worked. Gabe's absence had caused Martha to feel pressure to secure her financial legacy, recognizing the fragility of life.

"And the second surprise?" Elliott asked.

"Darby Ellis. She was not on my radar prior to the event. Nothing about her stood out. She did well in school but not exceptionally. She wasn't extremely popular nor unpopular. Her profile indicated that she was middle of the road, although she was an excellent student."

"And?" Elliott prodded.

Archer paused. "She was interesting. Her responses were interesting. One of the factors I didn't account for was that her family would be at the park. I believe she responded the way she did because they were in danger. That was a variable that was not considered in my experimental design. But then I did a little more digging."

Elliott didn't care about some tour guide. "So what's our status?"

"The program still needs a little tweaking. But it's close, very close." Archer smiled. "And I have to admit I am very intrigued by Darby Ellis."

Elliot frowned. "Why? She's no one."

Archer smiled. "Oh no, she most definitely is someone, as is her brother."

"Her brother?" Elliot asked picturing the tall, athletic young man.

Archer smiled, yet again looking so very human. "Yes, as it turns out , they're both on the list."

FACT OR FICTION

Thank you for reading *Predator Dominion*. I hope you enjoyed it. This is the first book in *The Shadow Directive Series*. There will also be a crossover in this series with *The Ancestral Code* series, as they are all set in the same universe. The first book in The Ancestral Code Series was *Hominid*. The second will be *Hybrid*. I hope you'll give them a shot.

Now, as with all my books, a lot of facts went into the creation of this novel. Many of the facts are listed below in no particular order.

Dangerous Animal Teams at Zoos.

Although not publicized, every zoo has one. They are composed of members of the zoo staff who are trained in firearms so that if there was a dangerous breach, they would be able to take down an animal that posed a risk to the public. They often include veterinarians, animal behavior experts, and marksmen with access to both tranquilizers and, when absolutely necessary, lethal force.

African Forest Elephants and Vibrational Communication.

This is true. African forest elephants are known to communicate using low-frequency rumbles that can travel long distances through the ground. They pick up these signals using sensory cells in their feet and trunks, enabling them to "hear" vibrations imperceptible to human ears.

Mating Between African and Asian Elephants.

Though extremely rare, mating between African and Asian elephants is biologically possible. It is however, unlikely to lead to a full-grown adult elephant. As mentioned in Predator Dominion, there's a virus called EEHV that is more likely to occur with the breeding between Asian and African elephants. The deadly form of herpesvirus affects primarily young elephants. It causes a fast-acting hemorrhagic disease that leads to internal bleeding, organ failure, and death—often within 24 to 72 hours if untreated.

While many adult elephants carry the virus without symptoms, it can reactivate and become fatal in calves. EEHV is now one of the leading causes of death among juvenile elephants in captivity and has been detected in wild populations as well. Early detection and treatment with antivirals can save lives, but the disease remains a significant threat to conservation efforts.

One documented hybrid, "Motty," was born in a British zoo in 1978 to an African bull and an Asian cow. Unfortunately, he died two weeks later due to health complications. While possible, the genetic differences between the species usually act as a reproductive barrier.

Sanctuary Kingdom.

Sanctuary Kingdom is entirely fictional, crafted as an amalgam of the best—and sometimes worst—ideas about wildlife parks and their ethical implications. While no such facility exists, many sanctuaries worldwide strive to offer humane alternatives to zoos or circuses. I did research on a lot of the security protocols and incorporated some into the book. In addition, I even created the *Fantastic Friends*. Check out the Predator Dominion book page at rdbradybooks.com to see them!

Spotted Hyenas.

Spotted hyenas are the largest hyena species, weighing up to 140 pounds and reaching lengths of nearly five feet. Despite their dog-like appearance, they are more closely related to cats. They are highly social animals, living in large matriarchal clans and covering extensive ranges. Though not endangered, they do face pressure from habitat loss and human conflict.

Hyena Intelligence.

Hyenas have demonstrated problem-solving skills and complex social intelligence, in some cases outperforming chimpanzees in cooperative tasks. Their intelligence is one reason they have thrived in harsh environments and outlasted many competitors.

Hyenas as Hermaphrodites and Female Dominance.

Female spotted hyenas are larger and more dominant than males and possess an enlarged clitoris that closely resembles male genitalia, making gender distinction difficult. While not true hermaphrodites, this trait plays a significant role in social hierarchy and reproduction.

Hyena vs. Human Antagonism Theory.

This theory posits that early humans and hyenas competed fiercely for food and territory. Fossil records show hyena bite marks on human bones and evidence of tool use on prey bones found in hyena dens, suggesting that the two species were locked in a survival rivalry that lasted millions of years.

Cassowaries.

Cassowaries are real, dangerous, and stunningly unique. Native to Papua New Guinea, Indonesia, and parts of Australia, these six-foot-tall birds are known for their aggressive behavior when threatened. The story of a cassowary fatally injuring its owner is, unfortunately, true.

Axolotls.

Axolotls are of course real. Wild axolotls are critically endangered, with perhaps only a hundred left in the wild. Captive axolotls, often white with pink gills, differ in appearance from their wild counterparts, which are darker. They exhibit neoteny, retaining juvenile traits into adulthood, including external gills and a permanent "smile."

The Defense Intelligence Agency (DIA).

The DIA is a real agency within the U.S. Department of Defense. It provides intelligence on foreign militaries and operating environments, supporting military planning and operations. Unlike the CIA, it is focused specifically on defense and military intelligence.

Tasmanian Devil Tumor Disease.

Devil Facial Tumor Disease is a highly contagious cancer that has devastated the Tasmanian devil population. Spread by biting, it leads to large, disfiguring tumors and is often fatal. Conservation efforts are ongoing to save the species from extinction.

Neural Implants.

Neural implants like Deep Brain Stimulation (DBS) have been used since the late 1990s to treat neurological disorders such as Parkinson's disease. Recent advances have also enabled amputees to control prosthetic limbs using brain-computer interfaces. Research in this area is rapidly advancing.

Mind Control Parasite.

Toxoplasma gondii, nicknamed the mind-control parasite, is real. *It* can significantly alter animal behavior, especially in rodents. Infected mice and rats often lose their natural fear of predators like cats—sometimes even becoming attracted to the scent of cat urine. This behavioral change increases the likelihood that the parasite will complete its life cycle in a cat, its definitive host. Scientists believe *T. gondii* may manipulate brain chemistry, particularly dopamine levels, to achieve this effect.

Internet Ads and Surveillance.

While dramatized in fiction, it is true that online ads are often tailored based on browsing history, location, and metadata. Algorithms can infer a surprising amount of information from even brief interactions online. Moreover, there's a great NOVA episode on how ads are aimed at us. Apparently, they first lay the groundwork, then we think about something and then an ad pops up. Mind blowing.

Tinfoil as a DIY Faraday Cage.

Tinfoil can block electromagnetic signals, including RFID and some Wi-Fi transmissions, when used correctly. Though a crude method, it works on the same principles as a Faraday cage, which shields against electromagnetic interference.

Ili Pika.

The Ili Pika is a real and extremely rare species of pika found in the Tian Shan Mountains of China. It's considered one of the world's most endangered mammals, with fewer than 1,000 individuals estimated to remain.

Thank you for reading Predator Dominion. I hope you enjoyed it. If you did, please leave a review. The second book in the Shadow Directive series, Final Payout, is now available for pre-order. Thanks for reading!

Until next time,

RD

BOOKS BY R.D. BRADY

Stand Alone Novels:

Hominid

Extinction Threshold

The Vienna Deception

Storm Rage

Operation Kringle

The Shadow Direction Series:

Sanctuary Kingdom

Final Payout

The Belial Series (in order)

The Belial Stone

The Belial Library

The Belial Ring

Recruit: A Belial Series Novella

The Belial Children

The Belial Origins

The Belial Search

The Belial Guard

The Belial Warrior

The Belial Plan

The Belial Witches

The Belial War

The Belial Fall

The Belial Sacrifice

The Belial Rebirth Series

The Belial Rebirth

The Belial Spear

The Belial Restored

The Belial Blood

The Belial Angel

The Belial Templar

The Belial Cipher

The Belial Devastation

The Belial Ghosts

The Belial Covenant

The Belial Heart

The Belial Witnesses

The Belial Trial

The Belial Sons

The Belial Fate

The Belial Alpha

The Belial Omega

The A.L.I.V.E. Series

B.E.G.I.N.

A.L.I.V.E.

D.E.A.D.

R.I.S.E.

S.A.V.E.

The H.A.L.T. Series

Into the Cage

Into the Dark

The Steve Kane Series

Runs Deep

Runs Deeper

The Unwelcome Series

Protect

Seek

Proxy

The Nola James Series

Surrender the Fear

Escape the Fear

Tackle the Fear

Return the Fear

The Gates of Artemis Series

The Key of Apollo

The Curse of Hecate

The Return of the Gods

R.D. BRADY WRITING AS SADIE HOBBES

The Demon Cursed Series

Demon Cursed

Demon Revealed

Demon Heir

Demon War

The Four Kingdoms

Order of the Goddess

Exclusive Content

Exclusive content is available only to members of R.D. Brady's mailing list. Sign up today!

B.E.G.I.N. – prequel novella (A.L.I.V.E. Series)

Belial Sacrifice - alternative ending (The Belial Series)

Dust – full length novel (The Unwelcome Trilogy)

Extinction Threshold - novella

Begin the Fear – prequel novella (Nola James Series)

Vienna Deception – excluded scene

Members who sign up for R.D.'s mailing list are also the first to hear when she has a new release and to preview book covers. Don't miss out!

ABOUT THE AUTHOR

Amazon All-Star Author R.D. Brady is the best seller behind over sixty pulse-pounding supernatural and science fiction thrillers.

A former criminologist and terrorism expert, she weaves cutting edge research and real-world intrigue—born from her academic work on terrorist ideology and life course criminology—into epic adventures where fierce women and brave men face ancient mysteries, unexplained scientific phenomena, and unrelenting action.

When she's not plotting high-stakes rescues, you'll find her teaching martial arts, logging miles as a dedicated runner, puttering around her garden, or spoiling her loyal canine companions. Under the pen name Sadie Hobbes, she also spins urban fantasy tales that keep readers on the edge of their seats.

Dive into her worlds now—and sign up at rdbradybooks.com for free books, exclusive content, and updates!

Printed in Dunstable, United Kingdom

66564040R00272